SO FAR AWAY

Also by Meg Mitchell Moore

The Arrivals

SO FAR AWAY

a novel

MEG MITCHELL MOORE

A REAGAN ARTHUR BOOK

LITTLE, BROWN AND COMPANY

NEW YORK   BOSTON   LONDON

Copyright © 2012 by Meg Mitchell Moore

Reagan Arthur Books/Little, Brown and Company
Hachette Book Group
237 Park Avenue, New York, NY 10017
www.hachettebookgroup.com

First Edition: May 2012

Reagan Arthur Books is an imprint of Little, Brown and Company, a division of Hachette Book Group, Inc. The Reagan Arthur Books name and logo are trademarks of Hachette Book Group, Inc.

The publisher is not responsible for websites (or their content) that are not owned by the publisher.

The Hachette Speakers Bureau provides a wide range of authors for speaking events. To find out more, go to www.hachettespeakersbureau.com or call (866) 376-6591.

Library of Congress Cataloging-in-Publication Data

Moore, Meg Mitchell.
  So far away : a novel / Meg Mitchell Moore.—1st ed.
    p. cm.
  ISBN 978-0-316-09769-7
  1. Mothers and daughters—Fiction. 2. Family secrets—Fiction. 3. Diaries—Fiction. I. Title.
  PS3613.O5653S6 2012
  813'.6—dc23   2011051322

10 9 8 7 6 5 4 3 2 1

RRD-C

Printed in the United States of America

For the girls: Adeline, Violet, and Josephine

SO FAR AWAY

I t was a Friday when the girl came into the Archives for the first time, the first Friday after they'd changed the clocks. Spring ahead, fall *back:* Kathleen had once learned some rhyme about that when she was a schoolchild, but she no longer remembered it. It had been some time since she'd been a schoolchild. This was early November, the leaves mostly down, lying wet and slick all over Boston.

Not so long ago, a few days, maybe a week, Kathleen had been out walking the dog in short sleeves, but today the sky—dark, glowering, low—seemed to be readying itself for some sort of inhospitable eruption. The planet appeared to be in a muddle, and she waited (they all waited) for something to happen.

Which it did. Not right away, but eventually.

Once when Kathleen's daughter, Susannah, was in kindergarten, she had come home with a song she'd learned about her place in the world: Universe, Earth, North America, United States, Massachusetts, Boston, South Boston. That was years ago, of course, before Susannah left, when she was still young, unblemished, unashamed to love her mother, with sturdy little legs and a smile that turned strangers' heads. There was a tune that went with the song, and some hand gestures. Kathleen thought of that now, imagining a camera zooming in on her, Google-mapping her all the way to her desk, and to the girl slouching in front of her.

This girl must not have heard the weather reports, because her jacket was thin and didn't look waterproof. The girl had long orangey red hair, and skin that was nearly transparent—Kathleen could see the tiny blue veins snaking along her temples—and even through the jacket Kathleen could see that she was very, very thin. Legs like toothpicks, a chest that was nearly concave, collarbones poking out from the skin. This was an arresting look. In fact she could have stepped right out of the pages of one of the catalogs Kathleen occasionally received in the mail (catalogs that were likely meant for Susannah, because certainly Kathleen, a woman of fifty-seven, a widow, had no need for a $170 dress with ruffled tiers of diaphanous silk).

The hair really stood out, because of the color, and the thinness was almost hard to take; the girl could have been just as easily headed for an eating disorder clinic as for the runway. But here she was at the Massachusetts Archives, which was, you had to admit, a strange place for a girl this age (what age? Kathleen wasn't sure) to be.

Neil was off somewhere, and the intern was helping somebody in the reading room. Later Kathleen was grateful for that; she was happy that she was the first one to talk to the girl, because what if somebody else had claimed her?

The girl held a cell phone in her hand, a tiny little thing but not so tiny that it didn't have its own minuscule keyboard, and occasionally she dropped her eyes to look at the screen. Kathleen listened politely as the girl explained what she was there for. A school project, she said. Researching her family tree.

"Ah," said Kathleen. "And you came to do it the old-fashioned way." She liked that.

The girl blinked at her. Kathleen could see that she had tried to camouflage the paleness of her eyelashes by using mascara, and that the mascara had clumped in one corner of her eye. She resisted the urge to tell her about that, and later that night, at home, with the television on and Lucy (a border collie, though about as far away from the border as you could get) resting on the rug near the fire, that was a choice she regretted. In the same situation, she would have wanted to know. The girl was also wearing, on slightly chapped and cracked lips, a shade of lipstick that was a little bit off.

"Old-fashioned," Kathleen repeated. "Instead of online." After a beat she added "Good for you" in an approving way, and the girl smiled at that, showing front teeth that seemed too big for her mouth.

And then Kathleen saw it! Just like that, the resemblance to Susannah. Not in coloring—Susannah was darker—and while Susannah was tall she wasn't as skinny, as coltish, as this girl, even when she had been this age. (Fourteen? Younger? Older?) But there was something about the mouth, the eyes, the expression. Something indescribable.

Thus encouraged, Kathleen went on. "Here's where you sign up for a visitor's badge." She pushed the form toward her. *Natalie Gallagher,* the girl wrote carefully, gripping the pencil harder than she needed to. Kathleen handed her a badge, and the girl—Natalie— put it on. "Now," said Kathleen, "your backpack isn't allowed in. You'll have to put your things in a locker." She pointed. "Then you can meet me in the reading room."

The girl slunk off, and returned a moment later, flushing. "It says I need a quarter," she said. "I don't have a quarter. So I put my stuff in the locker, but I couldn't get the key. Will I be able to get my stuff back? Without the key?"

"No quarter?" Kathleen said. She took her purse from the floor near the desk and rummaged through her wallet. "Here," she said, thrusting one at the girl. "You'd better get the key, just to be safe."

"Thank you," said the girl. She had manners.

A few minutes later Natalie appeared in the reading room with a sheet of paper in her hands. She pulled out a chair and sat across from Kathleen and regarded her with a gravity and a seriousness of purpose. They did not get many people this young in the Archives. Mostly it was older people: retirees with time on their hands, or people heading to Ireland who wanted to visit the village where their great-great-grandparents were born. Sometimes they got a Girl Scout or Boy Scout troop working on a badge. But a solitary teen? Unusual. Kathleen knew she was probably reaching, but this girl seemed like she had been sent from somewhere else as a messenger of sorts—a visitor from the Land of Susannah.

Kathleen had worked at the Archives for twenty-six years, since Susannah was a toddler. Part-time, at first, because she had to arrange for child care, and there was a certain point at which the cost of the child care would be higher than Kathleen's salary; she had to be careful not to reach that point. These were the things she worried about back then.

In those twenty-six years how many people had come to her looking to research their family trees? Hundreds, maybe thousands. Maybe more. She should have counted them. Why hadn't she counted? That would have been an interesting statistic to carry around with her, a way to measure the productivity of her life.

She retrieved some scrap paper from the pile and a pencil from the container of pencils and handed them to Natalie. Natalie took them both and tilted the paper at an angle and held the pencil above the paper, looking at Kathleen expectantly, as though this were an exam, and Kathleen the examiner.

"So," said Kathleen. "What's the assignment, exactly?"

"Oh." The girl shifted in her chair. "Well, no assignment, exactly. It's sort of an independent-study project. For extra credit, like. I'm the only one doing this. Other people are doing other stuff." She paused. "My father did some of this a couple of years ago, but I don't know, I guess I thought I could do something with it…" Here she gestured at a crumpled sheet of paper she had put on the table, crudely torn from a yellow legal pad.

"I see," said Kathleen, tapping the table with the eraser of her own pencil. "And where'd you come from? Where's your school?"

"Newburyport," said the girl.

"Newburyport! That's a haul, all the way down here from there. Somebody drive you? Your mother drive you?"

The girl looked down. "No," she said. "I came on my own."

"On your own? How?"

"Bus to South Station, then Red Line, then I took the shuttle."

"Oh," said Kathleen, impressed. "How'd you know to come here?"

The girl shrugged. "I Googled it," she said.

"I see. Then you must have seen…you probably saw that you can actually do much of this online, at least to get started."

"Yeah," said the girl. It was almost a whisper, the way she spoke. "But I wanted to come. I like the bus. And besides, I kind of wanted to get away."

Kathleen considered this. "Fair enough," she said. She went on. "If you don't mind, I'll use myself as an example. I've traced my family back to the early eighteen hundreds." The girl didn't react, so Kathleen continued. "How'd I do it? I took my time. Years."

Natalie said, *"Years?"*

"Years." This was one of the nuances of Kathleen's job: you couldn't ever be nosy, you couldn't ever show more interest in a person's family than he showed himself, but sometimes you had to encourage—even prod—in subtle and delicate ways. "To do research like I've done would be a major undertaking. But if you've got something to start with, well, in that case we might be able to go back a few generations pretty easily. And the thing about it is this. It's like pulling a thread that unravels and unravels. One loose thread, and you can unknit an entire sweater. Because everyone is a part of someone else's life story, once you find the connection."

Quietly Natalie said, "Geez. I don't know if I'm going to do all of that. I mean, I don't think I'm going to go, like, *overboard* on it." But Kathleen could see behind her eyes some glimmer of interest. Natalie finished, "I just want to get a good grade on the project."

Undaunted, Kathleen detailed some of her search, then continued. "When I got stuck, I thought my way out of it. I took other avenues to get the answer. And I'll show you what I got for it, if you wait here a minute." She left the room and walked back to her desk, where she kept photocopied sheets of her descendant chart. When she returned to the room she saw that the girl had her cell phone out again. This was strictly not allowed, but Kathleen let the transgression pass because as she drew closer she saw that the girl's shoulders were shaking; she was crying.

"Natalie?" She touched her gently on the shoulder, and the girl started. There was something like a caged animal in the look she gave Kathleen — she might have been baring her teeth. "Is everything okay?"

Natalie wiped at her eyes and, looking down, said, "Where's the bathroom?"

"Near the lockers, where you left your bag."

Abruptly Natalie stood, then set off toward the door of the reading room. Kathleen heard a *ting,* and when she looked down she saw that in her haste Natalie had knocked her cell phone to the ground. Kathleen picked it up, not meaning to read the message on the screen, well, okay, sort of meaning to read it, it was hard to pick the thing up without reading it, and she saw these words in the phone's window:

WE KNOW SOMETHING ABT U NATALIE

Out loud Kathleen said, "Huh?" She read it again, and then she put the phone on top of the table, and by the time Natalie made her way back from the bathroom, her eyes dry but the mascara now smeared beneath them, Kathleen had busied herself at one of the cabinets.

Just like that; it was that quick. She was involved.

※

"Okay?" Kathleen said when Natalie returned from the locker room. "Everything all right?"

Natalie shook her head and wiped fiercely at her eyes. "Fine," she said. "Fine."

"It doesn't look like everything is fine. *You* don't look fine." Kathleen spoke softly—Neil called this her Library Voice—and so when Natalie grasped at the phone on the table, knocking into the chair next to her, the sound was surprisingly loud in the quiet room. "I'm fine," she said. "But they're stupid."

"Who?"

"Stupid girls. The girls in my school. Everybody in my school is stupid. I hate them all." She said this harshly, and the hand that gripped the cell phone was white-knuckled.

Kathleen didn't know what to say to this. Some latent instinct arose in her; she had a mother's urge to draw Natalie to her, to cradle her head and kiss her hair. But of course she couldn't do that. Natalie would think she was crazy. She was now backing away from Kathleen, gathering her things, putting her phone into her jacket pocket. Kathleen said, "By the way. Why are you here instead of school?"

Natalie didn't miss a beat; she looked directly into Kathleen's eyes. "No school today," she said. "Day off. Teachers' in-service or something."

"Ah," said Kathleen. "I see."

Natalie fiddled with one of her backpack straps and pushed her hair out of her face. "Anyway. Thank you for helping me."

Kathleen could see now that Natalie had little gold hoops in her ears. Why was that sad? Earrings weren't sad. And yet the sight of them *was* sad to Kathleen: the innocence of them, this girl's small attempt to be beautiful.

"You're certainly welcome," said Kathleen. "That's my job. But I don't feel like I helped you much yet. We haven't really gotten started. Are you leaving?"

"Yeah. I have to catch my bus back."

"Well, do you think you'll continue?"

Natalie blinked at her. "Of course I'll continue," she said. "Like you just said, I barely got started. I didn't do anything yet. I'm not going to *stop*."

Kathleen fought the urge to put her hand on Natalie's jacket, to keep her there while she talked. "You know, you can probably get started from home. The indexes for a lot of facilities, ours included, are online. You have to go to the physical site for the primary source, of course, for the actual records. But I could walk you through some of it on the phone—"

Something in Natalie's face changed; there was a hardening. "Okay," she said.

"I didn't mean you *can't* come back."

Natalie sniffled and wiped at her nose with the sleeve of her jacket. Silently Kathleen pushed the tissue box toward her, and kept talking. Natalie ignored the tissue box. "Of course you're welcome to come back anytime. The whole public is welcome. I just meant that it's a long way, that's all that I was thinking. From New- buryport. If you don't have rides. Or maybe you'd have rides sometimes?"

"No," said Natalie shortly, unapologetically, lifting her chin an inch. "I don't have rides."

"In that case, I'll give you my card." Kathleen crossed the room to retrieve one of her cards from a little stack she kept near the pencils and the scrap paper. "That way you can get in touch if you want to. Email, call, however you want to do it."

Susannah's freckles were lighter, and disappeared altogether before she became a teenager. But again, there it was. Something behind Natalie's eyes that tugged at Kathleen's memories: Susannah as a toddler reaching out her arms to be picked up, Susannah as an eight-year-old on a bike with a white wicker basket, her braids flying out behind her.

"Here," Kathleen said. "I'll write my home number on the back." She did, and then under the number she wrote IN CASE OF EMERGENCY.

Natalie took the card from Kathleen and studied it. Then she said, "Oh, and…here." She held out a coin to Kathleen. "I didn't know I would get the quarter *back*. From that locker. So here you go."

"Thank you," said Kathleen. "But I wasn't worried about it, really." She smiled. "It's just a quarter."

"Well." Natalie scrunched up her face. "I don't like to owe people I don't know."

Kathleen was taken aback by something in the girl's tone, but she was impressed, too — it showed some resolve, the way Natalie straightened her shoulders and met Kathleen's gaze levelly. Kathleen took the coin. It was warm and moist.

She glanced up at the clock on the wall. "But wait. What time is your bus?"

Natalie shrugged. "They come every hour."

"Do you need to call someone, to let them know where you are? Your mother?"

Natalie looked down at her scuffed sneakers; her shoulders inched forward again. "My mother's dead. So I can't call her for anything."

"Oh, dear." Kathleen fixed her gaze on a spot on the side of Natalie's neck — there was a cluster of freckles there, lone and defiant, like a constellation in an otherwise empty sky. "I'm sorry to hear that," she whispered.

"Yeah, well, so'm I," said Natalie. She retrieved her phone from her pocket and glanced at it. Kathleen thought she saw her shudder. "I have to go," she said suddenly.

Kathleen said, "You know, it's going to rain, it might be raining already. Do you have an umbrella?"

"No." Natalie looked surprised at the question, as though Kathleen had asked her if she had an extra hand she might want to lend out.

"It's supposed to pour, Natalie. You'll get soaked."

Natalie adjusted the straps of the backpack and zipped her jacket to the top of her neck. She shrugged. "I'll be okay."

"No," said Kathleen. She thought of Susannah in a little yellow bumblebee-themed slicker, Susannah under a pink ballerina umbrella. "Take mine. I have a spare. Wait here." She didn't have a spare.

She went back to her desk to retrieve her umbrella. She half expected Natalie to be gone when she got back to the reading room, but Natalie was there, staring out into the middle distance, her cell phone tucked away somewhere. She took the umbrella from Kathleen. "Thanks," she said, and, in a gesture that was unexpected and surprisingly formal, she reached out her hand to shake. "See you."

"I hope so," said Kathleen, and meant it. "Come back, and we'll work on this together."

Natalie nodded.

Kathleen watched the girl's progress out the door. She made her way down the steps, slipping once and then catching herself with the handrail.

"Whoa," said Neil, appearing beside Kathleen, whistling. "Who's your friend?"

Kathleen shrugged, suddenly irritated by Neil, irritated by the weather, by Natalie's disappearance down the steps, by the rain, by everything. "I don't know," she said.

"Where'd she come from?"

"Newburyport." What had Natalie said? *I don't like to owe people I don't know.* That seemed like an odd thing for a young girl to articulate.

"Strange," said Neil.

"Yes," said Kathleen. *My mother's dead. So I can't call her for anything.* The poor girl. No wonder she looked so fragile and bewildered. So underfed! Poor thing, no mother. That explained why she was out in a rainstorm on a school day, why she was navigating Boston's public transportation system on her own. She had nobody to tell her not to.

※

Neil asked later why the girl wasn't in school.

"Teachers' in-service," said Kathleen. They were taking a coffee break in the little room upstairs. It was a coffee break where neither person was drinking coffee. For Kathleen it was water; Neil was sucking at the green beverage he'd brought with him — some sort of concoction that included kale and hemp seed, whipped up earlier that morning in his $500 Vitamix blender. ("For cleansing," he'd said.) "What did she want?"

So Kathleen told him about the project. "We didn't get very far at all," said Kathleen. "She said she had to get the bus back. Sort of odd, to come all the way here, for what was basically an introductory conversation." She was still thinking about the resemblance between Natalie and Susannah. It was chewing at her.

"Yeah, that's a shocker," said Neil. "Seems like kids do everything online these days."

Neil was somewhere in his thirties. Kathleen didn't know his age exactly, but it seemed to her he was too young to say "these days."

Kathleen nodded. "That's what I told her!" she said, feeling pleased with this evidence of solidarity between them. "Not just kids," she added. "Seems like most people do."

"Right," said Neil, and he took another sip of the smoothie. "And that's fine, in certain cases."

"Sure," said Kathleen. "A good start. But eventually you want the primary source."

"Of course you do," said Neil.

She liked Neil because he was a good and careful worker and because, though he was young enough to be her son, he shared her appreciation of the old-fashioned nature of their work, her respect for the rolls of microfilm documenting births and deaths and marriages, her taste for ferreting out the details.

Example: There was a time, a couple of years ago, when she had all but given up on one branch of her family tree; then she discovered that the Massachusetts Catholic Order of Foresters had life insurance policies going way back. Her missing link, a great-great-uncle, who had died in 1879, was listed as a member. And voilà, another branch of the tree opened. Neil was the first person she told, and his excitement was real. ("You smart little fucker," he said. If there was one thing Kathleen would change about Neil if she could, it would be his language. Salty. But he always apologized after.)

She liked Neil also because he never asked about Susannah. Neil seemed to accept the hole in her life without feeling the need to stick his finger into it, feeling around for the tender parts, the way most people did.

"Newburyport is a hike for a girl that age," said Neil.

"That's what I said," said Kathleen, pleased again. "She said she took the bus."

"Sure. The bus from Newburyport goes right into South Station."

"How'd you know that?"

He shrugged. "I know lots of things."

"Then the T, then the shuttle," said Kathleen. "She said she likes the bus."

"I like the bus," said Neil. "Once I took the bus all the way across the country."

"You didn't!" said Kathleen, impressed. She was always finding out interesting things about Neil, like that he knew how to cook lobster thermidor and that once in New Zealand when he was in his twenties he had jumped off a bridge with a bungee cord attached to his ankles. She thought that maybe that came with being gay, the sense of adventure. Once she said that to him and he had laughed and said, "You don't know many gay people, do you?"

Now he said, "So what'd you do? To help the girl."

"I told her the cold, hard truth." Kathleen smiled to show she didn't think the truth was either hard or cold. To her it was a delight, the purest kind of pleasure.

"Which is?"

"Which is if she really wants to do it the right way, she's going to have to come back here a few times," said Kathleen. "It can be a long slog. She might hit snags, dead ends."

"What'd she say about the long-slog part?"

"She said she didn't mind." There was eagerness in the way the girl had said that. Kathleen told Neil about that too. She had told Natalie to start by talking to her grandparents, if they were living. ("Nope," said Natalie. "All dead.") Then Kathleen had to explain that the Archives kept only the records from 1841 to 1920; to research her later generations she'd have to go to the municipal clerk's office or the Department of Public Health registry in Dorchester.

"What'd she say about *that?*"

"Taken aback, at first."

"Who isn't?" asked Neil. They got a lot of people who came to the Archives expecting to find everything there, expecting to fly through six generations on the first visit. But the system was confusing if you didn't know it intimately, the way Kathleen and Neil did. Early passenger lists for people arriving in Boston were held at the Archives. But census schedules from 1790 to 1930: microfilm copies of those were in Waltham. It was no easy feat, running all around the eastern part of the state, gathering that information. You had to be committed.

"But she seemed into it," Kathleen told Neil. "And then she just...left. I guess that might be the last we'll see of her." She didn't tell Neil about the cell phone, or the text. "But before she left, when she seemed excited about the project, a young person like that, it was enough to give you some hope about the world."

"Ah, Kathleen. You're always looking for a reason to hope," said Neil.

Kathleen said, "Well." She *didn't* say, "Can you blame me?" Susannah's hot little hand inside of hers, her hair in a braid down her back.

"You don't need to look so hard, you know." Neil smiled.

"Says you," said Kathleen.

Kathleen thought about the formal way Natalie had reached out to shake her hand. Natalie's hand was cold, and despite the length of the fingers, there was something birdlike about it; Kathleen felt that if she squeezed too hard she might break some of the fine bones just underneath the skin. You didn't always see manners like that these days, the world had become so casual. Different from how it was when Kathleen studied with the nuns.

On the lunch table somebody had left a copy of the *Boston Globe*. A headline caught Kathleen's eye: "Mexico City votes to legalize gay marriage."

Kathleen picked up the paper and studied it, studied the photograph of flag-waving activists all the way in Mexico City, the rainbow-colored banner—it looked like a parachute, really—that they held aloft. She had never been to Mexico. She scanned the article. "The Roman Catholics aren't happy about this," she told Neil. "Just so you know."

"The Roman Catholics are never happy about anything," said Neil. "Wouldn't you say?"

"I would." For the majority of Susannah's life Kathleen had forced on her daughter the same rituals that had been forced on her when she was a child: the sacraments, Sunday Mass, Holy Days of Obligation. Inside the top drawer of Kathleen's dresser was a framed photograph of Susannah in her First Communion dress, looking like a miniature bride in her veil (Susannah had insisted on the veil because her friend Lisa was going to have one).

She remembered clearly something Susannah told her after the service, as they were driving home. She said that her teacher had told them to expect a feeling of peace and joy to settle over them once they received the Host. "She said it would be wonderful," said Susannah. "A feeling like I'd never had before."

"And?" said Kathleen. Her hands tightened on the steering wheel.

Susannah sighed. "I didn't feel anything."

"Nothing?" said Kathleen.

"Nothing at all. It tasted like bread, and I didn't feel anything."

"Oh," said Kathleen. "Well." She didn't know what else to say.

Now on Sundays she woke up early and took Lucy for long walks through the Arnold Arboretum. Walking along the paths, surrounded by fall color or snow-smacked trees resplendent in winter, Lucy's ears flattened against her head the way they did in times of great exertion and concentration, Kathleen came as close as she ever did to worship. This was now her church.

Kathleen drank the last of her water.

"What's the news on Henri?" she asked. Neil finished his smoothie and put the cap back on the bottle. Neil and Adam were in the process of adopting a baby from somewhere. Guatemala, was it? No, that couldn't be it. The Dominican Republic? She could never remember. But she did know that the process was constantly being stymied by one bureaucratic detail or another. It seemed to Kathleen that by the time they actually got the baby he would be old enough for a driver's license.

Neil's partner, Adam, was a tall man with broad shoulders and thick black hair, the kind of man who would have been referred to as a catch by Kathleen and her friends when they were young. And look who'd caught him! Neil. Neil and Adam had Kathleen over to dinner occasionally, and she looked forward to those times perhaps more than she would admit to anyone. They lived in a brownstone in the South End, and if she didn't feel like getting her old clunky car out she could take the T in and walk to their building, past the trendy restaurants, the fancy boutiques.

Adam had some sort of job in finance and made pots of money. Because of this he and Neil could afford the sort of modern and expensive décor that to Kathleen's eye made the inside of their home look like a laboratory or an industrial kitchen. But never mind that: Neil was an excellent cook. In the summer he grew herbs in little clay pots on his deck so the salads and fish always had a wonderful flavor.

"Oh, *that*," said Neil, sighing, as he rose from the table. "Nightmare. You don't even want to know. It's a mess over there, in Haiti."

Haiti! Of course.

"But I do," said Kathleen. She supposed that once Neil and Adam procured their baby and began toting it around in a backpack, that would be the end of the dinner invitations, the end of the long evenings sipping wine inside the industrial kitchen. The end for Neil and Adam, too, of some of their habits. The end of the Sunday-morning jogs, the leisurely brunches after. Probably they hadn't realized that yet, how much a child changed your life.

"Actually, it's Adam handling the phone calls and all of that," said Neil. "He's better at it. I get completely stressed out. You can't imagine the red tape we're wading through. And all the time the baby is getting older and older! And we're missing out."

Kathleen nodded. She thought Haiti should just give the baby to Neil and Adam. But she didn't say that. Instead she said, "You'll want to do something about some of that furniture in your apartment, won't you?" She was thinking in particular about a glass coffee table with lethal corners. Imagine a baby toddling into that.

Neil squinted at her. "I guess so," he said. "Yeah, we need to do some babyproofing. But we've got some time. We're waiting for the call, and then Adam will fly down and handle the details. While he's gone I can make whatever adjustments we need to make for Henri. Then, boom: parenthood."

They went for a walk, as they often did. The wind was whipping the water in the harbor into a frenzy.

"This might turn into something," said Neil, peering at the sky. "What do you think?"

"I think it already has," said Kathleen, remembering the umbrella she'd given up.

They climbed the steps and Kathleen paused, as she always did, to admire the squat, fortresslike building, the letters carved into the stone: MASSACHUSETTS ARCHIVES. There was something about the beauty and permanence of those words that thrilled and awed her every time she looked at them. All the histories tucked away inside the building, all the individual lives recorded. Sometimes, when things were slow, she took a roll of microfilm, loaded it in the machine, and just looked. Death records from Boston in a certain year, for example. A man, age thirty-two, tuberculosis. A woman, twenty-three, in childbirth. Regular old cardiac arrest at age seventy, same as you might expect today. A fall down stairs, a fire, an automobile accident. Sometimes she lingered on the death records of children, reading the parents' names, the street address, the country of origin if they were immigrants.

She didn't do this every day. She didn't even do it once a week. Maybe once a month, maybe more. But she believed that sometimes it was necessary, even important, to remind yourself of the smallness of your life, your place in the world, the insignificance of it all.

Kathleen returned to her desk and pulled out her chair. The red light on her phone was blinking, and she thought, *Susannah,* but the message was from a woman in Bedford who was following up on a visit from the month before. She took down the information.

For a lark, she opened Internet Explorer and typed this into the Google box: Newburyport. Public School Calendar. Up it came. What grade was this Natalie in? She didn't know. Probably junior high school, maybe high school. Both schools had the same calendar. There was no holiday listed for today, no teachers' in-service. Natalie was lying.

Kathleen, the child of two dour Irish Catholics, had gone to a school where the nuns would rap you on the knuckles with a ruler if you were caught in a lie, and you took it, biting your lips to keep the tears back: then you ended up with sore knuckles and bleeding lips both.

She left her desk and went through the door to the reading room. There had been someone else there in her absence, and the trays with the scrap paper and pencils were out of order, but that person was gone now so she went about the business of straightening up. On the floor, close to where Natalie's cell phone had been, she saw a crumpled sheet of paper. She sat down at the table and flattened it as much as she could. This, she saw now, was the piece of paper Natalie had brought in with her.

Kathleen brought the paper back to her desk and spread it out next to her, pressing down hard to try to erase some of the wrinkles. Natalie's father had already done quite a bit of work on this. Natalie was born in 1996; that made her thirteen. And this *me* with the jaunty exclamation point, that must be Natalie's father.

Kathleen stared at the paper for a while, and then she tried to find her way back into the work she'd been doing before Natalie came in. IN CASE OF EMERGENCY, she'd written on the back of the card she'd given her. She wasn't sure why she did that, but later, after the rest of it happened, she was glad she had.

⁂

First on Natalie's list of things that made her sick: adults who always had to let you know what the rules were. Example: the man who sat next to her on the bus. The man had gray hair and wore a business suit; he reminded Natalie of her father. He was probably around her father's age, although it was seriously hard to tell with adults sometimes. He had on a fancy raincoat, and he was carrying one of those umbrellas that fold up into the size of a safety pin but open up into a giant golf umbrella. Natalie looked at him and immediately thought: banker.

He was typing away rapidly on a laptop. When Natalie turned on her cell phone he shot a disapproving glance in her direction and said, "No cell phones." He pointed to the sign at the front of the bus, which showed a cell phone with a big red X over it.

"Oh," she said. "Sorry."

"Don't apologize to me," he said, unsmiling. "I don't make the rules." He went back to his typing.

The bus's progress up 95 was slow and arduous, packed with commuters. The rain had slowed everything down. Natalie looked steadily out the window. She could see the brake lights of dozens and dozens of cars. The bus driver leaned forward toward the windshield. When the passengers boarded at South Station he had been jolly and accommodating, offering bottles of water from the cooler up toward the front, making jokes about the weather. But as the bus wound its way through the terminals at Logan, he clammed up, and so did the passengers, everyone intent on getting home, and now she could almost feel the tension emanating from the driver's seat.

She turned on her phone, surreptitiously this time, tucking it between her body and the window. Just to see the text one more time. WE KNOW SOMETHING ABT U NATALIE. From an unfamiliar number, no name identified with it.

She felt this like you would feel a punch in the gut: she felt hollowed out, almost gasping for breath. She had gotten almost the same text the day before, but she had chalked it up to a mistake; someone texting to the wrong number. This time, though, the text included her name.

The man hadn't noticed that she'd turned on her phone. (Second on her list: grown-ups who pretended to care but didn't really. The list was in no particular order.) She moved the phone a little bit closer to the man; she'd be happy to be called out again for the infraction, happier still to throw the thing out the window and allow it to be crushed on the highway. But he didn't notice this time.

Who knew something about her? Knew what?

It was warm on the bus, and Natalie felt her skin heat from the inside out.

Third on the list: her skin.

Whenever she complained about her freckles, her mother said, "Look at Julianne Moore! She's considered very beautiful. She's famous for her freckles." When Natalie asked her to come up with someone else, she never could; Natalie surmised from this that there was basically one person in the whole world who was considered beautiful with freckles, and it was Julianne Moore. It was not her, Natalie Gallagher.

But she digressed, as Ms. Ramirez liked to say. Ms. Ramirez was her English teacher, and she, by the way, had the most gorgeous skin Natalie had ever seen: it looked like caramel, and it was so smooth that Natalie imagined she'd never had a zit in her life. Also she had short hair, supershort, cut really close to her head, and you can't get away with that sort of haircut if you're not beautiful and if you do not have perfectly symmetrical features.

The boys in Natalie's class found this sort of beauty disconcerting: they wanted blond hair, pillowy lips.

Fourth on the list: the boys in Natalie's class, Christian Chapman excepted.

She had turned the sound off on the phone, so when the next text came in she felt the vibration against her leg. She didn't look: she wouldn't look.

She looked.

WE KNOW SOMETHING ABT UR MOTHER

Then another one, right on the heels of the first.

ASK UR MOTHER HOW OLD SHE IS

Both of these from the same number. Huh? Why was she supposed to ask her mother how old she was? She knew her mother's age: thirty-three.

But the third one was from a different number, one that Natalie's phone recognized. *Hannah,* the screen's display told her.

U DONT KNOW DO U? BUT WE DO

❉

"Hello, my lady," said Kathleen later that day. She was soaked, of course she was soaked, after giving away her umbrella, and on a day when she had taken the T to work instead of driving the Camry.

Lucy didn't answer, per se, but she did greet Kathleen at the door, stretching, coming to life after a long day's rest, the tags on her collar hitting against each other.

"And how was *your* day, sweetheart?" asked Kathleen. Lucy lifted her ears—they could stand up in triangles, or lie down flat on her head, like a rabbit's ears, depending on Lucy's state of mind—and looked at Kathleen. Kathleen said, "Yeah?" encouragingly, and then, "Really?"

There was a time, years ago, when Kathleen had paid a dog walker to take Lucy for a romp once during the day, but that proved to be expensive. Also, Kathleen didn't like the dog walker; she felt that the girl didn't understand Lucy's particular temperament, that she saw her standoffishness as an annoyance.

Truth be told, before they got Lucy, Kathleen had wanted a golden retriever, a leaner, a lover, a dog who couldn't get enough of you. She hadn't known anything about border collies when they picked Lucy out, but Susannah, some vestiges of the movie *Babe* lingering in her imagination, had insisted. She did all of the research, she chose the breeder, she called for directions to the farm in Connecticut where Lucy, tiny, still watery-eyed and clumsy, had risen on her stumpy little legs and wobbled toward them.

"She never plays with the other dogs," said the dog walker. She had some silly name that was also a color, like Cobalt or Coral. Stupid, Kathleen thought, to have a name like that, and although she understood that the girl had probably not named herself, still Kathleen held the fact of it against her. "She just wants me to throw the tennis ball, over and over. Or a stick, if I don't have a tennis ball. Or a leaf! A pebble. Anything."

Kathleen said, "And?"

Cobalt (Coral?) said, "And it's sort of sad for the other dogs, the labs and retrievers, even the standard poodle, actually *especially* the standard poodle. They want to play with her, and she wants nothing to do with them."

Kathleen, who did not particularly care if some dogs she had no responsibility for felt *sad,* said, "Well, she's a border collie. That's her temperament." Because she had come to understand Lucy, and to admire her for her intelligence, and to respect her space, the way you might respect the space of an artist or a writer, someone doing Very Important Work who needed time alone to think about it.

After that, Kathleen stopped calling Cobalt/Coral. Instead she got up early and took Lucy for a long walk around Castle Island, and took her out again when she got home from work. On weekends they ventured farther. That seemed to suit both of them just fine.

"Hello, my lady," she said again to Lucy now. She pushed her nose into Lucy's fur and stroked her along the sides of her face. She thought that some people who observed this ritual would think that she was crazy, to love a dog so much. But there was such peace in loving an animal. At night, when Kathleen turned off her light to go to sleep and heard the little snorts coming from Lucy's bed, the shiftings as she settled herself to sleep, and finally the deep, even breathing, she felt truly blessed and forgot about everything she had lost. This was love, for her, now. This was the love she had.

❋

Before that day, not too long before, came this day.

Here sat Natalie Gallagher: thirteen, tall for her age, young for high school (the cursed early admittance to kindergarten, never a problem before, now came at her with a pitchfork), skin that blushed furiously, betraying—always, everywhere, odiously—what she was thinking. Also: flat chest, flatter than flat, no sign of the burgeoning curves that seemed to be growing overnight in the bodies of girls like Hannah Morgan, Natalie's erstwhile best friend.

It was early October, though it could have been spring, so mild had the temperatures been. It was so mild, in fact, that Natalie's house, an old, crumbling colonial revival in the downtown area, which normally was drafty and chilly, with a creaking old heating system that had been updated in a patchwork way, had been surprisingly bearable.

Natalie supposed this was all due to global warming, which her Science teacher, Mr. Guzman, a tall, twiggy man with wool sweaters worn thin at the elbows, talked about at length any chance he got. And while she tried to take Mother Earth's needs into account most of the time, she couldn't help but revel—a little—in the mercy of the season, and in the fact that her teeth, when she wakened in her tiny slanted room, did not begin immediately to chatter.

But this was not Science class, this was English, and Ms. Ramirez stood at the front. Natalie sat toward the back, which she did in every class where the students were allowed to choose their own seats. Hannah Morgan and Taylor Grant had chosen seats near the door but toward the front of the room; this gave them the twin advantage of being able to leave quickly when they wished but also to waylay anyone else leaving if they chose to do so. Which, sometimes, they did.

In Mr. Guzman's class, seats were assigned, and he had placed Natalie front and center, where she felt as bare and exposed as a telephone pole sticking out of the snow. When, in the first week of school, the boy behind her had tapped her on the shoulder to ask her to sit down a little lower so he could see the board, her humiliation had been so sudden and extreme, and her blushing so furious, that she had to ask permission to go to the bathroom, and had then moved in what seemed like half time across the floor, as though through a viscous liquid.

No, she much preferred Ms. Ramirez's class, both for her position in the back of the room and for the subject matter, which stirred her imagination, which made her happy in a way that very few things did these days. So far they had read Sandra Cisneros and Shakespeare; also John Steinbeck and a rash of the Romantic poets. Ms. Ramirez had been going on for some time about an upcoming "independent-study project," to be worked on from now until January, whose details Natalie was hungrily awaiting. She was (she inched forward) literally on the edge of her seat.

"And now," said Ms. Ramirez on this day in early October. "What you've all been waiting for. Your independent-study assignment." The class groaned in unison. Natalie, who hadn't meant to, felt herself groaning along with them, carried along by their displeasure as though by a rip current.

Ignoring these signs of discontent, Ms. Ramirez went on with the details: due in mid-January, the assignment could be anything they wanted that taught them something.

"I want to know three things," Ms. Ramirez continued. "Why you chose what you chose, how you went about it, and what you learned doing it. That's it. Not so bad. You can really take the reins here, do something exciting and interesting."

Scarcely had Ms. Ramirez finished her sentence when Taylor Grant's hand shot up, and Ms. Ramirez, in her terse and (Natalie thought) wonderful way, nodded at her.

"Um?" said Taylor. "That's it? That's the whole assignment?" She glanced at Hannah Morgan, and in return she received from Hannah a look of approval.

Nine years and some months ago, on her first day of kindergarten, arriving, like the other kids, with an oversized backpack, a lunchbox tenderly filled by her mother the night before, and her heart in her throat, Natalie had first heard Hannah Morgan's giggle. The giggle had changed not a whit since then, but you could say, truthfully, that everything else had.

Eight years ago, beginning of first grade: Natalie and Hannah had declared themselves best friends. They were both only children. This was unusual — everyone else in their class had at least one sibling, many of them more—and they started a private club, the Only Child Club, with themselves as the sole members. They made business cards, red construction paper cut into uneven rectangles, and passed them out to their parents.

Also in first grade: the first play date at Hannah Morgan's house. Hannah Morgan lived in a big bright house on the other side of town. The house had a swimming pool and a gigantic kitchen and a massive carpeted basement whose centerpiece was a pool table imported from England. ("Snooker," Hannah told Natalie when Natalie, following her down the stairs, her mouth agape, could scarcely contain her amazement. "That's what they call it in England." This was said in an important, reverent tone that Natalie would soon learn Hannah adopted when talking about many of her family's possessions. Natalie couldn't think of anything in her own home that required such a tone, and for this she respected Hannah.)

Seven years ago: first sleepover. Hannah's bedroom had its own attached bathroom, with its own white cupboard into which Hannah's mother had set small white wicker baskets to hold Hannah's headbands and barrettes. Her bed had a yellow canopy. How Natalie envied Hannah that canopy, and the matching throw pillows, and the big pastel wooden letters spelling Hannah's name that were strung onto a white ribbon and hung on the wall.

In the morning Mrs. Morgan, a lovely, doting woman who wore expensive yoga clothes that gave the paradoxical impression of sweatless exertion, made them pancakes; they sat at the massive island and ate themselves silly, and then, holding their bellies, down they went to the basement to choose from Hannah's complete selection of Disney movies.

Hannah's eleventh birthday. Mrs. Morgan—Mr. Morgan being, as ever, unavailable ("working," both Hannah and her mother said as reverently as Hannah said the word *snooker,* and while it was never explained to Natalie exactly what he did, she knew that the work involved dealing with other people's money) — took them on a trip to New York City to see *Wicked* at the Gershwin. They ate big plates of spaghetti at Carmine's. They shared a double bed at the Marriott Marquis, where they were hermetically sealed forty-four stories high and bathed in ambient light from the neon signs, the glories of the city spread out before them. In the morning they sat in Duffy Square and polished off bagels as big as their heads, their friendship forever secure.

Or not.

※

It had been dusk when the bus started out from Boston, Natalie's journey from the Archives to South Station having taken longer than she'd expected, but now it was fully dark, an inky blackness replacing the craggy outlines of the trees along the side of the highway.

People always say that in Boston you're better off being on the road in a snowstorm than a rainstorm because at least people know how to drive in the snow, at least they take care. People didn't take the rain seriously, and then: *bam.* A string of cars laid out on the highway.

On the shoulder, there was a car that had skidded off the road and sat at a crazy angle, its hazard lights flashing.

A woman behind Natalie said, "Jesus Christ, does he know how to drive this thing in the rain?" Natalie couldn't tell if the driver heard her, but the woman had a North Shore accent and a loud, brash voice that let you know she hoped he did. For some reason, even though Natalie had lived in Newburyport her entire life, she'd always been a little bit afraid of such women: receptionists in the doctor's office or the school, clerks at the supermarket, women so loud and confident. Unafraid.

Her mother did not have this way of speaking; she hadn't grown up here. "Whisked away from the Kansas farmland" is what her father used to say, and it was true that Natalie's mother had lived most of her life on a farm, with real chickens scratching around in the dust, a horse in the barn, the whole deal. ("Not what you think," her mother said grimly when Natalie asked about the farm. "No red-and-white-checked aprons, if that's what you're imagining.")

"My wholesome midwestern beauty," Natalie's father called her. "Raised on whole milk straight from the cow. That's why her skin glows."

("What were you running from?" Natalie asked. "Never mind that," said her mother.)

Why had she told the woman at the Archives her mother was dead? She didn't know, not really, except that there was something satisfying in the lie, some power it gave her over her own story.

The bus lurched, and a voice from the back of the bus said, *"Jesus H. Christ."*

⁕

Four months ago: on a July morning so bright and hot and humid that even the birds seemed to be mollified, a morning so scorching that the garbage cans began to stink like tenement trash the moment they were set out at the curbs to be collected, Natalie's father moved out. He didn't go a great distance, just to Amesbury, just across the river, but as far as Natalie and her mother were concerned he could have been headed for Mars.

He moved first into a small, white studio apartment that belonged to a friend of a friend. When that friend reclaimed it, he moved again, into another apartment, which Natalie had yet to see, because she had been, for the past three weeks, studiously ignoring her father's phone calls and messages and requests for visits, having found, as her mother slipped deeper into the fog and haze that they may as well begin calling depression, that it was easier to be angry than sad.

When Natalie thought about that day, which she tried not to do often, the memory rose to her mind, unbidden: her father's grim determination packing his bags into his car, her mother's bedroom door tightly closed, its occupant ensconced in a state of desperate melancholy from which she would not emerge until later that evening, when they ordered take-out from Pizza Factory and sat together in the kitchen. Natalie's mother ate none of it, and Natalie, ravenous, bereft, confused, consumed four pieces, crust and all.

And from there: downhill, all of it.

After he left—two days after, because she spent the first day sitting on a bench near Cashman Park, looking out at the boats on the river—Natalie tried to call Hannah. But Hannah had become suddenly, astonishingly unavailable, even invisible. She was a regular missing person, and, when calls to Hannah's cell phone went unanswered, Natalie took to calling her home number directly and speaking to Mrs. Morgan. Hannah was swimming at the Ipswich Country Club with a friend (which friend, Mrs. Morgan did not say, leaving Natalie to exercises in tortured, anguished guesswork). The closest Natalie had ever been to a country club was the pool at the Y, which, of course, didn't count at all.

Then, suddenly, Hannah was gone for two weeks at a sleepaway camp in Waterford, Maine. (Where was Waterford, Maine, and why had Natalie never heard of the camp plan?) A bit of Internet research, conducted clandestinely in her room, although her mother, to be sure, was not checking in on her, revealed that the camp offered horseback riding and waterskiing; that there was an amphitheater-style campfire (what did that even *mean?*); that the dining room was large and rustic; and many other facts that, taken together, caused Natalie's throat to constrict and a low rumble to

begin in her ears. Hannah was away! Hannah had gone to this special place and had said not a word to Natalie about it. Not a word.
Witness the glories of the place, the toothy grins of the campers
featured on the website, happiness incarnate.

And it was that fast. Not quite overnight, but fast enough that
Natalie felt dizzy from it all, unmoored, unanchored, the way she
felt the first time she did a somersault underwater, when she didn't
know which way was up.

٭

Now Natalie closed her eyes and leaned against the window. She
was suddenly very, very tired. Truly, she wasn't worried about the
bus ride. She had always felt safe in cars driven by other people.
That probably came from all the times her dad used to drive her
around when she was little. He was in pharmaceutical sales and he
used to take her on calls. His territory covered a great distance—
up into New Hampshire, down through Boston and a little bit
south—and she'd fall asleep in the car, waking to find herself in
the parking lot of a medical office building, or in a strip mall where
a doctor's office was squeezed in next to a burrito joint or a hair
salon. "Wait here," her dad would say, and she knew enough not
to try to unbuckle her seat belt, not to open the door that he'd
locked. Sometimes he left her with a book to look at, or a toy to
play with, but sometimes he left her with nothing at all. She didn't
mind that. She had always had a vivid imagination; she and Christian Chapman had worked together on writing a book when they
were in kindergarten ("my early readers, my little Einsteins," the
teacher had called them).

Natalie remembered Christian in first grade, crying because
another boy had taken his kickball at recess. He had been small
then, and easily teased, with a little-boy buzz cut and a slender,
almost girlish body. In fifth grade he moved away. She couldn't

remember where. Was it Oregon? Montana? Somewhere wide open and exotic. He had recently returned. It all had something to do with his dad's job. During his absence Christian had grown, broadened, strengthened; he had taken up the skateboard and the snowboard, and the little-boy buzz cut had become fashionably floppy.

She sat behind Christian in English class now, and every so often, if she bent forward, she caught a whiff of something that could have been cologne or could have been merely the fresh clean smell of the outdoors but either way made her think of the snow-covered mountains or ranches from which he had just moved (it *was* Montana, definitely Montana).

Thinking about that, she must have dozed off because when she awoke the bus had passed Exit 56 on the highway and was approaching Exit 57.

Once, not too long ago, maybe last year, Natalie had said to Hannah, "Your house is so much *nicer* than mine." She said it in the gentle, teasing manner all the girls used sometimes, when they wanted the other person to disagree: My hair looks *awful* today. My butt looks *so big* in these jeans. You said that so the other person could say, No it doesn't, your hair looks great, or, Are you kidding me? I'd kill to be skinny like you. You wheedled compliments out of people, you made a little game of it. Everyone did it. But Hannah didn't play that time. She took Natalie's hand and said simply, "Stay here, then. Any time. What's mine is yours."

When was that? A year ago? Maybe less? Sitting in the bus, listening to the man next to her tapping at his keyboard—he had picked up his pace, a staccato *rap rap rap,* and he was frowning intently at the screen—Natalie could nearly taste the lemonade Hannah's mother brought out to them at the pool; she could see the glass pitcher sweating on the slate table, the bright stack of beach towels in the basket. Hannah's mother had once been a flight attendant ("back when it was okay to call us stewardesses"), and she still had a way of looking at you that made you think she could take care of everything, that she could find a spot for your overhead luggage even when you thought all of the compartments were full. Now her sole purpose seemed to be making Hannah and her father happy, and exercising in her lovely, matching Lululemon clothes.

Stay here, then. Any time. What's mine is yours. The feel of Hannah's hands on hers, the pillow sham grazing her cheek. (It was a double bed, big enough for two.) She remembered thinking, This must be what it feels like to have a sister.

In the absence of siblings, she and Hannah had created elaborate lives for their American Girl dolls, and intricate, complicated friendships among them. Now Natalie felt a sudden longing for those dolls and their tender, wide-eyed innocence, their gentle compliance with costume changes and tea parties and ornate hairstyles. The glossy catalogs that the company sent out. They had spent hours poring over those. You could get the palomino horse, which came with its own saddle! You could get a canopy bed! Natalie never got the palomino horse or the canopy bed or any of the rest of it. Truth be told, she didn't have a brand-new doll either. Hers was a castoff from a babysitter ("Are you *insane,* Natalie? Those dolls cost a hundred dollars!"), but she gamely brushed the doll's matted hair and tried not to notice the stain on her dress.

The bus pulled into the station. The man next to Natalie looked up and sighed, then glanced at Natalie for confirmation, as though they were complicit in their annoyance with the weather and the traffic. Still stung from his admonishing about the cell phone, she didn't meet his eyes.

"Finally," said the woman behind her. "For the love of God, I thought we'd never make it home alive." She spoke as if to someone, but when Natalie finally turned around to look the seat beside her was empty.

Natalie had planned on walking home, but her house was more than two miles away and the rain was falling so thickly it looked almost like a solid wall. She still had the umbrella from the lady at the Archives, but it didn't seem up to the task; using it would be like trying to cut a steak with a spoon (this was her father's saying).

She would have to call her mother.

***

Susannah had gone away on a rainy night. She didn't take an umbrella. A rain jacket, but no umbrella.

There had been a lot for the parents to worry about back then, a bunch of teenage suicides in Southie, one after another after another: a cluster, they'd called it in the news, as though they were talking about produce. The parents were on edge, the kids too: Who was next? When? Where?

Three weeks before the awful day, Deidre Jordan's mother calling her, *Do you know what our daughters are doing?*

And Kathleen, stupidly, hadn't known. She'd said, *What?*

Heroin, said Deidre Jordan's mother. *Drugs.*

Kathleen, not believing her, searching Susannah's room, her backpack, the bathroom cabinets, finding nothing, not a scrap of evidence, no needles, syringes, no plastic bags, nothing. Coffee grinders, she'd heard that was an accessory too. No coffee grinder, nowhere in the house.

Alcohol, she understood. She'd grown up around alcohol, two parents who drank more than they should have and then pretended nothing was wrong. But heroin? A mystery. And because it was a mystery and she didn't believe it and she didn't know what to do, she did nothing.

She called Deidre Jordan's mother back. *I think you're mistaken,* she told her. *I think you have my daughter mixed up with somebody else.*

※

Three weeks later, she was gone. How had this happened? Kathleen had worked this over and over and over again in her mind, and still she couldn't quite envisage the specifics of the situation.

Deidre Jordan had said…what? Come with me? And Susannah had gone.

※

It was Detective Bradford who had explained to Kathleen the difference between a missing person and a runaway. He was portly and mustached, and Kathleen pictured him eating food out of a can in a bleak studio kitchen: inhaling it, really, SpaghettiOs through the nose, canned green beans pierced with a fork and inserted into his mouth. But he was kind, and he took time with her, and though the fee he named at first was exorbitant he ended up charging her only half of it. ("Didn't do much," he said in the end. "Wasn't much to do.")

※

There was nothing for dinner, and nothing for breakfast the next day either, and it was raining too hard to walk Lucy.

"Sorry, old girl," Kathleen said. "I'm off to the Stop and Shop, and I'd invite you, but I don't think you'd be allowed in." Lucy seemed to understand. It was possible that she nodded.

The Stop and Shop was busy, the parking lot full of weary people pushing sopping wet carts toward even wetter cars. You'd think that there was a snowstorm coming, not just rain and more rain. The bananas had been ravaged, and Kathleen was poking through them, looking for a suitable bunch, when a voice behind her said, "Mrs. Lynch?"

She turned and saw a young woman. Familiar? She squinted at

the woman's curly dark hair. She was pushing a cart with a baby seat perched on top of it in that way that always made Kathleen nervous but apparently was very safe. (In Kathleen's mothering days, you carried your baby around or pushed it in a baby carriage — none of these complicated and ponderous pieces of equipment.) Yes, the woman was familiar.

"I thought that was you," the young woman said. She pointed at herself and said, "Melissa. Melissa Henderson. Susannah's friend." The girl leaned eagerly toward Kathleen and said, "God! I haven't seen you in I don't know how long."

Kathleen felt her face freeze in an unnatural smile. "Melissa," she said slowly, remembering. "Of course." Of *course*. Melissa Henderson, one of Susannah's best friends at one point: junior high, and early high school. The more she looked at the young woman under the unforgiving fluorescent supermarket lights (correction: unforgiving to Kathleen, not to Melissa), the easier it was to recall her fifteen years ago. She had an image of this girl and Susannah coming out of the bathroom with makeup on, laughing, all lip gloss and hair and perfume. Beautiful! Both of them. Beautiful hair, beautiful skin, beautiful and optimistic, all of life ahead of them.

"This is Mabel," this girl, Melissa Henderson, visitor from happier times, said to Kathleen. She turned the shopping cart around so that Kathleen could see inside. "My daughter." She laughed. "It still seems funny to say that, you know? Daughter. *Baby* doesn't feel weird. But daughter does. It seems so permanent, you know?"

Kathleen peered inside the car seat. The baby was very tiny, so new. She was wearing a small pink hat and was sleeping with intense concentration, one fist raised above her head. Kathleen felt a sort of reverence and peace descend briefly on her. "My Lord," she said. "She's so beautiful!"

"I know," said Melissa Henderson. "I mean, I think so too."

"It sort of takes my breath away," Kathleen said to Melissa.

Somewhere in the store, one of the fluorescent lights was blinking. Kathleen couldn't see it, exactly, but she could sense it pulsing in a nearby aisle. This baby's skin looked like it was made of silk. "Is she your first?"

"The one and only," said Melissa proudly. "And by the way, after delivering her I can't imagine going through *that* again. Ever."

Kathleen did not pursue this line of conversation. She did not believe in sharing details from labor and delivery. To her, these were private, excruciating moments, to be relived and remembered only in your own mind, if at all.

Instead she said, "What is she, about two months?" Kathleen couldn't stop looking at the baby. She wanted to pick her up and feel the heavy weight of her head against her neck.

"Three," said Melissa. "But she was born early. She's a real peanut."

The inside of the car seat was pink, and the blanket tucked over the baby was pink too. It was an oasis of pink. When the baby opened her mouth and made a little mewling sound Melissa plucked a tiny pacifier, also pink, from somewhere inside the car seat and put it between Mabel's lips. Mabel sucked twice and then let it fall out; not once during the entire transaction did she open her eyes.

"I imagine she keeps you plenty busy," said Kathleen.

"I'll say."

"They do, at first." Kathleen tore her gaze away from the baby and looked more closely at Melissa Henderson. She was still carrying some baby weight, that was clear, and who could blame her, but otherwise she looked only a little bit older than she had when she and Susannah had sat up in Susannah's room, the door closed tightly, doing God knows what. She added, "Though you look well rested enough to me."

"Well," said Melissa, "maybe that's because I'm visiting my parents. I've got some extra sets of hands." She went on from there: she lived out in Oregon now, on the shores of some lake Kathleen had never heard of, and her husband worked for Nike. They went hiking all the time. Biking. Skiing. "Not so much anymore," she allowed, casting a loving look inside the car seat. "But of course this is even better." At the end of her monologue Melissa Henderson sighed blissfully and said, "We love it so much there, we'll probably never move back here."

It was then that Kathleen felt the first stirrings of envy for Melissa Henderson, for her lakeside home, her beautiful baby girl, her healthy skin. The mention of her parents and the extra set of hands they were providing to care for the baby. (How Kathleen would love to provide an extra set of hands to help care for a grandchild! She would love it so much, it hurt to think about it.)

Melissa looked expectantly at Kathleen: it must be her turn to speak, but she had no idea what to say.

Slowly, inexorably, the envy that had sprouted began to morph into something more foreboding. Melissa Henderson's presence here; the lovely, pink accoutrements in the car seat; even the smattering of freckles across Melissa's adorable little nose: all of this seemed to showcase so blatantly the things that Melissa had become and Susannah had not. Wife, mother, lakeshore resident. How was it that these two girls, at one time walking in tandem on the same path, had diverged so dramatically?

"Hey," said Melissa suddenly. "Do you remember when you took us to the movies that time? What'd we see? Do you remember?"

Kathleen didn't recall at first, but after a moment there emerged a cobwebby recollection of Susannah and Melissa behind a container of popcorn, a jug of soda as big as Texas, their heads pressed together, the two of them whispering madly, while Kathleen sat slightly apart, an observer, a glorified wallet. (But glad to be there! She remembered that. Glad to be there.)

Melissa snapped her fingers. "It was *Home Alone*! I remember now. That freaky little kid, remember?"

"Ah," said Kathleen. She did remember. Who was that little twit who played the kid?

"Macaulay Culkin," said Melissa. "God, that was forever ago." Melissa leaned toward Kathleen in a way that was both conspiratorial and, Kathleen thought, a little too familiar. "Crazy," Melissa said. Then she continued: "Did he die? Or was that someone else?"

"I'm sure I don't know."

"No, he didn't die. That was one of the Coreys. Feldman, was it? Oh, I don't know. What's it matter, right?"

"Right."

In an effort to disguise her envy, Kathleen cast her eyes about the produce section, at the orderly stacks of oranges and apples and lemons piled atop one another in a way that seemed to be precarious and unstable. The bananas she would give up on—there was not a suitable bunch in the lot of them.

She could have taken her leave, but she didn't; she waited for the question that was surely coming next.

Melissa Henderson was now so close that Kathleen caught a whiff of a subtle and expensive perfume. Melissa arranged her features in an expression of sympathy and understanding, and her voice seemed to change an octave. And here came the question, as though Melissa had just thought of it, as though the whole conversation had not served as a prelude to this. She tilted her head at Kathleen and asked, as casually as if she was asking about where in the store she might find the quinoa, "How's Susannah these days?"

How's Susannah!

How's Susannah.

These days.

The temptation, of course, was to fill in a whole life for Susannah, a string of successes both personal and professional. *Living in*

San Francisco, Kathleen could have said. Or Chicago. Working in banking or accounting. *Busy, busy. Married? No, not yet. But dating someone serious.* She could invent a dog for her, perhaps, a designer breed like a Labradoodle or a Woodle (it was true, Kathleen had recently heard that there was such a thing as a Woodle).

In no hurry for all of this, she could have said, gesturing to indicate Melissa's baby, her cart full of groceries. Diminish it, that's what she could have done with the gesture, indicating that Susannah was bound for things larger and better.

But she didn't. She kept it enigmatic. She averted her eyes and looked down at her own shopping cart, and said, "She's fine. Thank you."

Melissa's eager expression became serious and thoughtful. In a whisper as soft as corn silk, she said, "You don't know, do you? You're not in touch?"

"No," admitted Kathleen. "No, we're not. I don't know."

Melissa said, "I didn't think so." She reached down and adjusted the baby's blanket—no need, really, it was perfectly arranged—and said, fiercely, "I blame it on the other girl." She stroked the baby's cheek and then continued, "I know she's okay, though. I feel it."

Kathleen said, "You feel it?"

"I do," said Melissa staunchly. "I do."

"Thank you," said Kathleen, wanting to believe her.

"I know it must be so hard for you," continued Melissa.

"Thank you," said Kathleen again. But what she thought was: You don't know. You can't know. Kathleen had to keep her eyes averted. The faraway fluorescent light kept up its ferocious blinking, all the worse for being impossible to locate. Kathleen's head was beginning to hurt.

She looked again at the baby, who had stirred and resettled herself as much as the confines of her bulletproof car seat would allow.

The baby lips were like a little puff set in the center of her face, like a little dessert. Kathleen had to stop herself from bending down and breathing in the baby's scent. In the folds of her neck she could see where a little milk was caught—breast milk, judging from the size of Melissa's breasts.

And just as suddenly as the envy had emerged, it began to disappear. It wasn't easy, being a new mother, and despite Melissa's breezy exterior she was of course going through the most major transition of her life. It wasn't Melissa's fault if Kathleen and Susannah had lost each other. Kathleen could be kinder.

Softly, still looking at the baby, at beautiful little Mabel, she said, "It's almost enough to make you believe in the world again, a baby like that." That was the best she could do, but it seemed like it was enough, because Melissa Henderson gave her a sincere and open smile.

After they parted, Kathleen turned and watched Melissa's progress down the cereal aisle. She watched her bend lovingly over the car seat, and she was overcome by such feelings of despair that she thought she might have to sit down.

But of course there was nowhere to sit in a grocery store, and nothing for Kathleen to do except continue on her way, pushing the cart ahead of her, trying to ignore the squeezing in her heart.

꙳

Natalie stepped inside the station. The man behind the counter who handled the parking for the commuter lot peered at her. On a table next to him sat a coffeepot sizzling on its metal stand, a stack of Styrofoam cups, sugar packets. The man said, "You just come off that bus?"

She nodded and picked at a hangnail.

"You have a way home?"

Natalie nodded again. "I'm going to call my mother."

She sat on one of the orange chairs and turned carefully away from the man. Slowly, cautiously, she turned on the phone. No texts. She dialed her home number. The phone rang once, twice, three times. No answer. She put the phone on her lap, thinking.

Then a text came in. This one said: DONT U WANT TO KNOW WHAT WE KNOW?

The man cleared his throat. "She's not there?"

"She's there," Natalie said. "Probably just in the bathroom. I'll call back." She couldn't stop looking at the text.

"Coffee over there if you want it," said the man.

"Thanks," she said. "I'm not allowed to drink coffee." How old did he think she was? Why did she have to be so *tall?* (Thing number five that made her sick: her height.) Where was her mother?

"We used to have some cocoa packages," the man said. "You like cocoa?"

She did like cocoa, but she shook her head, and anyway she liked the real kind, made with milk and actual whipped cream, not the powdered kind with the fake little marshmallows. Hannah's mother used to make them the real kind, after they went sledding down the hill behind Hannah's house.

"I could probably find the packets," he said. "Might have a box of them in the back."

Natalie looked around the small room and thought, In the back of *what?*

She felt a sudden and unreasonable rage at the man, who was clearly trying to be helpful, who did not seem to be a pervert or a freak, although of course you never knew. He wore a wedding ring; he was somebody's husband. Probably somebody's dad too. Natalie looked at him, the thinning hair, the paunch that showed beneath his blue shirt. "No," she said. "I don't like cocoa. But thank you."

The man nodded and shrugged. "Suit yourself," he said.

She braced herself, glancing at her phone again.

Another text: WE KNOW UR SECRET

She felt sick to her stomach. She hit delete, delete, delete, the whole series of them, off into the ether. Her hands were shaking so much that it was tricky to push the buttons.

What secret?

This time her mother answered on the third ring.

"Mom," she said, and she could feel the man looking at her. Again she turned away. "Mommy," she whispered. "Can you come pick me up? At the bus station?" She didn't know where that came from: she didn't remember the last time she had used the word *Mommy*.

She listened and then she said, "It doesn't matter. Come in your pajamas. You don't have to get out of the car."

She said, "I *know* it's raining. I was going to walk—no, the *bus* station, not the train station. Up on One-thirteen. Yeah, that one. No, there's a little building. I'm sitting inside."

She knew the man had been listening, and after that she couldn't meet his eyes, so she waited outside.

It was hard for her to stand up straight. Her knees felt weak.

She waited under the awning, which kept the rain from landing on her head, but the rain was coming in at such an angle, and the wind was so strong, that there was nothing she could do to protect herself: by the time her mother pulled up she was soaking wet.

※

Nearly a week later, on Thursday, when early November had given way to the soggy middle of the month, raining again, Kathleen's phone was ringing when she opened the door after work. She raced for it, Lucy following her, ears up. She had the thought that it might be that girl from last week, Natalie Gallagher. ("How do you live without caller ID?" Neil had asked her once. "I would *never* answer the phone if I didn't know beyond a shadow of a doubt who was on the other end.")

"When are you going to get a cell phone?" said Carol when she answered.

"I have a cell phone."

"When are you going to turn it *on?*"

"It's on." (It wasn't.)

"Sure," said Carol. "Anyway, I'm just calling to remind you that I'm picking you up at eleven on Saturday." Kathleen hadn't known Carol when they were younger, but she imagined that her friend had always been the way she was now: coiffed, adorned, painted, alarmingly energetic. They had met five years ago in a knitting class. Kathleen was going through what she called her "extracurricular" phase; besides the knitting she'd taken Beginner's Italian at the Center for Adult Education, and also a wine-tasting class. None of these had stuck (she kept getting the Italian mixed up with her dormant high school Spanish; she got the knitting yarn hopelessly tangled; in the wine-tasting class, every wine had tasted the same to her and she had never, for the life of her, seen the "legs" you were supposed to see on the sides of the glass after you sloshed it about).

But Carol had stuck. Underneath the makeup and the Chanel suits was a sardonic air that Kathleen appreciated. Also Carol knew how to keep her mouth shut. Kathleen had told her once about Susannah, then told her she never wanted to talk about it again. Carol nodded crisply, took Kathleen's hand briefly and then dropped it, and that was that.

Carol took Kathleen places she'd never been and most likely wouldn't ever have gone without her: to dinner at Radius, for drinks at the Oak Bar, to a charity auction at the Ritz-Carlton. She took her into Neiman Marcus at Copley Place, where Kathleen had no intention of shopping, and Kathleen watched while Carol tried on (and purchased!) a blouse that cost $198.

Carol had a husband and three grown children, a passel of grandchildren, a couple of cats. Carol's house was a Tudor in Newton with a yard of such grandeur and magnitude that you could truly call it "grounds." ("Saddled," Carol said, "with all of this," and it was with some envy that she talked about Kathleen's "solitary existence." Kathleen didn't know "how lucky she was, sometimes," to be able to come and go as she pleased.)

Recently Carol had given gobs of money to some sort of organization that empowered young girls, and so she was invited to bring a guest to a luncheon at a swank downtown hotel.

Kathleen thought about Melissa Henderson bending over the car seat.

"Wear something semi-nice," said Carol. "Not flashy, but nice." This was clearly a joke: Kathleen didn't own anything flashy.

"Got it," she said. "Eleven."

"You know what? Let's make it ten thirty. I think there's a walk for something or other on the Common. You know how it is: those things suck up all the parking."

※

Thing number six that made Natalie sick: the way things could change so quickly, and nobody gave you any warning. One day Hannah Morgan was your best friend, and the next day she was not. One day your father was there, and the next day he was not. One day your mother was functioning like a normal mother, making you breakfast in the morning, showering, washing and drying her hair, putting on a little makeup maybe, and the next day she was in bed, shades pulled down, the day one long night.

※

Almost a week had gone by since Natalie's trip to the Archives, and in the interim she'd made no progress with her independent-study project. None whatsoever. She'd gone to school, she'd come home, she'd joined her mother for "dinner" (she had to put the little air quotes around the word each time she thought or said it because she wasn't sure the desiccated fish sticks, the gummy pasta, actually qualified), she'd done her homework, gone to bed, gotten up. Lather, rinse, repeat.

There had been no new texts; she'd allowed herself to believe the ones she'd gotten on the bus the week before hadn't really happened. (What secret, what about her mother? Didn't matter, maybe she'd imagined the whole thing, she'd deleted them, there was no record.)

Then. Friday, after English, Natalie at her locker, fumbling on the floor for a dropped piece of paper, stood up and almost knocked into Taylor Grant, so close was Taylor standing to her. She seemed to be standing *over* her, although Natalie was by far the taller of the two. And behind her, like a lieutenant, like a bodyguard, Hannah Morgan, looking carefully into the middle distance.

"Hey," said Taylor softly. "You never answered our texts, Natalie!" She was so close that Natalie could feel Taylor's breath on her neck, could smell the minty scent of her gum, and also some perfume, really pretty, she had to admit.

Natalie said, "What?"

A little louder, as though talking to her deaf aunt Betty, Taylor said, "Our *texts*. You never answered."

Around them swarms of students moved by; Natalie could see them out of the corner of her eye, but they melded into one, a symphony of color and sound.

Later she thought of that moment as where it all began, all of it, the whole terrible mess, crystallized into an instant, the instant she met Taylor's eyes (she had to look down to do this) and said, in a voice hard and even, "I don't know what you're talking about."

"No?" Taylor looked at Hannah. "She doesn't know." Hannah

gave an infinitesimal shrug, barely a movement. "About your *mother*, Natalie. We know how old your mother was when she married your father."

"What?" Natalie's mouth was dry; she felt her throat constrict. *"What?"*

Taylor continued: "We think it's creepy, you know." She leaned closer to Natalie—it was amazing that was possible, she was so close already—"And illegal too, you know. She was practically a *child*."

Natalie gathered enough of her voice to say, in a hoarse, unnatural whisper, "My mother is thirty-three."

"Yeah?" said Taylor. "Are you sure about that?"

The drumming in Natalie's ears was now so loud that she couldn't believe nobody else could hear it. She looked at Hannah, and what she saw there made her misery complete. Hannah wasn't going to do anything to help Natalie. Hannah was scared of Taylor. She was terrified. Hannah looked like she'd looked when both girls were nine years old, about to step onto the Yankee Cannonball at Canobie Lake.

But then Hannah did something with her face, something that transformed the fear into a smooth mask of unconcern. God, it was terrifying, the way she could do that, like magic, but not regular magic: black magic, the worst kind. There was a swirl of mint and perfume, there was glossy hair tossed over shoulders, and Natalie stood for a moment longer, even though she knew she'd be late for her next class. She was shaking. She finally understood the expression "her knees knocked together" because that's what hers were doing, knocking together like one was a hammer and the other a nail.

Christian Chapman came down the hallway, alone, late too, not looking very worried about it. He stopped in front of her. "Hey. Natalie. You okay?"

"Yeah," she said, and tried to smile. "Sure, yeah, fine."

Once, on one of the nature shows she used to watch with her father, she had seen a lion with its prey (a warthog, maybe?), bandying it about before finally killing it. It looked like sport, she remembered that. She turned to her locker; she gathered her things for the next class. But she couldn't shake the image of the warthog lying limply on its side, eyes closed, waiting for the fatal bite.

Number seven on the list of things that made her sick: Taylor Grant.

�֍

Carol knocked more loudly than she needed to on Kathleen's door—more loudly than she needed to because Kathleen was dressed and standing in the kitchen eating toast smeared with a gorgeous orange marmalade.

"Have some," said Kathleen, pointing.

"No," said Carol. "Thank you. I've got my makeup on."

"Suit yourself," said Kathleen. She held up a finger. "Just hang on a minute. I've got to brush my teeth."

"The food will be crap," Carol said once they were in her cream BMW, fresh vacuum marks visible on the carpet. "So you'll be happy you had the toast. But the cause is good."

"*I* don't mind," said Kathleen. "I'm not in it for the food. I'm in it for the company."

"I'm just happy to be out of the house," said Carol. "I've got my son and daughter-in-law visiting from New York, the two kids— my God, the mess they make! I mean, I love them to death, but. Stuff everywhere, everywhere! I don't think they keep their own house that way, in fact I know they don't, but in my house I guess anything goes."

"Which kids are these?" asked Kathleen politely. She could never keep it straight.

"The twins," said Carol.

"Ah," said Kathleen, no more enlightened than she had been.

Carol turned onto 93. The trees were suddenly bare and stark against the sky, the leaves that were there just a week ago had been wiped clean away.

"How's your week been?" asked Carol. "Anything new in the world of dead people?"

"Oh, *stop*," said Kathleen. "You're just jealous that I'm gainfully employed. But one thing did happen, the end of last week." And then she was telling Carol all about Natalie's visit. "It's the strangest thing, I can't stop thinking about her."

She paused, and fiddled with the handle of the glove compartment door. "She reminded me of Susannah, you know. There was something about her that was so similar, I can't put my finger on it. I keep wondering if she'll come back."

She told Carol about the cell phone too, and the crying. "I don't know what it meant," she said, "the text. But it didn't seem right. It seemed ominous."

"Oh, *God*," said Carol. "I was just reading something about that. Cyberbullying. Awful stuff, just awful. You hear about it everywhere. Makes me glad my kids grew up when they did. Not that there weren't plenty of dangers then—" She glanced at Kathleen. "Sorry."

Kathleen waved a hand at her. "I know. Nothing for you to be sorry about."

"But it's different nowadays," said Carol. Then she said, "Isn't it strange, that we're old enough to say *nowadays,* and it seems perfectly natural? When did that happen? I feel like I'm still nineteen most of the time, until I look in the mirror."

"Yeah," said Kathleen. She didn't remember what it felt like to be nineteen; some days she felt ninety.

They were quiet then. Carol exited the highway and began to wind her way through Chinatown. She drove expertly. She opened her window a couple of inches, but not enough to threaten her hairstyle. "Tall air after a good hard rain," she said. "Is there anything better?"

***

After Gregory died, Kathleen had, for a time, given up on noticing the natural world. Why should she? The natural world seemed to her to be an extension of God, and God, by taking Gregory away from her, had failed her, and had failed Susannah, too, leaving them adrift, unanchored, looking at each other like a couple of baby birds abandoned in a nest. Small chirping mouths, empty stomachs, tiny little scrabbling talons.

Except only one of them was a baby, of course, and Kathleen was the adult meant to look after the baby. But how could she look after a baby when she had a giant hole in her heart, when she woke up at night shivering, unable to get warm no matter how many blankets she used or how high she turned the thermostat?

After, the doctor said that there was no way anyone could have known about Gregory's heart condition. Not only undiagnosed but undiagnosable, he said, looking at Kathleen, though not so much at her as through her, as though on the other side of her lay the answer to some important question that somebody else in the room had asked him. One of those freak things, he said soberly. This doctor couldn't have been much older than Gregory. His wedding ring was shiny and a little too big: he was probably a newlywed. He said, "I'm sorry I can't give you any more information than that." He made a move toward Kathleen, and it seemed for an odd instant like he might embrace her. Then he backed away. His actions were uncertain, like those of a teenage boy, but his words had authority and clarity. Finally he held out his hand and shook Kathleen's. Later that seemed strange to her, as though they had engaged in some sort of business transaction.

Kathleen's mother came from Pennsylvania to help out with Susannah, who was two. Not a baby, really, after all, though the image of the chirping baby bird in the nest remained with Kathleen. Susannah was old enough to say, "Where Daddy go?" but young enough not to pursue it if nobody offered a reasonable explanation. Which, of course, nobody could, because there was nothing reasonable about it.

Kathleen was supposed to rest when her mother arrived, but she found she couldn't. The only way to make it bearable to was to keep moving. So she walked around Marblehead, where they lived. She took long walks to the town beach and sat on a rock looking out at the angry gray water. It was late fall, the leaves had gone from the trees, and the waves seemed to be yelling at one another.

Sometimes she walked to the library and looked in medical books to find photographs of human hearts. Healthy hearts, diseased hearts: all of these she studied. Nowadays, of course, you would just go on the Internet if you wanted to learn anything about the heart. But back then Kathleen sat at a scratched brown table, her toddler napping at home, the librarians busy around her, and opened one book after another, trying to understand.

The funny thing was that after looking at so many photographs you'd think she would have the image of a human heart fixed firmly in her mind. But whenever she called up the picture of Gregory's heart what she saw was a heart that a child would cut out of red construction paper: crooked, imperfect, a little bit torn around the edges.

There were people in the town who watched her walking. They said it was time for her to move on from Gregory's death and to focus on her daughter. She knew this because her mother, who overheard some of these things on the playground or in the grocery store with Susannah, had no compunction about repeating them. In fact she seemed almost gleeful about it, energized by it, describing the women, their hand gestures, their harsh words.

Kathleen didn't believe in ghosts, not exactly. But sometimes in the night she was woken by a sound in her dark, quiet room. It was the sound of Gregory laughing, and her laughing with him. More likely a memory than a ghost, but real enough that she sat up in bed and turned the bedside light on, looking for the source of the noise. How she and Gregory used to laugh back then! Before Susannah was born, and then after, when they were a happy triumvirate. Laughing, laughing, all the time—until their sides hurt, until they gasped for breath.

This was all by way of saying that Kathleen had once been happy and had once been young and sometimes it was only when she looked in the mirror that she realized that she was neither of those things anymore.

Eventually her mother returned to Pennsylvania, to her own life, to Kathleen's father, whom she had left to his own devices, opening "goddamn cans of soup" for dinner—he was hopeless at taking care of himself. It was understood that Kathleen's mother had offered Kathleen all of the help she could reasonably offer, that it was now to be Kathleen and Susannah against the world.

Listlessly, Kathleen began looking for work. She didn't find any. But she wasn't looking that hard; there was nowhere nearby she could picture herself working. Not a shop or a restaurant, not the little grocery store in town. The library didn't need anyone. Then where? She didn't want to commute to Boston—she'd have to find someone to look after Susannah for all of those extra hours she'd spend driving.

Just like that, it was decided for her. She got a call from a lawyer. An aunt she had never heard of had left her property in South Boston. Rather, the aunt was Gregory's aunt, and she had left the property to Gregory, but of course it was Kathleen's now. This seemed like something out of a novel: an aunt she had never heard of. An aunt with property! A small house, the first floor of a three-family, with two tiny bedrooms, one bathroom, an outdated kitchen. But it was to belong to Kathleen, all of it, even the little scrap of yard, which had given over completely to weeds.

It wasn't difficult to leave Marblehead. The apartment was a rental, and anyway so much of the town reminded Kathleen of Gregory: the crooked little houses along the downtown streets, a certain slant of light that hit the rocks along the beach just before sunset.

They drove south. Once they were through the worst of the Boston traffic, Kathleen felt something in her loosening. Susannah was sleeping in the backseat, and Kathleen could see the curve of her lovely toddler cheeks in the rearview mirror. This was a new beginning.

After a couple of months there, the differences between the two towns started to gnaw at her a little bit; she had replaced the narrow little streets of historic homes with grimy, leaning three-families. They were outsiders, doing their best to fit in. Kathleen wondered sometimes what would have happened if they'd simply stayed put in Marblehead. Would Susannah have found someone like Deidre Jordan, or would someone like Deidre Jordan have found her? Was what happened inevitable, preordained? Or simply a consequence of Kathleen's decisions?

She got the job at the Archives, found a suitable day care for Susannah.

Slowly it returned to her, her ability to notice the world around her. She reveled in it again! The leaves in the autumn, colors so bright they hurt your eyes. The water in the harbor outside the Archives. She loved it in all moods: sparkling with the sun, severe and foreboding during a storm. She grew to love Southie too, after a time. The toughness of the people there was something she could appreciate.

Work became her focus: work, and Susannah's happiness, both of which she pursued with equal fervor. They got a dog, Lucy's predecessor, the beloved Murphy, a mutt. She went on dates! Life, love, all of it seemed possible again. Years went by like this, the two of them against the world.

And then it all went wrong.

⁂

"Mom," said Natalie on Saturday morning. "Mom, it's a beautiful day. You should get up." She yanked on the shade's cord to raise it. "The sun's out," she said. "It's not raining."

Her mother shielded her face with her hand. "Sweetie, just a minute. Let me wake up a little bit."

Natalie sat carefully on the edge of the bed and took a deep breath. "Mom?"

"Yeah?" Her mother's eyes were closed.

"How old were you when you married Dad?"

Her mother opened her eyes. "What? Why?"

Natalie thought of Taylor's breath on her neck, her minty gum, the texts.

U DONT KNOW DO U? BUT WE DO

"I was nineteen, Natalie. You know that. I was young. Twenty when I had you. I'm thirty-three now." Her mother didn't meet her eyes when she said that. She was shielding herself again from the sun.

"Yeah?"

"Yeah. Natalie, what's this all about? Why are you asking me?"

"Nothing. No reason."

"Natalie, honey, can you make me a cup of coffee? Lots of milk and sugar?" She let her head fall back against the pillow. "Thanks, sweetie. Then I'll get up, promise."

⁂

Somehow it didn't occur to Kathleen that this might be difficult. It didn't occur to her after they parked in the Common Garage. The hotel parking garage represented "highway robbery," said Carol, sighing, so they would park here, and Kathleen didn't mention the Neiman Marcus blouse, though it was hard not to. It didn't occur to her, as they trooped gamely across the Public Garden, what they were going to, or what that meant.

"A girl-power thing," said Carol. "You know."

"Didn't you say girl *empowerment?*"

Carol waved a hand. She walked quickly, and Kathleen struggled to keep up. "Isn't that the same thing?"

"Is it?"

"I don't know," said Carol. "But walk faster. We're going to be late."

What they were going to, it turned out, was some sort of celebration of young girls who had done important and amazing things, proceeds going to a corporation that empowered girls, whatever that meant.

"Oh," said Kathleen softly, understanding finally when they walked into the hotel lobby, whose occupants seemed to divide neatly into two distinct groups: women over fifty (perfumed, silver-haired, stockinged, bejeweled) and girls in bright orange T-shirts with the name of the charity—Girls Alive!—emblazoned across the chests.

"Hello!" they chirped to Carol, to Kathleen, to everyone entering. "Welcome!"

"Thank you for coming!"

"This way please!"

An adult must have told them to do that.

"Are you okay?" said Carol, peering at Kathleen. "You look strange suddenly. Like you're going to cry."

Kathleen wondered how she looked to everyone there. Regular, like someone to whom nothing had ever happened. As though there were such people.

"Don't be ridiculous," said Kathleen gruffly. But she couldn't bring herself to meet Carol's gaze, nor could she meet the eyes of the girls in the orange T-shirts. All those brilliant eyes, all those hopeful, uplifted faces.

Kathleen was fine during the lunch—tired, overdressed chicken Caesar salads, Carol had been right—but after, when a couple of women got up to introduce the girls they were honoring that day, all went swiftly and irrevocably downhill. The keynote speaker was a woman with an ultrashort, all-gray hairstyle, the kind Kathleen always admired but knew she could never pull off; she was CEO of such-and-such Boston-based business (Kathleen missed the name). Organizations like this were so important, she said, because society was not always kind to girls. Society did not always let them know how much they could accomplish; society did not always set them free. All around them, this woman said, girls were in danger.

Natalie (poor motherless Natalie, adrift, bereft) looking at her cell phone. Susannah crumpled on the corner of her bed, burrowing into the wall.

Kathleen could no longer hold it together.

All around them, girls were in danger.

Kathleen rose from her seat and signaled to Carol that she was going.

"Bathroom is that way!" sang a girl in the back of the room, a girl with glorious dark skin. (Hispanic? Cuban? Gorgeous.) She was in danger too! Didn't she know it? They all were.

Some time later, a stranger knocked on the stall door.

"Excuse me. Are you okay in there? Do you need something? Do you need me to call someone?" Beneath the stall door Kathleen could see black pumps, nude stockings. Through the crack where the stall door met the frame, a gray suit was visible. From the ballroom came applause.

"No," she managed, although of course she was lying.

"Sure?" The gray suit moved a bit; the black pumps shifted.

"No, thank you, I'm fine."

Lying through the stall door, lying through the crumbs of salad croutons in her teeth.

Long ago Natalie's father had laid some wide boards out on the basement floor, which otherwise was just dirt—it was a glorified crawl space, really, and it had been years since Natalie could fully stand up in it. In one corner a sump pump tried gamely to keep out any water that crept in, but without the boards it would have been hopeless: everything would have been ruined long ago.

Thing number eight that made Natalie sick: fathers who did jobs like that and then left anyway.

But the boards worked, and this was where the Gallaghers kept their bins with the Christmas ornaments, old paperwork that didn't have anywhere else to go, outgrown clothing waiting its turn to be donated.

Thing number nine that made Natalie sick: living in a tiny, crumbling house. All around them, during Natalie's childhood, neighboring homes were purchased and renovated: walls knocked down, kitchens enlarged, spacious family rooms carved out of impossible spaces. In one lot on the next street over, an old home was torn down entirely to make way for a faux-Federalist mansion so big it strained against the property lines like a fat lady in an old suit. While theirs sat, untouched, peeling. Ancient, the same as it had ever been.

"Why don't we do something to our house?" she ventured once. And her mother said, "Do you think we're made of money?" This was before Natalie's father left, and Natalie's mother must have seen something in her face, some sort of wound, because she continued more softly, "This house has been in Daddy's family for ages. He doesn't want to touch it." It was hard to remember it now, but it had existed once: the tenderness when her mother talked about her father.

Instead of touching it, then, he had just left it: left the two of them there, flailing. Staggering through their days, living inside the house with the crooked doorway ("Original!" her father said cheerily, pulling at it when it got stuck), the sash windows ("Annoying," said her mother, "I can't get the one in the living room to close all the way"), the peeling clapboard ("Period," said her father; "Disgraceful," said her mother).

You reached the basement not via a regular staircase but by lifting up a strange little door near the kitchen and descending a short set of uneven steps. You had to have a flashlight with you—there was a bare bulb hanging from the ceiling that was not quite up to the task—and you had to descend slowly, feeling for the next step with one foot while you balanced the other on the higher step.

All of these things Natalie did on Saturday after she brought the coffee to her mother, who had fallen back asleep, one arm flung above her head, her mouth slightly open, emitting a quiet wheezing.

The first box she found was full of her first-grade artwork, and was labeled as such in her father's neat hand. In her family it was her father who was the organizer, the saver, the bill payer. In other families it was different, Natalie understood that. Hannah Morgan's mother, for instance, could not pass a Target or a Walmart without running in for some sort of container to hold something: it was an addiction. If you opened up any desk drawer in the office in Hannah's house you'd find dozens and dozens of file folders, all labeled, all containing exactly what they were supposed to contain, nothing more, nothing less.

Natalie pulled the string next to the bare bulb and miraculously the light struggled to life, though she needed the flashlight as a supplement. She opened the box of artwork and found a picture of a grinning snowman. The smile, which she was certain she had intended to be cheery, was ghoulish. She studied the block letters that made up her name; she could remember writing them, could feel the pencil in her grip, smell the scent of the shavings from the sharpener. In first grade she would have been—what? Well, only five, because of starting kindergarten early. Five! A baby, really, working away on this snowman, laboring over the odd angle of his mouth. It was enough to make her cry. Had she been happy then? She couldn't remember. But she thought she had.

She sat back on her heels and looked around her. She peeked into most of the boxes—Christmas decorations, baby clothes (absurdly tiny), old toys (plastic rings, a few tattered stuffed animals, a train that, she remembered, used to sing some sort of song about bad luck or hard knocks), tin canisters that at one time lived on the kitchen counter but that had been removed during some massive clean-out. ("All this clutter," said Natalie's father. "Making me crazy.")

In the far corner of the basement was an additional bin, a pale blue Rubbermaid, and this one was labeled in her mother's writing. *Misc. papers, Carmen, old.* Natalie had to work to get it out of the corner. It was wedged in there pretty tightly. Inside the box was a picture of a girl. She recognized her mother immediately because of the way her mouth turned automatically up at the corners. She flipped the picture over. *Carmen,* it said. *1989, Cimarron, Kansas.*

She sat for a moment, breathing heavily. Strange. Unless she was doing the math wrong...her mother would have been twelve or thirteen in 1989, but this girl looked no older than nine or ten.

Underneath the photo was a piece of paper that said "Birth Certificate, State of Kansas" with her mother's maiden name, and her mother's parents' names (Natalie's grandparents, long dead, she'd never met them), and the date and place of birth: June 13, 1976. There was the name of the hospital, St. Catherine Hospital, Dodge City, Kansas, and a gold seal with the word OFFICIAL going around it in a semicircle. Okay, that made sense. The date on the photograph must be wrong, that was all. She wished she had the sheet of paper her father had written his family tree research on; she'd left that at the Archives.

But. Underneath the birth certificate was a plain black photo album, and underneath that was another birth certificate, nearly identical. Except this one had the name of a different hospital — Western Plains Medical Center — and the gold seal was raised instead of flat. Also: the date of birth was different. June 13, 1979.

Natalie's head was spinning, she thought it might spin right off her neck and roll off the boards into the muck in the corners of the basement.

She stood abruptly and knocked her head against the ceiling. Damn her height! One of the tallest girls in the freshman class, despite being the youngest. Double whammy.

WE KNOW SOMETHING ABT UR MOTHER, said the text. But how did they know this? She hadn't even known. *We know something about your mother.* So they knew — what? That Natalie's mother was younger than she professed to be, that she had two birth certificates, one showing her real age and one her fake age? And why did that matter, to anyone else but Natalie and her mother? Why did they care?

She put the photograph back in the box, and the photo album with it. The birth certificates she folded up and put in the pocket of her jeans, both of them. If her mother had been born in 1979, as one birth certificate said, then she was only sixteen when she married Natalie's father—not nineteen, the way Natalie had always thought. And that meant—what? That it was illegal, what her parents did? And if so, so what? That still didn't answer the question of why anybody cared.

Sixteen. That was only three years older than Natalie was now. When she was eight her favorite babysitter had been sixteen, a junior in high school—Natalie remembered the babysitter, Francine, she went by Francie, as a gum-chewing, busty girl in short shorts who braided Natalie's hair and, when she got her license, drove her out to Plum Island to sit on the beach. It was from Francine that the American Girl doll had come. She thought of the juniors in her school now. Sure they seemed older than Natalie, older than Hannah and Taylor too, but old enough to be *married?* To become mothers? No way.

Natalie's head was beginning to hurt.

She cast her flashlight once again across the basement. In one corner (she had missed this before) a pair of skis leaned against each other. Who skied? She didn't, never had. A few plastic beach buckets—purple, red—now aged and cracked. She remembered digging with them on the beach at Plum Island, making sandcastles with her father, her mother stretched out on a beach chair (her mother's skin always tanning, never burning, never freckling, God, how jealous Natalie was of that!).

And then. And then! In the darkest corner, the one farthest from the naked bulb, a cardboard box, bent with age, the brown faded nearly to white, one corner rippled like corduroy where it must have gotten wet and then dried again because it wasn't on the boards, officially, but sort of tucked away behind them.

She felt a strange humming in her ears. The box wasn't labeled, and when she bent to lift it, it almost collapsed in on itself, so she ended up bumping it up onto the boards and then dragging it toward her.

And inside the box was another box, metal, black, with a faded flower design on it, and an ancient piece of masking tape with something scrawled across it, she couldn't read what. She opened the box, half expecting to find another box inside of that, like those Russian dolls, what were they called? The nesting dolls. Hannah had a set on her dresser, red circle cheeks, little bow mouths, brought back by her father from one of his many business trips.

There was no additional box, though, just a black spiral notebook, nothing written on the front of it, and inside pages and pages of writing. When Natalie opened the notebook, a sheet of paper fell from it—no, more than one sheet, a bunch of sheets, but this paper was so thin it was hard to tell how many, and these papers looked much older than the notebook itself. She shone the flashlight on the box, but there was nothing else in there, so she put the papers back in, then she removed the birth certificates from her pocket and put those inside too, closed the box, and carried the whole thing upstairs.

She felt like she'd been on a long journey and she half expected to emerge, like Alice in Wonderland, in an entirely different world from the one from which she had departed. But everything was just as she'd left it. The kitchen table with stacks of mail on it, the dingy towel hanging crookedly on the handle of the stove, the elderly tap dripping its syncopated rhythm. And from the rest of the house: silence. No mother tapping around upstairs, no music playing, no television. Just silence, plus the thudding of her heart inside her rib cage.

※

"I'm coming in with you," said Carol, piloting the BMW toward Southie after the event. "To make sure you're okay." Carol eased the car onto the highway, not looking, not really, to see if other cars were coming.

"I'm fine," said Kathleen. She could feel the Caesar salad churning around in her belly.

On the last day of their Beginner's Knitting class, when they were supposed to be finishing their scarves, Carol had pulled out all of her work—hers had been a terrible scarf, bumpy, uneven, really a disgrace to scarves, and to knitting in general—and had said to Kathleen, "Screw this. Let's go for a drink." And so they had: Irish coffees at The Black Rose. ("With every tourist in Boston," said Carol. "But who cares! The coffees are the best.")

"Or better yet," Carol said now. "Come home with me for the afternoon. I'll make you tea. I'll get off the highway right here..."

"Carol, I'm *fine*."

Carol peered at her. "You don't look fine. You don't *seem* fine. You seem strange."

"I'm fine. I'm perfect. I've never been better. I just need to lie down."

※

Thing number ten that made Natalie sick: the way half the English class thought the independent-study project from Ms. Ramirez was a joke. No, more than half. Most.

Most of the freshmen class didn't like Ms. Ramirez because she held them to standards that some students believed to be impossibly high and because she did not, like some of the other teachers, buy into preconceived notions of success and popularity. These notions, for example, said that girls like Britney Thompson and Hannah Morgan and Taylor Grant were always going to do well and that Finnegan Davis, who had greasy hair that emitted a faint odor of poverty and neglect, was never going to.

(On her ring finger Ms. Ramirez wore a small, tasteful diamond; she was said to be engaged to a soldier deployed to Afghanistan, though she never spoke of the soldier or of an impending wedding—indeed, reading aloud from *Romeo and Juliet,* she seemed almost to straighten her slender shoulders and to read with some coldness the line *"O that I were a glove upon that hand, that I might touch that cheek!"*)

After Ms. Ramirez gave the assignment for the independent-study project, after Taylor's hand shot up and after she said, "Um? That's it?" and after Ms. Ramirez set her lips carefully together and gave the smallest sigh of impatience, Taylor continued, unbowed, "Can you give us, like, an *example* or something?" Ms. Ramirez said, "Certainly. You can...let's see. You can write a collection of poetry. You can go to a museum in Boston—the Museum of Fine Arts, let's say—and choose a painting that speaks to you, then write me a paper about why. You can write a short story. You can outline a novel. But these are just ideas. I think what I'd value most is if you were to think of something I didn't just mention, go off in a different direction. Challenge yourselves. Learn something."

A low rumble of protest rose from the class: a novel! Who did she think they were? Seniors?

"I know that seems vague," Ms. Ramirez continued. "But the vagueness is purposeful. I want to push you—you're freshmen, but you're smart, you can handle this—to learn things for yourselves."

Later, after the bell rang, Natalie was packing up her things, and heard Hannah Morgan say, *"I'm* going to write some poetry." And then, more quietly, "So easy. What a joke."

※

Natalie opened her laptop and fired up a fresh Word document. The laptop had been a gift from her father for the school year ("To start you off on the right foot"), though Natalie thought of it more as a good-bye present, a crumb he threw her on his way out the door.

Why you chose what you chose, Ms. Ramirez had said. How

you went about it. What you learned. Natalie felt energized by the prospect of answering these questions.

She typed, *Family Tree.* She typed, *Why I chose what I chose.* She thought about that for a few minutes, then began her first, halting sentence. *I chose what I chose,* she typed, *because.*

She pulled the black box from under her bed, where she'd hidden it, and then her mother knocked on the door. She shoved it back under the bed.

"Come in," she said. Her mother opened the door a crack.

"I'm going to bed. Came to say good night." Her voice was rough in the semidarkness of the hallway.

"Okay," said Natalie, but her mother didn't leave. Natalie didn't look up, just continued typing. *Because there are too many secrets.* That sounded idiotic. She deleted it. *Because my father left us.* Worse. Delete. *Because I want to know where I came from.* She let that one stand and considered it, studiously ignoring her mother's presence in the hallway.

Her mother entered the room and said, "What are you working on?"

Natalie turned her body slightly away. "School project," she said.

"Oh." Her mother sat carefully on the edge of the bed. Her hair was lank and unwashed, unstyled. Her beautiful hair. The hair was what Natalie's father had fallen in love with first, he always said. Her mother's beautiful hair first, and the rest of her after. My Kansas rose, he called her. Carmen, my Kansas rose.

There was a time — oh, a few years ago, maybe — when all of Natalie's friends' mothers were getting short, stylish haircuts, shorter in the back than in the front, swinging around their faces. Natalie wanted her mother to get one too, but her father begged her not to. "You're younger than those women," he said. "Prettier. You stay as you are." So she'd kept it long. For him!

Natalie's mother looked out the window — Natalie hadn't drawn the shade—and said, "Can you believe how early it's getting dark these days?"

Natalie said nothing, stared at her computer screen, and against the unwelcoming wall of silence, her mother pushed: "Nat. I'm doing my best. You know that, right?"

It was the first time in recent memory her mother had used her nickname, the first time she'd sat this close to her, looked at her directly. Natalie's throat caught.

"Sure," she said. "Yeah." Something—pity, maybe—covered her so thoroughly and unexpectedly that she almost couldn't breathe. She said, "Do you remember when Dad was doing that thing with his family tree?"

Her mother looked at her blankly.

"Let's see...no I don't."

"Oh."

"Why?"

"No reason. Just wondering. For a school thing."

"I don't." Her mother offered Natalie a wan smile. "But I swear that there are days when I don't remember my own name."

Natalie made a deep, unhappy sound.

"I'm kidding." Her mother put her hand over hers. "Nat, I'm just kidding."

"I know," said Natalie, but she wasn't sure if that was true. Everything about this moment made her feel like crying: the circle of light from the lamp on her nightstand, the shadow it threw on the rest of the room, the black box hidden under her bed. Even her mother's face, the gray pouches that had recently formed under her eyes, marring the beauty of her skin. All of this made her want to burrow under the covers and weep like a little girl.

Her mother straightened and pushed her hair back from her face. *First the hair,* her father had said, *and then the rest of her, that's how I fell in love.* How Natalie envied her mother's coloring, the way that, with the right makeup, she looked Spanish or South American or something unidentifiable but equally exotic, not farm Kansas. "You can ask Daddy yourself."

"Maybe."

"You should call him."

"I'll ask him tomorrow."

"Tomorrow?"

"Remember? I'm seeing him tomorrow." Thing number eleven that made Natalie sick: mothers who couldn't remember anything. Natalie took a deep breath. She said, "I found something in the basement."

Her mother, who had been examining her fingers, looked up, startled. "What do you mean?"

"I found something, in a box, with your name on it."

"What kind of box?"

"A box with papers inside. *Papers.* Birth certificates. Mom. There were two birth certificates, with two different years for you." Watching her mother, she felt as though the two of them were trudging together up a long dirt path.

Her mother stared back down at her hands. "But, Nat, I don't understand. What made you go looking for that?"

"Someone said something to me. At school."

"At *school?* How did they know, at school?" It was true, then.

"I don't know." Natalie kicked the metal box under the bed, sending it skidding closer to the wall. "But you have to be eighteen, to get married in Massachusetts. I looked it up. You always told me you were nineteen when you got married. But you weren't, you were sixteen. It was *illegal,* what you did."

"But how'd they know at school? How'd anyone know?"

Natalie looked squarely at her mother. "I don't know. You tell me."

Then came a sound from Natalie's cell phone, which was on her nightstand—they both started at that. "Just a text," said Natalie, but she could feel her voice shaking when she said it. *Here we go,* she thought. *Here we go again.* She wanted to pick up her phone and look at the text, but also she didn't. Really what she wanted to do was throw up, or run away.

Her mother tapped her forehead with her fist. "Oh, *God.* I think I know what happened."

"What?"

"Once, a long time ago, I told Hannah's mother."

Natalie felt her stomach drop to the floor. "You *what?*"

"I told Hannah's mother. This was forever ago, years ago, one of those endless play dates, you know how those used to go on when you were young? Afternoon into the evening, your dad was traveling for work, so was Hannah's dad—"

Carmen paused and looked at the ceiling, and into the silence Natalie said, in a voice she hardly recognized, "And then what?"

"And then her mother got out the wine, and we ordered pizza for you girls, and we sat there forever while you two played. I think we even put a movie on for you...God, I forgot all about this."

"Mom. I don't care about the movie. What happened?"

"Well, then we got to talking. She's pretty charming, you know, Angela is, and I guess I just told her..." Carmen reached out and touched Natalie's hair, and Natalie pulled away. "Sweetie, just because I was young when I married your father doesn't mean I didn't love him. My God! I loved him more than anything."

"Yeah but."

"Yeah but nothing. Your father saved me. He saved me, Natalie! I needed saving. I was so ready to leave home, and he came along—"

"He saved you from what?"

"It doesn't matter."

"It does matter."

"Why?"

"It matters to me."

Carmen sighed and twisted a piece of her hair around her finger. "From an unhappy home, unhappy people. My father drank, Natalie, and it wasn't an easy house to grow up in." She drew in her breath, then let it out slowly. "There was a lot of...there was a lot of anger."

Natalie considered this; somehow, they had never talked about it. She should have worried more about her mother as a little girl, but instead she thought of the long-ago play date, the secret that had been released. After a beat she said, "What did your parents do? When you left?"

"They stopped speaking to me. It was a huge scandal. Keep in mind, Nat, the town I grew up in had about two thousand people. That's like three of your high schools, the whole town. Tiny. When somebody runs off with an older man—a pharmaceutical salesman!—it causes a ripple."

Natalie was silent, waiting for her to go on. Then she said, "So that was it? You never talked to them again?"

"I tried to contact them. After you were born, that's when it became really important to me, for you to have a family, some roots."

Natalie thought of her father's family tree, hastily begun and then forgotten. She thought of the rows and rows of cabinets in the reading room at the Archives, and the records they contained, all those people, all those families, intertwined. She thought of the notebook she'd found and not yet read: could her roots be there? She said, "So then what?"

"They didn't want to hear from me. I felt terrible about that. Here you were, this beautiful little baby, so tiny and pure..." Carmen's voice broke off there. "I felt so sad for you, no relatives, your father's brother, your uncle, moved to Australia so long ago. He started a whole different life."

Natalie knew about this, her Australian cousins, whom she'd

never met; they were older, with beautiful exotic names: Barita, Kolora, Larra. "And Daddy's parents were already dead when you were born."

Natalie knew about this, the car accident, her grandparents riding together down 95, in an early summer fog, the truck, overturned in front of them, that they couldn't see in time. "And that's why we've never gone back there."

"That's why."

Natalie chewed at a cuticle. "I always thought it was just because your parents died."

"Well, yes, but that happened when you were older. When you were a baby, they were still alive."

Natalie thought about this: a set of grandparents all the way out in Kansas, alive and well when she was born, grandparents she had never known because they were so consumed by anger. She felt it suddenly and acutely, the absence of these strangers.

"Did Dad know? How old you were?"

"Of course he did."

Natalie wasn't sure if that made it better or worse. "But sixteen is so *young*..."

"I know," said Natalie's mother. "It seems that way now. But I was an old sixteen. An old soul." She smiled. Natalie did not smile back. "Maybe I was young, honey, but I knew what I was doing. I loved your father so much."

Natalie snorted. "Lot of good that did you." Her mother gasped at that, and Natalie didn't apologize. (Thing twelve: people who expected an apology when they were the ones doing something wrong.) She said, "How come you never told me?"

"Well, it was a complicated situation. It seemed better not to go into it."

Natalie stared hard at the wall.

"I didn't mean for this to hurt you, Natalie. I certainly didn't mean for anyone to find out. Honestly, I didn't think anyone would care."

"I know you didn't." What else could she say? And yet. Her mother had given Taylor and Hannah ammunition, and for that she couldn't forgive her.

Carmen kissed her on the forehead; Natalie accepted the kiss but did not return it.

"Don't stay up late," her mother said, and under her breath Natalie said, "What do you care?"

But it wasn't exactly under her breath after all, because her mother turned back, and there was a different sort of edge to her voice when she said, "Don't judge things you don't understand, Natalie."

Natalie didn't answer. As soon as her mother left she dove for the phone on the nightstand.

WHAT R U DOING 2NITE, LOSER?

She wanted to run after her mother and give her the phone, have her take it away until the morning, or forever. There were kids whose parents didn't allow them to have their phones at night. There were kids whose parents monitored everything. Hannah and Taylor clearly did not have those sorts of parents; neither did Natalie. She croaked out one word: *Mom?* But her mother had gone, had disappeared into her room, didn't hear.

⁂

Later, in the dusk — the gloaming, wasn't it? — Kathleen rose from her bed, where she had fallen asleep for nearly an hour. She hated sleeping at that time of the day because waking in the near darkness made her feel discombobulated, almost depressed; she'd always been that way, even as a child, and Susannah had too, inconsolable upon waking after she had napped too long.

Kathleen removed her computer from its berth on her nightstand and carried it out to the living room. It was an aging Mac laptop, a hand-me-down from Neil, who was constantly, at Adam's insistence and with his financial backing, upgrading various technologies in their home. But it served her purposes just fine; any emails she needed to send were generally of a business nature, and she sent them from work. She didn't use the Mac very often, though she had, at Neil's suggestion, swung for the high-speed Internet access that was offered along with her phone service.

While she waited for the computer to start up (this process was lengthy and clamorous), she turned on the television. Not because she liked television particularly, but because she wanted to hear some voices. It was the local news (grim), followed by the weather (grimmer), followed by a random smattering of national news (a bus carrying marching-band members in Arkansas had crashed, national unemployment numbers were at a new high, swine flu had reached a remote Alaskan Eskimo village). "Jesus," said Kathleen. "How is that even possible?"

And then, grimmest. Kathleen sat up straighter. The suicide of a fourteen-year-old girl in Des Moines who had asphyxiated herself in her parents' garage after being tortured by her classmates online. Ashley Jackson, the girl's name was, and the photo that accompanied the story was a school photo, that was clear because of the background of too-bright leaves.

"Unthinkable," Kathleen said aloud, and Lucy, lying at Kathleen's feet, lifted her ears. The banner under the photo read, *Cyberbullying*. Kathleen imagined this girl, Ashley Jackson, getting ready for school in the morning, choosing her outfit, combing her dirty-blond hair in the mirror of the school bathroom. Ashley Jackson was not a freak. No acne, no extra weight. Normal! If you looked at her a certain way you might even call her pretty. Smiling, in this photo, a wide, toothy smile. And now dead.

⁓

Later, much later, Natalie padded down the hallway to her mother's room, where the light from the television cast a glow on the bed, illuminating her mother's supine form. Carmen's mouth was open, her head was tilted back, and her breathing was deep and even. Amid the nightstand clutter—an old *Us Weekly,* a water glass, two different kinds of moisturizer, an empty Kleenex box, a string of gold beads—Natalie saw a pill bottle, which she plucked from the detritus and carried back to her room, pausing on her way to turn off the television.

In her bedroom she undid the cap to the pill bottle and poured a couple of the pills out into her hand. The pills were salmon-colored with an *A* in the center and a little squiggly line next to the *A* that reminded her of the *tilde* that went over the *n* in Spanish words. She read the writing on the bottle: the pills had been prescribed to Carmen by her doctor, a creaky primary care physician with offices in the Towle Building on Merrimac Street. The directions said: Take one before bedtime. Natalie couldn't say for sure, but judging from her mother's deep breathing, her nearly catatonic state, her difficulty waking in the morning, her mother had taken more than one, often took more than one.

Natalie put a pill in her mouth, moved it around, then spit it back out. She closed the shade and lay as still as she could in her bed, tired but not sleepy. She listened. From her mother's bedroom, silence. From the first floor, the bangs and hisses as the old radiators struggled.

She took the black metal box out from underneath her bed, where she'd hidden it (hidden it from whom? nobody was monitoring her movements) and removed first the birth certificates, then the notebook. She opened it. The light here was better than it had been in the basement, and she was able to make out the writing inside the front cover. *Bridget O'Connell Callaghan,* it said. *Newburyport, Massachusetts. 1975.*

She read the first few sentences of the first page. This was difficult, because it was all in cursive, and Natalie never had reason to read cursive, and also the letters had faded so that she really had to strain to make them out. Difficult, but not impossible.

I am writing this down because this is my story. I don't know if anyone will read it. Maybe it's better if nobody does. But I have a long life behind me, and maybe not so much ahead of me. And I think it's important for the truth to be out there. So I will start now and maybe by the time it's my turn to go I will have it all down, the truth, the way it really happened, because if I don't do this nobody will ever know. There were only ever two other people who knew my secret, and both are gone before me.

It took her a long time to work through even this small section. "Geez," said Natalie. "What the hell?" she said.

She thought of the Archives, and of the woman who had helped her there (she still had her umbrella). She rummaged in her backpack until she found the card. IN CASE OF EMERGENCY, Kathleen Lynch had written, with a phone number on the back.

Was this an emergency?

Maybe, maybe not.

She dialed.

Kathleen switched off the television and turned her attention to the computer. She was going to, as she sometimes did—okay, as she often did—search for Susannah. All of her previous searches had come up empty, but that didn't stop her from trying again. She said, "Hello, Google, my old friend," and into the search bar she typed *Susannah Lynch.* There was a junior high school Susannah Lynch who had placed second in her state cross-country championship a few weeks earlier in Virginia. There was a Susannah Lynch who was born in 1823 in Somerset, England. Also a painting by a Susannah Lynch that was about to be sold at an auction in Wyoming, and Kathleen felt a stab of hope when she saw it. Her Susannah had never been a painter before, but was it possible? Was it? No, it was not: further investigation revealed that Susannah Lynch the painter was sixty-two years old and had gone to art school in Germany. There was a Susannah Lynch, age forty-eight, who was running for local office in Tennessee on a platform of redistributing government money in some way other than how it had been distributed in the past. No dice.

Kathleen cleared the search bar and typed *Ashley Jackson*. Google returned dozens and dozens of results—the media had seized on this story, and accompanying each version was the same picture.

Kathleen sighed. She thought she'd been through the saddest things in the world—dead husband, vanished daughter—but this was sadder.

"The saddest thing in the world," she said.

When the phone rang she started.

"Hello, darling," said Carol. "I'm checking in on you. You didn't seem quite right today."

It was hard for Kathleen to hold her voice steady, but she did, looking the whole time at Ashley Jackson's picture.

Somebody had tucked a gift from the tooth fairy under this girl's pillow; somebody had held her head when she was sick at night; somebody had watched her perform in a dance recital or sing in a school assembly or score a goal at a soccer game. Somebody had read her letters to Santa, filled her Christmas stocking. And now she was dead.

"I'm *fine*," she told Carol. "I promise you, I am perfectly fine."

She hung up and went back to her computer, but all she could find there was evidence of girls in trouble, so she got up and stretched and called Lucy for a walk. She was hooking on the leash when the phone rang again, and this time she picked up and said, "Carol! I told you I'm fine—"

But it wasn't Carol. She tilted her head, listening.

"Oh!" she said. "Natalie Gallagher." She glanced at the clock; it was nearly ten. "Natalie Gallagher. I thought you had disappeared! I thought you had fallen off the face of the earth!"

She nodded vigorously; she put her hand to her throat. *"Yes,"* she said. "Yes, bring it down. What? As soon as you can. And if you can't, I'll come to you."

⁂

It was after eleven when Natalie went downstairs to the kitchen, where, in the dark, the appliances seemed to be leering at her. She turned on a single light and rummaged around in a cabinet until she found the boxes of Ziploc bags, remnants from an earlier life, when her mother used to pack her lunches for her. Now that job was left to Natalie, who forgot half the time. Into the bag she poured a few of the pills she'd taken from her mother's room. How many would be enough to have on hand but not enough that they would be missed? She shook the pills out. Six, eight, a dozen. How many?

⁂

The arrangements for Natalie to see her father were currently haphazard; her parents weren't divorced, only separated, so they made their own rules. Natalie supposed that when they got an actual divorce the arrangements would lose their suppleness and become more formal, worked out by a fictional character in Natalie's head called the Judge. The Judge was kindly and benevolent and looked a lot like Detective Lennie Briscoe on the reruns of *Law & Order* Natalie and her mother occasionally watched.

It came to her, the idea, very late at night, after she'd talked to Kathleen Lynch on the phone, after she'd put the pills in the baggie and put the baggie in her backpack for safekeeping, after she'd turned her phone on again, then off, then on again, and while she was thinking about her visit with her father the following day.

("Avoid clichés whenever you write," said Ms. Ramirez. "If someone's said something the way you're about to say it, *think of a different way*.") But Natalie couldn't banish the cliché; she saw the lightbulb suspended somewhere above her head. Her father! He was the answer. He had moved not only out of their house but to a *whole different town*. With a *whole different high school,* where she could begin a *whole different life,* away from Taylor Grant, away from Hannah Morgan, away from all of them. She felt a momentary pang about Christian Chapman, but that dissolved quickly.

A memory kicked in, her father holding his arms out to her as she jumped into some pool (whose pool, or where, she didn't know). Her father on Christmas morning in a Santa hat, passing out presents.

She walked to the mirror over her dresser. Who was she, really, to criticize her mother for not keeping herself together? She hadn't washed her hair in a couple of days, and her lame attempts at makeup were ruined by her foraging in the basement, all the dust that had stirred up: there were black streaks of mascara running down her face, there was lipstick smudged in the corner of her mouth.

She opened the notebook again.

My name is Bridget O'Connell Callaghan. I was born Bridget O'Connell in County Kerry, Ireland, in 1905. In 1925, at the age of twenty, I came over to America to work in service for the

Turner family of High Street, Newburyport, Massachusetts. My sister Grainne sent money for my passage, as she had come over herself to work in service two years earlier. She married and left service just before I came over.

Sometimes I am grateful to Grainne for doing that for me. Sometimes I wish she had never done it. Sometimes I wish I had stayed in Ireland. I always wanted more, when I was there. I was greedy, greedy, greedy, and what was there was not enough for me.

But I remember it! I remember dancing with my sisters at the parish festivals. I remember the days when the master dance teacher would come to our village on his bicycle, and teach us new steps, around the house and mind the dresser, we used to say, you could say that to any Irish immigrant of my vintage today and they'd know exactly what you meant. I remember learning the Saint Patrick's Day dance and dancing with my sister Fiona. She was a great one for dancing, Fiona was, and caught onto the steps so much quicker than I did. I always envied her that, and how happy she looked when she was dancing, her hair flying out behind her, her cheeks pink.

Sometimes I wish I never wanted more than what I had back in Ireland. But that wasn't enough for me, and I wanted.

My parents are dead, God bless them, and so too is Fiona, as well as my dear husband. It is one of the greatest sorrows of my life that I never saw Fiona again after leaving Ireland, and that is the greatest sorrow in a life that has seen no shortage of sorrow.

But also no shortage of joys.

Grainne is two years older than I am and lives in the city of Lynn, not far from me. My sister Siobhan married a boy from our village and lives there still. My sister Claire never married, but she cared for our parents until they died.

Declan would not like to know that I am writing all of this down — he was of the school of thought that says keep the past in the past. I think that is fine for the most part.

Except.

I had a scare with my health recently and I thought I might die. I didn't die. It turned out to be a simple situation, a problem with my appendix, which was then removed, but the idea that I might pass on from this world to the next without ever telling this story worried me, I couldn't stand the thought of it, of going to my grave with everything a secret.

That expression had always sounded strange to me, "going to my grave," as though you pack a suitcase and board a train to get there.

Even if nobody ever reads this, even if I hide this in a box and hide the box somewhere in the house and nobody finds it, it will be enough for me to know that the story has been told.

You could say there were lots of things that led to what happened.

But it all started on Christmas Eve, 1925, so I will begin my story there.

Natalie's eyes were heavy; she couldn't keep them open. She let the notebook fall to the floor. It was all she could do to reach over to the nightstand and switch off the light.

☀

"You know," said Kathleen to Lucy, "I've never found anything worthwhile in my basement. And believe me, I've looked plenty of times."

Lucy stared impassively back at her.

Kathleen washed her breakfast dishes and rooted around in the closet for her boots — she wanted to take Lucy to Castle Island.

But just as she was getting ready to go, Neil called; he wanted her to go to Magic Beans with him and look for a crib.

"I'd love to," she said. "But isn't that Adam's department?"

"God no," said Neil. "I'm not letting him come on any more shopping trips. He put me on an *allowance,* Kathleen. Can you believe it? He thinks I'm going overboard."

"Are you?"

"Definitely. Also he's in a volleyball league, Sunday games."

"Volleyball!" said Kathleen.

※

Her mother was still sleeping, dreaming her Ambien dreams, her eyes twitching behind her eyelids (Natalie had checked), but Natalie, who had been up with the birds, was dressed and ready to go, ready to talk to her father, ready to begin this new chapter of her life. She didn't know how it was that she'd never thought of this solution before, but now that she'd thought of it she could scarcely think of anything else.

An *outing,* her father had christened it on the phone, when he called to finalize the arrangements, as though he were a camp counselor, and she a camper.

Natalie stood outside for a few minutes, waiting, but she wasn't dressed warmly enough. The storms of two days before had left behind a new world, refreshed, scrubbed clean, but colder too.

Back inside she studied the cracks in the living room wall. She could bid these good-bye, and also the slanted floor in the kitchen: on to bigger and better things. Well, not bigger, necessarily. But newer—surely her father's apartment was newer than this house. On to *newer* and better things.

If she moved in with her father, if she switched schools, she wouldn't have to complete the project. She wouldn't have to do all of the hard work Kathleen Lynch had described. She would be free of all of it. She would miss Ms. Ramirez, but there would be other teachers to take her place, other projects.

Her father would be her savior, his Lexus a chariot to carry her away from here.

The Lexus pulled up. Not in the driveway, where you would park at your own house, but along the curb, the way a visitor would park. Natalie could see him at the mailbox, scrutinizing the post for signs of disrepair, and then he squinted up at the house. He squatted and inspected something on the surface of the driveway. From her vantage point Natalie could see the place on the top of his head where the hair was thinning. You couldn't really tell that by looking at him from the front, so she felt she was privy to an important and telling detail: her father was aging.

"Hey!" said her father when she appeared. "There she is!" He never said things like that to Natalie; he never addressed her in the third person: he was nervous. But he looked the same as ever, though he wore a cautious, hopeful expression she recognized from the days of the sales calls. This expression he always replaced, upon approaching the door of a medical office, with one of unruffled composure.

His winter coat was different from the one she remembered he had the previous year—newer, darker, woollier—but his aftershave smelled the same as ever, and when he bent to kiss her on the cheek she experienced a brief spasm of recognition, or maybe even love.

He had a package for her: a Wii console and two games to go along with it.

"What for?" she asked. "It's not Christmas yet."

"No reason," he said, shrugging.

The games were Family Tennis and something called *Gold's Gym Cardio Workout*. (Really? Did he think she needed to *lose* weight?) She didn't like video games. She didn't care about the Wii.

The fact that her father didn't know that, that he didn't seem to know her at all, exerted a pressure on her head. But she had her eyes on the prize.

"Thanks," she said. "It's great."

"Really?" Her father breathed in deeply, then exhaled.

"Sure. Really."

So unfitting was this gift that it was as though he had bought it for someone else but had happened along Natalie in the interim and changed his plan. And where was she to play these games, if she were to play them at all? In their tiny antique living room? In her bedroom, where there was no television? In her mother's bedroom, in the midst of the unmade bed, the collection of pill bottles, the heap of unwashed clothes? She brought the boxes inside and put them in the kitchen, and when she returned her father was tapping his keys against the leg of his pants, looking up at the house. She had a second to study him unnoticed, and he wore an air of distraction, but as soon as he saw her he rearranged his features into a jovial expression. Watching the sudden transformation, Natalie couldn't help but think of Hannah Morgan near the lockers.

"Ready?" he said. "Natty Nat Nat. You ready?"

She bristled at this and put on her own jolly mask: two could play this game. "Ready, Freddy," she said. And then, borrowing a phrase he used to say, "Ready as I'll ever be."

※

The river to their right was silent and cold and gray in the emerging morning. In the sky, a violet streak, the singular remnant of the sunrise, hung in the sky. Natalie fixed her gaze on that.

"Dad?" said Natalie. "Do you remember when you did some of that family tree stuff a couple of years ago?"

"Huh?" He wasn't really listening to her. (Thing number thirteen: grown-ups who didn't really listen.)

"Your family tree. Didn't you do something with your family tree?"

"Oh, yeah, that. I got on a kick about that awhile back. Early midlife crisis. I started thinking about my parents being gone, feeling rootless, my brother so far away. I wanted to figure some stuff out. I don't think I got very far. I remember a lot of question marks."

"Do you remember someone named Bridget?"

"Bridget? I'm not sure. I don't know. Why are you asking?"

"School project. Do you know who lived in our house, before we did? I mean like a long time before we did?"

"Natalie, I don't know, I'm sorry. My mother inherited it, I know that, and we moved in when I was eight or nine, but beyond that..."

His voice was sharp; the hand not on the steering wheel was tapping on the console. All of these things Natalie recognized, from the sales calls, as signs of nerves.

She had been about to ask him about her mother, about the birth certificates, when she heard the sound of a text on her cell phone. Her father glanced over. "Want to get that? One of your friends calling?"

She snorted. "Nooooo. Just a text." Same as the night before: she wanted to look, but she didn't want to know.

She had also been about to ask him about moving in with him, but that could wait too, for just the right time.

"Listen," her father said, too loudly. "Listen, before we get back to my place." (*Our* place, she thought.) His voice had softened, and he was looking at her kindly, and she could see, somewhere behind his eyes, the gentle and patient person who had taught her to ice-skate at the Bartlet Mall, who held the back of her bicycle seat as she wobbled along on her bike that first, exhilarating time without training wheels, around the tennis courts at Cashman Park.

She said, "Yes?" Probably he needed someone to take care of him, a feminine touch around the apartment. She could cook, a little. She could make omelets. She'd want to get registered in the new school before classes began in January.

But he was saying... what?

"There's something I want to tell you about," her father said. She watched his Adam's apple working. She felt suddenly like his voice was coming from very far away. "I suppose I should say *some-one*," he corrected. "I suppose I should say, there's *someone* I want to tell you about."

There was a lump in her stomach, in her throat.

Hadn't she known? She watched enough television. She had read plenty of books. It was the plot of nearly every story ever written: someone else. There was someone else, someone besides her mother. There was always someone else.

So he wasn't her savior after all. She should have known.

The phone dinged again: that's what it did when you didn't look at your text, it kept dinging and dinging to let you know it was there.

※

The new apartment was in a mill building that had been turned into living spaces. "A feeble attempt at cachet," was how her father described it to her on the way there, turning partway to look at Natalie and then returning his eyes to the road. (Thing number fourteen: stupid adult jokes that are not funny.)

Her father hadn't loosened his hold on the steering wheel; she could see small white circles on his knuckles. They crossed the chain bridge into Amesbury. From the bridge Natalie could see the river, inhospitable now, despite the emerging sunlight, though in the summer it would fill with boats. They turned left after the bridge and continued on the road along the river, and she was grateful for that because it gave her something to do, looking out at the fancy houses with their fine stone walls, their beautiful gardens. When she was little she had imagined living in one of these homes, spreading herself out in a spacious bedroom. The car sloshed through puddles, sending dirty water in sprays around them and on the windshield.

After they turned away from the river and toward the downtown, Natalie's father said, "So, look. Natalie. As I was saying. When we get to the apartment, there's going to be a woman there I want you to meet." She didn't turn toward him: she wouldn't. The sun hitting the pavement made shapes that danced in front of her eyes. She felt dizzy. He went on from there: this had nothing to do with Natalie, or how much he cared about her. His relationship with this woman, this woman named *Julia,* was separate from all of that.

When he said Julia's name he faced Natalie and reluctantly she met his gaze before he turned his eyes back toward the road. There was a signal—a light behind his eyes—that made her realize that something very big and important had changed. When she heard the word *relationship,* a wave of nausea washed over her. She thought she might have to ask him to stop the car to allow her to be sick on the side of the road. If there was a new relationship, if there was a woman named *Julia* (Natalie couldn't say the name in her head without adding the italics), there would be no room for Natalie.

Natalie's father pulled into a large parking lot, into a space with the number 33 painted on it in bright yellow paint. She got out of the car slowly. A phrase traveled through her head: *This is madness.* She had no idea where she'd heard such a phrase, or why, but the drama of it seemed perfectly fitting to the occasion. Madness.

Her father walked around the car and opened her door. It was a courtly, gentlemanly gesture that she had forgotten him capable of. Suddenly she remembered all of the sales calls when she sat in the car and watched him disappear into a medical office, and the way he'd always look back at her and wave.

The sun had risen quickly and dramatically, and Natalie's father lifted his hand to shield his eyes from the glare. "Listen," he said. "I know this might come as a surprise to you, all of this. Hearing about Julia."

She stared hard at the building in front of them. A real estate agent's sign stuck into the ground advertised sales and rentals. "It's nothing," she said, trying her best to erase the weight of the news with her nonchalance. "No big deal." That sounded just mean enough without being whiny.

"Hang on," he said, bending down. "Your phone fell out of your pocket."

He picked it up. Another text sound. "Here," he said, smiling broadly. "This thing keeps going off. You must be popular."

⁂

The salespeople and the other customers at Magic Beans must have thought that Kathleen was Neil's mother. Or maybe an overbearing mother-in-law, insisting on being involved. The store was packed, and everywhere you turned there was a belly in a different size: a cantaloupe, a soccer ball, a beach ball. On top of each belly, a fresh, rounded face, and attached to each fresh, rounded face a husband.

"Do you feel strange being in here?" whispered Kathleen.

"No," said Neil. "Why, should I? And why are we whispering?"

They didn't buy a crib; in the end Neil couldn't decide on one without Adam. After, they went for coffees at the Panera across the street.

"I hate to sound so old," said Kathleen, "but in my day we didn't have baby stores like that. The money that goes into having a child these days! It's staggering."

"I know," said Neil. "But it is what it is."

"Our biggest expense was a bassinet," she said. "I remember that."

Susannah had slept in that bassinet her first four months. Kathleen had set it next to her own bed so she could more easily care for the baby in the night, and she remembered how fearful she'd been to fall asleep those first few weeks, scared that she'd miss some warning change in Susannah's breathing. She'd thought then that that part would be the worst for her and Gregory to get through, that once Susannah had emerged from that stage fat and happy, taking deep, regular breaths, sleeping soundly and regularly and intently, that they were in the clear. Ha!

This seemed like a dangerous path to traverse, so Kathleen cast about for a way to change the subject. "Hey," said Kathleen. "Remember that girl who was in at the end of last week?"

"The one with the cell phone?"

"That's the one. She called me! Last night. She found something in her basement, an old notebook."

"I've never found anything in my basement," said Neil morosely. "And believe me, I've looked, plenty of times."

"That's what I said," said Kathleen. "Earlier today, I said the exact same thing to Lucy."

"What'd you tell her?"

"Lucy?"

"Wiseacre. *No.* The girl."

"Natalie. I told her to bring it down. I told her we'd have a look at it with her, you and I."

"Good," said Neil. "And we will."

"I told her you are the king of reading supposedly indecipherable writing."

Neil stirred his coffee. "You did? You told her that?"

"I did."

"Kathleen Lynch, I'm flattered."

"Well, it's *true*."

⁂

Natalie's father explained that they would have taken the elevator to his apartment but that the elevator, like other parts of the building, was still under construction. All around them were piles of sawdust and toolboxes and other evidence of renovation: a bucket of white paint in the hallway, dots of primer on the wall, a ladder. Natalie tried to make herself think, *I wouldn't want to live here anyway*.

"This is how I get my exercise now," her father said as they walked, but he seemed not to be up to the task, because they stopped and rested between the third and fourth floors.

The apartment was on the fifth floor. Her father fumbled in his pocket for the key, but before he could insert it, the door opened and there she was. *Julia*.

"Come in!" she said merrily, and Natalie's father leaned forward as if to kiss her but then must have thought better of it because instead he gave her an awkward clap on the shoulder and ushered Natalie in front of him.

Julia had a small flat face and an upturned nose that, when she turned to the side, made her look like a little girl. But in fact she looked nearly a decade older than Natalie's mother. Didn't you always hear about men leaving their wives for younger women? But this was the opposite situation. WE KNOW SOMETHING ABOUT U.

Julia was not beautiful, but she was pretty in an ordinary way, like a person you would see in a magazine advertisement for yogurt or a practical car that could hold the whole family. She was dressed almost entirely in beige: beige pants, a soft beige sweater, beige boots featuring a big gold buckle. Her honey-colored hair was cut to her chin in a swingy style, and she gave off the pleasant smell of recently applied perfume.

"Natalie!" she said, smiling. She had a gap between her two front teeth, the kind that, nowadays, they would sort out immediately with braces. "I'm so happy to meet you, finally." When she said *finally,* she turned a wry smile in the direction of Natalie's father; her face, when she smiled, reminded Natalie of a dance teacher she'd had long ago, when she'd done such things as take dance classes, before they'd all realized she was a klutz. *Reach up to the sky, girls, like you're trying to touch the clouds!* Julia held out a hand to shake Natalie's, and her grasp was firm and confident. She held on a little longer than Natalie was expecting, and when she released Natalie she clapped her hands together like a child expecting a birthday present.

She seemed not to notice Natalie's silence, nor that of her father; she just talked right through it, eliminating it altogether. "I thought we could go out for pizza," she said—again, the cheery tenor to her voice, the display of childlike enthusiasm. "Natalie, do you like pizza?"

"She loves pizza," said her father, before Natalie had the chance to answer. Natalie nodded slowly—she did love pizza, though she was loath to admit it here—and looked around the living room. The furniture was beige, too, as though it had been dressed to match Julia, and it had a boxy look to it, with identical light wooden arms on the sofa and chairs. It looked like furniture you would find in a doctor's office or a hotel lobby, plain and inoffensive and slightly uncomfortable. On the squat table lay two glossy gardening magazines and a picture book about downtown Newburyport; it was these, more than anything else, that led Natalie to believe that somebody else had furnished this apartment. Glossy magazines were not her father's style.

"There's a great pizza place not far from here," Julia said. "Flatbread? But you probably know that. You don't live far." After a beat she added, "We can walk there. If it's not raining. It's not raining, is it? They say it's supposed to rain again later—"

Natalie didn't answer the question about the weather, but her father did ("Sunny as a beach day in July!"). Natalie had been to Flatbread. She had been once with her parents, long ago, and once with the now-odious Hannah Morgan and her mother on a school night when Hannah Morgan's father was away on business. "I have to go to the bathroom," said Natalie. It was hard to get the words out, because the urge to cry was so strong.

Julia pointed down a slim bright hallway with a door on either side. "The bathroom's on the left," she said.

Once out of view of the living room, Natalie opened the door on the right and was astonished to see a mattress on the floor, heaps of clothes piled here and there. This was in such stark contrast to the living room, with its tidy matching furniture. There was a card table that held a mound of change and, incongruously, a couple of packets of ketchup, the kind you got with take-out food, and also a pair of glasses that must have been Julia's. They had bright red frames and were open, as though someone had put them down for just a minute and planned to be right back.

Natalie crossed the hallway to the bathroom, which was small, barely big enough for the sink, the toilet, and the shower. But the ceilings were high, as they were everywhere in the apartment, and on one side of the toilet was nailed a handsome white cabinet with big silver knobs shaped like stars. Natalie, who did not actually have to go to the bathroom, opened the cabinet and saw a razor next to a red-, white-, and blue-striped can of Barbasol; an unwrapped bar of soap; and, on the top shelf, which she had to stand on her tiptoes to access, a collection of moisturizers in matching white containers.

The moisturizers were labeled in elaborate black script. The brand was unfamiliar to Natalie, but she sensed that the whole collection was expensive. She reached up for one tiny bottle. It was devoted entirely to the delicate skin under and around the eyes. All of this must belong to Julia. Not only that, but the whole collection had been purposefully hidden from Natalie, who, after all, was taller than Julia and still had to stretch to reach it.

So. Julia was not here merely to greet Natalie, and to take her to Flatbread for pizza. Julia was a representative from her father's new life, the one he'd built since leaving them. Or perhaps — though this was a thought she allowed herself to entertain for only a fraction of a second — even before. Julia was living here, with Natalie's father. They were living together. There was no room for Natalie.

On the back of the toilet Natalie saw a light green bottle of perfume with an unpronounceable name in gold block letters. This, they had forgotten to hide. She pulled off the knobby gold top and recognized the scent that Julia wore. Then she sprayed a little in the air in front of her, the way her mother had showed her to do once, and walked through it.

A knock on the door. "Nat? You okay in there?" It was her father. His use of her nickname infuriated her, even more than the Natty Nat Nat back at her house had. She yanked open the door.

"What?" she said furiously.

Her father was taken aback by her tone, she could see that she'd hurt him. Good. He stepped back, then stepped toward her again.

"Natalie," he said gently. "Honey." He opened his arms to her beseechingly. "Nat. Come in here. Sit down." He reached around her to turn off the bathroom light.

He led her into the bedroom. There was nowhere to sit except for the mattress, so she sat cross-legged on the floor, and he did too. He took a deep breath and exhaled slowly.

Natalie stared at the floor and said, "She's living here. Julia. She's living here, right?" The moisturizers lined up in the cabinet, the perfume bottle on the toilet tank, the easy confidence she had in the living room. Even the way she matched the furniture! These were clues, all of them.

Her father didn't answer.

There was a pause, and Natalie, looking around the room again, saw a neat pile of women's clothes folded in the corner. On the top of the pile was a black lacy bra. She stared hard at the bra and tried not to cry. She hadn't known that women as old as Julia wore lacy underthings. It seemed pitiable and gross. How old was she? Forty? Older? Pathetic.

"Nat," said her father. "One thing you have to understand is that things between your mother and me haven't been good for a long time." He opened his palms and lifted his hands to the ceiling.

"But you *left* her," Natalie spat. "You left us."

"Natalie, honey, it's more complicated than that."

"How? How is it more complicated? You. Left. Us."

"Well." He sighed and drew his hands through his thinning hair. "She left me a long time ago."

"*What?* No, she didn't. She's right where she always was."

"In her mind, is what I mean. She stopped being the person she was."

The unfairness of this struck Natalie like a blow. She felt dizzy from the imagined impact. "I don't even know what that means," she said.

Her father sighed again and looked around the room, as if for an escape. "It's complicated."

"You already said that." She stared at her hands. She had a feeling that if she didn't look up, her father might stop talking and they could carry on as they had been. They could continue the charade that everything was okay.

"Someday you'll understand. When you're older."

Natalie kicked at a pile of clothes on the floor, sending sport shirts tumbling. Her father ignored that and focused instead on her face with an open, sympathetic look that made Natalie want to scream. "I *hate* when grown-ups say that."

"Natalie."

"Why do grown-ups always say that? It's stupid. It's a stupid, shitty thing to say."

He let the cursing slide. "Natalie. Just because I'm the one who actually left, the one who walked out the door, well, that doesn't mean that I'm the only one at fault."

Cautiously she said, "What do you mean?"

"Well, for one thing, I wanted to have more children, a bigger family. So did your mother, at one time."

Natalie felt a gentle vibration begin somewhere in her stomach, almost like there was a subway moving under the apartment building. But there was no subway, just her father's voice in the quiet room.

She said, "So. Why didn't you?" Her voice sounded unfamiliar to her, low and dull.

"Well," her father said, "your mother...your mother didn't want to. She found it very overwhelming, being a mother." He glanced at Natalie. "Not because of *you*. But babies are difficult, for some people. Mothers can go through a depression. She wasn't well for a while after you were born. She hasn't been well, I mean completely well, for a really long time."

Natalie said nothing, absorbing all of this, and her father said, "I'm sorry. Maybe I shouldn't have told you that."

Natalie thought of Hannah Morgan, of their Only Child Club. Once they had made buttons and worn them to school. This was a long time ago, of course. Even if they were still friends now, which obviously they were not, they were too old for such foolishness. But how proudly Natalie had worn the button, and what solidarity she'd felt with Hannah Morgan, because they both understood that deep down this was not how they wanted things to be.

Her father continued. "But I need you to understand that your mother and me, together, we were unhappy. For a long time." Natalie felt her mouth twist into something ugly. Her father must have seen this because he said, "Oh, not with *you*, honey. But with each other. And that's not how I wanted to live out my life, unhappily. Neither does she."

"So, what? You just leave her? Find something better?" She gestured toward the living room. What was *Julia* doing out there, anyway? Browsing through one of the glossy magazines? Straightening the tan pillows? Sitting perfectly still, trying to listen?

"No. I'm telling you it's not that simple."

"Well, maybe not. But look at you. You're happy enough. But she's not!"

"It might take longer—"

"Some days she doesn't even get *dressed*," said Natalie. This was her ammunition, and she fired it as hard as she could.

Her father put his head in his hands and rubbed at his temples. "Really?"

"Really. Most days."

Softly her father said, "Jesus Christ." He looked at the ceiling. Abruptly he straightened, then got to his feet and shook his clothes as though he'd been eating at a picnic and needed to clear the crumbs. "Natalie. Your mother needs help, to get better."

"Help?"

"Medication, a therapist, maybe both. She promised me she was going to do that, but now I see that she hasn't."

"She doesn't leave the *house*," whispered Natalie.

"Well. We're going to make sure that she does." Natalie's father looked around the room, but it was unclear what he was looking for, and eventually his eyes landed once again on Natalie and he opened his arms to her.

She remained where she was. She said, "Who's the *we?* You and *Julia?*"

Her father studied her. Then he lifted his shoulders—it was almost imperceptible, the motion—and said, "Not we. *Me.* I will do it." Then he said, with a false brightness in his voice, "We can talk about all of that later. For now, how about some pizza?"

"No," she said. But she was starving, and her stomach was making little grumbling sounds. She unfolded her legs and rose from the floor.

Her father grasped her elbow awkwardly and led her toward the door. "Honey, I know I already said this. But I mean it. This is all very complicated. When you're older, you'll understand it better."

"Why do you all say that, all grown-ups? Why is that your excuse for everything?" She took a deep breath. "When I'm older, I won't understand because I won't even think of you at all." It was the worst thing she could think to say to him. The worst! And she added to it, twisting the knife. "Not at all," she repeated.

That felt good. It was the only thing that had felt good to Natalie in a very long time, but it felt really good. It felt amazing.

❈

Natalie didn't come, she didn't bring the notebook down, and after a few days of waiting Kathleen let herself stop thinking about it. Just like that, it was almost Thanksgiving, and the stainless-steel sky was so low it looked like you could reach right up and touch it.

Kathleen was having Thanksgiving dinner with Adam and Neil and some of their friends. She had offered to bring a pumpkin pie, and she was going to make the crust from scratch, a recipe she'd seen in *Eating Well* magazine (Neil would appreciate it, if he took a break from his green smoothies long enough to try it), but looking through her cupboard on the day before Thanksgiving she realized she didn't have any whole-wheat pastry flour. After work she'd have to go to the grocery store, along with every other last-minute idiot south of Boston, but there was nothing she could do about it now, because she was due at work in half an hour.

"Well, Lucy?" said Kathleen, getting ready for work. "How do I look? Okay?" Lucy's chin was on the floor, and her eyes followed Kathleen as she moved around the kitchen. "Lucy," said Kathleen. "You haven't eaten your dinner." Typically Lucy ate in the middle of the night, like a person with an eating disorder, someone ashamed to consume in front of others; Kathleen would hear the crunching, oddly comforting, break into her dreams. But today Lucy's bowl was full. Kathleen would be late if she didn't get a move on; she didn't stop to ponder Lucy's bowl.

On the sidewalk a man ran by her dressed in shorts — shorts! — which seemed to Kathleen too optimistic, but indeed she did feel overdressed in her thick winter coat. She unwound her scarf and stuffed it in her pocket. "Global warming," she said dismally, to nobody.

At work she was well settled at her desk when Neil walked in.

"Sorry, boss," he whispered, and she could see that the skin underneath his eyes was pouchy and gray.

She said, "Neil! What happened to you? For heaven's sake, turn right around and go home. You look terrible. Are you sick?"

He leaned two hands on her desk; he hadn't shaved (that was unusual) and she thought that it was possible he was wearing the same sweater he'd been wearing the day before. "Not sick," he said gruffly. "I'm exhausted."

"Why?"

"We were up all night — talking, fighting, talking. I don't think I slept more than ten minutes. And then Adam got up and went to work, the bastard."

This was interesting. Kathleen perked up. "Fighting? About what?"

"Oh, everything. Henri. Plans. Arrangements. Fatherhood. Anything you could think of, we fought about it. Which day care to use."

"You don't have that sorted out yet?"

"Not really. Well, it depends on your definition of *sorted out*. Mine and Adam's are apparently very different."

"Neil!"

"I know, I know. We have our names on some lists. We're on it, really we are. But apparently Adam thinks one of us should leave our job to care for Henri."

The door opened and in walked a middle-aged man with a hat tipped over one eye, making him look like some shady character in a film noir. But when he took off the hat he became a regular man, balding, paunchy, in search, no doubt, of some piece of genealogical information he had been sent to retrieve by an elderly and unwell relative. Kathleen nodded at the man—the intern was greeting him—and turned her attention back to Neil.

"And this never came up before?"

"Maybe it did. Maybe I wasn't paying attention."

"Neil," she said. "Don't quit on me. Don't you dare."

"No," he said vaguely. "Of course not." But underneath his words she could sense a sort of giving in.

"*Neil,*" she said.

"I know!" he said. "I don't want to, believe me. But it's complicated. It's all a lot more complicated than I realized. I mean, even just *getting* him—that's turning into its own circus. Adam might go over there in a couple of weeks to try to sort things out."

"And come back with him?"

"Maybe. We don't know. Or maybe we'd both go back later to get him. Who knows? It's hard to say."

Kathleen could see a figure walking up the outside steps. The figure looked familiar, the height, the posture, but from this distance she couldn't be sure—was it?

"Oh, Neil," she said. "I'm sorry. It seems awfully difficult." And she meant it. It did seem difficult. Adopting a child! Complicated. Having your own child: also complicated.

(Susannah turning sullen and angry, her usual sunny demeanor vanished; money missing from Kathleen's wallet, jewelry from her room. Kathleen absorbed these signs, and she dissected them, trying to ascertain their meaning and what to do about them. She thought she had time to figure out a plan. But she was wrong. She didn't have any time at all.)

Then the door opened and the figure moved closer.

"Neil!" she stage-whispered. "That's her, the girl with the notebook. That's Natalie."

Neil looked up briefly. "Yeah?" he said.

"Too tired to care?"

"Yeah," he said. "I'm just going to stagger over to my desk and sit down for a minute. And then I'm going to hit the coffee machine, hard."

Kathleen watched Natalie's slouching progress across the floor. An expression came to her mind: *bent but not broken*. She rose to meet Natalie and when she reached her and said hello she saw that the girl's eyes were rimmed with red. Crying, or cold? But it wasn't very cold out; she thought again of the man running in shorts. So crying, then. And who wouldn't be crying, with a dead mother? Natalie looked to Kathleen like some sort of bedraggled animal. She wore the same jacket she'd been wearing a few weeks earlier, but it was dirtier, as if its owner had met with unexpected obstacles. The hair was the same, the brilliant orangey red, but it was pulled back with a rubber band. Absent, today, were the meager attempts at makeup; without these Natalie looked both more innocent and older.

"Well!" said Kathleen, trying to sound carefree and unconcerned, as though she hadn't been wondering where Natalie had been. "Hello again!"

Natalie blinked at her, and her face wore a vaguely surprised expression, almost as though she had been carried into the Archives building in her sleep and had awoken suddenly to find herself there.

"Have you brought what you found in the basement?"

Natalie nodded. "I brought it. But. I've been trying to read it for, like, *days,* but I can't read much of it. It's taking forever. It seems sort of hopeless. Plus I don't even know what I would do with it if I read it, what kind of project it would be."

"Oh, nothing is hopeless," said Kathleen. She didn't really believe this (lots of things were hopeless), but it seemed like the right thing to say. She looked closely at Natalie. "And why aren't you in school?"

"Early release."

"How early? It's only eleven thirty now. And you came all the way from Newburyport..."

"I don't know. Early."

Kathleen let that one pass. She'd been lied to before by a teen-age girl; no reason she wouldn't be again.

Natalie looked suddenly stricken. "Why? Do I need an appointment?"

Something in her eyes made Kathleen relent. (She was a girl without a mother, for the love of God! Go easy on her.) "No, of course not," she said. "I just meant that if you've been trying for days and days with no luck, you could have come in sooner, we would have helped you. But that's okay, we'll get to work now." She gestured toward the empty reading room. "So why don't we have a seat and take a look."

They settled themselves at their usual table and Natalie pulled from her backpack a black spiral-bound notebook. She had bypassed the locker ritual this time, an infraction Kathleen did not point out, so transfixed was she by the notebook.

"I wrapped it in tissue paper," Natalie explained.

"Good idea," said Kathleen, touched by that little detail, the responsibility and maturity it displayed. This poor dead mother, whoever she had been, however she had died, had taught her daughter well.

Kathleen began to read. She stopped and looked at Natalie. "How far did you get?"

"I don't know, like, two pages."

Kathleen bent closer to the book. Natalie sighed, and there was something so adolescent about the sigh, so reminiscent of Susannah's own sighs at that age, her frustration at life's little cruelties or indignities, that Kathleen thought she might cry. But she organized herself enough to say, "What is it?"

Natalie chewed at her fingernail. Her nails were ravaged, some of them bitten all the way down to the quick, and Kathleen had to stop herself from suggesting that Natalie leave them alone. "Nothing. I just thought this would be easier." Her posture really was terrible. It was a shame to think she might grow up slinking around like this, embarrassed by her gorgeous height.

"You thought what would be easier?"

"This. All of this." Natalie gestured to indicate the reading room, then the main lobby; her gesture even seemed to include the wide expanse of Massachusetts Bay that lay beyond the windows. "I thought I could do some sort of amazing project, really impress my teacher."

"And why can't you?"

"I don't know," said Natalie. "All I have is this book, and some stupid research my father never even finished—"

"Okay," said Kathleen. She closed the notebook and rested her hands on top of it. "So what is it exactly that you want to do?"

"I don't know. It's independent study. I guess I can do anything. I thought I could do something really cool, like research my whole family tree, go back and back and back, but it took me so long to get here even this one time..." She blinked her eyes rapidly and looked at the ceiling.

"But you have to produce...something, right?"

"Yeah. But other people are just writing a poetry collection, dumb stuff like that. I should just do that. I'm not sure why I'm here."

In a voice as gentle as she could muster, Kathleen said, "And sit up straight, will you?"

Natalie looked wounded—wounded like a little bird, like the birds in the nest Kathleen used to compare herself and Susannah to after Gregory's death.

"I'm sorry," said Kathleen. "It's just that tall girls tend to slouch, and it's a terrible habit to begin so young. My daughter was tall. Was. Is. Is tall. She got it from her father." She gestured toward her own body. She was of exactly average height on a good day. "Obviously."

Natalie did straighten, pulling her shoulders back to reveal the lines of her collarbones. This too seemed birdlike, somehow, though birds did not, to Kathleen's knowledge, have collarbones. Natalie looked interested. "And does she hate it? Being tall?"

"Sometimes when she was young, I think," said Kathleen. "But she grew into it. You mostly end up growing into your own body, whatever body you get."

"What about now?"

"What do you mean?" Kathleen busied herself with looking down at the notebook, because she was trying to delay the question that surely, inevitably, Natalie, like Melissa Henderson before her, would present next. To distract herself she thought about how strange it was that something like this notebook had once been new—purchased in a store, taken home, with fresh, blank pages.

"I mean, what about now. Does she hate being tall now?"

"I don't know," said Kathleen.

Natalie persisted. "Well, ask her."

"I can't ask her. I lost touch with her."

"You lost *touch* with her?" Natalie pulled her eyebrows together, but her eyebrows, like her eyelashes, were so light—without the makeup they were almost invisible—that the look did not carry the force that Kathleen imagined that Natalie believed it carried.

Can of worms, thought Kathleen dismally. Can of worms.

"You don't talk to your own *daughter?*"

"Well," said Kathleen. She shifted in her seat. "It's more complicated than that. It's really... complicated." She turned her attention back to the notebook.

"Yeah, but that's really sad," said Natalie. "Right?"

The cell phone was not in evidence, but a buzzing sound emanating from Natalie's backpack took her attention—briefly, but thankfully—away from Kathleen.

"Shit, sorry," said Natalie. "I meant to turn that off."

"Get it, if you must," said Kathleen. She looked around at the empty room. "There's nobody here." She lowered her voice. "But you were supposed to leave the backpack in the lockers, like last time."

"Sorry, I for*got*," said Natalie.

The noise came again. Kathleen pictured the phone acting like a phone in a cartoon, jumping inside the backpack, little lines radiating from it.

"Go ahead and answer," said Kathleen. "Really. It won't bother me a bit."

"No," said Natalie.

"What if it's someone important calling?"

"It's not." Natalie set her lips firmly and shook her head.

"How do you know?"

"Because it's a text, not a call."

"Oh," said Kathleen. "How do you know that?"

Natalie sighed gently, indulgently, the way you might sigh at an old lady in bed at a nursing home as you bent to lift the water glass to her lips—*Just one more sip, Aunt Mary, or you'll be up all night in the bathroom*—and said, "I have it set to make different sounds."

"Oh," said Kathleen. "I guess I'm showing my age and my ignorance. One or the other. Maybe both!" She'd meant it to be a little joke, but it was clear Natalie was not going to fill in the silence with a laugh so Kathleen provided one herself, engaging in an awkward, wheezing sound that immediately after she wished she'd kept to herself.

"I'll turn it off," said Natalie. "It's hard to concentrate." But she didn't turn it off, and the buzzing continued. Kathleen took this opportunity to change the subject. "You know who we need?"

"Who?"

"Neil, that's who. He's a genius at this. I told you that, right? I'll be right back."

She returned with Neil, his grouchiness improved slightly by two cups of coffee from the Keurig machine in the lunchroom (this was a far cry from the Nespresso machine he and Adam had at home, but in extreme circumstances he used it anyway).

"This," she said to Natalie, who was studying her phone, "is Neil. Neil, Natalie."

Neil gave a theatrical bow. It was enough to make Natalie smile. Kathleen thought he was going to kiss Natalie's hand, as though he were a commoner visiting her court, and she the queen, but instead he pulled out the chair next to her, brandished his magnifying glass, and said, "So you're the one with the treasure. May I?"

Natalie smiled and pushed the notebook toward him. From the other room, phones were ringing, and two people had appeared out of nowhere, waiting to sign in.

"I'll just go and see what's going on out there," said Kathleen, backing away. Neither Neil nor Natalie looked up. "Okay, then," said Kathleen. "I'll just be out here, if you need me."

She looked through the glass after she exited the room: Neil and Natalie, heads together, looking down. Something about this picture seemed right.

✳

For a long time they sat there. Neil came up with a plan. "If you want," he said, "I'll read it out loud, and you can write it in your own handwriting, so you have a copy."

"Yeah? Okay. You can read it just like that, no problem?"

"I don't have many talents," said Neil. "But this is one of them."

Neil started from the beginning, and it didn't take long for him to get to the part where Natalie had left off:

> Even if nobody ever reads this, even if I hide this in a box and hide the box somewhere in the house and nobody finds it, it will be enough for me to know that the story has been told.
>
> You could say there were lots of things that led to what happened.
>
> But it all started on Christmas Eve, 1925, so I will begin my story there.

"Here's where I stopped," whispered Natalie. It seemed appropriate suddenly to whisper.

"Okay," Neil whispered back.

> This is what I remember. Christmas Eve, cold, and the wind coming off the Merrimac, hard and driving, blowing my hair back from my face. I was Bridget O'Connell then, hatless, and gloveless too, and late to boot. I walked as quickly as I could, and every so often I attempted to break into a run. But I had hurt my ankle the day before, twisting it on the servant stairs, and now it was tender and swollen and I could run only a step or two before the pain forced me to slow.

There was a song going round and round in my head. *I saw three ships come sailing in, come sailing in, come sailing in . . .*

Anna played that song over and over again on the Victrola, she'd been playing it since the beginning of December, and I, despite my determination not to love anything that Anna loved, had grown very fond of it.

I turned from the post office onto State Street, past the shops and on toward the dignified homes, then onto High Street. It was just past two in the afternoon, but I could feel the darkness coming on already, the evening rushing to overtake the day.

Of course I wasn't meant to be calling her Anna, I was meant to call her Mrs. Turner, and I did, to her face, but in private I called her Anna. Because despite what Anna, with her volunteer work, with her letter writing, with her morning naps, thought, the two of us were more equal than anyone wanted to believe. I knew that.

And Charles should have been Dr. Turner, but in my dreams he was Charles. There were many of those dreams, and they were secret, so secret I hadn't told anyone, not my dear friend Norah, who worked in service for a wealthier family a quarter of a mile away, not my sister Grainne, who had encouraged me to come over from Ireland and who was married to a Cork boy and living, chubby and complacent, in Lynn.

I saw three ships come sailing in . . .

One time I came into the parlor to dust and saw Anna dancing the baby around while that song played. She was singing too. I had never heard Anna sing. She had a beautiful voice, lovely and sure. This was a surprise because I loved to sing, and I sang throughout much of my workday, and more than once I encountered Anna's stare as she came around the corner. The Protestants, my mother told me, didn't care for music the way the Catholics did.

The baby, James, was laughing with his mouth wide open so I could see the little stumps of teeth that were beginning to come in. When I entered, Anna stopped, and James stopped laughing, and for a second both regarded me seriously, as though I had walked in through the wall. Then the baby put his fat dimpled arms out to me and made the little mooing sound he sometimes made. Anna handed him to me and swept out of the room, shaking her skirts.

It was nothing, really, an incident that should have been easily forgotten, an ordinary moment in an ordinary day. And yet after that time I found I often thought of that, of the way Anna looked with her head thrown back, her hair coming loose from the pins. I could see the girl Anna might have been not so long ago. I could see, however briefly, the girl Charles had fallen in love with.

That was a few weeks ago, of course. Before I found the blood on the sheets.

Natalie's fingers were starting to cramp: she never wrote this much by hand, almost everything she did for school was on the computer. She hadn't written this much since second grade, Mrs. Foster's class. She remembered the teacher's fleshy neck and the way she opened her mouth really wide when she laughed. Natalie's other hand held the notebook open, while Neil ran his forefinger down the page as he worked out the words.

"Okay?" said Neil.

"Yes," she said. She shook her fingers to loosen the muscles. "Keep going."

Ah, Charles had said when I first arrived at their home, a Bridget named Bridget. Because that was the name they gave to all the girls over from Ireland, they called them all Bridgets, and while I should have been able to laugh that off, the terrible coincidence of my name, the way it made something I always thought was individual to me common and everyday, I often felt a flame of anger when I heard it. How funny, Charles said. We got the actual Bridget! The real thing. But he hadn't sounded mean when he said that, the way some might, there was something kind behind his eyes when they caught mine.

Christmas Eve, then. I forced myself to walk faster. All that way to the post office and back on a sore ankle. Underneath my stockings the ankle was swollen and purplish blue, and the buckle pressed into the tender skin in just the wrong place. But there was a letter from home for me, and that made it all worthwhile.

I was tired, I remember that. I remember so much about that day, and the weeks and months that followed, and yet I can't remember what I did last Christmas. I am sure my son Patrick, who is a brain surgeon, would have some sort of explanation for that.

Natalie put the pencil down and flexed her hand. It *hurt*.

"You okay?" asked Neil.

"Well," she said, "not really, no." She made a fist, released it, made another fist. "I'm not sure I can keep writing."

"Kids these days," said Neil. "Bunch of wimps." But he smiled when he said that. "You know, when I was in college, one hundred and eighteen years ago, we had to write all of our exams in a little blue book. And I was an English major, so those were some long exams. Essay questions, all of them, hours and hours of writing. I remember I had a callus on my middle finger the size of a boulder. Well, never mind. I wonder if they still do that? No, there's no way. Nobody would survive it."

"I don't know," said Natalie. College seemed impossibly far in the future.

"You know what?" said Neil. "Forget the writing. You look like your hand is about to fall off. Why don't I read, and you just listen. We'll transcribe it another time."

"Okay," said Natalie.

I had risen at five that morning, which was half an hour earlier than I normally rose. Because of the holiday there was plenty to do. Besides the usual — the table to set, the breakfast to prepare, the beds to air out and make once the family had risen — there was Christmas baking to finish and a spit-and-shine all over the house, for there were guests expected that evening, Dr. Turner's family coming up from Boston. His difficult, beautiful sister, Elsie, and her husband.

At last I arrived at the house after my trip to the post office. There was Anna, standing in the doorway. Two of the children were swirling around her, pulling on her skirts, and in her arms she held James. The older two were Harry and Edward. So many boys! Boys everywhere in this house. I remember that when I arrived the previous March, still woozy from the ship, and from the trip up from Boston, I was unprepared for all of this masculinity; I hardly knew what to do with it. My home back in Kerry was dominated by women, even after Grainne departed for America: my mother, sharp-tongued and assertive; my sisters Fiona and Claire; and little baby Siobhan, who was no longer a baby, really, because she had just turned five, but in my mind a baby she would remain forever.

In the presence of so many females, my father, with his wide, freckled cheeks, his work-worn hands, seemed to fade and recede, year by year, into the background.

But these boys, the Turner boys! They frightened me. They had their father's quick dark eyes, and his lean build, and the oldest one, Harry, had a way of looking at you that made him seem far older than his years. It could set your teeth on edge, that look.

Edward was more physical. Once he bit me on the leg so hard I bled.

The baby was different. I loved James unwaveringly. I loved his fat pudding face. I loved to bury my face in the warm folds of his neck and blow gently, and I loved the eruption of a laugh that came from deep in his belly when I did that. That I could feel such love for someone I bore no relation to was a fact that astonished me. But there it was.

Here's something nobody in the Turner home knew: in the middle of the night I woke and tiptoed down the steps from my attic room and into James's room. Every night I did this; despite the fatigue, something pulled me to James's room. I checked the rail of the crib to make sure it was fastened tight. I checked the windows to make sure they were closed and locked. And then I stole back to my room, barely breathing, lest Dr. Turner or Anna emerge from their room and see me in the hallway.

Why did I do this? I don't know. But somehow James felt as close to me as he would have had I given birth to him myself. And I to him, I believed that, which made what happened later all the more unspeakable.

"What happened?" asked Natalie. "What's she mean?"
"I don't know."

Already, at nine months, though he could not yet walk, James showed signs of being a dexterous climber. He had ways of pulling himself up and over things, belly first, his whole chubby face intent on gaining the object he desired. He had a fire in him, and I felt a responsibility to keep him safe from himself until he was old enough to spot the dangers in the world on his own. Soon he would walk, and then he would run, and then he would no longer be a baby. My baby. That's how I thought of him! As mine. Can you imagine if Anna knew I thought of him that way?

There was a game we used to play where James crawled away from me outside his bedroom, looking back to see if I was following, laughing when I did. Sometimes I crawled too, and that made him laugh even harder.

Anna was horrified the time she caught us playing that game. "Bridget!" she said. "Whatever are you doing?" Her lips had gone cold and white.

I righted myself, standing and smoothing out my skirts, straightening my hair, forcing my expression from laughter into gravity. "Oh, we are only playing, ma'am. No harm in it." A latent giggle exploded from James, and he looked from one of us to the other: were we still playing?

"Only playing! No harm in it! He could have fallen right down the front stairs."

I felt my face grow warm. "I wouldn't let that happen, ma'am. I always catch him in time."

"I should think you'd know better." Anna's face hardened. "Even you." His mother's harsh tone and the fact that the game had stopped conspired to make James start crying. Anna went on: "Maybe it's done differently in Ireland, but in America we protect our children from harm."

"Yes, ma'am," I said, looking down. "That's the same as we do in Ireland."

"Tell me, Bridget. Did you grow up in a home with stairs?"

I shook my head.

"I didn't think so. Did you grow up in a home with a stove? With automobiles driving outside on the street? With a river within walking distance?"

No.

"Then you don't know. You can't know. The dangers we face—"

"We have the hearth fire, ma'am," I said. "There's plenty of danger there." I meant that sincerely, but I knew as soon as I said it that Anna would take it as impudence.

"The hearth fire," spat Anna. "Hardly the same."

After that, Anna made Dr. Turner fashion a wooden gate to go against the front stairs. The gate had a small hook that fastened into a ring on one side of the stairs, and you had to lift the ring out of the hook to open the gate and insert it again to close the gate.

"Can't have the doctor's son taking a tumble, can we?" Dr. Turner had said when he nailed the thing together. He winked at me when he said that. I couldn't tell if he was trying to make light of what he thought was a necessary precaution, to make me feel better about things, or if he truly thought Anna was making a lot out of nothing. Either way I was glad of his winking, and when he smiled at me after I felt something drop in my stomach: an unfamiliar sensation to which I couldn't give a name.

Back to Christmas Eve, then, and me coming in from the post office. I could see by Anna's face that I was in trouble. This was not unexpected. I felt the letter in my coat pocket, caressed the corner of the envelope. Anna began talking even before I reached the doorway so the effect was that of watching a film from the street, with Anna as the actor. I had been to see *The Gold Rush* with a couple of the Kerry girls earlier in the year at the Strand on Pleasant Street, and that's where I got the comparison. There's no theater there anymore, of course, but when I walk by the spot where it was, on my way to where the post office now stands, I still remember how we laughed and laughed, the girls and I.

As I drew closer I could begin to make out the words. The beds, something about the beds. I felt my cheeks heat up. I had forgotten to do the beds! Anna's face was red, and there was an angry squiggle in the center of her forehead. The anger made Anna uglier, and I took some pleasure in that, for she was not a very beautiful woman to begin with.

"Bridget! It's Christmas Eve. We'll soon have the house filled up with visitors —" Here Anna paused to shake Harry off her skirt, and he looked at her, wounded and befuddled, and began to cry. "And I can't get anything done with the children here, not a single thing. You must know that."

I did know. I thought of my mother back in Kerry, in our cramped little home, so different from the homes here in America. Back there the roof had only recently been thatched. The lot of us were stuffed in so tightly that I knew my sisters' smells, the sounds they made while they slept, their wishes and disappointments, as well and maybe better than I knew my own. Our dear mother! Poor, yes. Hardworking, certainly. Tired, much of the time. But not angry like this. Never pinched and angry, like Anna.

James reached his arms toward me, his plump, delicious arms. When I was alone with him, I pretended to eat them and he laughed and laughed. He was a great one for laughing, James, and his laughter was the brightest part of my day. James, and then the master, of course, Charles, Dr. Turner. I smiled.

"Bridget! Faster. What are you smiling about, then?"

"Nothing, ma'am. I didn't know I was." I walked up the steps. I had swept those steps that morning, as the sun was just beginning to rise. I had been awake for so long that that seemed like yesterday. I was often so tired at the Turners' house, and the work was so monotonous, and so physically demanding, that the days melted into one another, one task becoming the next, infusing even my dreams with their tedium.

I think a few things led to what happened. The first is how much I loved the baby. James. I loved that baby so much that I never thought I could love another baby in the same way, even when I had my own not so long after that. I did, of course, love mine as much, but I didn't know if I would.

The baby, my baby, was also named James.

"What?" said Natalie. "I don't understand." Once she had stopped trying to write down what Neil was saying, his reading picked up pace; Kathleen had been right, he was a genius at this, reading through the spidery writing just as easily as most people read through the newspaper. How'd he do it? She didn't know. But she felt as though this was a real, honest-to-God story, something true and dramatic, not just a dusty notebook from the bowels of her basement. When was the last time an adult had read something to her? When had her parents stopped reading to her at bedtime? When she learned to read herself, she supposed, kindergarten, first grade. Had she been on her own at bedtime that long? She supposed she had. This realization was suddenly woeful and telling to her, a signal of the end of her childhood that she hadn't noticed enough to mourn.

"I don't understand either," said Neil. "But I bet if we keep going, it will all become clear. You game?"

"Yup," said Natalie. "I'm game."

I have never spoken of the events of that time, the winter of 1925 and the spring of 1926, to anyone. Declan knew what happened, of course, but he never asked me to talk about it, and so I never did. He was wonderful that way, the sort of husband you wish for your daughters: kind and loyal and unwavering.

It is funny which memories your mind keeps and which it discards.

I remember—I will always remember—the shoes that Elsie wore to dinner on Christmas Eve in 1925. They had silver buckles. I had never seen anything like those shoes.

After all that happened later, I forgot the shoes; I forgot nearly everything about Elsie and Arthur. Or if it wasn't forgetting, exactly, it was a pushing down of certain details, a burying. I didn't think consciously about Elsie or her beautiful and ridiculous costume until very recently, long after those fashions had gone out of style, when I came across a pair of similar shoes in the window of an antiques store in New York City. Funny, said one of the women I was with, how something that used to be current fashion can become an antique! Something that was fashionable in our lifetime.

I thought I heard once that in order for something to be considered an antique it had to be one hundred years old or older, but I didn't say anything. The woman—her name was Helen—was close to my age, and I did not know her well. We came together on a bus trip, one of those excursions planned for groups of older women who have lost their husbands and are looking for some way to pass their time.

Yes, I said, I suppose everything becomes an antique eventually, and I sighed in a world-weary way that was meant to mask the thumping in my chest, the sudden rush of blood to my cheeks.

This was . . . oh, a couple of years ago. I was, as I am now, gray, veined, a widow, my Irish accent greatly diluted from years and years of living away, dressed in a cardigan and sensible slacks: the uniform of my current life, but with a new blouse underneath the cardigan in honor of the bus trip to New York City.

I must have had a look of some consternation on my face because the young woman who was in charge of the trip took my elbow and asked if I was all right. This young woman, Nell, was cheerful and freckled, with a wide, moonlike face and curly reddish hair held back with a headband. She could have been a girl from the village, she could have been that, swinging around in a ceili, though her feet turned in when she walked. Back in Ireland in my day, they'd put your shoes on the wrong feet on purpose to correct that; there was a whole family, the Murphys, walking around with their shoes on the opposite feet.

I don't think they do that anymore.

I said that I was fine, but really I wasn't, because there was something rising in my throat, constricting my breathing, and I had to take three rapid inhalations, and then I had to put my fingertips against the shopwindow to steady myself. It was all there suddenly, carved out of very old memories. What part of the brain is it that held your old memories?

My son Patrick had told me once; he is a brain surgeon. Imagine that! My son, slicing into people's brains. It's not brain surgery, people said of something that was not considered very difficult, in the same way they said, It's not rocket science. That was an old joke in our family before Declan died. There he'd be, trying to fix the toaster or change the filter in the furnace, and struggling with it for one reason or another, and he'd say, It's not exactly brain surgery, is it? His Irish accent so much more persistent than mine, for some reason. I think that's because I read so much, I was reading all the time, and when I read I put a different voice into my head.

What Declan meant by the joke was how did the two of us come to have a son smart enough to become a brain surgeon. And how did we? I don't know. It was just one of those things.

You would have thought James would have been the one to become the brain surgeon.

In New York City that day I stared at the shoes and around me I felt the crush of people on the sidewalk, heard the taxicabs honking and the buses coming to whooshing stops along the curb.

"Just buy them already," said Helen cheerfully. "I'll go in with you." She made a motion toward the door of the shop.

"No," I said. "I don't want to buy them."

"Why not? What's the harm?" Helen laughed. What was she so happy about? Why was everyone around me always so happy?

"I don't want them," I said, maybe too sharply. "I'm just looking."

"Well, ohhhh-kay," said Helen, drawing out the word, making a face that made her look suddenly juvenile, an adolescent's expression on an old lady's features.

My memory was keeping me from remembering the name of the part of the brain that held the memory! In another circumstance perhaps I would have been able to appreciate the irony.

Patrick told me once that the sense of smell is tied more powerfully to memory than any of the other senses. So you can catch a whiff of a perfume your mother used to wear, or of a food you ate at a carnival years ago, and immediately you might be transported to that time and place. Everyone experiences that, Patrick said, casually, almost laconically, gesturing toward his nose. But there are scientific reasons behind it.

What smells had there been that night? The roast, of course. The fire. The cigar smoke on the men, after they came in from looking at the car. Elsie's powder. Dear little James's baby scent.

In New York City that day, I turned away from the shoes, away from the window, and I began to follow Nell and the rest of the group back to where the bus was waiting to take us to Times Square for a matinee: some play I had never heard of, a musical, something cheerful, because it was assumed that the elderly were always in need of cheering up. Which maybe we were.

Was it the same with sounds? I remember the noise of Arthur's coupe pulling away from the house when he took Dr. Turner for a ride — there was that, and the honk of the horn, one two three, like he was playing a song for everyone left inside. ("Showboater," said Anna grimly, and Elsie laughed.)

And later, at midnight, the church bells ringing, signifying the start of Midnight Mass, which of course I could not attend.

After the antiques shop I climbed aboard the bus. The driver was solicitous, holding out a hand for each of us, though when he got to Nell, who was bringing up the rear, she laughed, revealing a set of crooked bottom teeth, and said, "I think I can manage. But thank you."

The hippocampus, that was it! Patrick showed me a picture once in one of his textbooks from medical school. The hippocampus outlined in bright green, like a pea pod set in the middle of a plate of spaghetti. "This is a lateral view," he said importantly. "Two of the lobes have been removed so you can see this."

"Ah," I said, marveling at his knowledge, at his ease with this mysterious organ.

I sat by myself, placing my coat and pocketbook next to me. I settled back against the plush seat, resting my head against the crinkly paper that had been set there, ostensibly for reasons of sanitation. I closed my eyes so that if Helen tried to meet my gaze I would be spared the effort of vocalizing my wish to be left alone.

Imagine that: a lifetime of memories living inside something that looked no bigger or more important than a pea pod. The hippocampus.

"This lady can *write*," said Neil. "Don't you think?"

Natalie nodded. She didn't want to speak; she wanted Neil to keep reading. She felt that speaking would be like breaking a spell.

I remember other things.

I remember the way the paperboys used to deliver the newspaper to apartments on the third floor; the customer would lower a nickel wrapped in white paper down on a string and the paperboy would take the coin and tie the newspaper onto the string to be raised back up.

I remember when you could take a trolley out to Plum Island. I remember the bootleggers down by the wharf—the speakeasies with their walkways hidden by tall bushes—the music on the gramophones, people dancing the Charleston. I remember there were brothels down there too. It seems impossible to me sometimes, but all of these things happened in my lifetime.

And so did the rest of what I'm about to tell. It's as if I wrote the events of that year on a piece of paper and folded the paper into tiny squares and put it in a pocket of my brain. But they are always with me somewhere and now that I have decided to write about them I feel like I have unfolded the paper and am reading it anew.

I remember things about Ireland too, even though I never made it back there. I remember the way my sister Fiona's hair smelled when we lay together in the bed in the family cottage. I remember her breath on my cheek. I remember the color of my mother's everyday shawl. If ever I hear a bit of Gaelic spoken I remember what it was like to hear that all the time, everywhere, and I remember how hard we worked to learn English, and penmanship, and the dances. I remember the parish dances, and how we looked forward to those.

Other things, I have forgotten, or put in the wrong order.

I remember a fiddle playing, I remember someone singing "Molly Durkin."

But who was singing, and where?

"I'm a decent honest workingman as you might understand/ and I'll tell to you the reason why I left ol' Ireland/'Twas Molly Durkin did it/when she married Tim O'Shea..."

In America, I remember working until my back ached, until my hands ached, until my brain was blurry. I have never in my whole life worked as hard as I worked that year in the Turner house, my first year in America, I have never again been so tired to the core, to the deepest part of my bones.

And I was also never so happy as at certain times during that year.

I remember the time Anna pushed me. She was walking by me on the stairs, and the stairs were narrow: it was always difficult for two people to pass at a time. You had to push a little bit to get by. But she pushed more than she needed to, and I slipped and I fell down. I hurt my ankle.

This was the day before Christmas Eve. Anna knew that I was hurt, but she never acknowledged she had anything to do with it.

Norah, who was my dearest friend at the time, in service for another family, told me that she could tell that Anna hated me because I was pretty. I was! I can say that now, because I am no longer. I have no photographs of me from that time, I wish I did.

Anna was cruel to me, and I wanted what she had, and when I found out I could take it I did. That was the second thing that led to what happened. Can you blame me?

You should blame me. I blame myself. Somebody died because of what I did.

"Wait, *what?*" said Natalie. "Did you say somebody *died?*"

"Holy *shit,*" said Neil. Then, "Sorry."

"That's okay," said Natalie. She felt like she was holding her breath. "Who died?"

"I don't know," said Neil. "But I can't wait to find out."

The third thing was that I got careless with what I had, once I had it. As people do.

·⁣᠅⁣·

Kathleen came in and said, "Neil, there's a phone call for you."

"Adam?"

"No. Female. Research question. Follow-up from something or other."

"Can you take a message?" He didn't look up when he said that.

She said, "Yes, sir. At your service." She stood there for a moment and said, "Making progress?"

"Oh yeah," said Neil, still not looking up. "Serious progress."

"You need my help?"

"No," said Neil, still looking down. "I think we've got it."

The next time she came in, Kathleen said, "Neil? Keep an eye on the desk, will you? I've got to run out for my pastry flour. Day before Thanksgiving, it's going to be nuts out there. I don't want to put it off."

Neil looked up then; he said, "Sounds like a nightmare. Better you than me."

"I'm making the pie for *you,* sir. You and your fancy friends."

"Right," said Neil. "In that case, off you go."

Natalie wasn't used to grown-ups talking like this to each other, in this gentle, teasing way. She didn't know what to do with it so she stayed quiet, with her eyes focused on the notebook, and when Kathleen had departed Neil kept reading.

I let the roast cook for too long, that Christmas Eve, and that was my first mistake. But I'm getting ahead of myself. I believe that is what happens when all of these memories come out, tumbling over one another. What would Patrick have to say about that?

Never mind about the roast: I will start after dinner on Christmas Eve, when I began carrying the dishes into the kitchen to prepare them for washing.

No, I will start before that, when Dr. Turner's sister, Elsie, and her husband, Arthur, arrived.

There was no love lost between Elsie and Anna, anyone could see that, but when Elsie came in the front door I could scarcely take my eyes off of her, so transfixed was I by her long silver coat and the short black hair curving out from under her hat.

"Well!" Elsie said, handing her coat to Charles, who handed it to me to hang in the closet. Elsie kissed Charles on the cheek, then grasped Anna by the hand and kissed her too, then looked around as if for someone else to kiss. Her gaze settled briefly on me and then she looked away, and Charles said, "Oh! You haven't met our girl from Ireland, our Bridget," and he pushed me forward. Elsie nodded crisply at me and took off her hat and I could see the fringe that was cut bluntly across her forehead. The older boys Elsie did not kiss, but she rubbed them on their heads in a distracted, almost frantic way, as if they were dogs who had come too close to her on the street and whose intentions she mistrusted.

"Well!" she said again, smiling. "You're all looking well. Aren't they looking well, Arthur?" Arthur was standing behind her. He was ten years her senior; he was tall and dark and unsmiling and he wore a double-breasted suit. Though he wasn't unfriendly, he also wore a preoccupied expression that made him appear to be thinking about matters more serious than the ones currently before him.

He was some sort of businessman — this much I had picked

up from listening to Charles and Anna talk about him. ("I don't trust him," Anna said, and Charles said, "Does it matter if you do? Elsie is madly in love." To which Anna said, "If you call that love," and after that they moved out of my range and I heard nothing else.) In fact in the present circumstance Arthur seemed to be an accessory more than anything else, a bystander who had been sent into Elsie's orbit to observe rather than participate. That was partly because of the way his hat sat, slung low over his eyes, but also because of the way he stood a little bit apart from all of them. When he removed his hat and handed it to me I caught a whiff of something—cologne?—that spoke to me of an exotic and captivating world. Until that point I knew no men who wore cologne.

They had come up from Boston in Arthur's new coupe, and perhaps that accounted for the slightly breathless way Elsie had entered the house: all this motion, now halted.

"Aren't they, Arthur?" said Elsie. "Looking well?" She was smiling eagerly at all of them, but without her gaze truly settling on any one of them in particular.

"They are," Arthur said finally, and Charles said, "I've got to have a look at that car, Arthur," and both men left together through the front door. When they did, Elsie said in an exaggerated voice, "God! Men and their cars." Anna, who was bending down to smooth Edward's hair, did not answer.

Well, they were beautiful, so lovely to look at, both of them, that I couldn't stop staring. I believe Elsie was the most beautiful creature I had laid eyes on up to that point, and perhaps even to this day. There were the shoes, which I've already mentioned. I couldn't stop staring at the strap, and also at Elsie's stockings, which were beige, with some sort of embroidery around the ankle.

Dinner came next. As I've said, I let the roast go for too long.

I knew immediately when I cut into it, but there was nothing to be done, so I forged ahead, sawing at it awkwardly—I had not yet learned how to cut the meat properly, and I was too proud to ask Anna to show me—and then I lay the pieces on the serving platter and carried the plate into the dining room, my heart ricocheting. But Anna said nothing, she just took the platter from me, hardly looking at it, because she was listening to Elsie.

Elsie was saying, "Well! Where do you think we're going next month? Monte Carlo, that's where." She pulled on her husband's sleeve. "To the opera. Isn't that right, Arthur?"

Arthur nodded.

"Oh, Arthur, what's the name of the opera? I can't keep it straight in my head."

"*The Spellbound Child*," said Arthur.

"That's it!" said Elsie. "I can never remember the name. Why can I never remember the name?"

"Because you smoke and drink too much, my darling. It's going straight to your brain," said Arthur, and they were all silent for a beat, waiting for Elsie's reaction. I had heard Anna speak of Elsie's great temper. She was known for it, and apparently unembarrassed by it. When Elsie ended the silence by tossing back her head and laughing, the very furniture seemed to bend forward in relief.

On my way back to the kitchen I tried to imagine my mother and father talking to each other the way Elsie and Arthur talked to each other. I could not. I tried to imagine Anna and Charles talking that way. I couldn't do that either, nor Grainne and her husband, nor anyone else I knew, in Ireland or in America. Elsie and Arthur seemed to have stepped straight out of a movie screen. Anna made a sound that could have been a cough, and then she said, "Bridget! We've only got the meat. I guess we'll have the vegetables now too."

"Yes, ma'am," I called, and I paused just over the threshold to the kitchen, long enough to hear Elsie say, "She's beautiful, your girl. Isn't she beautiful, Arthur?" I didn't hear Arthur answer, but I could hear that Anna said something in a fierce whisper, and then I heard Elsie laugh, the same way she'd laughed at Arthur, and I clattered the spoon against the vegetable dish more loudly than I needed to. My face was warm, and when I entered the dining room again I kept my eyes cast down.

The rest of the meal passed quickly: from the dining room to the kitchen and back, dining room, kitchen, back. And all the while I kept my eyes on the clock hanging over the sink: seven o'clock, then eight o'clock, then half past eight, and still they sat. The boys grew fidgety and finally they were permitted to leave the table, and to open the packages that Elsie and Arthur had set beneath the Christmas tree. For Edward, a spinning top with pictures of clowns and teddy bears painted on the side. And for Harry, a model aeroplane kit. For James, there was a wooden pull toy, but he was growing tired and ornery, pushing his head back against Anna's shoulder and rubbing his eyes with his fists, and he didn't care about the present.

"Give him to me," said Elsie, turning to Anna with arms outstretched. Anna placed James into her arms, but the passing around made James inconsolable. You could see that Elsie knew nothing about how to comfort a child; she was clearly irritated by the way James thrust his fists toward her neck, and the way he put his wet face right into her beautiful dress.

"Well," said Elsie to Anna, sliding a napkin between the baby and her dress. "Perhaps you should take him back."

"Better off giving him to Bridget," said Anna. "That's the one he really wants."

When I was clearing the remains of the dessert, Elsie took out her compact and examined her face in the mirror, making her lips into a kissing shape and blowing gently. Then she removed a lipstick from her bag and pressed it to her lips. This was astonishing to me — I had never seen a woman apply makeup in public. At the dinner table!

There were a lot of dishes. Anna had the fine china out and the silver too, and the serving dishes and all the rest of it. My ankle had swelled up and was throbbing. I could hardly walk on it, but Anna didn't seem to notice. Or if she noticed she said nothing.

My heart was at home that night with my family in Ireland. I was thinking of the distance that separated us and the journey that it took to get here, the tediousness of the voyage, the inspections after arriving, the loneliness, something as simple as my usual cup of tea difficult to find because suddenly everywhere there was coffee.

I was thinking of Fiona and how much she wanted to come over to America to do the same thing I was doing, just as I had followed Grainne. I remember that I had been waiting for a letter from Fiona and that it had finally arrived that day but that I had not yet had time to read it. I remember that I had been having strange dreams about Fiona. We all did that, had dreams about people we'd left behind, the girls and I talked about it all the time when we were together. It was a very common consequence of being so far from home. But my dreams of Fiona had gotten very odd, more gruesome and puzzling: Fiona's face floating under a murky body of water, her hair spread out behind her like a fan. Fiona riding on horseback into a wood, looking back, shouting something at me that I couldn't understand.

All my sisters were dear to me, but Fiona was the dearest, we were the closest out of the whole family, she and I. We had that special bond.

I was thinking of the Midnight Mass at Rathmore and the way the sky would look after, cold and dark and lit up with stars like it is there. The stars weren't the same in America. It was enough to make me want to cry, and I am not a crier, never have been and never will be. I cried only twice during the whole time I lived in the Turner household: once that Christmas Eve, and once on that terrible night, stumbling outside in the dark.

"What night?" said Natalie. It was hard for her to breathe. Neil said, "I don't know."

"Keep reading!" said Natalie. "Neil, keep reading!"

⁂

On a whim Kathleen collected Lucy from home and made her a cozy bed in the backseat of the car. She did that sometimes so that Lucy wouldn't be alone all day. Working-mother's guilt, she called it, only somewhat facetiously.

This made her later than she had planned to be for the Stop and Shop, which, true to form on the day before Thanksgiving, was like the middle of a bad dream: the full parking lot, the harried people dashing from car to store in the dwindling light, the drivers pulling in and out of spaces, hardly looking, the ghastly fluorescent lights inside the store illuminating the scowls on the clerks' faces.

"In and out," said Kathleen sternly to herself. "Just in and out, beeline it toward the baking section."

Next: the bright voice behind her. "We've got to stop meeting like this."

She turned. "Melissa. Melissa Henderson." Again. What were the odds? "You're back in town."

Kathleen didn't want to get snagged in a conversation; she wanted to pay for her pastry flour and get back. The Archives was due to close at four thirty. But Melissa Henderson appeared to be settling in for a conversation.

"I never left, actually. Seemed silly to fly all the way back right before the holidays, and my husband was working anyway, and so here I am!" Melissa Henderson looked a little crazed.

"Where's—" Kathleen had forgotten the name.

"Mabel," Melissa supplied. "Home. With my parents. She hasn't been sleeping great. I don't even need anything! I just had to get away." There were puffy mauve pockets under her eyes, and her hair was in a sloppy ponytail.

"And this is where you came to get away? The day before Thanksgiving?"

"Yeah, I know. Crazy. I wasn't thinking, I sort of forgot about Thanksgiving somehow. But it's weird, right? That I saw you here twice. Unless you're here all the time."

"I'm not," said Kathleen. "Not all the time."

"Sort of cosmic." Melissa Henderson grinned, a wild-eyed grin. Was she a little manic?

"Right," said Kathleen. She peered at Melissa. "Is everything okay? You look a little—"

"A little nutty?"

"I was going to say *tired*," said Kathleen. "A little tired."

"Oh." Melissa sighed. "Tired, yeah, I'm tired." She leaned on her shopping cart, which, Kathleen noticed, was perfectly empty. She said, "This mothering thing is kind of hard, isn't it, Mrs. Lynch?"

"That," said Kathleen, "is the understatement of the year."

"Tell me it gets easier," said Melissa.

"It gets easier," said Kathleen. But what she was thinking was, *You have no idea how hard it gets.*

Melissa smiled, a genuine smile, less crazy; she seemed cheered by Kathleen's lie. Kathleen decided to allow her that solace, however false. Melissa straightened and gripped the handle of her shopping cart. She said, "Hey, you have a happy Thanksgiving, Mrs. Lynch. Give my best to . . . well, to whoever."

Whomever, thought Kathleen.

⁂

"Keep reading!" said Natalie again.

So Neil kept reading.

My next mistake came soon after that. The gravy boat, which I was carrying to the sink to wash, slipped from my hands and clattered to the floor, shattering. The conversation in the dining room stopped, and I held my breath, waiting. Then I heard a murmur, and I could make out a few words here and there. *Clumsy* was one of them. *Vase* was another. I knew what that was about, I broke a vase in the bedroom the first week I was there. I was dusting. Anna said that it was not important that day, but I could see by the set of her mouth and the way her eyes grew small and squinty that it was. Then somebody—a male—said "fumble-fingered." Was it Dr. Turner? Arthur? One of the boys, making their voices deeper than it typically was? After that there was a small outburst of laughter.

I turned on the tap. I thought Anna would be in soon enough to see about what had shattered, and she would add the broken gravy boat to the long list of my transgressions. Poor Bridget, who couldn't do anything right. I bent to collect the pieces from the floor. But I reached too quickly for one of them, and I cut my hand. Without thinking I wiped my hand on my dress, and this added to my indignity, because now I had blood on my dress, and Anna wouldn't want me to continue serving at the table unless I changed.

But it wasn't Anna who came in, it was Dr. Turner. So involved

129

was I in picking up the pieces of the gravy boat, and in trying to regain my composure, that I didn't hear him enter the kitchen, and I didn't know he was standing there until I saw his shoes in my line of vision.

I looked up.

"Oh, now," said Dr. Turner. There was something yielding in his voice that I hadn't heard before, and something else that was unfamiliar: a tenderness, I think you would call it. Something thumped deep inside me.

He said, "It's just a dish, Bridget. No need to cry about it."

"I'm sorry," I whispered.

"It won't be the end of us, you know, if we lose a gravy boat." I had heard this jocular tone before; he used it with Harry and Edward sometimes, and occasionally when he read portions of the *Daily News* aloud at the breakfast table. But never with me. Nor with Anna.

He said, "What is it, Bridget?" and I pointed at my ankle, whose swelling you could now see through my stocking.

I had never noticed before that there was a light strip of brown in one of his blue eyes. I guess I'd never looked at him directly so close up, nor he me. Once I noticed the brown strip, I couldn't stop looking at it.

I probably have some of this conversation wrong—this happened fifty years ago—but what I remember, what I imagine I remember, is that he said, "What good is it having a doctor in the house if you don't make use of him?" And he pointed me toward a kitchen chair, which was higher than the stool.

He unbuckled my shoe gently and slid it from my foot, then rolled down the stocking. I winced when he touched my ankle, and I saw that it had turned a purplish green color. There was a mark across it from where the buckle had been pressing into it. It seemed like such an intimate thing he was doing, holding my ankle like that. He whistled, low and long. "Bridget! This looks painful."

I nodded. I was trying not to cry, but in fact the trying made me cry harder.

He said, "I'll wrap it. I have bandages in my bag."

Then he said, "They won't notice if you go on upstairs after I wrap it. Not Elsie and Arthur anyway. They won't notice anything. They're well into the rum." From the dining room I could hear loud laughter, both female and male. Dr. Turner rolled his eyes in a way I suppose was meant to signify that there was a joke between us. And I guess maybe there was.

"Holy shit," breathed Neil. "Scandalous. Is this going where I think it's going?"

Natalie didn't know. But before she answered, Kathleen came in and said, "It's nearly four thirty, you two. We're about to close."

❋

Back at the Archives, Kathleen stood for a moment outside the reading room and watched Neil and Natalie, the two Ns, their heads close together, bent over their work. She felt a stab of something, probably jealousy, that was the only emotion that really stabbed you. Also regret. Regret stabbed too. But this was definitely jealousy, even though she had been the architect of this scene. (Let's call over Neil! she'd suggested. "He's a genius at this.")

All around them girls were in danger. And obviously she was ill-equipped to help: look what had happened the last time she'd tried. She thought of Susannah in the bath, playing with a yellow ducky, Susannah climbing aboard the school bus, turning to wave, all the hope and optimism in the world on her face. It went so quickly from that to the rest of it, it took your breath away.

When Susannah left she took with her a few items of clothing. Two pairs of jeans. A navy blue sweatshirt that said GAP across it in white letters. A rain jacket with a hood. Things she didn't take: Her toothbrush. The little white polar bear with the black nose she'd slept with since infanthood. A suitcase, nor, as far as Kathleen could tell, anything to carry her belongings in.

Things she did not leave: A note, an explanation, an apology. A good-bye.

Now the regret was stabbing too.

Better, after all, to leave Natalie to Neil, to unsullied, about-to-become-a-father Neil. Maybe he wouldn't wreck it.

She tried to keep her voice steady when she said, "It's nearly four thirty, you two. We're about to close."

Neil stood and stretched and placed a hand on Natalie's back in an avuncular way. "Great work," he said.

"But I didn't do anything."

"Well then, great work by me. And now I must check in with my better half. Although today that's questionable. You're coming back, right? Another time? So we can keep going? This is gold, what you've got here. Kathleen, you won't believe what's in here."

But Natalie was looking up at the clock on the wall. "Oh *crap*," she said. "I'm going to miss my bus."

Kathleen cleared her throat. "Where's your bus leave from? South Station? I'll give you a ride."

"Yeah," said Natalie. "But you don't have to—"

"Oh, nonsense," said Kathleen, motioning toward the window. "I drove in today. It's completely dark out. It won't take me more than ten minutes. And you're...how old?"

"Thirteen."

"Thirteen! Your—" Kathleen had to stop herself because she had been about to say, *Your mother wouldn't like for you to be traveling like this in the dark*. But after all, the girl had no mother, the mother was dead and gone, this girl was practically an orphan. (Surely there was a father, though, right? Somewhere, there must be a father.) So she amended her sentence to make it, "You're tall for your age," at which Natalie winced, and then Kathleen wished she had kept her mouth closed entirely. *If you can't say anything nice,* her own mother used to tell her, *don't say anything at all.* To soften the blow of the "tall" comment, she said, "Don't worry. We'll get you to your bus."

And then a surprising and amazing thing happened. Natalie shrugged and said, "Okay. Thanks." But she met Kathleen's eyes levelly, and it seemed that some understanding passed between them, some recognition of what Kathleen might do for Natalie, or even what one day they might do for each other. The look departed quickly, Natalie's eyes becoming once again hooded and shadowy, the eyes of a newly minted teenager, but it was enough for Kathleen that it had been there at all.

Kathleen thought, *She just needs someone to take care of her.* Then she thought, *Don't we all?*

Susannah in a Girl Scout uniform, Susannah locking herself in the bathroom, Susannah in a car, on a whale watch in Boston Harbor. Susannah in her toddler bed, waking in the night from a bad dream, her arms around Kathleen's back, her lips on her neck, chubby cheeks in a little creamy face.

It was so quick, from that to this, the blink of an eye.

※

It was fully dark when they left, and the campus adjacent to the Archives was mostly deserted, the University of Massachusetts students off for the holiday. There was no moon and the harbor was a hulking shadow, nearly invisible. Kathleen, leading the way to her car, suddenly remembering, said, "By the way. How are you with dogs? I have my dog, Lucy, with me."

"You have a dog?" Natalie stopped on the Archives steps. "I

love dogs. I *really* love dogs. I would love to get a dog. But I'm not allowed."

(Of course not, thought Kathleen. The dead mother, the fractured family. Who would want to add a dog to that scenario?)

"Well," said Kathleen. "I guess that's understandable."

"Do you keep her in your car all day?"

"No, no, just since I went to the store. She's had this rasp. I didn't want to leave her all day....Oh, never mind, I'm sure it's nothing, but anyway, she's in the car."

Kathleen unlocked the door for Natalie, who slid in and turned immediately around to greet Lucy. "A border collie!" she said. "I love these. These are sheepdogs, right?" Then, sagely, soberly, as though she herself, perhaps in a past life, had been responsible for the care and feeding of a border collie, "These dogs need a lot of exercise. If you don't give them a job to do, they'll find one themselves, and it might not be one you like."

Kathleen turned the key in the ignition and said, "How do you know so much about border collies? And fasten your seat belt."

"I know everything about dogs," said Natalie. "All kinds of dogs. In grade school, when we used to go to the library and pick out a book every Friday, I always picked a dog book. I know everything about most breeds." She said this with a certain amount of bravado, almost an arrogance, but it was endearing.

"Have you ever had a dog?"

"No," said Natalie, shaking her head. "Our house is too small. And my mom is allergic." Kathleen glanced at her. "Was allergic. Also, no yard. But I know I'd be a really good owner. I just know it. I'm meant to have a dog. Someday I will."

"Someday," said Kathleen, "someday you'll be an adult, making your own decisions. And you can do whatever you want."

Natalie said, "Yeah." Morosely.

"Off we go," said Kathleen. "Into the gloaming."

To which Natalie said, "Huh?"

"The gloaming. Dusk. It's supposed to be a magical time. Have you never heard that expression? It's the name of a movie. Also a short story or a novel, I can never remember which."

No response; Natalie had twisted in her seat and was rubbing the white stripe between Lucy's eyes. Lucy was pressing her head into Natalie's hand, and the dog's expression was one of supreme contentment.

"Well, I suppose we are far past the gloaming now anyway, aren't we, and into actual night." (Chatty, Kathleen, aren't we today?) "What are we, a month from the solstice? Less? Three weeks? Sometimes I feel like Daisy Buchanan, waiting for the shortest day of the year and then missing it. Although she's waiting for the longest day of the year, not the shortest."

Kathleen stole a glance at Natalie, who was staring blankly at her; the car's interior lights had come on when they opened the doors but had not yet gone off.

Natalie said, "Who's Daisy Buchanan?"

Kathleen said, "Haven't you read *The Great Gatsby*?" And then, because Natalie's long legs seemed to be cramped in the front seat, she said, "You can move back, you know. There's a lever on your right, just above the floor."

Natalie obliged and said, "No, I haven't read *The Great Gatsby*. We don't read that freshman year."

"That's something to look forward to." Kathleen looked behind her—no need, really, for the parking lot was empty except for her car—and said, "But I suppose it's all about Harry Potter for kids these days, is it not?"

Natalie shrugged. "Not really. That's for little kids." Kathleen remembered Susannah, newly out of diapers, standing on a footstool in the bathroom to wash her hands. *I'm a big kid,* she'd say. And later, trolling slowly down the sidewalk on a bike with training wheels. *See? I'm a big kid.* The irony, of course, was that once children stopped making such pronouncements was when they actually were big.

Kathleen took a mental walk through the book section of the *Globe,* the posters she saw on her rare visits to the mall. "Or vampires, right? Is that what you and all of your friends are into?"

"I guess," said Natalie. "I don't know." She chewed at her fingernail, and Kathleen had the urge to reach out and pull her hand away from her mouth. She resisted.

Then Natalie's phone let out a series of musical sounds, suggesting a song that was vaguely familiar to Kathleen. "See?" said Natalie. "That's a phone call. Different sound." But she ignored that, too.

They were on the Expressway now and Kathleen, who hadn't had reason to drive to South Station for some time, leaned forward, peering out at the signs. "I *think* I want Exit Twenty," she said. "But would it hurt them to make it a little clearer, where I'm supposed to go?"

Natalie didn't answer.

Kathleen exited and followed Lincoln Street. There, at last, was the sign she was looking for. She turned left from Kneeland onto Atlantic, without giving anyone quite enough warning, in front of a shiny Mercedes, and the driver's face appeared in the window, pale and irate. She glanced quickly at Natalie, but she seemed not to have noticed. A woman hurried by, carrying a paper grocery bag with a baguette sticking out of it.

"Looks like a movie set," said Kathleen. "You never see anyone actually walking around with a baguette sticking out of their bag, do you?"

Natalie said, "I guess not."

"God, the traffic," said Kathleen as they neared the station. "Thanksgiving. Planes, trains, automobiles. You know that movie?"

Natalie shook her head.

"Before your time."

The phone sang again and Kathleen, trying to discern whether there were different entrances for trains and buses — she thought there were — said, "Don't you want to answer that?"

"No," said Natalie, and Kathleen glanced over at her to see that her lips were set in a tight, thin line.

"Go ahead," said Kathleen. "It won't bother me a bit."

"That's okay. It's nobody I want to talk to."

They drove on in silence, finally pulling up alongside South Station. Kathleen looked behind her for a parking garage entrance, or a ten-minute drop-off spot.

"The gloaming," said Natalie, looking out the window on her side of the car. "Is that what you said?"

"Yes," said Kathleen. "The gloaming. But we're far past that now. It's certainly night now —"

"I know," said Natalie quickly. "I know that. But I like the way it sounds. It's sort of...I don't know. Beautiful and depressing at the same time. Do you know what I mean?"

"I do," said Kathleen. "Ominous, in a way. But hopeful too, right?"

"Exactly!" said Natalie.

It was dark enough in the car that she didn't think Natalie could see her fully unless they turned to face each other. So Kathleen allowed herself a smile so wide and expansive that it felt like a silly grin, like an exaggerated clown face, the sort of smile that might, if it stayed too long on your face, give you an ache in the jaw.

※

She was still smiling like that when she sorted out the parking situation and turned into the garage. Here was her precious cargo, safely delivered.

"What are you doing?" Natalie, who had been rooting through

her bag, stopped and looked out at the parking garage, then back at Kathleen.

"I'm going in with you." Kathleen lowered her window to retrieve the ticket from the mouth of the automated dispenser.

"Why?"

Kathleen parked, turned the key, silenced the car, felt behind the seat for her purse. "To check the bus schedule. To make sure you're not waiting here alone."

Natalie grimaced. "They come every hour."

"But what if you've just missed one? It's—" Here Kathleen pushed up the sleeve of her coat to look at her watch. "It's five twenty. What if one left at five fifteen?"

Natalie shrugged. "Then I'll wait until six fifteen."

"No." Kathleen shook her head. "No, absolutely not. I'm not leaving a thirteen-year-old girl alone in South Station at this time of night. At any time of night, the day before Thanksgiving. It's going to be nuts in there."

"But Lucy—"

"She'll be fine."

Natalie sighed and made a great show of clambering out of the car. Was this petulance or some sort of grateful acquiescence? Kathleen hoped for the latter, feared the former, and decided reality must fall somewhere between the two. And anyway it didn't matter, because they were on their way out of the car together, navigating the stairs of the parking garage, heading toward the bus terminal.

※

Kathleen was glad she'd insisted on going inside. Because Natalie had just missed the bus up to Newburyport, and the next one did indeed not depart until six fifteen.

"Don't bother arguing," she told Natalie, leading her back in the direction of the parking garage. "It's my fault you're here so late, my responsibility, I kept you there working with Neil. I'm driving you home."

"No you didn't," said Natalie. "I kept myself there." But Kathleen noticed that she wasn't arguing.

☀

They settled themselves back in the car and Kathleen pulled out of the parking garage, first paying the attendant, whose laconic "Have a good night" was shortened to something scarcely recognizable: maybe just the word *night.* Perhaps a bedtime wish. *Night-night,* she used to tell Susannah. *Don't let the bedbugs bite.* Apparently bedbugs were on the rebound, she'd read that somewhere.

On the way out of the parking garage they talked more about Lucy: her eating habits, where she slept, what she'd been like as a puppy.

It occurred to Kathleen that what she had beside her in her car was a child, what the airlines would call an unaccompanied minor, and though Kathleen was accompanying her, she wasn't sure that this, in the eyes of the law, or of her parents (*parent,* she corrected herself, just one parent), was a reasonable situation. It occurred to her that if she were stopped by anyone, what she was doing might be construed as kidnapping, pure and simple. But she was in it now, on Atlantic Avenue, then off it, heading north, and she couldn't very well abandon the girl now that she'd brought her this far.

"Isn't there someone you should call? To let them know you're safe, that you're on your way home?"

"Not really," said Natalie.

"Your father?"

Natalie made a sound (a snort?). "He's at work."

"Someone else, then? A neighbor? Does anyone look after you when your father isn't home?"

Natalie sat up straighter. "I look after myself."

Kathleen said, "Of course you do."

Tick me up, Susannah used to say when she had trouble pronouncing her *P*s. Mommy, mommy, tick me up.

Kathleen was thinking about how wonderful it was to have a child beside her in the car again. (Was this girl a child? Of this Kathleen wasn't sure, for in her memory thirteen was the witching age, when girls could head either way.) She was thinking all of this when Natalie, having heard some sound that Kathleen didn't hear, rummaged in her backpack, pulled from it the cell phone, looked at it, and made a strangled, anguished noise.

"Natalie? Is something wrong?"

Natalie shook her head mutely and turned to look out the window.

"Natalie?" said Kathleen. "What is it?"

She expected huffiness or reticence; she expected to be shot down, to be told, in no uncertain terms, to mind her own business. But the tears came instantly, and Natalie, her voice shaking, reaching up every now and again to stroke Lucy's chest (Lucy having moved closer so both paws were now resting on the console, but remaining grave, almost presidential), began to talk.

✹

There was plenty of time for the story—more than enough, buckets of extra time—because every person who had ever lived in or near Boston and who had ever had a family to visit for Thanksgiving was now on the highway with them. But besides her kitchen, making the healthy version of pumpkin pie, where else did Kathleen have to be? Nowhere. So she listened.

"Well," began Natalie in a trembling voice. "There's these girls in my school...they've been doing mean things."

Kathleen held her breath and then let it slowly out. The moment felt large and important. "What sorts of mean things?"

"Sending texts and stuff. Really horrible texts. Making fun of me, calling me ugly, that sort of thing. Stupid stuff."

"Ugly! But you're gorgeous."

Natalie stared straight ahead.

Once a friend had told Kathleen that if you had anything to talk about with your teenage daughter you may as well do it in the car, "when they're looking straight ahead, when you're *both* looking straight ahead, nowhere to run, and you don't have to face each other." Kathleen had tried that with Susannah. It hadn't worked. But maybe now it would. Kathleen said, "Who are they? Do you know them?"

"Yeah," said Natalie. "Well, one of them. One of them used to be my best friend."

"Your best *friend?*"

Natalie was pulling at a strand of hair. "Yeah. But then she got to be friends with this other girl, and she's really popular, and… well, it all started after that."

"Natalie, that's terrible." Kathleen said. She thought of Ashley Jackson, the school photograph, the bright fake trees. "What about the school? Can't they do something to help?"

In answer to that Natalie emitted an abrupt laugh, almost a guffaw, and then set her lips more firmly. "Yeah," she said. "Yeah, *right.*"

"Have you told anyone?"

Natalie looked horrified. "No! Who would I tell?"

"Your…father?" Kathleen eased her car ahead slowly toward a minivan with a rooftop car carrier. Stuffed to the gills, that car must be.

Natalie slumped down in the seat. Kathleen wanted to tell her to sit up straight, that the seat belt wouldn't protect her that way, but she didn't. The phrase *choose your battles* marched through her mind. Someone had given her that advice with Susannah. That hadn't worked either.

"No," said Natalie. "That would be worse. That would be awful. If they thought I *tattled* on them."

Kathleen moved her car ahead a quarter of an inch. At this rate they wouldn't get to Newburyport until Christmas.

"Well, what kinds of things do they say? In these texts?"

"Oh, I don't know. Stuff. The ugly thing, or that maybe I forgot to take a shower because they thought they smelled something when they walked by, or that I shouldn't talk to this guy named Christian. Stuff about my m—" She broke off.

"About your...?"

"Nothing, never mind. It's all stupid stuff."

"Stupid stuff, yes. But it hurts."

Natalie nodded rapidly and pressed her fingers to her eyes.

"And one of these girls was your best friend? For how long?"

Natalie drew in a shuddering breath. "Forever. Since we were little, kindergarten. I don't know what happened, I really don't. I mean, I do know, sort of. She wants to be friends with these other people, and I'm not good enough for that—"

"You mean they *think* you're not good enough," said Kathleen. She passed the minivan on the right and stole a glance inside: a grimacing father at the wheel, the mother turning around to pass a sippy cup to the backseat. God, the holidays!

"Yeah. Whatever. It doesn't matter if it's true or not." Kathleen couldn't argue with that logic. Natalie continued. "The thing is, Hannah, that's the one I was friends with, I don't think she really wants to be that mean, I think she just gets caught up in it when Taylor, that's the other girl, is around. But she's always around."

"You know, that can be tricky, those female friendships at that age. I mean, my daughter—"

"Yeah?" said Natalie eagerly. But Kathleen couldn't do it, couldn't talk about Susannah.

⁂

The difference between a missing person and a runaway, Detective Bradford told Kathleen, was that a missing person wants you to look for them. And a runaway doesn't. (Only she remembered that he said, *A runaway don't.*)

"The missing person, the police are gonna pursue. The runaways, they don't. There's just too many." He shrugged his beefy shoulders, and she wanted to cry against him, wanted to press her cheek against his plaid shirt. "That's why you hired me, to do the stuff the police don't have time to do."

He took out a pad of paper and a bleak little pencil covered with bite marks and said, "Pertinent details, please."

Kathleen, looking to the ceiling, breathing very rapidly, couldn't speak at first. She croaked out three useless, incomplete sentences: "She just walked out. She took her Gap sweatshirt, her rain jacket, two pairs of jeans, and she followed her friend Deidre Jordan out the door. That's all I know."

Deidre Jordan's family stopped talking to Kathleen soon after, Kathleen told him.

"Couldn't take the memories," said Detective Bradford, nodding soberly. "Very common."

"Where do you think she is?"

"She could be anywhere."

She had thought he was a fortune-teller, an angel sent from heaven. But really he was a doughy man in a plaid shirt, a man who had to sit with his legs apart to accommodate his belly.

※

What did Kathleen wish she'd done differently with Susannah? Aside from everything. She wished she'd believed Deidre Jordan's mother when she called. She wished, when she discovered it was all true, she hadn't waited so long to formulate a plan. She wished she hadn't been alone in it: she wished Gregory had been there to help her. She wished she hadn't gone to the corner store.

Sometimes she wished she'd killed Deidre Jordan, to protect Susannah from her.

Not really, of course.

But sort of.

She wished she'd done something.

※

There was a sudden break in the traffic, and Kathleen drove on for several minutes. She lost sight of the minivan. "Well," she said carefully, "maybe if you get her—what's her name? Hannah?—alone, maybe you can talk to her."

Natalie shifted. "Yeah. Maybe. You think so?"

"Sure! Sure, I mean, if she used to be your best friend, I'm sure she still *likes* you. Maybe she just doesn't understand how hurtful all of this is to you."

Kathleen reached into the backseat, past Lucy, for her purse and handed it to Natalie. "I have tissues in there, if you don't mind wading through to find them."

Natalie found the package, extracted one, and blew loudly. "You think that would work?"

"I do," said Kathleen. "I think it's worth a try."

Finally they reached the exit for Newburyport.

"I've never been here," Kathleen said, turning off the highway where Natalie gestured. "Isn't that funny? It's not so far away from where I live after all. And people say it's a beautiful town. Is it beautiful?"

"I guess," said Natalie. "Beautiful enough." She had grown quiet. In the passing glow cast by the streetlights she appeared drawn, the hand in her lap still clutching the offending cell phone.

All around them, girls in trouble.

"Hey, are you hungry? Yes? Me too. I'm starving. What do you say we get something to eat?"

"Uh, sure."

"Is there somewhere to go to get ice cream? Do you like ice cream?" Susannah had loved ice cream. Maybe still did.

"Yeah. I love ice cream." It was enough to make you break your heart, the way Natalie's face brightened at that. Simple pleasures.

"So we'll do that. And then I'll take you home."

"Okay." Natalie was looking straight ahead. Kathleen observed the curve of her cheek, still childlike, plump, even in one so thin. She thought of Susannah in the backseat as they drove away from Marblehead for the last time.

"You name the place, and we'll go."

"Well," said Natalie. "Most of the good places here are seasonal. They'd be closed. But there's a Friendly's in Amesbury, really close."

※

Not long after Deidre Jordan's mother called, there came signs Kathleen couldn't ignore. There was money missing from Kathleen's wallet, and from a shoebox on the top shelf of her closet where she kept an emergency stockpile of cash. Susannah had a runny nose with no other signs of a cold. There were strange bouts of unexplained euphoria, then the opposite, when Kathleen could hardly rouse her for school. She was a senior, due to graduate in May. She was so close.

Kathleen took a day off from the Archives. She waited for

Susannah to come home from school, and she cornered her near the door.

"Let me see your arms." Susannah was right-handed; it was the left arm that would have marks. It was unseasonably warm for April, but Susannah was wearing long sleeves. Kathleen reached out to her and Susannah pulled away.

"No. Mom, *no*. Jesus." Susannah lifted her arm like she was about to strike Kathleen. Kathleen reeled a little bit from this but recovered, came at her again. "Let me see your arms."

"Get *away* from me. God, Mom, what is this? What the hell?"

Kathleen didn't know, at the time, that it was the last time she would hear Susannah call her Mom. Kathleen reached for Susannah again. She tried to speak softly. She said, "Susannah, if there's something wrong, let me help you. I can help you."

"I don't want your help," said Susannah. "I don't want anything from you." She went into her room, slammed the door, locked it.

To stop herself from beating down the door, from saying unspeakable things, Kathleen left the house. She had to figure out what to do: next steps. She walked to the corner store. Moving down the sidewalk, she felt like she'd lost her equilibrium. It was a struggle to stand up straight. The rain didn't help, and though she had an umbrella the wind kept knocking it out of her hands.

Kathleen didn't need anything at the corner store. She would buy milk, even though she didn't trust milk from the corner store, and toilet paper, even though it was fantastically overpriced.

Deidre Jordan's mother had been right. Kathleen was so angry she was shaking. She had survived a dead husband only to be felled by this, by Deidre Jordan and the pestilence of Southie, a place she'd thought would be a haven for her and Susannah. Deidre and Susannah were due to graduate the next month — they were *so close!*

On the way back she tried to catalog sweet little things she remembered about Susannah, the better to help her. She tried to think about the little chirping birds in the nest. She tried to think about the first time Susannah wrote her name, the wobbling, painstaking letters a mile high. She thought about the first lost tooth, the first time on a bike without training wheels, the first time she'd read a chapter book, driven a car, made her bed, made an omelet, said a sentence in Spanish with a perfect accent.

But Kathleen was so angry. And she didn't know what to do.

When she came back, Susannah was gone. It was that fast. Kathleen went out for milk and toilet paper and it was a fifteen-minute errand but it was long enough to lose her daughter.

※

Kathleen and Natalie were ensconced in a sticky red booth. It was early, and they had the place pretty much to themselves. The waitress had a fabulously outdated bouffant hairdo, and her ample breasts strained against the polyester of the uniform. In a cigarette-addled voice, she asked, "Ice cream, or a meal?"

"Ice cream," said Kathleen. "Just ice cream."

They spent some time looking through the massive menus. Kathleen saw that Natalie was looking at the kids' page. She pointed at the clown sundae. "I used to love these when I was little," she said. There was a wistfulness in her voice that made Kathleen's heart crack.

"Get one!"

Natalie hesitated. She rubbed her fingers on the menu. Finally she said, "Nah. They're for little kids."

"*I* don't think so," said Kathleen. "I think they're for anyone who likes clowns. And sundaes. Get one."

"Nah."

"I'll get one too."

"You will?"

"Sure." Kathleen signaled to their waitress. She pointed at the menu. "One question," she said. "These clown sundaes. Do you have to be a kid to get them?"

The waitress tapped her pencil on the ordering pad. "*I* don't care what you get," she said. "Just order quick." She squinted at the clock on the far wall. "Shift change coming up."

"All right, then," said Kathleen. "Two clown sundaes, please."

When they had their sundaes Natalie inspected hers and Kathleen said, "So. Is it how you remember it?"

"Yeah. Exactly." Natalie smiled, and Kathleen could see what she must have looked like at age seven or eight, with missing front teeth and scabs on her knees from falling off her bike. She thought that you could do that with most people, if you looked hard enough: find the child in the adult.

"Hey, thanks. For bringing me home."

Kathleen, trying to play it cool, said, "Not a problem. Really."

They ate in silence for a few minutes, and then Natalie said, "You must think I'm crazy, the way I keep going down to the Archives at weird times." She tapped the spoon against the metal bowl and picked out one of the Reese's Pieces eyes with her long fingers.

"You? Not at all. I'm glad you came. You're no crazier than any-one else."

"Really?"

"Really. We've all got our own brand of crazy."

"Tell me one crazy thing about you."

Kathleen had an image of herself twenty-eight years ago, a young wife, a new mother, not sure how to calm Susannah down from her crying jags. She said, "When my daughter was very young—oh, maybe six weeks or so—she was a terrible sleeper. Colicky. It was awful. There was this one time when my husband had to travel for business, and I wasn't getting any sleep. I was out of my mind. So once I put her in the car and I drove south. She was sleeping, and I was scared to stop. I didn't want her to wake up. So I kept driving. I drove all the way to New York City. But I had never driven there, and I got scared, just on the outskirts. So I pulled over at a rest stop, and I fed the baby. Then I got the biggest coffee I'd ever had in my life, and I drove back. Nine hours in the car." She couldn't tell if that was crazy enough for Natalie. But it was something.

Natalie squinted at her and said, "Why are you so nice to me, anyway?"

Girls in trouble, thought Kathleen. Girls in danger.

"I don't know," said Kathleen, making herself busy with her wallet. To the waitress she said, "Shift change, I know."

The waitress said, "Appreciate it," and Kathleen tipped her extra, because she felt inexplicably lucky.

✳

"Bear right," said Natalie after they pulled out of the parking lot. "Back on the highway, then take the next exit." She lowered her window and lifted her face to the wind. Kathleen allowed her this, and Lucy nuzzled her way in, pointing her nose out the window.

So far this town was no more beautiful than any other suburban outpost: a redundant collection of gas stations, a Dunkin' Donuts from which emanated, even at this time of day, the faintly nauseating smell of overly sugared coffee, of doughnuts boiling merrily in fat.

Kathleen tried for some conversation. "What are you doing for Thanksgiving?"

Natalie shrugged. No mother home whipping up mashed potatoes, rolling out a piecrust. She said, "Relatives?" and Natalie nodded.

Susannah had gone through a vegetarian phase; Kathleen remembered a questionable meal when she was thirteen or fourteen, a tannish, tasteless log called Tofurky: it had been like chewing on old leather that had been left out in the rain.

"It gets better," Natalie said, and for a second Kathleen thought she had spoken aloud, she thought Natalie meant the Tofurky, until she specified, "The town."

And indeed as they continued on past one shopping center and then another—grocery stores, a nail salon, a dry cleaner, a Market Basket—the predictability began to give way to statuesque old homes, Federalists and Victorians, all, it seemed, meticulously decorated with tasteful fall displays illuminated by perfectly placed spotlights. Did Natalie live in one of these? (Had the author of the notebook?)

"No," Natalie said. "Keep going." Then, eventually, "Turn here, left."

Natalie directed her to turn right next, and then said, "Okay, so. You can pull over." Kathleen did, though the street wasn't quite wide enough and a driver passing her honked his displeasure. Natalie said, "I'm just around the corner. I'll get out here."

"Here, on the corner? But why?"

Again Natalie shrugged. "Just because. No reason. I can walk up. It's right there." She pointed to a narrow street full of old, crooked homes. "I can see it from here. See? With the porch light on. You can turn around right here. It'll be easier to get back to the highway." (The porch light on, but no mother waiting, what was sadder than that?)

"I'd rather make sure—"

But Natalie was out of the car already, clutching her backpack, stuffing her phone in her jacket pocket, saying, over her shoulder, "Thanks a lot for the ride. Thanks a lot."

Kathleen watched Natalie cross the street, then watched her turn the corner and climb the steps to the house she had indicated. MILK STREET, the sign said. Kathleen could see an injured shutter, hanging like a loose tooth, on the house Natalie was entering. Natalie fumbled for a key in her backpack and worked it into the lock (poor motherless girl, a latchkey child). Susannah had been a latchkey child too, what else could you be when your father was dead and your mother was working? For a long time Kathleen had blamed all that had happened on that. But Deidre Jordan had *not* been a latchkey child, so there you go. No rhyme or reason to it.

Lucy let out a low whine and then turned and settled herself in the backseat. Kathleen thought again of Ashley Jackson, the wide smile, all the hope in the world in her face. She thought of Susannah. All around them girls were in danger, you could lose them in the blink of an eye.

❦

Later, at home, Kathleen was fumbling on the floor of the passenger seat for an errant tennis ball of Lucy's that had rolled out of view when she'd stopped short in the horrendous pre-Thanksgiving traffic that she followed all the way home. Bumper to bumper was an understatement, a euphemism: this had been more like bumper *on* bumper. Bumper over bumper, bumper glued to bumper.

When she reached for the ball she felt something else on the floor. A book: the notebook, which must have fallen out of Natalie's bag during her hasty departure, or when she had fumbled for her phone. She brought it inside and set it on the kitchen counter.

❦

As Kathleen rolled out the crust for the pie, she thought about Natalie, and about what she could do. She could get the notebook back to her. She could help Natalie with those girls at school, those bullies. She wasn't sure how, but she'd figure it out. She could make a healthy pie to bring to Neil and Adam. She paused to curse the healthy piecrust recipe—a crust with virtually no fat was difficult to roll, impossible to crimp. But the filling, if she could be so immodest, was delectable.

She held out the spoon for Lucy to lick, but Lucy just stared at her, uninterested. "No pressure," she said, and Lucy settled herself down in the corner, gazing up at Kathleen with a look that could only be described as melancholy. "Cheer up, old girl," said Kathleen. "We're going to be all right, you and I."

See? She could do this. All was not lost. She had a second chance.

⁂

On Thanksgiving Natalie and her mother dined at the Chinese restaurant downtown: cashew chicken and egg rolls among the goldfish and the hovering waitstaff. Besides the two of them, there was a merry table of five adults knocking back the contents of a scorpion bowl; other than that, the place was empty.

⁂

The day after Thanksgiving Natalie woke early, just after six, and lay in bed, listening. There was nothing much to hear, just some warbles from a few birds outside her window. She thought the birds would have all flown south by now, but maybe they were confused by the constantly shifting temperatures. She thought about the picture Mr. Guzman had shown them, a polar bear clinging grimly to a piece of ice no bigger than a picnic blanket. Or maybe not all birds flew south. She didn't really know.

It was overwhelming, to think about the birds and the polar bears. Better to start small, with her own problems, of which there were plenty. Maybe Kathleen Lynch had a point. Maybe if Natalie got Hannah alone, outside of school…well, maybe she could talk to her.

Twenty to seven. The birds had ceased their warbling. Perhaps

152

they were having breakfast, or off to Starbucks. She opened her bedroom door and listened. Nothing. Not even the sound of the television from her mother's room, which meant her mother had gotten up to turn it off before she fell asleep for the night. That was a good sign. She moved down the hallway and opened her mother's door a crack. The room was dark, tomblike, the shades completely drawn. She could make out her mother's shape in the bed, under the quilt.

"Mom?" Her voice sounded strange, otherworldly, in the quiet and dark room. The shape in the bed didn't move. Once Natalie's eyes got used to the lack of light in the room she could see the pill bottle on the nightstand. She felt her heartbeat step up its pace. *My mother's dead,* she had told Kathleen the first day, and then she had stuck to the lie. What if…

She opened one of the shades, inviting the watery morning sunlight in.

Then her mother rolled over, opened her eyes, used her hand to shield her face. "Honey?" she said. Her voice sounded thick, like she had swallowed cotton, or like Natalie's voice sounded when she had strep throat.

"Mom? How many of these did you take?" Her mother pulled the clock toward her. "Six forty-five," she said. "Natalie, what the hell?"

"How many, Mom?"

Her mother pushed herself up on an elbow. "What? Take of what? Oh, *those.* Just one, one before bedtime. That's all I ever take. God, Natalie, it's *early.*"

"Sorry," said Natalie. "Sorry, Mom. I didn't realize it was so early. Go back to sleep." Her heart was still hammering away inside her rib cage. She let the shade down.

She used the bathroom, brushed her teeth, got dressed. She grabbed her backpack from her room. By the front door she collected her ski jacket, boots, hat, gloves — she could see frost on the grass in her neighbor's yard. Maybe that's what the birds were warbling about, maybe *they* were saying, *What the hell?*

It was only a couple of blocks to the edges of the downtown, and another couple to Starbucks, where Natalie ordered a hot chocolate with the money her mother gave her every so often these days, without explanation or instruction—*hush money,* as Natalie thought of it, because she had heard that term somewhere, in a movie, although she didn't know why she would need to be hushed. Really it was Hannah Morgan and the rest of them who needed to be hushed. She should give *them* hush money.

She took one of the good upholstered seats, one of the coveted seats, but she didn't let herself feel apologetic about that.

She turned on her phone.

Well, there it was, like a bowling ball to her gut, like a scalpel slicing into her heart. This one came from Taylor, whose number she now recognized, whose name she had even entered into her phone alongside the number. DID U HAVE A GOOD THANKSGIVING? EGG ROLLS? WITH UR TEENAGE MOTHER? Someone had seen her—someone had walked by and seen her eating Thanksgiving dinner with her mother in the Chinese restaurant. There was another one after that: U R SUCH A LOSER!

The texts had come in the middle of the night, while she was sleeping. Like her mother, sleeping, dead to the world. She thought of her mother's salmon-colored pills. She deleted the messages.

Next to Natalie a man in a business suit was unwrapping a breakfast sandwich, and because of where she was sitting the scent traveled directly to her. She didn't realize until that moment how hungry she was. But there seemed to her to be a sort of dignity to her hunger as she sat and contemplated what to do about Hannah Morgan. To give in to the hunger, to stand up and pull the dollar bills out of her pocket, to count them, to order herself a breakfast sandwich: all these actions seemed like the dishonorable path. She had bigger battles to fight.

Maybe Kathleen Lynch was right. The only way to do it—the only way to survive this, and to move forward from it—was to appeal to Hannah, to get Hannah to get Taylor to stop. She studied the walls, where an exhibit from a local photographer hung: framed prints, for sale. One in particular caught her eye. It was a close-up of a tree branch in the rain, the droplets made enormous, bubble-like, by the lens. Hannah couldn't *really* hate Natalie—that was impossible. It was not so long ago that they had been best friends. If Natalie could just get her alone, if they could talk the way they used to talk, maybe things could go back to the way they had been.

Natalie had nearly finished her hot chocolate, but always there was that puddle of chocolate in the bottom of the cup. She removed the plastic top and studied the remains of her drink, then attempted to scrape the chocolate up with a coffee stirrer. This didn't work. She tipped the cup to her lips and swallowed as much of the chocolate as she could access, then replaced the top. She could do this.

They had been so close once, Hannah and Natalie. Surely Hannah needed only a reminder of that closeness, and Natalie would be welcomed back into Hannah's house, into her beautiful bedroom, her lovely attic. She would be hugged again by Mrs. Morgan, she would smell her perfume in the night as she bent to tuck the girls in. All of this was so appealing to Natalie that she could hardly wait to get outside and begin making things right.

And why not walk to Hannah's house today? Natalie had nothing better to do. She liked to walk—walking suited her body, her long stride, her temperament. Moving, in her opinion, was always preferable to staying still. She had her iPod in her bag; she would listen to music, and it would make the time go by faster. Hannah was probably, like Natalie, at loose ends on this day off from school, this orphan day between Thanksgiving and the weekend. With nothing to focus on, with no siblings to keep her entertained, perhaps she was feeling as lonely, as unmoored, as Natalie herself was. The Only Child Club, victorious, once again.

⚜

Natalie crumpled her cup and wedged it into the garbage can outside Starbucks. It was now nearly eight thirty, and State Street was coming alive: a woman unlocking the door of the shoe store, a golden retriever dragging its owner along the sidewalk. Across the street, in Market Square, the Christmas tree, the lights strung but not yet lit, stood tall against the slate gray of the sky, and a small girl, a toddler, dressed from head to toe in purple snow clothes, stood with her mother, looking up at it, pointing. On Sunday the town would gather by the waterfront to watch Santa come in on the boat; the high school bands would creak out a few holiday tunes for the parade; the tree would be lit for the first time. Natalie remembered shivering there with the rest of them, in happier times, each of her mittened hands in one of her parents'.

Watching the mother and child, Natalie felt something pass through her, a tremor of anticipation or relief. So uplifted was she by the beauty of the day, by the love she felt so suddenly and intensely for her town, for her fragile, sleeping mother, and for Hannah Morgan and their upcoming reconciliation, that she felt as though it had already happened, as though she'd passed straight through the awfulness and arrived, unscathed, improved, better for the journey, on the other side.

⚜

"Come shopping with me," said Carol, and Kathleen wished she hadn't answered the phone.

"Oh, Carol. I don't think so."

"What'd you take the day off for, then? If you're just going to sit around?"

"I'm not sitting. I'm getting ready to walk Lucy."

"The sales are out of this world. They are *giving* stuff away at the Arsenal Mall."

"*You're* at the Arsenal Mall? Isn't that a little low-end for you?" A mass of contradictions, Carol was. "And I thought you had to get up at dawn for those sales."

"Don't make fun," said Carol. "I'm an equal-opportunity sales shopper. And you do have to get up at dawn, to get the good stuff. I did, I'm up, I'm still out."

"You *what?*"

"I already bought a flat-screen for my son and his wife. I almost got in a fight, real fisticuffs."

"I don't think so . . ."

"It'll be fun! We'll get coffee. Coffee with *Baileys*. Or whatever you want. My treat."

"Oh, Carol. Thank you, but I really don't want to."

The truth was she had nobody to shop for. Lucy was easy: a bag of tennis balls, two rawhides, and done. Neil never wanted anything much; Adam made enough money that they could buy what they wished. She and Carol went out for a nice lunch instead of buying each other gifts.

Kathleen remembered Susannah painstakingly writing a letter to Santa the year she was seven, her last year of truly believing. She had been studying for her First Reconciliation at the same time and so her letter was a mix of request and confession: *Dear Santa, I apologize for all of the bad things I have done over the past year but except for the bad things I have been a really good girl and I was wondering if you could get me a little bit of presents.* Somewhere in her bedroom closet, in an old shoebox, Kathleen still had that letter.

"So there's nothing I can do?" Carol said. "To convince you?"

Kathleen should have held on to that innocent time in Susannah's life a little bit longer.

"No," Kathleen said. She set Bridget's notebook on the kitchen table next to her computer. "No, really, there's absolutely nothing you can do to convince me."

Neil had put in a bookmark, one of the scraps of paper from the reading room, to hold the spot where he and Natalie had left off. And Natalie had left her transcription folded up inside. It was easier to read that than to decipher Bridget's handwriting, because Natalie's handwriting was really very neat, which was nice to see; Kathleen was surprised anyone learned to write these days. So Kathleen caught up on Bridget's story (she could tell where Natalie's hand had tired and she had stopped), and then she moved ahead, stopping after each paragraph to type what she'd read into the computer.

For a moment every sound around me was magnified: the ticking of the clock, James's fussing in the dining room, the clatter of Edward's spinning top against the floor. I didn't dare look up, so I trained my gaze on the black and white checks on the kitchen floor.

Dr. Turner said, "Bridget. You go on and put James to bed. Then you go and rest. I'll tell Anna. Can you manage James, with your ankle?"

I said that I could, although truthfully I could manage only barely.

Dr. Turner collected James from the dining room and brought him in to me. His eyes had a thin band of red around them from crying and his hair was sticking up in little tufts. He quieted when I pressed him to my shoulder, and I sat back down in the chair for a moment to rock him and to rest my ankle before starting up the stairs. His head fell heavily against my collarbone.

"Remember to close the gate," Dr. Turner said, and I said, "Of course." As simple as that.

I breathed in the scent of James's hair and his skin. He could have been one of my sisters sleeping there — he felt that familiar. He felt like a part of me, his weight completely giving in to mine. He felt like my own child, and I loved him with a fierceness that I imagined was like a mother's love, although I did not know at that time what a mother's love felt like.

I think I sang to him that night, as I often did: "Over in Killarney, many years ago, me mother sang a song to me, in tones so sweet and low." Anna didn't like when I sang Irish songs to the children; Anna wanted me to sing "Twinkle, Twinkle, Little Star" and "Baa, Baa, Black Sheep," nice English songs with English pedigrees.

I sang, "Oft, in dreams I wander, to my home again, I feel her arms around me, as when she held me then."

By the time I finished the song I missed my mother with a nostalgia so strong it felt like a pain. I thought of the letter from Fiona: not long now and I would be able to read it.

The skin on my hands was cracked and raw from the cold and also from the work. I remember that I was ashamed of this. I remember that Grainne had told me to rub butter on them, to make them softer. I remember that I told Grainne that Anna would never permit me to use butter for my own purposes, and if I did it without her knowledge surely she would catch me. She kept track of such things. In Norah's house it was different — there were so many servants there that sometimes one or another of them could get away with something without it being noticed, and they all watched over each other, like a family. I always envied Norah that.

By then I had given up all hope of Midnight Mass — even if I had been permitted to leave the house, my ankle would not have allowed me to walk to church.

After I dressed for bed I read the letter from Fiona. Fiona had enclosed a photograph of herself just as I had requested and I looked at it for a long time. It was heartening to me to see her there in the photograph, looking so well. I began a letter back to her. I was so tired that it was impossible for me to write for very long—my head was heavy on my neck, and my body kept pitching forward until I startled myself out of sleep. But there was so much I wanted to tell her. In particular I wanted to describe— before I forgot—Elsie's powdered face, her plum lips, shaped into a Cupid's bow so that the effect was of a mouth that was permanently ready to be kissed. Also her eyes, outlined with a smudgy black and dusted with gray and green shadow. Imagine showing up at home on Christmas Eve dressed like this! You would be laughed out of the church, out of the town, you'd be the talk of everyone for weeks. I wanted Fiona to know about that, to know how different it was here.

It was much later when he came to me.

I think I had fallen asleep when there was a knock at my door and I sat immediately upright, my heart racing. I thought it was Anna, come to scold me for leaving the dishes downstairs.

But it was Dr. Turner. Charles.

I opened the door.

"Bridget," he said. "Bridget, it's all right, really it is."

I don't think I said anything at all; I think I just stared.

Then he said, "You are so beautiful, Bridget." The way he said my name sent a strange sensation through my body. He brushed his fingers against my cheek, and he drew them under my chin and turned my face toward his.

That was the beginning of it.

It was difficult, later, the next morning and the next morning after that and all of the other mornings that came, to reconcile this man with the man who sat at the table at breakfast, eating a soft-boiled egg out of an eggcup.

And I came to see that there was a greediness in me that I hadn't known about. Without that greediness, there would have been none of the rest of it.

❋

It was Mrs. Morgan who answered the door.

"Natalie!" she said. "You look like you've been through a war!" She peered around Natalie to the street. "Did your mom drop you off?"

Softly, apologetically, anticipating Mrs. Morgan's pity before she actually witnessed it, Natalie said, "No. I walked."

"Walked! That's got to be four miles! What'd you do that for?" Mrs. Morgan was dressed, as always, in a perfectly matched Lululemon outfit, a lavender sweatshirt and a lavender tank just visible underneath. This costume was proof to Natalie that though she'd been away from this house for a long time some things remained exactly as they had been. That was comforting.

"Well, never mind why, come *in,*" said Mrs. Morgan. "But take your boots off right inside. And for heaven's sake, look at your jeans! You're a mess. Did you walk all the way from your *house?*"

"From downtown," said Natalie. "Starbucks."

"Good Lord, sweetie, no offense but that was kind of nutty of you, was it not?"

It was, Natalie acknowledged this. She nodded. In her defense, though, when considering the distance to Hannah's house she hadn't counted on the fact that as the day grew warmer some of the puddles that had frozen overnight would begin to melt into an angry gray slush. Crossing the 95 overpass, where she'd been splattered with that slush, she realized that she hadn't thought through her route carefully enough, and there was a spot—no sidewalk—where she had to cross over the on-ramp to the high-way. That experience had left her numb and trembling and now that she had reached her destination she could have fallen right into Mrs. Morgan's arms, so relieved was she at having arrived, tattered but basically unharmed. She bent to unfasten her boots.

"Sit down, honey," said Mrs. Morgan, shepherding her toward the lovely brown woven leather bench that stood near the front door. How many times had she and Hannah come in from school and tossed their backpacks on that very bench? How many times had Natalie's mother gotten mad at them for getting the bench wet? *This will never dry!* she'd cried, pointing at the water spots. *It's completely ruined, you two.* Oh, to have Mrs. Morgan mad at her again. To be in trouble in this lovely house, among all of these lovely things. And anyway the bench had always dried, was never ruined.

"Socks too, honey," said Mrs. Morgan. "I'll get you some slippers from the mudroom—we've got extras. If I'd seen how wet you were I would have sent you in that way, but I guess it's too late for that now."

"I guess so," said Natalie. She rolled up her socks and stuffed them inside her boots, but Mrs. Morgan, watching her, made a clucking sound and said, "Give those to me, sweetie. I'll wash them and Hannah can bring them back to you at school."

For a minute, consumed with getting off her wet things, and with talking to Mrs. Morgan, and with looking around her to get a sense of what had changed in her absence, Natalie had forgotten her purpose in coming, the reconciliation with Hannah she was about to engender. But at the mention of Hannah's name, her heart pulsated. She wondered what Mrs. Morgan knew.

"It's been so long since you were here, Natalie. Just the other day I was asking Hannah about you." Mrs. Morgan had her hands on her hips and was surveying Natalie kindly, indulgently. So. She didn't know, then. She didn't know anything! Natalie felt immensely cheered by this. If Mrs. Morgan didn't know anything, then perhaps somehow Natalie had made it all up. Perhaps this was normal, dropping by like this—perhaps a return to the real normal was possible.

"The girls are upstairs," said Mrs. Morgan, and Natalie felt a little catch in her gut at that. *Girls?* Why the plural? "On the computer or something," Mrs. Morgan added, and she rolled her eyes in a way that Natalie thought was meant to signify some sort of complicity, the two of them, Natalie and Mrs. Morgan, against the world. "I suppose you came to join them."

Them. More than one girl up there: not just Hannah, slouching around in her bedroom, bored out of her mind. Now Natalie slowed her motions, taking her time with the slippers Mrs. Morgan held out to her, spending several seconds tucking the laces carefully inside of the boots. How to escape from this situation? With Mrs. Morgan there watching her, how could she put her boots back on, ask for the coat Mrs. Morgan had already whisked away, resume her sodden trek? And at the same time, how could she walk all that way in reverse?

Well. There was simply no way. She couldn't leave. That was all. She was here. The realization arrived abruptly, like a punch to the stomach. This was a mistake, but she was in it now.

She stood, finally, and Mrs. Morgan, who was still watching her, said, "Well, goodness, Natalie, I believe you've gotten even taller!"

"Thank you," said Natalie, though she wasn't sure it was a compliment. Indeed she felt, next to the petite Mrs. Morgan, as though she'd grown three solid feet since she'd last been here. Or perhaps, like Alice in Wonderland, she had grown out of proportion to her surroundings. Taller! Taller! Taller!

There was a lovely smell wafting out of the kitchen—cookies? some sort of cake?—and Natalie tried to focus on that, and on the Christmas decorations in the foyer, the lovely silver bells hanging from the newel post, the artificial tree that stood where it had always stood in the corner of the foyer, because the real one, the fantastically tall one, would be in its spot in front of the living room window, with the tasteful white lights that would come on automatically when dusk arrived. Mrs. Morgan was a great believer in beating the Christmas rush. The tree went up on Thanksgiving night, when the presents were probably already purchased, wrapped, stored.

Natalie tried to think about all of this—Christmas! festivity! joy, etc.—instead of concentrating on the feeling of the blood moving too quickly through her body. But she couldn't stop it, and it didn't take long for Mrs. Morgan's form in front of her, her lovely lavender sweatshirt, to begin to wave and tremble. Mrs. Morgan's face, suddenly, seemed to be not her own face but geometric pieces of it, like a Picasso. Natalie was thinking how strange that was, and how like the painting of *Guernica* they'd studied in Spanish class, when everything went black.

❈

So much for a quiet day at home with Bridget's notebook: the phone rang again. Kathleen let the machine pick it up: she thought it would be Carol again. But it wasn't Carol, it was Neil. "Kathleen, my dear, the Archives is *no fun* without you. And you left your pie plate at our house last night. I left it on the porch, in a Trader Joe's bag, but if you don't come for it, no biggie, I'll bring it Monday."

The phone's ringing had brought her momentarily out of Bridget's world. That was okay with her, she felt like she needed a break, a chance to process what she'd read.

Pie plate, she thought. *I'll go get that pie plate.* She gathered Lucy and her leash and coaxed the Camry to life. She parked a few blocks away from Neil and Adam's brownstone, wanting to give Lucy the walk. Some of the buildings, the shops especially, had already made their first tentative motions toward holiday decorating. It all made her feel festive; perhaps she shouldn't have turned Carol down.

Outside the brownstone, next to the Trader Joe's bag, there was a large cardboard delivery box. She checked the return label. Pottery Barn Kids. This must be a gift; she took Neil and Adam for people who would order from some obscure, independent shop she'd never heard of. She peeked inside the front windows, where the monochromatic curtains had been drawn back, revealing the pristine living room. She couldn't see the gunmetal kitchen. She felt like a Peeping Tom; she grabbed her bag and walked Lucy back to the car, but Lucy was walking more slowly than usual, her ears folded back against her head. She stopped once and sat down and then, after a moment, rose and regained her pace.

The phone was ringing as she unlocked the door to her house. (Must get that caller ID after all. Suddenly she was getting popular.)

Natalie was crying, which made it difficult to understand her, but she repeated her words again until finally Kathleen understood. "You were wrong," she said. "The advice you gave me, it was wrong."

※

It wasn't long before she came to—Mrs. Morgan told her she was out for only half a minute—but it was long enough for Hannah and Taylor to hear the sound of Natalie falling and come running down the stairs to see what the commotion was. So when Natalie opened her eyes, she had three sets of eyes looking down at her: one caring, one suspicious, one vacant.

"Thank *God!*" said Mrs. Morgan. "Nat, sweetie, I was about to dial nine-one-one. In fact I still might." Her face had fallen into creases of concern, and up close like this Natalie could see the furrows over her nose, and the lines radiating out from her eyes. Tiny threadlike lines, even, above her lips, that Natalie had never noticed.

"No," said Natalie, pushing herself up on one elbow and surveying with some confusion the scene before her. "No, don't. I'm fine. I just—" But she didn't know what to say. She just what? She didn't know what had happened.

Mrs. Morgan was kneeling on the ground, cradling Natalie's head. Natalie could smell her perfume, that sweet, familiar scent. Mrs. Morgan felt around gently in Natalie's hair and said, "Oh, honey. You've got a bump on the back of your head. No, don't get up. Not yet. Let me get a pillow for you while you pull yourself together."

While you pull yourself together. Humiliation.

Mrs. Morgan continued: "Actually, Hannah—run and get one of the couch pillows, will you? I'm going to get some ice. Natalie, you stay right here. Don't move."

Hannah, who had been crouching next to her mother, had so far said nothing. She stood and looked down at Natalie; from Natalie's vantage point Hannah appeared to be as tall as a redwood tree, and as powerful and foreboding. "Sure," she said to her mother, but she was looking all the time at Natalie. "Sure I will." She stood for another several seconds, considering Natalie with an expression that was part sneer and part bewilderment, and then she was gone.

Thus Natalie was left alone with Taylor Grant. It occurred to her that both Taylor's first name and her last name were the names of presidents. Suddenly this seemed terrifically ironic to Natalie, Taylor not being the brightest bulb, but she didn't realize she was smiling, laughing, even, until Taylor said, in a harsh and ugly voice, "What's so funny, *Natalie?*"

Natalie had no answer to this question. It was all too much to bear: the fainting, the laughing, her inadvertent insulting of Taylor. This too she would have to pay for—she would have to pay for all of it, and the price would be high. The long walk she had undertaken and must now undertake in reverse. The reconciliation with Hannah that clearly was not going to take place. She closed her eyes.

When she opened them Hannah had returned with the pillow from the living room. It was one of the lovely orange pillows with which the two of them used to build complicated forts. Hannah was holding it in such a way that Natalie couldn't tell if she was going to put it under Natalie's head or suffocate her with it.

Under her head, it turned out, though more roughly than Mrs. Morgan would have done, and before Hannah straightened she leaned close to Natalie's face. "*What*," she said, "are you *doing* here?"

Natalie was no longer sure, so muddled was she from the fall and the general confusion and disappointment. For not only did Hannah have plenty of friends at school who were not Natalie, she had a friend right here in the house, usurping Natalie's place, eating Mrs. Morgan's cookies (they really did smell divine), sleeping next to Hannah in the canopy bed, receiving Mrs. Morgan's gentle forehead kisses in the night, if indeed Mrs. Morgan still delivered them. Hannah had plenty of everything. She did not need Natalie.

But Hannah's question hung in the air; Natalie could almost see it there, cold and unyielding. She cast about for an answer. There must be some reasonable explanation, some way out of complete and utter mortification. It was evident that there was to be no saving her friendship with Hannah Morgan, but surely there was some way to save herself.

Before she found one, Mrs. Morgan was back with the ice, and Hannah smiled sweetly, angelically, when Mrs. Morgan said, "Oh, good, you got the pillow, thanks, honey." Then, "Yes, that's a good one, that's nice and soft," inspecting it. She helped Natalie first to a sitting position on the floor and then to the brown braided bench, where she rubbed small circles on Natalie's back. She pressed the ice pack to Natalie's hand and guided her hand gently toward her head. "Keep this there," she advised. "That's quite a lump you'll get if you don't. Now, why don't you tell me what could be going on with you, for you to faint like that."

There was a profound silence during which Natalie's audience of three stared at her, and after several seconds of this she attempted an explanation: "It's nothing. I just didn't eat much — and then I walked a long way. It was a really long walk."

"You *walked* here?" said Hannah.

Mutely, miserably, Natalie nodded. Hannah and Taylor exchanged glances. They didn't say anything, but they didn't have to. The implication was clear: *freak*.

Hannah exhaled and considered Natalie. After a minute she gestured toward Taylor and said, "Taylor's parents had to go out of town." Then, narrowing her eyes at Natalie: "She had to spend the night!" Beside her, Taylor nodded her affirmation, studying her fingernails. That, thought Natalie, explained the middle-of-the-night texts. They had been together, the two of them, in this house, concocting new ways to torture her. While she was alone in her narrow bed, with her narcotized mother softly snoring in the next room.

"Oh," said Natalie, holding the ice pack to her head, which, in truth, was beginning to throb. She pressed harder with the ice. It was easier to focus on the physical pain than to listen to Hannah, who was still talking.

"Plus we had some planning to do."

"Yeah?" Natalie tried to sound uninterested but really she was dying of curiosity. Not literally. ("Don't ever use the word 'literal' when you don't mean it," Ms. Ramirez had said. "You are not literally climbing the walls unless you are at a rock-climbing gym. You are not dying of thirst. This was not literally the straw that broke the camel's back.")

Hannah was saying, "I'm going skiing in Vail. With Taylor's family. Over Christmas." Natalie's head began to throb with more vigor and intensity. Was it possible that the ice was making it worse?

She lowered the ice pack, but then Mrs. Morgan, who was sitting sentry beside her on the bench, gently and firmly guided it back to her head, saying authoritatively, "The swelling comes right away if it's coming, you know. Keep it here." She waggled a finger at Natalie. "I've had medical training, remember? From the airlines."

Natalie had forgotten that Mrs. Morgan had ever been anything other than what she was today: pre- or post-yoga, gentle, concerned, ensconced comfortably in this beautiful home, where she had raised a beautiful daughter who had stealthily transformed herself into Taylor Grant's partner in crime.

Hannah and Taylor had taken on identical postures, with one foot—the left—slightly in front of the other, as though they were on a stage, about to begin a duet. Natalie thought, Christmas in Vail! Mrs. Morgan leaned closer and adjusted the ice pack on Natalie's head. Her perfume, so recently a reminder of all that Natalie loved and missed about this house, had become cloying.

How was this possible, for Hannah to go skiing with Taylor Grant and her family? Hannah was, like Natalie, an Only Child, and she couldn't leave at Christmas, but there was Mrs. Morgan reaching over from the bench to smack Taylor lightly on the leg, saying, "I can't believe you're taking my baby from me at Christmas. But Vail! Who could say no to that?"

"That sounds nice," said Natalie, who did not know how to ski, and was not sure when Hannah had learned. But inside she was roiling. Had the world gone insane? Was everybody against her? Oh, how her head hurt. It seemed that since she had rung the doorbell she had been traveling down, down, into the depths of her misery, and that she had finally reached the bottom.

Natalie studied the fuzzy pink slippers. They were as clean as if they had just come out of the package, and something told her that they had. "After we get you iced up I'll drive you home," said Mrs. Morgan. "I think you should rest. I'll talk to your mother, make sure she keeps an eye on you. She might want to take you in to see the doctor."

Natalie's mother wasn't even out of bed yet, and what would Mrs. Morgan think if she came stumbling down the stairs in her pajamas and opened the door on this scene: an injured daughter, a reluctant caretaker? What if Hannah and Taylor came along for the ride? What if they were *watching?*

"That's okay," said Natalie. "You don't have to talk to her. Really, I'm fine. I'm totally fine."

Mrs. Morgan said, "Well—" and stood up, considering Natalie. "It's just sort of strange, to faint like that. Even if you were hungry. Even if you walked a long way." Then she said, "Oh my *God,* you're hungry! Of course, you just said that. Let me get you something to eat. Better yet, come into the kitchen."

Natalie rose from the bench and followed Mrs. Morgan toward the lovely smells, the site of so many pancake breakfasts, pizza dinners, after-school snacks. She was hungry. She was ravenous. The hot chocolate at Starbucks seemed like a very long time ago, and before that was — what? When had her last meal been? She couldn't remember. The Thanksgiving dumplings, she supposed.

The island, which was long and curved the whole length of the kitchen, looked the same as it always had, clear and gleaming, more stools than necessary lined up like obedient children waiting to be inspected before church. *For all the kids I never had,* Mrs. Morgan used to say ruefully about the stools. She had said that often for a few years and then abruptly she stopped saying it.

Hannah and Taylor hadn't followed them. Natalie heard their feet pounding on the way upstairs. Mrs. Morgan, peering into the oven, was saying, "Of course *I've* had to give up the carbs and the sugar completely, but not you girls, you're all just twigs—"

Next to the oven, on the wide expanse of luminous countertops, were several trays of cookies: sugar cookies shaped like

Christmas trees and snowmen and angels, peppermint bark, and some sort of green and black balls — chocolate mint, it turned out, when Mrs. Morgan loaded up a small square plate and set it in front of Natalie.

This was a lot of cookies for a family of three, especially this early in the season. Suddenly this seemed very sad to Natalie, all of these cookies, nobody to eat them. Probably Mrs. Morgan would keep baking them, even while Hannah was off in *Vail.*

Thing number fifteen that made Natalie sick: rich people's ski vacations.

Without asking, Mrs. Morgan filled a glass with milk and passed that to her too. "Eat!" she commanded. "My God, Natalie, you need some meat on your bones. You'll waste away. I wish I had that problem. I can pack some up for you to take home with you."

"I'm eating," said Natalie, and she was. She was entirely enjoying being fed and comforted, coddled. She was even enjoying the slippers. But combined with the sense of being cared for was the understanding that this part would end and immediately after that the rest of her life would commence. She was thinking about this when Mrs. Morgan leaned over the island, fixed her gaze on Natalie, and said, "You're not in any trouble, are you?"

The relief that flooded Natalie was nearly palpable, and she looked into Mrs. Morgan's eyes. It seemed somehow that they too had become lavender, like her exercise clothes. Here was someone who knew. Here was someone who cared. And here was someone with the power to do something about it. In trouble! Yes, she was in trouble. She was in serious trouble, and it was trouble of Hannah's doing, and she needed a way out. She was forming the words in her head when Mrs. Morgan continued, "You're not...I mean, there isn't any possibility that you're *pregnant,* is there, Natalie?"

Natalie couldn't keep the shock, the mortification, out of her voice. "What? *No!*"

Mrs. Morgan held her hands up like she was stopping a bus. "Hey, okay," she said, smiling, "I just had to ask. You know, you hear these stories about young girls sometimes, too young, and the fainting—well, I just had to ask. You understand."

"Okay," said Natalie, wondering how she could recapture the look of benevolent concern Mrs. Morgan had recently bestowed on her, and how she could tell her about the real source of the trouble.

At the same time another thought struck her. If Mrs. Morgan thought it possible that Natalie could be pregnant, did that mean—could that mean?—that Hannah was having sex, had had *sex?*

No. It was impossible. Natalie was thirteen years old. Hannah and Taylor were fourteen, but they were *freshmen*.

None of this would do. There was no way, especially after this, that she could sit in the car next to Mrs. Morgan while Hannah and Taylor stayed behind, plotting Natalie's further social demise. Because of course they would turn what had just happened into grenades.

"I'm all done with the ice," she said to Mrs. Morgan, holding out the pack.

"Okay, then. I'll just pop this back in the freezer, and then we'll get your things together."

Mrs. Morgan stepped out of the kitchen and called up the wide and gleaming stairway, "Hannah, why don't you grab a pair of your socks for Natalie? Hers are soaked."

"Okay," came back Hannah's sweet reply. Though Natalie tried not to listen, she tried with all her might not to listen, she was sure she heard first the girls' voices and then the dissolution into laughter.

"I'm just going to pee real quick," said Mrs. Morgan, and it was then that Natalie remembered the easy way she had with talking about bodily functions, and how that had alternately delighted and embarrassed Natalie when she was younger.

The hammering in her head picked up tempo. Mrs. Morgan

called, "Grab yourself some cookies for the road! I'll just be a minute!" (She hadn't closed the door to the bathroom, and Natalie remembered that because Mr. Morgan was never around, Mrs. Morgan and Hannah acted like sisters.) Natalie slipped down from her stool and stood uncertainly in the center of the kitchen.

Finally she managed a strangled *no thank you* and then she was on her way to the foyer, removing the slippers, stuffing her sockless feet into her boots. Luckily her coat had not been, as she thought, whisked away to the expansive mudroom (labeled baskets, copious hooks); Mrs. Morgan had hung it on the handle of the front door, so she was able to grab it and put it on.

She had her hand on the doorknob—a lovely copper affair, "hand-hammered," Mrs. Morgan had once told her, although Natalie didn't know what that meant—when she heard Hannah say, "Natalie!" Her heart lifted briefly and she turned to see Hannah making her way quickly down the stairs, without Taylor. Here was her chance. She searched her mind for the right way to say it, but Hannah spoke first, casting furtive glances over her shoulder.

"Natalie," she said. "Watch out. She has a picture of you." Natalie stared at her, not comprehending. "She took a *picture* of you. With her phone. While you were passed out."

Slowly Natalie began to understand. "Hannah. You can't—you have to stop her. You have to make her stop."

Hannah made an expansive gesture to indicate the stairway, perhaps her room, who knew what else. "I can't."

In her face Natalie saw her former best friend—just for a second, but clearly enough that she knew she hadn't imagined it.

"Natalie, I can't stop her. She's going to do what she's going to do. I just wanted you to know—"

"But why me, Hannah? Why me, out of everyone? I mean, the thing about my mother, but—?" Natalie was desperate, *desperate*. She would do whatever it took to turn this thing around.

Hannah glanced up the stairs. "Nat," she said. "If it wasn't you, it would just be somebody else."

"Yeah, but. But can't you do something to make it not me? Can't you?"

Hannah shrugged. "I can't, Nat, I can't do anything. It is what it is."

"But I was your best friend. We were best friends! Why are you doing this to me? Why are you letting Taylor do it? Why are you bringing my *mother* into it? Why does she care about my mother?"

Hannah gazed at her, impassive. "She doesn't care about your mother." Hannah's voice was as even and emotionless as that of the lady who gave the weather forecast on the morning news: a blond, bland voice with nothing behind it.

And there was the answer Natalie had been searching for that day in the basement, when she found the birth certificate, when she found Bridget's notebook. Even as she asked she knew: the answer was that there was no answer. There didn't have to be an answer, or a reason. People did what they wanted to do, and you couldn't stop them. "Then why—?"

"It's just a weakness she found, that's all. Just something to focus on. I can't help that."

Then Taylor's voice: "Hannah? What are you doing down there?" The top of the stairs and the wide-open second floor overlooked the foyer; Taylor stood there for several seconds, regarding them. Rapunzel, Rapunzel, let down your hair, thought Natalie. Let down your hair so I can climb up and scratch your eyes out.

"Nothing!" said Hannah. "I'm coming right back up." Taylor disappeared, and Hannah lowered her voice an octave and said to Natalie, "Listen. You have to pull yourself together. Start washing your hair, pay attention to what you wear."

Natalie was taken aback by this. Feebly she said, "I wash my hair."

Hannah appraised her. "How often? Never mind, it doesn't matter. You know what I'm saying."

"But. Will you do something, about Taylor? Can you erase the picture, get it away from her?"

"I can't, really," said Hannah, without real feeling, the way you might answer if someone asked you whether you liked *Glee*. "It's not up to me. It's not my phone. She could have made ten copies by now anyway. It doesn't matter if I erase one of them."

Natalie had nothing to say to this.

"Just…pull yourself together. It'll be better for you that way. Don't make yourself pathetic."

Then Mrs. Morgan's voice: "Natalie! Sorry I'm taking so long. I forgot I still had a pan in the oven. I'll be right there to take you home."

Hannah turned and retreated up the stairs, her progress so rapid and silent that it was as though she hadn't been there at all.

Natalie tried to keep the trembling out of her voice when she called back to Mrs. Morgan, "I'm just going to walk! Thanks for everything!" She opened the door and let herself out, walking down the porch steps and around the mail truck.

She thought she heard someone calling her name when she was three houses away, and she imagined Mrs. Morgan's face at the door, the wrinkle in her brow all the more pronounced because of her bafflement, but she persevered, walking faster, the whole trek ahead of her: the cars, crossing the on-ramp to the highway, all of it. She would press on. She couldn't show a crack in her shell. She wouldn't. She would build herself a suit of armor, she would become impenetrable, as hard and unyielding as a rock. Like the mighty cockroach, she would survive, after the rest of them had gone.

Bad stuff, bad stuff, this was bad stuff.

She walked faster. Her feet were cold. Hannah had never brought down the clean socks. She knew she would never get her own back. Mrs. Morgan would wash them and dry them, perhaps as lovingly as she washed and dried Hannah's things, perhaps not, but Hannah would never deliver them.

Of all the things that had gone badly about the day thus far, clothes were the least important. But it was the thought of her orphaned socks, held hostage in that beautiful house, rolled together on top of the state-of-the-art washing machine, that finally unleashed her tears.

She stopped outside Hannah's neighborhood and rummaged in her backpack for Kathleen Lynch's card. She flipped it over: on the back, Kathleen had written her home number and the words IN CASE OF EMERGENCY.

With trembling fingers, she dialed. This was an emergency.

No answer.

She tried again, and again, stopping a few times on her walk, and finally Kathleen answered, on the fifth or sixth ring, and she sounded breathless, as though she'd run for the phone.

Natalie had told herself she'd hold it together ("Pull yourself together" was Hannah's cold admonition, and Mrs. Morgan had said the same thing, though more kindly). She wasn't even sure what she was asking for, by calling. "You were wrong," she said. "The advice you gave me, it was wrong."

And then she hung up.

※

Natalie hung up before Kathleen had the chance to say anything— she didn't get to tell her she'd left the notebook in her car, didn't get to ask her what had happened. She cursed her lack of caller ID. ("You're not quite a Luddite," Neil had said to her once. "But you're close.") Natalie had written a number on the sign-in sheet at work, as all visitors did, but Kathleen didn't have access to that now.

She'd have to wait for her to call back. It was all she could do.

It was too early to pour herself a glass of wine. But Kathleen felt shaky.

She opened her computer. Her search for Susannah Lynch returned the same results as her last search had: nothing new under the sun, people who want to stay hidden stay hidden, Detective Bradford had been right about that.

No sun here, though: it was just early afternoon, but already the dusk was coming, the gloaming. What had Natalie said? *Beautiful and depressing at the same time.*

"You can say that again," Kathleen said to Lucy, who was lying on her side on the kitchen floor. Sometimes Kathleen felt bad for Lucy; sometimes she thought she was doing wrong by her. Here was a dog bred to roam the moors of Scotland, over hill and dale, fully engaged and employed, and because of Kathleen she was lying on an urban floor, no closer to a flock of sheep than Kathleen was to the gates of heaven, if such gates existed. Which probably they didn't. Lucy coughed then, and Kathleen said, "Excuse you, ma'am."

Not that Kathleen had taken Lucy straight out of Scotland. She'd come from a breeder in Connecticut, and anyway Kathleen believed that nobody in the world, Scottish or otherwise, farmer or not, would love Lucy as much as she did. She said, "Right, old girl?" and Lucy rolled her eyes toward Kathleen.

The next thing she couldn't help. She typed in "Ashley Jackson" and pulled up news stories she hadn't seen last time. She studied again the original school photograph and found a few additional photographs: Ashley Jackson as a toddler (heartbreaking), as a kindergartner, her two front teeth missing (also heartbreaking), wearing a Santa hat: saddest of all. She read more about it: there had been a boy, and that's why her classmates were tormenting her (of course there was a boy, there was always a boy). There was talk of the parents suing the school; there was talk of forming a "task force" to study the problems that had led to the bullying going on for so long; there was talk of antibullying laws being passed. But for Ashley Jackson's parents, what? Just an empty bed, maybe a toothbrush still in its holder. Heartbreaking.

After Susannah was gone, Kathleen had left her toothbrush there for weeks and weeks, until the bristles dried and shriveled. Then she threw it away.

She searched the photos for some sign of prescience in Ashley Jackson's face. In it she was standing with a boy and a girl, different ages, younger than Ashley, presumably siblings because all three shared the same smile. When had this photo been taken? Did Ashley know she was going to end up as a grim statistic, an actual poster child? Kathleen could find nothing in her face, her toothy, open smile, to indicate that she had.

Now, surely, it was not too early to open the wine.

"Don't mind if I do," she said. It was a red, a Chianti, which was the only sort she remembered from her wine-tasting class, so that's what she bought all the time now, because it made her feel sophisticated and international.

Now, what to do about Natalie? If Kathleen didn't have her number she couldn't very well let her know that she had the notebook. She'd have to wait for Natalie to contact her again. Had she realized yet that she was missing it?

Her glass was empty. "Don't mind if I do," she said again as she refilled it; she knew she'd already made that joke, but there was only Lucy to hear, and Lucy didn't care about repetition (look how many times she'd bring the same grimy tennis ball over and drop it at your feet, the world one big Groundhog Day to her).

She typed "cyberbullying" into the search bar. Google told her that there were more than 2 million results. "Jesus," she said. She changed it to "cyberbullying experts," and the number dropped significantly: 255,000. Still!

She scrolled through the results and after some time located an expert who seemed knowledgeable and approachable, a professor at a small college in the Midwest, who listed his email address alongside the inventory of publications in which he'd been quoted, plus those articles on the topic he'd written himself, which had names like "The Bully Without a Face" and "The Growing Problem of Cyberbullying." The professor's name was Jacob Paterson. The photo on his college's website showed him to be wan and bespectacled, and therefore, for some reason, benign in a way that Kathleen found comforting. If this man could have all the answers on the topic, then how bad could it be?

She drank more wine and kept reading.

It turned out that Professor Paterson did not in fact have all the answers. In one interview he actually said, "I don't have all the answers." Another interview: "Children can be very cruel. Teenagers too. And that's always been the case. But the tools they have are more powerful than anything they've had in the past—they're lethal." In still another interview his answer to the question of what school administrators could do to combat bullying was so rife with equivocation that it was rendered, in Kathleen's opinion, completely useless. But he said one thing that struck a chord with Kathleen. "It's a complicated terrain these schools are navigating," he said. "Nobody quite knows where the lines are."

After some internal debate she wrote an email. "Dear Professor Paterson," she began. "A young friend of mine is being bullied." But that sounded creepy, almost predatory. She deleted that text and typed, "My daughter is being cyberbullied." Then she stopped. What was she asking, exactly? She didn't know.

She wrote, "I don't know what to do. Can you help?"

She sent the email. Neil had set all of the sounds on the computer long ago, and Kathleen had never changed them. The sound of an email going out was a *whoosh*: you could almost see carrier pigeons taking off from a rooftop, wings flapping.

By the time she looked up from the computer, dusk had given way almost entirely to darkness.

"Hey, pup," she said to Lucy. "Let's get out of here."

It occurred to her as she and Lucy trolled around the neighborhood — a ghastly oversized crèche already in evidence in one yard, a brightly lit snowman in another, plastic, all plastic, the world had gone completely plastic — that although she didn't have Natalie's phone number she did know where she lived. Natalie had pointed out the house on the narrow street, among the old crooked homes.

Not now, of course: the second (third?) glass of wine had gone to her head. But soon. She'd drive up there, she'd bring the notebook, and she'd make things right.

※

By the time Natalie got home she was starving and wishing she'd taken Mrs. Morgan up on her offer to pack up some cookies, or that she'd stopped at the Dunkin' Donuts or one of the gas-station convenience stores. She held out a little bit of hope for the natural grocery store on High Street — a gluten-free scone or a ready-made tofu burrito, either of these would be preferable to hunger, but a small sign on the dark green door told her that the store was closed for the long weekend. Without the socks, her boots rubbed against the big toe of her left foot; she could feel the ominous beginnings of a blister. She was angry (at Kathleen Lynch, for the bad advice, at Hannah for ignoring her pleas, at Mrs. Morgan for her cluelessness, at her socks for staying behind when she really needed them), humiliated (about the fainting), and scared (about what Taylor

Grant would do with the picture). It was an unpromising trio of emotions.

She entertained a fantasy that her mother would be up, dressed, baking Christmas cookies. She would say something like "Hello, lovey!" (Not a phrase common for a Kansas-farm-girl-turned-New-Englander, but which Natalie allowed into her fantasy nonetheless.) Then she would usher Natalie to a seat at the table and serve her warm cookies fresh out of the oven. The cookies in this fantasy looked a lot like the ones Natalie had consumed at the Morgans' house, although standing in for the mint balls were peanut butter crisps.

After Natalie had eaten, she would repair to her room, where she would pull out Bridget's notebook and effortlessly read the whole thing (take that, Kathleen Lynch) and then begin the genealogical research that would lead to Ms. Ramirez's praise, and to Natalie's independent-study project being held up as the paragon of all independent-study projects.

She sustained the fantasy all the way home, and even as she unlocked the door and entered her house, but it was revealed to be fiction when she heard the sounds of the television coming from her mother's room. The kitchen was dark, the stove unused. No peanut butter crisps here.

Natalie made herself a peanut butter and jelly sandwich (close enough) and carried it up to her room. At least she could spend some time with the notebook, maybe get ahead of the project.

But when she opened her backpack she didn't see the notebook anywhere. Not in the main compartment, not in the side pocket with the baggie of Ambien and her cell phone. It was nowhere.

This was the final straw. She thought the final straw had been the experience at the Morgans' house, but she was wrong. This, apologies to Ms. Ramirez, was going to be the straw that broke the camel's back.

She wondered if the notebook could have fallen out of her backpack somehow. She pictured it flying over the highway overpass, flattened by the evening commute or the holiday shoppers on their way back from the mall. Now she had no notebook, no independent-study project, no friends.

Her phone rang. She expected Kathleen Lynch again (she wasn't going to answer), but she saw her father's name in the caller ID window. She pressed the answer button and didn't say anything.

"Natalie?" said her father. "Nat, are you there?"

She didn't trust her voice not to catch. Finally she said, "Yeah," but her father was already talking over her, "Hey, kiddo, we missed you yesterday, but I know it was important for your mom to have you there with her..."

Natalie bristled at the word *we*. There was an expectant pause that Natalie did not fill. Her father went on: "So hey, I wanted to talk to you about some holiday plans..."

Into this pause she said, "Okaaaay," drawing the word out in a way (obnoxious) that she knew bothered him.

"Listen, I wanted to figure out a time to celebrate with you, because it turns out I'm going to be away *on* Christmas, on the actual day."

She inhaled slowly. "Where?"

"Well. Uh. Julia, you see, has some family near DC, and I told her I would make the trip with her, you know. I figured you'd be with your mom, and then we could have another celebration a different day, an extra-special celebration."

"Dad, I'm not five," she said. "You don't need to say 'extra-special.' You don't need to try to trick me."

"Trick you!" His voice was jovial, insistent. "I'm not tricking. I mean it."

She was silent.

He went on. "And also, we'd like you to spend New Year's Eve with us. Okay? Natalie, okay? We'll take you someplace nice, maybe in Boston, out to dinner. We'll really have a good time."

We. She said, "An extra-special good time?" She knew that was snotty of her, but she couldn't help it, she was unspooling.

"Natalie. Come on. Don't be like that." This he said in his Other Voice, the get-in-the-car-right-now-we're-going-to-be-late voice that she remembered vaguely from her childhood.

Insincerely she said, "Sorry."

He seemed to accept that. He said, "Okay. Okay?"

"Okay."

This was the final straw. Not the Morgans' house, not the socks, not the notebook, this. So: no notebook, no friends, no Christmas, no father. This was the bottom.

Her father's voice changed timbre. "Did you get that Wii hooked up yet? You having fun with that, you and your friends?"

The box was in the corner of her room; she had forgotten about it.

She had a different sentence at the ready, something about how she didn't care about the Wii, would never care about the Wii, he could have it back if he wanted (that would wound him), but what was the point? She said, "Yeah, lots of fun." With her *friends*. An image came to her mind of Hannah Morgan and Taylor Grant crashing around in Natalie's antique living room, whipping around a paddle. It was almost — not quite, but almost — enough to make her laugh.

He said, "So, New Year's Eve, okay? We can plan on it?"

Quietly she said, "Sure." And then more loudly, the teenager's answer to everything: "Sure, whatever."

*

Later, at her mother's behest, Natalie pulled down the attic stair-way to fetch the Christmas tree (artificial) and the ornaments. It seemed *almost* festive, with the dim light in the living room obscur-ing the wayward tilt the top half of the tree seemed to have — as if it were a real tree, as though some forest creature had gnawed at the trunk halfway down. Many of the ornaments had been home-made by Natalie herself in an earlier, happier era. Here was the oversized gingerbread man with the flamboyant red bow. And here, the tinfoil star, a tattered loop of red yarn stuck through a hole in the top.

"Aww," said Natalie's mother, holding it up. "I remember when you made this, in first grade."

But first grade reminded Natalie of Hannah Morgan. She hid the star in the back, against the wall.

*

"Phone call," said Neil. Kathleen was at the photocopier; she motioned that she'd be right there. "Sounds urgent," he said.

Kathleen thought, *Natalie!* She thought, *Finally.* She said, "Really?"

"No," Neil said. "I'm just kidding. It doesn't sound urgent. I think it's your crazy friend Carol." He peered at her. "What are you doing? You look guilty."

Kathleen said, "Guilty? Don't be idiotic, Neil." She was photo-copying Bridget's notebook, page by page, and trying to be surrep-titious about it. It was a long process, she'd been doing it in stages for two weeks, a few pages at a time, but it was worthwhile too: she wanted to have her own record of it before she brought it back to Natalie. She was almost finished. She had expected Natalie to call looking for it, but she hadn't, and anytime Kathleen had called the number she had, the number Natalie had written on the form the first day, nobody had picked up.

She said, "Neil, if it's Carol, will you tell her I'll call her back? In just a few minutes. And you look exhausted. Still. Again? Aren't you sleeping?"

"Not much," he said, backing away from her. "Hardly at all."

She shook her head, looking down at the photocopier. "You're supposed to stop sleeping *after* the baby arrives, not before."

He said, "I know. Tell that to Adam."

When she had finished her photocopying she put the pile of pages in her desk drawer and called Carol back.

Carol answered on the first ring. "Play hooky with me."

"What? I can't! Carol, I'm at work."

"Work, schmurk. That's why I called it hooky. I'm bored out of my head. I've finished shopping for my grandkids. In fact my daughter-in-law has laid down an ultimatum: no *more,* she said. There are fourteen days to go until Christmas, and I don't know what to do with myself. If you don't play hooky I'm just going to start eating chocolate."

"Is that a threat?"

"Sort of. Meet me after work, then. Let's poke around Fancuil Hall. I hear the tree is amazing this year."

"I can't. I have to go up to Newburyport."

"Newburyport? What for?"

She didn't want to tell. This felt like her story. She said, "Nothing important. Drop something off."

"Want company? I could do some shopping up there."

"Nooo…"

"Fine," Carol said. "Have it your way. But be careful driving. There's supposed to be snow coming later."

"Really? Snow?"

"That's what they say."

The nameless, faceless *they*. They never had anything good to portend. It was always bad weather, a terrible flu season, a declining economy.

When she hung up Neil said, "What are you going to Newburyport for?"

"Do you always listen to other people's phone conversations?"

"I can't help it. Adam says I have the ears of a bat."

"Yeah?"

"And by that he means I have good hearing, not that thing where your ears don't lie flat. That's for real, you know. A medical condition."

She said, "Okay." She wasn't really listening. She was trying to figure out how many more hours Lucy could be alone. Not that many. She decided to bring her along in the car with her.

"I saw a special on it once, I think it was the Discovery Channel."

"Neil," she said. "When you go home, get some sleep. You're starting to sound loopy."

"Can't sleep. Too much to do, to get ready for Henri. We have to stain the crib, and there's a whole bunch of stuff we have to buy—"

She said, "Neil, he's not going to care if his crib is stained or not."

Neil stared morosely at his computer. "I know. But we care."

"Well, don't care so much," she said. "It's all going to be fine."

"Promise?" He reminded her of Susannah sometimes, of the hopeful look she used to get in her eyes when she wanted to know if what she was wearing was okay or not. This was a *very* long time ago, back when Susannah solicited her opinion. Maybe she was the loopy one.

Against her better judgment she said, "Of course it is. I promise. It's all going to be fine." She looked at the clock. Then she said, "Hey, Neil?"

"Yeah?" He turned.

"I have to go home and get Lucy first, but I could use the company on the drive up to Newburyport. You want to come?"

※

For a good long time, several days, Natalie let herself believe that Hannah and Taylor weren't going to do anything with the photo Taylor had taken. Maybe, after all, Hannah had been mistaken: maybe there was no photo at all. Maybe Hannah had deleted it. Maybe Taylor had dropped her phone in the toilet when she was slinking out of her skinny jeans. Maybe they had chosen another victim. Maybe Natalie was free and clear.

In English class Ms. Ramirez asked about their progress on their independent-study projects. Natalie grimaced, thinking of the lost notebook. Nobody volunteered an answer, and Natalie, struggling to make herself small, felt her face redden. She thought Ms. Ramirez was going to call on her, and she had nothing to say. But happily Ms. Ramirez focused instead on Emily Middleton, who was ghostwriting an autobiography for her dog. Emily Middleton, who had been chubby in elementary school and was now positively fat, though not friendless, wheezed slightly as she talked, and, when she was done, sat back and exhaled softly.

"Wonderful," said Ms. Ramirez, apparently without irony. "I look forward to reading that."

Watching this strange turn of events unfold, Natalie had to wonder. Why was Emily Middleton not drawing the ire, the scorn, of Hannah Morgan and Taylor Grant? Taylor, who was absent-mindedly twirling a piece of her hair around a finger, which, because it had been straightened into a state of preternatural silkiness, fell immediately into place when she let go of it, seemed not even to notice that anyone was talking. Why should Emily Middleton (an autobiography of her *dog?*) fly under the radar while Natalie could not? It was unfair: terribly, hopelessly unfair.

Christian Chapman stopped Natalie in the hallway. "Hey," he said. "Natalie. What are you doing, for the independent-study project?"

His eyes were dark brown, very dark, you could get lost in those eyes. The hallway was crowded, kids moving around them in all directions, but she and Christian Chapman could have been on an island. He was taller than she was, and she was grateful for that; it was unusual. There was something nice about the way he smelled—it was probably just the laundry detergent on his gray T-shirt, but it was lovely.

She tried to slow her breathing; her hands, holding her English notebook, were sweating. She said, "Oh, I'm not sure. I was working on this one thing, but—" She didn't finish the sentence because suddenly there was someone behind her, and then a thrust, and she felt herself pushed into Christian Chapman. Her notebook flew out of her hands and landed several feet away, and she nearly lost her balance and went down in the hallway.

"Geez," said Christian. "What the hell was that?"

"I don't know," she said, bending down for her notebook, gathering herself, pressing her hands to her flaming cheeks. "I didn't see anyone. Did you?" She couldn't reach the notebook.

He scanned the hallway quickly. "Nope." She could see after that that his attention was gone: it was too late to have the conversation, too late to tell him about Bridget and the lost notebook. Better to say good-bye and slip away with what remained of her dignity. Which was minimal.

Just seconds later she felt her phone buzzing. U R SUCH A LOSER DIDNT I TELL U 2 STAY AWAY????

Did they? *Had* they? She didn't remember anything about that. She was playing a game where the rules were constantly shifting.

Then, a few seconds later, WHY R U TALKING 2 HIM??

HE DOESNT LIKE U WHY WOULD HE

And one more: U BETTER WATCH OUT!!

⁕

Later, toward the end of the day, when she was gathering her things at her locker, Taylor Grant approached. Hannah was with her, and, watching them draw near, Natalie was reminded of a diorama she'd made once at Sunday school, back when she went to Sunday school at the Universalist church, where the kids got to go down to the basement during the service, to the ammonia-scented common room, and work on some sort of craft among the kind, gray-haired, paisley-attired church volunteers. One week they received a shoe-box and a bunch of small plastic animals that they were to line up by twos, the shoebox acting as a stand-in for Noah's Ark. She thought of that now, Hannah and Taylor, two by two, two by two, into the ark, in perfect unison, two by two.

"Hey, Natalie," said Taylor. She spoke quietly: she might have been whispering a secret to Natalie, she might have been soothing a baby to sleep. Then, even more softly: "Did you see your Web page?"

"My *what?*"

"Your Web page. Did you see it yet?"

What Web page?

Hannah said to Taylor, "I thought you took that down."

Took *what* down?

Taylor ignored Hannah and stepped closer to Natalie. Natalie thought she was going to reach out and strike her, but instead she lifted a section of Natalie's hair and inspected it. She said, "Is there something in your *hair?* Is that peanut butter?" Natalie said nothing: she had gone mute. She was shaking, but she had gone mute.

Taylor continued to study the hair, as though she were a scientist and the hair a microscope slide. "Natalie," she said, as softly as a spring wind, as sweetly as a mother, "When was the last time you washed your hair?"

"*Tay*lor," said Hannah. "Come on, let's go."

※

"God, dark out already," said Neil. "Unbelievable. Geez. New-buryport! What a haul. What are we going up there for, again?"

"Errand," said Kathleen, and Neil, bless his heart, didn't demand more than that.

They settled into a comfortable silence. As they crossed the Zakim Bridge, Kathleen, thinking of Natalie, and allowing herself, for a moment, to imagine herself as a savior, experienced a sensation of optimism and serenity. This feeling remained with her all the way up Route 1, past the strangely defunct motels with their wrecked signs, hanging like untended broken limbs.

"I guarantee you someone's been murdered in each one of those motels," Neil said.

"Neil! What a thing to say." Kathleen signaled and moved into the left lane.

"What? Look at them, and try to tell me it's not true."

"Okay," conceded Kathleen. "Okay, maybe you're right." FREE HBO, said the sign outside one motel. TRACTOR TRAILER PARKING, said another. WEEKLY RATES.

"Who *stays* in these?" asked Neil. "I mean, really."

A woman in a gold-flecked Sienna cut off Kathleen's car; they were so close that for an instant Kathleen could see, inside, three unoccupied car seats.

"Happy holidays, lady," said Kathleen.

"Merry merry," Neil agreed. They passed the Prince Pizzeria. "The leaning tower of pizza," said Neil. "God, I *love* Route One. Don't you just love Route One, Kathleen? Did you ever get called Katie?"

"No," she said. "Never." This was a lie: Gregory used to call her Katie, but thinking about that made her stomach twist.

The red letters on the white sign outside the pizzeria read, HAPPY BIRTHDAY, SUSAN MCDONALD. They passed the Hilltop Steak House. "They go through forty-five thousand pounds of beef in a single week there," said Neil.

"How do you know that?"

"I read it somewhere. I know lots of really useless information."

In the backseat, Lucy, coiled into a semicircle, slept.

Closer to Newburyport, Kathleen's serenity and optimism turned to trepidation. She had a task of great import ahead of her: to convince Natalie's father that Natalie was in trouble. Who was she to think she could butt in where she didn't belong? "*Jesus,* sweetheart," Carol had said to her when Kathleen told her about Susannah all those years ago. "You got the double whammy: husband *and* daughter. How is it that you seem so normal?"

"That's only on the outside."

"Yeah," said Carol, uncharacteristically speechless. Then, after a moment, "How could it be anything else?"

Who did Kathleen think she was, to think that she could get involved in this mess with Natalie?

Then again, who was she to think she couldn't?

She swung off the highway and followed the street signs to downtown. But she lost her bearings and turned left onto a wide street with a Catholic church, a funeral home, and a building that must have been a church in a past life but now appeared to be a trendy restaurant. She drove past a glittering Christmas tree in the center of a square and oodles of little shops, similarly bedecked.

"Cool," said Neil. "These little towns do it up right at Christmas, all class."

In her head, Kathleen practiced. *Hello. Mr. Gallagher? Hello. My name is Kathleen Lynch. You don't know me but...*

She regained her bearings and retraced the route she'd taken when she'd come here with Natalie, her sense of direction kicking in at just the right time. Gregory had no sense of direction, he always said he could get lost going straight on a one-way street, and he could, but she was better.

A couple more turns, and she pulled over. "There it is," she said. "Natalie's house."

"Ooooooh," said Neil. "So that's what we're doing here. What, just dropping by?"

"I have her notebook, Bridget's notebook."

"You do? All this time? You little sneak! Where's her house?"

Kathleen pointed: the injured shutter and the pitiable mailbox, the rusted red flag halfway raised. She turned off the ignition. Neil unbuckled his seat belt, and Kathleen gathered herself and said, "Neil? You know what?"

"What?" He had opened his door, was on his way out.

"This might sound strange to you, but I think...I think I want to go in first. Alone."

"Yeah? Why?" He sat back down.

"Well." Kathleen couldn't really put it in plain words. "It's hard to explain," she said finally. "I don't want to freak anyone out, you know?"

"Okay," he said. "No biggie." He was so amenable. Neil: guileless and innocent, like a little boy with a cowlick. "I'll poke around town, come back in a bit."

"Want to walk Lucy?"

"Sure. Come on, girl." She handed him a plastic bag from the stash inside her glove compartment.

"She won't go here," said Kathleen. "She's particular, likes her own spots. But just in case. Do you know where you're going?"

"Sure I do," he said. "I've been here before, remember? The downtown is"—he pointed—"that way. And I know there's a bookstore on that street we drove down, near the big Christmas tree. I'll check out the bookstore."

"You sure?" Suddenly, despite what she'd said, she didn't want to go to Natalie's door alone.

"Positive. You go ahead. Do your thing. Deliver your notebook, make the world right."

⁓❋

Kathleen stood for a moment outside the house, gathering herself. Practicing.

Mr. Gallagher? I'm here because I believe your daughter is in trouble.

I want to help.

I want—

"Oh, hell," she said finally. She tried an old trick from her childhood, something you did to make yourself go under the water in the pool or a lake when you were reluctant. You said, *One, two, three,* and then you jumped. You just plain didn't let yourself not jump. You didn't give yourself another option.

She remembered the quick inhalation of breath, the shock of the cold water, and then the feeling of emerging, triumphant, shivering.

She said, *One, two, three.*

She approached the house.

I am here to help you save your daughter, Mr. Gallagher. She's in trouble.

One, two, three. And under.

She knocked.

⁓❋

Natalie couldn't bear the thought of doing this in her little bedroom, in her cold little house, so she had grabbed her laptop and headed right to the library. The first floor seemed too public—preschoolers wandering in and out of the children's room, must be

193

some sort of story hour, she almost tripped over a snowsuited toddler sucking on a pacifier. In the ominously named Teen Loft, a *Twilight* poster urged teens to read (thing number sixteen on the list of things that made Natalie sick: *Twilight* posters. And why did they use a poster from the *movie* to get you to read a *book*, it didn't make sense, nothing made sense, and that was number seventeen on the list of things that made her sick). Chairs set up in a way that was meant to allow for quiet conversation—that was too, well, too teenage, too obvious, so she headed to the carrels on the third floor, which were deserted.

She opened her laptop. There was a ringing in her ears, and she felt warm under her arms, in the crooks of her elbows, behind her knees. Maybe she was getting sick—maybe she was getting the swine flu, although you weren't supposed to call it that anymore. It had some formal name with letters and numbers that Natalie could never remember.

She'd start with the basics: Google, her name, her town.

And there it was: too easy.

There was a photograph, a close-up of Natalie's face, as unflattering as you could get, taken from above. Her eyes were closed and her face was slack. There was a little stripe of sweater showing, and she recognized it from the day she'd been to Hannah's house.

On the top, in glaring red letters, were the words: WELCOME TO THE WE HATE NATALIE GALLAGHER PAGE! Then a smiley face that flashed off and on.

The photo wasn't the worst of it. It was the comments that appeared below. *U suck,* said one.

What a loser!

U will never get a boyfriend, said another.

I am LMAO at this, said one.

None of the comments had real names attached to them, just screen names and numbers (like the swine flu), so it was impossible for Natalie to know who had seen this, who had commented, who was involved.

She saw, in the picture, a string of drool in the corner of her mouth. Only a matter of time before somebody seized on that, enlarged it or altered it, made it into something worse than it was.

I don't know her, said another comment, *but I am LMAO anyway.*

LMAO. Laughing my ass off.

We hate Natalie Gallagher.

Welcome to the.

She closed the laptop and looked around the library. The third floor was an open setup, and from her vantage point she could see the tops of the librarians' heads, the people in the second-floor carrels. A twenty-something, male, was engaged in some sort of elaborate game with flying creatures whizzing through a tunnel. An older woman gazed at a bunch of pictures of babies on her screen: grandchildren, probably. Outside the window Natalie could see the tops of a few bare trees and, beyond that, a giant lighted wreath on the outside of the bank.

She looked at the sign in front of her:

THANK YOU FOR NOT

EATING

DRINKING

USING YOUR CELL PHONE

What about dying? Could you die, here in the carrel?

She was getting warmer and warmer; she had to get out of there, into the fresh air. Maybe she really was coming down with the swine flu. She sort of hoped she was. Maybe it would get really bad, maybe she'd have to go to the hospital, stay there for a while, maybe she'd lose consciousness. That seemed preferable. Anything seemed preferable to this.

※

The woman who answered the door had coloring that was different from Natalie's—darker eyes, darker skin—but there was something of Natalie in the shape of her eyes and her mouth. She was young—under thirty, or right around. She was unsmiling, and she fixed Kathleen with a cloudy gaze.

Wait, thought Kathleen.

Kathleen cleared her throat. "Hello," she said. "My name is Kathleen Lynch. I'm looking for Natalie Gallagher. Do I have the right house?" She drew her shoulder bag closer to her body. She had the notebook in there, she had a legitimate reason to be here, standing on this doorstep, in this neighborhood, in this town, talking to this woman who, despite her coloring, looked enough like Natalie to be her—

"Mother," said the woman. "I'm her mother. Who are you?"

"*Oh*," said Kathleen. "Her mother. I thought you were dead."

※

Natalie sat on a bench in Market Square, near the giant Christmas tree. It was cold, but she had her heavy ski jacket on, not that she'd ever skied, not that she had plans to ski, but in this town it was a necessity: the uniform of the New England teenager. She didn't mind the cold, not really, she minded the heat more. That probably had something to do with her stupid pale skin. (Thing number eighteen.)

"Hey," said a voice belonging to someone who was walking toward her from Inn Street. "Hey, Natalie. Natalie Gallagher."

She recognized the voice, she recognized the posture, wasn't that—

Christian Chapman!

"Hey," she said, sitting up straighter.

He moved closer and said, in that casual, slouchy, wonderful way he had, "Whatcha doing?" Without asking he sat down next to her. He might have been out for a run or going to the gym; he smelled like sweat, like clean, wintertime boy sweat.

"Nothing," she said. "Just out for a walk. Thought I'd look at the tree."

He said, "So, hey, we never finished talking about this. What's going on with your independent-study project?"

"Oh," she said. "That. Yeah, I don't know. I might start mine all over." She thought of the notebook, thought of Bridget, thought of Kathleen and the bad advice that had led to the Web page she'd just seen. She felt sick to her stomach.

"I haven't started mine," said Christian. "But hey, I'll just do it over vacation, right?"

"Right," she said. Christian obviously hadn't seen the Web page. But it was only a matter of time. How long? She said, "You aren't going away, over break?"

"Naw," said Christian. "I wish. I'd love to go out west with my board."

She said, "Hannah Morgan and Taylor Grant are going to Vail. But you know that, right?"

"Nope," he said. "Why would I?"

"Aren't you...aren't you and Taylor sort of, together?" She thought that's what the texts had been about: she thought she was supposed to stay away from Christian because he'd been claimed already.

"Together? Me and Taylor? No way."

The smile that Natalie hid as she turned to the side could have lit up the Market Square Christmas tree, could have lit up the entire town.

Christian said, "What are you doing now?"

"I don't know. This."

"I'm going to get a piece of pizza. You hungry? Want to come?"

Of course she wanted to come! She was starving.

They walked to the Upper Crust, their breath making dragon smoke in the air, and sat across from each other at one of the little square tables. Was this a date? Natalie wasn't sure. Maybe not, but still it was something. He *definitely* hadn't seen the Web page. What would happen when he did?

"Those dogs are great," said Christian, looking out the window. "Border collies." Natalie was rooting in her bag to see if she had enough money to pay for her pizza; by the time she turned around she didn't see anything.

"Where?" she said.

"Oh, a guy just walked past with one. He's gone now."

Funny coincidence, thought Natalie. "Yeah," she said, "those dogs are great. I know one."

※

"I'm Kathleen Lynch."

"I heard you say that," said the woman, Natalie's mother; she seemed to Kathleen, who was struggling to reorder her thinking, to be part ghost, risen, Christ-like, from the dead. "But *who are you? How do you know my daughter?*"

"That," said Kathleen. "Well. I work at the Massachusetts Archives. I've been helping your daughter with a school project." Here she gestured at her shoulder bag, as though it were a clear plastic Ziploc, as though the woman could see the notebook inside. "I have something that belongs to her, something she left behind."

"Hang on," said the woman. She turned into the house and

called out, "Natalie! Nat!" They both waited and then she said, "She's not here. I'm not sure where she is, but she's not here."

"Oh…"

"I can give her whatever it is you have."

Kathleen shifted on the stoop. She cleared her throat again. One, two, three: *jump*. "Actually, I'm here for another reason too. I was hoping I could come in and talk to you for a few minutes. About Natalie."

⁂

They got two cheese slices, one each, though Natalie could have eaten more. She concentrated on folding the piece in two to keep the cheese from dripping out.

Apropos of nothing, Christian Chapman said, "I'm staying at my dad's tonight."

"Yeah?"

"My parents split. Divorced."

"Your parents are divorced?"

"Yeah," he said. "Yours?"

"No." She thought of Julia's lacy black underthings, her perfume in the bathroom. "Well, not yet. But they're separated. So I guess almost."

He nodded sagely. "It's not so bad, you'll see. I mean, it sucks moving your stuff around, and you forget shit at one place, but… I don't know, it's okay. My dad buys me tons of snowboarding stuff. Out of guilt. There's a lot of guilt. You gotta play off the guilt. And me and my brothers, we're in it together, you know, so that's okay."

She nodded and said, "I don't have any brothers."

"Yeah," he said. "I remember that. Cousins?"

"Not that anyone keeps in touch with. They're far away, in Australia." She thought of her father's pathetic little family tree, scratched out on a piece of paper and then abandoned. He was probably looking for the same thing: a connection. But then, of course, he found *Julia*.

"That's cool."

"But I never see them."

"Bummer."

"I know."

He said, "What do you think of Ms. Ramirez?" and then, before she had time to answer, "Kind of a tough bitch, right?"

"I don't know," she said. "I think she's all right."

After a beat he said, "Yeah. No, you're right. She's all right."

When they were finished eating they parted; Christian's dad was renting a basement apartment on Marlborough Street ("a real shithole, but whatever"), and Natalie turned toward home.

The Web page was awful, really terrible, so bad that she didn't even know what to make of it, what to do, but until Christian Chapman saw it she thought she could pretend that it didn't exist, had never existed.

How long until he saw it, though? How long until everybody did? And what would come next?

※

Stand firm, Kathleen, she told herself. *Katie*.

Kathleen followed the mother—born again, risen from the dead—inside the front door, through a small living room (artificial tree, ornaments mostly homemade), and into a galley kitchen, long and thin, with a rectangular oak table and three chairs. Three chairs, like Goldilocks and the three bears. A father bear, a mother bear, a Natalie bear. But where was the Natalie bear?

On the kitchen table sat a stack of mail, though calling it a stack was rather generous; really it was a mound, or a small mountain, with envelopes of all shapes and sizes mixing casually with supermarket circulars, catalogs, a sample of Oatmeal Squares cereal.

"I'm sorry," said Kathleen, as Natalie's mother motioned toward one of the chairs, "I didn't get your name."

"Carmen." She extended a hand and they shook, though it seemed late in the game for that, and also inadequate.

"Carmen," said Kathleen. "Any relation to the opera?"

Carmen seemed not to have heard; she neither affirmed nor denied; she motioned to the table, and dutifully Kathleen sat. Carmen's eyes seemed hazy and unfocused, the way Lucy's had the time, some years back, when the vet had to put her on tranquilizers to keep her from aggravating a strained leg. Was Carmen all right?

When they were both seated, Carmen said, "Wait." (And although, in fact, nobody was speaking or moving, and there was nothing to wait for, Kathleen waited.) "Wait," she said again. "Let me get this straight. Natalie said I died? She said I was *dead?*"

"Well," said Kathleen. But what else was there to say? "Yes," she said finally, and, because she didn't want to meet Carmen's eyes, she cast her gaze around the kitchen. Aside from the mail mountain the kitchen was tidy enough, but in the unfresh way of a kitchen that had not been used properly in some time. The rectangular sponge propped against the side of the sink was desiccated; the dish towel hanging on the oven handle had a forlorn, hopeless look to it, as though it had been abandoned by a lover.

Carmen curled her lip up. This too made her look like Natalie; it was like seeing Natalie's face on an olive-toned, dark-haired body. Carmen took a deep breath.

"How did I die?"

"I don't know," said Kathleen. "She didn't say. I guess I assumed cancer—"

"*Cancer?*"

"No!" Kathleen held up a hand. "She didn't say. I just assumed."

"Oh. I see."

"It's always cancer, right? I mean, with a young parent. Cancer or car accident. Right?"

"I don't know," said Carmen. She studied her hands, which were folded on the tabletop.

Kathleen said, "So! What's Natalie up to today?" She almost called her *our Natalie* but thankfully she stopped herself in time: what an overstepping of bounds that would have been. She was thirsty; she wished for water, but none had been offered.

"Not home from school yet," said Carmen.

Gently Kathleen said, "It's five thirty. It's dark out."

"It is?" Carmen looked startled. "Well, then, I'm not sure where she is. With her friends, I guess."

Kathleen knew better.

If the mother lived here, alive and well (or alive, anyway), maybe the father lived elsewhere. That might explain the untended mound of mail, the unused kitchen. *H. Gallagher*, Kathleen could see on one of the envelopes.

Carmen said, "You said you have something of Natalie's?"

"I do," said Kathleen, patting her shoulder bag. "Something she left behind with me. But really I wanted to talk to you about something else. Or, actually, I thought I'd be talking to Natalie's father."

"Good luck with that," said Carmen evenly.

Kathleen waited.

"He doesn't live here anymore."

Kathleen nearly shouted, *Aha!* But she didn't; her mind was buzzing along.

How to lead into the trouble at school, which now had a name (cyberbullying) and a professional attached to it (Professor Jacob Paterson who, Kathleen was certain, was at home, standing in his midwestern kitchen, a gaggle of children swarming around him)?

Her head hurt. She was so thirsty.

She said, "Do you think I could...may I have some water, please?"

"Of course," said Carmen. She rose, dislodged a glass from the cupboard, filled it from the tap. "Sorry, I should have offered. I've been...I've been a little out of it lately."

Best to be frank, thought Kathleen. Best to come right out with it. One, two, three: under.

"I think Natalie's having some trouble at school," she said. "I thought that someone close to her—someone who knows her well—should be aware of it."

Carmen said nothing, just blinked at Kathleen in her strange befuddled way.

So Kathleen began to talk. She talked about the text messages. She talked about the way Natalie broke down in the car with Kathleen. ("Wait," said Carmen. "You drove her home? She doesn't even know you!") She told her about Professor Paterson's website, and the information about cyberbullying it contained. She even told her about Ashley Jackson. ("I'm sure you've seen the story on the news," but Carmen shook her head, no, no she hadn't, she didn't watch the news.) When Kathleen was finished, she took a long, deep, shuddering breath, and waited.

Carmen said, "Let me get this straight. You're a total stranger—"

"Not a stranger to Natalie," Kathleen broke in. "I'm helping her with a project."

"I haven't heard anything about any project."

"Maybe," said Kathleen, "maybe she didn't tell you. If you've been distracted—"

"So you're a stranger," said Carmen again. "But you come to my house, and you tell me about what's going on with *my* daughter?"

"That's right," said Kathleen, holding her ground. "I thought someone should know."

"It doesn't sound so terrible me," said Carmen. "What, some texts, some emails? How bad can that be?" She shifted in her chair. She was very thin—Kathleen could see her collarbones jutting out, like Natalie's.

"It is," said Kathleen. "It is that bad. I mean, it can get that bad. Ashley Jackson—"

"I don't know," said Carmen, "why you keep talking about someone I've never heard of. I'm still not really sure what you're doing here."

"It's all over the news—"

"I told you, I don't watch the news."

"With all due respect," said Kathleen, "maybe you should."

"This stuff never happened to you in high school? You never got teased? God knows I did. But it's part of growing up. You move on, you forget."

"Yes, but."

"Do you think I didn't go through this? You think you didn't? Everybody does." Carmen rose from her chair and looked steadily at Kathleen until she rose too, gathering her things.

"I think it's different now," said Kathleen. "I really do." Kathleen paused, unsure how to frame the question. One, two, three. *Under.* "So are you going to do something? I mean, what are you going to do?"

There was a new resolution in the way Carmen walked Kathleen to the door, and Kathleen found herself following her like an obedient child. "I'm going to take care of it. I'm going to tell her to turn off her phone, her computer. It will work itself out."

"But—"

"Think about it. When you were a kid, if you can remember that far back"—here she seemed to take in Kathleen's silver hair, the sagging skin that Kathleen was sure was in full view in the unforgiving overhead light—"did you want your *mother* messing with your affairs?" She gave the word *affairs* an inflection, sort of flat, almost southern, that Kathleen couldn't place. But she wasn't from around here, that was certain.

Kathleen had her hand on the doorknob. She turned and said, "Maybe not. But I think this is a different ball game kids are playing now." She paused. Two. Three. Under. "And if you lose your child over this, you will never forgive yourself."

Carmen took the door from her. "Nobody's losing anything," she said. "I'll take care of it." Thinking about it later Kathleen had the sense that she had been swept out royally, as though by a queen.

Neil was standing by the car, leafing through a book with a bright green cover. "Look what I found!" he said. "*Life in Newburyport, 1900 to 1950.* That little bookstore is fabulous. The Book Rack. I could have spent a thousand dollars in there."

"Back on the road," said Kathleen, unlocking the car door. She tried to steady herself, although she was reeling.

"And they allow dogs. Lucy got a treat. She didn't eat it, though. Doesn't she like those?"

Kathleen glanced at the biscuit in Neil's hand. "Yeah, she loves them. Must not be hungry."

"Maybe she lunched with the ladies." He tipped his head toward the house. "How'd it go with Natalie?"

"Natalie's not home."

"Did you leave the notebook?"

"Of course I did." She hadn't. She didn't trust the mother. She said, "Do you mind driving? I've got a headache, suddenly, a bad one. Straight out of nowhere. Feels like there are staples in my brain."

"I don't mind," said Neil. "Sweet little ride like this." He tapped the book he was holding on the hood of the Camry.

"Oh, stop," Kathleen said, but she felt herself begin to soften.

In the car she closed her eyes and leaned back in her seat. Again down 95, then onto Route 1, the leaning tower of the Prince Pizzeria, the red letters against the white sign. Happy birthday indeed, Susan McDonald, thought Kathleen. And many happy returns. It was beginning to snow, Carol had been right, the mysterious "they" had been right, and the traffic immediately slowed, a line of brake lights marching down the road.

She had not saved Natalie, she had not saved anyone, she had certainly not saved Susannah. *I have to get out of here,* Kathleen had said that night. Screamed, really. *I have to get out of here for a minute.* She'd never felt such rage in her life, it was like a fire. And when she returned, ready to fix things, ready to make a plan, Susannah was gone. Two pairs of jeans, a navy blue sweatshirt that said GAP across it in white letters, a rain jacket, no toothbrush. No note.

"Want to stop for something to eat?" said Neil. "Hilltop? Big plate of beef for you?"

"No," she said softly. "No, I'm sorry, just drive, please, Neil. Just drive."

She thought she might cry, there in her car, cruising toward Boston and then eventually through the city, past it, over the Zakim. What had changed, really? Nothing. But everything.

⁂

"Natalie," said her mother, knocking on her bedroom door. "Nat, I need to talk to you."

Natalie said, "What?" As surly as she could manage. She had her laptop open; she was looking at the Web page. It was like poking at a wound: it hurt, and yet she couldn't stop doing it. When her mother opened the door she closed the laptop.

"Are you hungry?"

"No."

"Well, did you eat?"

"Yeah. I ate downtown."

"Oh! That's nice. What'd you eat?"

"Nothing. Pizza. It doesn't matter." She thought of what her father had told her about her mother: *She stopped being the person she was.*

"By yourself?"

"With a friend."

"Which friend?"

"Doesn't matter."

"Natalie, is anything going on at school?"

"What? No. *No.* Why?"

"Well, some lady stopped by."

"Some lady?"

"Kathleen something. I forget. She said she was helping you with a school project."

"She came *here?* Today?"

"Yes. While you were out. And she said … she said you might be in some trouble. At school."

"I don't know what you're talking about," said Natalie.

"If there's something going on, you need to tell me."

"Nothing is going on. It's fine. Everything's fine." She closed her eyes, and on her eyelids she saw the We Hate Natalie Gallagher page. The ghastly blinking smiley face.

"All I know is, this strange lady stopped by, talking about a project that I've never heard of—"

Something sudden and searing rose up in Natalie. *LMAO* at this. She said, "She's not strange. And anyway, what do you care?"

Her mother looked perplexed. "What?"

"You're barely here."

"I'm here all the time …"

Natalie sighed. "That's not what I mean. I mean *here.* In spirit. How am I supposed to tell you anything?" She thought of Hannah

Morgan's kitchen, Mrs. Morgan's racks of Christmas cookies on the gleaming counter. She thought of the slippers, just out of the package. She thought of riding in Kathleen's car, Lucy's paw on the console between them. Under her breath she muttered, "It's like living with a ghost."

Her mother said, "What?" and instead of saying, *Nothing,* as she easily could have, Natalie said, louder, "It's like living with a ghost." Her heart was beating rapidly, and her hands were sweaty once again. She said, "Did she leave anything for me? Kathleen Lynch? A book?"

"A book? No. She said she came to bring something back to you, but now that I think about it, she didn't."

Bridget's notebook. "Are you sure she didn't?"

Carmen rested against the doorjamb. She was wearing one of her usual costumes, old jeans and a ratty sweatshirt with the name of a college nobody they knew had ever attended. "I'm sure," she said. "You can check the kitchen, but I'm sure."

They were silent for a moment, watching each other, like two animals about to go on the attack. "I don't care anyway," said Natalie. "I don't want it anymore. I'm not working on that project."

"But what did she mean, trouble at school?"

"Nothing," said Natalie. "I don't know. I'm fine."

She thought, *Do something. Help me. Figure it out. Do something.* But she couldn't say it. (Why had Hannah said to Taylor, "I thought you took that down"?)

"Nat—"

"I said I'm *fine.*"

"Natalie."

"What."

"She said you told her your mother was dead. You told her I was *dead.*"

Natalie had no reply to this and so she said nothing. How long until everyone saw it, how long until Christian Chapman saw it?

She wished she could reach inside the computer and wipe the gleaming string of drool from her mouth.

"Natalie. Why would you say something like that? To a stranger?"

"I don't know," said Natalie. "It just came out. And she's not a stranger. We were working on a project."

Carmen was silent, looking down, twisting her hands together. "Natalie," she said finally. "Do you wish I was dead?"

"*What?* No, God, Mom, of course not. I don't know why I said it, okay? It's not a big deal. I said I'm sorry."

No answer, just the twisting hands, the fingers pulling at one another.

"Mom, I'm sorry." Natalie wanted to reassure her mother, but at the same time she wanted to be reassured herself; together, the two impulses canceled each other out.

Carmen walked to the window and placed the palms of her hands flat against the windowpane. "This snow," she said. It was almost wistful, the way she said that. Then she turned to Natalie and considered her for several seconds. Finally she sighed and said, "You're so beautiful. You know that, right? How beautiful you are?"

"No, I'm not," said Natalie. It made her angry that her mother could be so divorced from the truth. Didn't she know better? Was she really, truly going off the deep end? She thought of the website, the flashing smiley face.

"Oh, honey," she said. "You are. You'll see that when you're older. I'm not sure I tell you that enough. I should tell you all the time." Her father had said the thing about when she got older. How was it that all of this mysterious stuff was going to be apparent when she was older? It wasn't, that was all, it was all bullshit, just something grown-ups said.

"Yeah."

"Maybe you'll be off school tomorrow, with the snow."

"Mom, tomorrow is Saturday."

"Oh! That's right, I forgot." Carmen laughed, but her laughter had a tinny quality to it, like somebody on a television show pretending to laugh.

She turned from the window. "Natalie, did you say something to your father?"

"About what?"

"About me, about something being wrong with me."

"I don't know, maybe."

"I'm just sad, you know." Her voice caught. "There's nothing wrong besides that. I'm just really, really sad."

"Mom—" Did her mother know about Julia?

"I'm going to go to the doctor, to get some medicine. I have an appointment next week. Your father made the appointment."

"Yeah?" Then, after a beat, "Mom? Why did you marry Dad? So young, why did you marry him so young? Why'd you have to lie about it?"

Her mother turned back to the window. She said, "Natalie. Don't judge things you don't understand." Then she sighed and said, more softly, "I'm sorry. Like I told you before, your father saved me, Natalie."

"But you didn't say from what."

"From home, from an unhappy home, unhappy people. If I didn't lie about it, well, I wouldn't have gotten out. And I had to get out. When I met him I was...what? Three years older than you are now. A baby."

"And what was he like then?"

"Oh, Nat. He was so handsome. Charming. I would have followed him anywhere the day I met him, anywhere at all. He was in town for a medical conference—"

Her voice trailed off, and for a second this seemed like Natalie's old mother, the mother Natalie's father had fallen in love with. So what if she was young when she'd married him? She had loved him, he had loved her, and then it didn't work out. It happened all the time: Look at Christian Chapman's parents. Maybe there was nothing so odd about their story.

The next thing she knew, Natalie was telling her mother about it, about Hannah and Taylor and the texts. She almost, *almost,* showed her the Web page, but she couldn't bring herself to look at it again, so she stopped there. She didn't look at her mother while she was talking; she looked straight ahead at the wall in front of her, then up at where the wall met the ceiling, a spot where the paint was peeling. It had always been peeling in just that spot; when she was younger she called it dragon's skin.

After that it happened fast.

Her mother said, "That's it."

"That's what?"

Carmen held out her hand. "Give it to me."

"Give what to you?"

"The computer."

Natalie's heart beat faster. *"What?"*

"And the phone. Give me your computer and your phone."

"But I—"

"*Natalie.* We didn't have problems like this when I was a kid. We didn't have all of this stuff to have problems with. Give me the computer. Give me the phone."

Natalie had no strength to articulate anything, and in the background of the whole conversation was the Web page, a hot little ember burning. *I don't even know her. LMAO anyway.* She didn't believe anyone anymore. She said it again, same thing she'd said to her father, the teenager's answer: "Yeah, okay. Whatever." She gave her the computer, lifted her phone from the nightstand, handed it over. Obeyed.

※

All the next day Kathleen stewed and shifted. She took Lucy for a long walk around the harbor. She waited, though she didn't know what she was waiting for. She called Neil to see if he wanted to go to a museum—there was an exhibit on Toulouse-Lautrec's Paris at the MFA, and something at the Athenaeum. But Neil didn't answer. Didn't she have another friend she could call? No, she did not. No friends.

Not true. She had Carol. She called Carol; Carol's house had been chosen to be on some Christmas showcase tour and she was in a mad frenzy of preparation. ("Holiday tour, it's really called," Carol said. "But I'm calling it a Christmas tour and anyone who doesn't like that can *just stay home*.")

She perused the food section from the previous Wednesday's *Globe* and cut out four different recipes, then made a shopping list from them. Then she shopped. She bought mushrooms and steak for mushroom, barley, and steak soup. She bought walnuts, pecans, and almonds for a spinach salad with spiced nuts and blue cheese. Glazed pork roast? Why not! Into the cart went a four-pound boneless pork loin and a jar of gourmet spicy mustard. And for dessert: raw almonds, eggs, and flour to make almond biscotti.

Kathleen kept her eyes open for Melissa Henderson and her little pink baby; she felt betrayed when they did not appear.

The girl at the checkout, a teenager, fifteen, maybe sixteen, was telling a story to the pimply kid who was bagging the groceries. "So then I was, like, is he going to call, or not? And he didn't call, so I was, like—"

Stop! Kathleen wanted to yell. *Stop being so vulnerable, stop being so stupid!*

All around her, girls were in trouble.

She cooked for nearly three hours. She brushed the pork loin with the mustard mixture. She cut the biscotti on an extreme angle, the way the recipe instructed. She cut it perfectly, if she did say so herself, so that none of it crumbled.

While she worked she tried not to think of Natalie, or of Natalie's mother. She should be able to do more for Natalie, but could not. She should have stood up to Natalie's mother, but had not. Would Natalie's mother tell her that she had been there? Maybe, maybe not. She checked the barley. Was it barely tender, the way it was supposed to be? Yes, it was. She heated the broiler and brushed the steak with olive oil.

She found herself thinking of Bridget O'Connell, standing in a kitchen so many years ago, preparing a meal, same as Kathleen was doing now.

The wind picked up and beat against the side of the house; she could hear the wind chimes on the front porch clanging. There was something comforting about being inside the house, quartering crimini mushrooms, measuring out sherry and beef broth to pour into the soup pot. She felt like Laura Ingalls, safe inside her prairie home.

I can do this, she thought. I can survive. I am a survivor.

But when she was finished, and had laid all the food out before her, she realized that she had nobody to share it with. (How was it possible that she was only now realizing this?) Rapidly the comfort dissipated. She was alone in the kitchen, with enough food for a complete dinner party, and she was not hungry.

She studied the pork loin, plucked a pecan from the spinach salad, admired the angle (extreme!) of the biscotti. She sighed. She covered the pork with foil and wedged it on the bottom shelf of her refrigerator and emptied the salad into a Tupperware container. She put the cover on the soup pot and left it on the stove while she walked Lucy again through the remnants of yesterday's snow.

(Lucy did not appear to require this walk, or even to want it, but Kathleen did.)

When she returned she pulled out the laptop and checked her email. There was nothing from Professor Paterson, nothing from anyone. Natalie had lied to her about her mother. Susannah had gone. Everybody was a liar, everybody was a disappointment.

She pulled the notebook from her bag and poured herself a glass of wine. "Well, Lucy," she said. "Looks like it's just you and me, pup." She nodded at the notebook, contraband, someone else's belongings. "And you, Bridget," she added, as she opened the notebook.

We had a long winter that year, loads of snow, and suddenly it was over. April passed; May came. Along High Street the gardens came into bloom, and people were outside all the time. James turned one, and then he was fourteen months old. He toddled along, holding my hand, up and down the sidewalk. He said small words — *cat, car* — and pointed with his chubby little fingers. At night I took extra care putting him in his crib; again and again I checked to be sure the gate Dr. Turner had built was fastened because he could climb up or down anything. "My little Houdini," I called him, leaning over to kiss him.

Once I bent down and whispered in his ear, "I wish you were mine." I thought I would have to be careful about that because soon enough he'd be able to repeat to Anna anything I said to him.

He had all his teeth by then, or nearly all. He bit his brothers and he laughed about that too, and soon we were all laughing, because it was impossible for even the most bad-tempered among us to stay angry at him.

Because of Charles, I was happier, and I did the work better for being happier.

Dusting in the parlor, I sang, "On the banks of the roses, my love and I sat down/And I took out my violin to play my love a tune."

"What is it?" said Anna sharply. "What are you so happy about?"

"Oh, nothing, ma'am," I said. "Just a letter from home, it's cheered me up." I swept the front steps with extra care; I scrubbed the pots with vigor. My hands got even more cracked and dry from the scrubbing and I stole a little butter to rub into them; I didn't want Charles to notice the rough skin.

Anna had gray pouches around her eyes, and the skin looked like it was stretched too thin over her cheekbones.

Once I almost called him Charles instead of Dr. Turner in front of one of the boys. I stopped in time, but I could feel myself blushing furiously and I had to step outside under the pretense of beating the doormat against the side of the house. When I think about that winter and the spring that followed, I think of being very still, waiting, in my little room, waiting for Charles. He didn't come every night. And anyway I think my memory has played tricks with me there. Really I was hardly ever still. I think I was moving all the time. And I was tired all the time too, because my work didn't cease. I was careful not to complain about it, not wanting Anna to suspect. I did as I was told, always as I was told. In a way I think I was apologizing to her, for what I was doing.

It was that winter that Declan Callaghan came to do some work for the Turners, when Charles's practice had become busy. He did odd jobs around the house — a "jack-of-all-trades." I don't know what the jobs were, I never paid attention, but when I imagine the man he was back then — a boy, really, not so much older than I was — I picture him with a hammer, going about the house, whistling. Smiling. His hands broad and freckled, like my father's hands — not like Charles's hands, a doctor's hands, long-fingered and graceful.

"He's stuck on you," Norah used to say, because she had taken to using American expressions whenever she could. (She said, "All wet." She said, "Cat's meow." She called money "dough." She went, when she could, to the speakeasy down on Liberty Street. She cut her hair.)

"Him?" I said. "A Cork boy? Norah!"

"What? You don't think he's dashing?" (That was another one: dashing.)

"I don't," I said.

I didn't.

And then. Washing the Turners' sheets again, I saw the blood. I knew what this meant. I turned my face to the wall over the laundry and bit my fist to push down the urge to scream.

On the same day I noticed that Anna was pale and tired—she stayed away from me, and away from the boys, and she shut herself up in her sitting room with her letters, not coming out for meals, not coming out for anything. I didn't mind taking James from her. I almost cried for her, looking at the slouch of her shoulders, looking at the veins protruding from her pale hand on the stair rail.

But I hated her too.

And for a few days I hated Charles.

I had been a fool to think he had given her up for me when really he had us both.

For three nights I refused him and on the fourth night I did not.

He said, "Bridget, Bridget, it's you that I love. You know that." And then it didn't matter about Anna or not Anna. It didn't matter who else was in the world when we were separate; it mattered only that when we were alone, it was just us. Why was that enough?

I think I willed it to happen, if such a thing is possible. I think it was that night that it happened.

As I set out in the beginning of this writing, I don't expect anybody will ever read this account. I am writing it for myself. Otherwise I would perhaps be concerned about what people would think
or whether anybody would believe that it was real, the love between
Charles and me. But it was real. I was there, and it was real.

I didn't think about the future. When you are young you think
either that nothing is permanent or that everything that is
important to you will continue like that forever. Both ways of
thinking are dangerous.

"I'll say," said Kathleen. "You've got that right."
Lucy, lying on the floor, coughed.

⁂

"Hey, Nat," said Taylor on Monday after English. "You haven't
answered any of our texts. What's wrong? Not friends with us anymore?" She indicated Hannah, standing at her side like a lieutenant, as the other part of the *us*.

"Hey," said Natalie mournfully.

"Didn't you get our texts?"

"No," said Natalie. "I don't have my phone."

"Oh, poor Nat! What happened? Did you lose it?"

She thought about her mother taking them away. "Yeah," she
said. "I lost it."

Taylor studied her and then said, "Bummer." She followed that
with "How's your *mother?*"

"Fine."

"She get her driver's license yet? Can she *vote* yet?"

Taylor made a crazy sign with her hand and looked over at Hannah
for affirmation. Natalie could feel her cheeks start to warm; she wanted
to lift her hand to her face, to cool it down, but didn't want to call
attention to it. And yet. She remembered her father's long-ago

217

admonitions to stand up for herself. This, like the importance of sitting up straight at the dinner table, of writing thank-you notes, of using *Mr.* and *Mrs.,* had been drilled into her from an early age by her father.

Nobody likes a weakling, he told her one time, driving home from a sales call, gripping the steering wheel, the wormlike vein above his temple popping out. *People can smell fear, like a dog they can smell it. You've got to get ahead of it, every time.*

Gathering every morsel of bravado available to her (admittedly, a very small amount, and not easily accessed) and looking first Hannah and then Taylor directly in the eyes, Natalie said, "Listen. Why don't you leave me alone. I didn't do anything to you." But, horror of all horrors, she could not hold her voice steady, and the last word came out in a gruesome combination of whine and almost-cry. Taylor snickered, and looked at Hannah.

Natalie pushed past the girls, making unwitting physical contact; unwitting, too, was the proximity to their perfume, a scent — unfamiliar, expensive — that could have come from either one of them but likely came from both, since Hannah and Taylor apparently now shared everything.

She walked away, and after a few steps she turned around. They were both bent over a phone. Already.

She thought again of the warthog and the lion, the relief the warthog might have felt after the final bite, the pain so close to being over.

⚜

On Tuesday, at nine o'clock sharp, the phone at Kathleen's desk rang.

"Kathleen Lynch," she said, as cheerily as she could manage.

"It's Natalie Gallagher."

"Natalie! I'm so glad you called." All was not lost, then. Here was her second chance. (Third, fourth? Did it matter?)

"Do you have my notebook?"

"I do! I have it."

"It doesn't matter. I don't want it. I'm all done with that stupid project. I'm not doing it. That's not why I called."

"But—"

"You went to my *house?*"

"I did. To drop off the notebook. But then I forgot to leave it, I'm so sorry—"

"You talked to my mother. You told her everything I told you."

Kathleen felt a drop in her stomach.

"Thanks a lot," said Natalie.

"You're welcome," said Kathleen, in a small voice.

"I wasn't being *serious,*" said Natalie. "I'm not *really* thanking you."

Kathleen had figured that.

Natalie continued, "What I told you in the car was *private.* If I wanted to tell my mother about it, I would have told her myself."

Kathleen had the sensation of a ship listing, veering off course. Fix it, she told herself. Straighten it out. She said, "But I thought your mother should know. Actually I thought your father should know, because you told me your mother was dead…"

"*You* thought! What do you know?"

"I thought—"

"She took away my phone. My computer. I'm calling from my home phone."

So: not in school then. Better not to bring that up.

"All of it. She took away everything. Now I don't know what they're doing to me, they could be doing anything."

Kathleen was silent: she had no words.

"What if she tells my father?"

Kathleen didn't know. So there was a father in the picture. H. Gallagher from the mail pile, the jaunty *me!* in the scrap of genealogy Natalie had brought in the first day. Carefully she said, "Well, what if? Maybe—"

"And what if he goes marching into the school and says something? They'll know I'm a rat. They'll crucify me."

Kathleen hadn't thought about that. "Natalie."

"I thought you were my friend. I *trusted* you. I told you all that stuff—"

Kathleen knew even as she spoke that she should not engage in battle. "I was trying to help."

"Yeah, like you helped your own daughter."

This was like a punch. Natalie was crying now: Kathleen could hear the great gasping breaths. But she steeled herself. "You don't know anything about my daughter."

"I know a little bit. Neil told me some of it. I know she ran away from you."

"She ran away. Not from me. It's more complicated than that."

"Yeah. Right." Natalie was still crying.

"Natalie. I was trying to help."

"Well, everything you do to help, you mess it up. It's the same with all grown-ups. It's the same with everything." And she hung up.

Kathleen stood there, clutching the phone.

Deidre had said...what? "Come on, Susannah," and off they'd gone? She'd packed the Gap sweatshirt, the jeans, the rain jacket; she'd left the toothbrush.

Detective Bradford had said, "If a runaway doesn't want to be found, she usually manages not to be found." The air was light and sweet when he told her that, the promise of summer not far off. "That doesn't mean there's no hope for finding her," he said. "I just like anyone in your situation to know that, right from the start."

※

Christmas Eve. Natalie and her mother were invited to her mother's friend's house. The friend had young children, three of them, all aged five and under, and Natalie could think of nothing worse, nothing sadder and simultaneously more irritating, than watching these children in their sugared-up, pre-Santa state of excitement. No thank you.

Still, she was happy to see her mother dressed in a red blouse, a black skirt, makeup on, hair brushed and washed. ("It's only been ten days on the medication," she whispered to Natalie, whispered as though someone was listening, as though anyone at all ever listened to them, "but I think I can feel a little bit of a difference.")

She rapped on Natalie's door and opened it without waiting for an answer. "Natalie! Is that what you're wearing?"

Natalie was lying on her bed, reading *The Great Gatsby,* which she had checked out of the library, and Kathleen had been right, it was the longest day of the year that Daisy always waited for. Summer solstice. She looked down at her clothes, then up at her mother. "I'm not going."

"You're not? Of course you are. I told Nancy..."

"I told Dad I'd go with him. He's picking me up soon." She was lying, of course; her father was in DC with *Julia.*

"He is? He didn't mention—"

Natalie shrugged as if to indicate that she didn't know what had or hadn't transpired between her parents.

"Listen," said her mother. "Are you ready for your phone back? Your computer? I'm going to give them back." She disappeared momentarily and then reappeared, holding both out to Natalie. "I want you to know I wasn't punishing you—"

But Natalie wasn't listening; she took the phone, took the computer. There was a small clot of fear underneath her collarbones. After her mother left, she fired up her computer—hands shaking, heart hammering. She typed her own name into Google but paused before hitting Enter. She couldn't do it. She didn't want to know. She wouldn't do it.

She erased her name and typed in "Vail, Colorado." She clicked on "images" and saw a gigantic melon of a moon rising in a cobalt sky over a glittering village. She saw beautiful people holding snowboards and consulting trail maps. She saw exquisite Christmas lights in trees along an immaculate Main Street, and a lovely outdoor skating rink surrounded by tan buildings so beautiful and pristine that they looked counterfeit.

Why was she doing this, pressing the bruise? She didn't know. Vail was paradise, and she was not there. Others were.

She held her breath and turned on her phone. The battery was nearly drained; she'd have to find her charger.

Thirty-seven text messages. Make that thirty-eight: another came in just as she watched.

She didn't read them. She found the button, then closed her eyes while she pressed it. Delete, delete, delete.

⁂

Kathleen invited Neil for Christmas dinner. It was just the two of them. Adam, having worked through some of the bureaucratic red tape, had left the day before to secure the adoption of little Henri.

She had already had it out with him, the thing about telling Natalie about Susannah. He apologized; she forgave—it was difficult to stay angry with Neil, and anyway they'd made the plans for the holiday weeks before and she couldn't very well uninvite him now.

Kathleen unearthed some very old red place mats that she hadn't used in years. She threw them in the dryer on the de-wrinkle setting. At the Stop and Shop she picked out a simple poinsettia wrapped in shiny gold paper to set in the middle of the dining room table. She wore a red sweater with a snowman crocheted into it, and little snowman earrings; dressing in her room before starting dinner, she felt positively festive.

She had a small tree — real — that she had purchased in the parking lot of a gas station off Route 93; it was being sold by the Boy Scouts, a group of polite young men wearing khaki caps and olive green pants and eager smiles. Kathleen had taken their careful dress, the line of patches on their still-skinny arms, as a sign that the tree was in good health and would last all the way to the New Year. But two days after the tree's homecoming its needles began to brown and to drop as if it were the star of some piece of autumnal performance art. Even so, she had pulled a box of ornaments from the basement and done her best to bedeck it. She acknowledged that her anger at the smiling Boy Scouts was unreasonable, but no less fierce for that. She thought she should have gone grander, better, with the tree, or not bothered at all.

She had a glass of wine while she set the table, while she dressed the chicken and peeled the potatoes and prepared the cranberry sauce — made from scratch, with pecans and currants and raisins added. It was the same cranberry sauce that her mother, and her mother's mother before her, had prepared on both Thanksgiving and Christmas. She worked from a stained index card propped up against the counter; the card was yellowed with age, and it made her think of Bridget's notebook.

She tried not to think of Susannah — the wine made it difficult; the more she drank, it seemed, the more porous her thoughts became — and where she may or may not be this Christmas Day. But her mind, despite her efforts, seemed intent on creating and playing a montage from Christmases past. Susannah, front teeth missing, hair messed, ripping into a box that contained...what? Kathleen could not remember. Susannah, a near-teenager, slender and long-legged, proffering to Kathleen a gift she'd made at school, a small wooden jewelry box, which sat now inside Kathleen's top dresser drawer, and which held the tiny gold cross Kathleen had given Susannah as a First Communion gift. Susannah, age sixteen, sitting beside Kathleen at Christmas Eve Mass, her hair dyed jet black, as dark as night, darker even, her face pale beneath the hair, which only partially covered up the line of earrings marching up the length of her ear.

She thought of Natalie Gallagher and wondered how she would pass the day. With her mother? With her father? With nobody, alone in her bedroom, with just her cell phone for company? With relatives, an extended family that Natalie had never mentioned but that Kathleen imagined might swoop in at such a time, taking the poor, semi-orphaned girl under their collective wing, offering her solace?

Before she could continue this line of thinking all the way to its end, the doorbell rang and there was Neil, holding a bottle of Malbec in one hand and a bouquet of daisies in the other.

"Well!" she said. "Merry Christmas."

He held out the flowers. "You told me once they're your favorite flower, and I couldn't resist when I saw them."

"Oh, Neil. Daisies! In December—"

"I *know*," he said. "Terribly un-environmental of me. How many gallons of fuel did it take to get these from wherever to here? Forgive me, Mother Earth." He bowed. "And Merry Christmas."

"Well," she said again. "*Thank* you."

"I like your sweater. It's very—"

"Very what?" She crossed her arms protectively over the snowman.

"Very, oh, I don't know. Midwestern."

"*Neil!*"

"In a charming way. Don't worry, you can pull it off. You've got the class for it."

("I bet you used to be a knockout," Neil said once to Kathleen. And Kathleen had thought, *Used to?* He hadn't meant anything by it, had only meant to compliment her, but the words hurt.)

Neil perched at the counter while Kathleen put the chicken in the oven. He had brought an iPod, and an iPod speaker, which he plugged in at one of the kitchen outlets, and soon enough the kitchen was filled with Diana Krall singing "White Christmas."

"And tell me again why you didn't go with Adam?" said Kathleen, opening the Malbec. She knew from her wine class that she was supposed to decant the wine to let it breathe, but she felt a childish, petulant delight in pouring it straight out from the bottle. She fussed with the daisies for a minute, finding a vase under the kitchen sink, and eventually she replaced the poinsettia with them, relegating the poinsettia to the bathroom.

"Oh, because it could take weeks," Neil said. "I had to let him have this. As much as he complains about it, he loves sorting through bureaucracy. I'd be useless at this point, and grouchy to boot." He pulled his face into something approximating a grimace. "And anyway, my boss is sort of a stickler when it comes to vacation time. I doubt I'd get the time off."

"Oh, stop," said Kathleen. "Smart aleck."

"And when things are sorted out, and Henri is ready to come home, I'll fly down to meet them. And we'll all come home together."

"One big happy family."

"Exactly."

"Well," said Kathleen. "Happy families. I'll drink to that." She raised her glass to Neil's, and she tried not to sound wistful, or envious, although she felt, along with the muddled holiday cheer, a little bit of both.

※

Later, dinner cleaned up, leftover chicken offered to and declined by Lucy, Neil departed, she checked her email for a response from Professor Jacob Paterson. Nothing. She accessed his university Web page—she had bookmarked it, and even the creaky Mac was able to bring it to the fore quickly—and studied his photograph again: the glasses, the pale, flat face. It seemed he had something to tell her. But what? He likely had his own family with whom to celebrate the holidays: his own wife cooking him his own roast chicken, perhaps in her own holiday sweater, his own children tearing about, playing with their new toys, breaking them, probably, the way all children did on Christmas Day. Crying about it after, as they all did too.

She had more wine. What had Natalie said? *You don't talk to your own daughter.*

She typed into Google the name "Natalie." Of course this returned hundreds of thousands of results. Natalie Portman seemed to be the most popular of those, and Kathleen spent some time looking at her, admiring the elegant lines of her face, her wide, open smile: true beauty. Then she entered "Natalie Gallagher"; there seemed to be plenty of Natalie Gallaghers in the world. Then, to narrow it further, "Natalie Gallagher Newburyport."

And then.

Here was Natalie Gallagher, the girl Kathleen now thought of as *her* Natalie. There was a photograph, a close-up of Natalie's face, as unflattering as you could get, taken from above. Her eyes were closed and her face was slack. Was she lying down? Asleep?

The photo wasn't the worst of it. It was the comments that appeared below. Kathleen felt sick looking at all of this. Had Natalie seen it? If she had, how could she stand it? But what if she hadn't? She should tell her, make sure she was aware of what she was up against. Or she should tell *someone*. Someone at the school, an administrator who could help. She even went so far as to rise from her chair and walk toward the phone. But it was Christmas night! No school administrators would be around, not tonight, and most likely not for the next week; they were all home, like their students, like Kathleen herself.

Lucy came into the kitchen, her nails tapping against the hardwood, and stood, gently whining, by Kathleen's side.

꙰

It was dark on the street save for the Christmas lights on at many of the houses. Neil had observed once that it seemed that the less money people had, the more they spent on holiday decorations. Kathleen thought that was an obnoxious thing to say, and she told Neil so, but really wasn't it true? Witness, two blocks over from her house, the multifamily, in front of which she now stood. It was similar to Kathleen's building, but decorated with such flamboyance, such an extravagance of lights — bright white reindeer prancing across the roof, a trio of angels gamely blowing trumpets in the front yard, a giant wreath covered in red lights — that the house itself seemed to give off a noise.

Kathleen wobbled a little on the sidewalk, caught at the leash. Perhaps (probably) it was the wine, but the longer she stood there on the sidewalk, the more Kathleen felt herself overcome by a searing sort of clarity.

"Somebody should do something," she said. An idea was forming in her mind, and she now saw herself as the young girl's savior, as a knight of sorts, maybe not a knight in shining armor but an older, female knight, in black dress pants and a midwestern-style Christmas sweater: a knightess. "Somebody's got to do something for that girl," she said, and Lucy, sitting respectfully beside her, cocked an ear in a way that signified both interest and support.

·ᐟᐠ

Christmas night she typed, "Dear Professor Paterson: I'm sorry to bother you again, but I am worried that my last email might not have reached you." She stopped. She wrote, "I am pasting it into this email, just in case." Then she wrote, "I have tried to help my friend, but I'm afraid I wasn't able to." Then she deleted the word *friend* and replaced it with the word *daughter*. She traveled into the bowels of her Sent folder to retrieve the original email, and dutifully pasted the text. She pressed Send and heard the *whoosh*: the carrier pigeons doing their work. Where was he now? Finished with his supper, perhaps settling down to relax in his living room (beige, it would be beige) with his wife, surrounded by pictures of his kids doing the usual kid things: selecting pumpkins at Halloween, jumping into an aquamarine pool at somebody's birthday party, bundled up by the front door in snowsuits. Weather in the Midwest could be unpredictable.

She Googled Ashley Jackson again. She found more details. There had been hateful texts; there had been Web pages, pictures, nasty comments posted anonymously. And there had been Ashley Jackson, alone in her parents' garage, turning the key in the ignition. Sitting back, waiting, unable to go on.

"The cruelty of kids at this age should not be underestimated," said an expert quoted in the article (the expert was not Professor Paterson). "They don't always understand that their actions have consequences."

She wished she hadn't sent the email to Professor Paterson yet; there was something she wanted to add.

She wanted to add, *I am afraid something bad is going to happen.*

She picked up the notebook again.

❈

Elsie and Arthur returned from abroad. They had a new car, a Duesenberg roadster in gleaming black.

"What happened to the old one?" asked Dr. Turner.

"Crashed it," said Arthur.

"Drunk," said Elsie. She shrugged. Arthur smiled.

"Well," said Anna. "Where'd you go? On your travels?"

Elsie laughed and said, "Where didn't we go?" and Anna said sharply, "Just answer the question, Elsie."

Arthur said to Dr. Turner, "Whoah. What's eating her?"

I, clattering around in the kitchen, knew what was eating Anna.

A few minutes later I heard Elsie say, "What happened to your girl—what was her name?"

"Bridget," said Dr. Turner, and it was a secret thrill to me, to hear him say my name in general company. "She's still with us." Still with us: that was a thrill too.

Even with that comment, and the little lift it provided, I felt a certain heaviness in my limbs. Balled up, as Norah would say. Not quite right. I knew where this came from: the lack of sleep, the nights with Charles, my inability, sometimes, to fall to sleep after he'd gone. Then there was the extra work I did in the mornings, the care I took with the beds and the sweeping, so that Anna could accuse me of no wrongdoing.

"There you are!" Elsie said when I entered with the soup. "You haven't gotten any uglier, have you?"

Arthur said, "Elsie!" and Elsie said, "What? She hasn't." Then, to me, "You'd better watch yourself around the young men, you know. They're likely to take advantage of you." She cast a sidelong glance toward Arthur. "Believe me, I know how the male mind works."

"Now, Elsie," said Dr. Turner. "I'm sure Bridget is perfectly capable of taking care of herself."

My hands were shaking. I put a soup bowl down a little too hard in front of Dr. Turner, and a bit of it sloshed over the edge. I could feel Anna glaring at me, but I didn't meet her eyes, and Dr. Turner wiped at the spill with his napkin without saying a word.

"You can't imagine what we saw there, in Europe," said Elsie after they'd eaten. She was smoking a cigarette at the dining room table. Harry and Edward watched her, transfixed, quiet, for once, as if in the presence of royalty. "You really should go, Anna. You and Charles should go to Monte Carlo."

Anna snorted. "Me! In Monte Carlo. How am I going to manage going to Monte Carlo?" I thought I saw something in her expression: a wistfulness.

"Arthur lost all of our money, of course," Elsie went on. "He's a wretched gambler."

"Did not," said Arthur, unbothered.

"You did!"

"Not all of it."

"Enough."

"Plenty more where that came from."

A silence fell after that, and James banged a spoon on his high chair and said, "Up."

"We saw the Fitzgeralds," said Arthur. "On the Riviera."

At this Anna perked up. "The Fitzgeralds! What was that like? Was she very beautiful?"

Again James said, "Up," and I lifted him from his chair.

"Into the kitchen," I said. "You've got food all over your face."

Elsie said, "They were both beautiful. Straight out of a movie. Out of a dream, really. But crazy, I guess. She is."

Everything swam in front of me for a moment: it seemed like

the entire living room was made up of tiny vacillating dots. I heard someone say my name, but the sound seemed to be coming from very far away. Then it grew closer and closer and the room came back into focus. They were all looking at me — the whole table.

"Bridget!" said Anna. "You look quite strange. Go into the kitchen and sit down for a minute. Put the baby down."

"Yes, ma'am," I whispered, and I obeyed, but I looked first at Dr. Turner. His eyes were now locked on his plate, and he was tending to his food as carefully as I imagined he might tend to his patients. Would he look at me? I remained a few seconds longer than I should have, to see if he would. He didn't.

A few minutes later Elsie entered the kitchen. I was washing dishes at the sink. Elsie's perfume preceded her; I didn't need to turn around to know she was there.

"Bridget," said Elsie. "Listen here. Are you in some kind of trouble?"

Slowly I turned. Up close like this I could see the white base of Elsie's makeup, and the black liner around her eyes. I looked at the edge of Elsie's eyes, where the makeup was smudged, to avoid looking at her directly. Then I looked down again and wiped at the counter with the rag. I said, "What do you mean? What kind of trouble?"

"You know what I mean."

This time I met Elsie's gaze directly and didn't look away when I said, "No, I'm sorry. I don't know."

Elsie moved closer — so close that when she narrowed her eyes I could see the charcoal shadow shift. "Play dumb if you want to. But you're not going to get any help from them with anything."

I said nothing.

"Well. If you change your mind and decide that you are in trouble, you talk to me about it."

"Yes, ma'am."

"There are things I know—people I know, too. You talk to me, do you understand?"

"Yes, ma'am," I said.

"Elsie," she said. "Call me Elsie. I'm not your mistress."

"Elsie," I said softly. "All right. Elsie."

⁂

The day after Christmas, Natalie awoke to something of a miracle: her mother, up before her, showered (showered!), hair styled, making pancakes. Natalie was starving, but she eyed her mother suspiciously over her plate. This woman before her, the near stranger in the kitchen brandishing a spatula, *looked* like her mother, even sounded like her mother. But she did not seem like Natalie's mother.

"What's going on?" she said warily.

"Well!" her mother said brightly. "I thought we could spend some time together."

"Really?" said Natalie. "Um, okay." But what she really wanted was Bridget O'Connell's notebook back, even though she'd told Kathleen that she didn't. She wanted Ms. Ramirez to turn her beautiful dark eyes toward her and say, *Natalie, what a wonderful job you've done here. You should be proud.* She wanted Christian Chapman to be impressed; she wanted Hannah Morgan to be envious.

But it went beyond the project, of course. She thought of her mother's parents, desolate and unhappy on their Kansas farm, tangled in their own anger. She thought about her father's parents, talking about something regular, like the weather or what to have for dinner that night, coming up on the fog-covered overturned truck on the highway, seeing it too late to do anything about it. This had been part of family lore for so long that she'd never actually taken the time to think it through, how terrifying it must have been, that last glimpse of a prone truck before you slammed into it.

That's why she'd been so interested in the notebook, and so excited to have found it: she figured there was some sort of connection there, something tying her to another person. She felt a need, as intense as an itch, to find out what that connection was. She had a father who had (sort of) deserted her; she had a mother who had (definitely) been deserted by her family. So no matter how far in the past this connection to Bridget O'Connell Callaghan was, if it existed at all, it had the potential to be something—to tether her to someone.

And then she'd messed that up too, by leaving the notebook behind, and by telling Kathleen she didn't want it. That wasn't true, of course. (Thing number nineteen that made her sick: lies, other people's, but hers as well. Also—thing twenty—failing, and failing was exactly what she was going to do when Ms. Ramirez learned that she had nothing for the independent-study project, nothing to show for the weeks and weeks of supposed work.)

※

They went to the North Shore Mall. Natalie's mother bought her two new sweaters and a pair of jeans at Abercrombie. For herself, at the makeup counter, she allowed herself to be talked into three new lipsticks and a concealer stick. ("Your skin is *gorgeous,* ma'am," said the bejeweled and perfectly made-up salesgirl, speaking through lips coated with a heavy layer of what she said was Viva Glam II. "But these dark circles—let's get rid of them!") Natalie, standing to the side, grimaced; her mother straightened and beamed into the close-up mirror, looking at her distended cheeks, every pore and follicle illuminated.

"I'll take it," said Natalie's mother. "And the Troublemaker lipstick, too." (Who was this mother?)

On the way home, they stopped at Trader Joe's, where Carmen stocked up on dark chocolate caramel wedges, organic strawberries flown in from Mexico, three tins of *queso fresco.*

But Natalie didn't want three tins of *queso fresco;* she wanted Bridget's notebook back. Maybe she should call Kathleen. Maybe she could get back down there and retrieve the notebook, visit the Archives again. She'd liked it in the Archives. She'd liked the formidable stone of the building's façade, the flag whipping ferociously in the winter wind, the water in the harbor choppy and defiant, the way, Natalie imagined, the water had looked in the ancient seafarers' tales they had studied with Ms. Ramirez at the beginning of the semester. (*Boring,* pronounced Hannah Morgan, and Taylor Grant echoed her: *Yawn.*)

⁕

After Trader Joe's, Natalie's mother pulled into the parking lot of Qdoba. Qdoba! When had Natalie's mother last eaten a full meal? But here she was ordering the Ancho Chile BBQ Burrito, a Diet Coke to go with it. Was her mother doing all of this for her, because of what Kathleen had told her about Hannah and Taylor? Or was it the medicine?

When they were seated at the white table, still slick and pristine from the washrag Natalie had seen an employee rub energetically against it, her mother, not quite looking at her, said, "So. I wanted to tell you."

Natalie thought, *Here we go.*

Her mother said, "I got a job."

Natalie studied the tortilla chip in front of her. With every effort to make her voice sound casual, even devil-may-care, she said, "Oh yeah?"

"Right before Christmas, at Talbots. I went in there, and it turned out someone had just quit—it was luck, really. And I can walk there. The lady said"—here she beamed—"that I had a good eye."

Natalie said, "Oh," and used a little plastic fork to remove a black bean that was lodged in her teeth.

"Isn't that good? Nat?"

But Natalie was intent on the bean in her tooth; the plastic fork was not up to the task, its tines too thick and unyielding, so she gave up and inserted a fingernail.

"Earth to Natalie!" Her mother reached over and knocked softly on Natalie's skull with her knuckles. It was an old joke from Natalie's childhood, but today Natalie found this abhorrent instead of amusing. She pulled away.

This hurt her mother: she saw that instantly. But she let the wordless insult lie because what she could have said instead was far worse. She wanted to say this: Too little, Mom, and too late. Because wasn't it true that her mother's lie about her age was the first thing Taylor Grant and Hannah Morgan had chosen to exploit, opening a fissure in Natalie into which they could insert whatever weapon they chose, to probe, and then to maim her further? Wasn't all this, at the core, her mother's fault? It had to be somebody's fault.

Her mother said, "Aren't you happy for me? Sweetie—"

Natalie said, "I guess." Artfully, she shrugged.

Natalie felt something dark and ugly gnawing a hole inside her. It was bullshit. All of it: bullshit. Her parents, both of them. Kathleen Lynch, who wasn't even helping when she said she would. Hannah Morgan, who could do something about Taylor Grant but refused to. Mrs. Morgan, too blind to see what was going on. Ms. Ramirez, praising an idiot like Emily Middleton, who was writing her dog's autobiography. All of them full of the same bullshit. Pretending to help, but doing nothing. Bullshit bullshit bullshit.

Natalie stared hard out the window at the traffic going by on

114, streaming from the mall parking lot, from the Target, from everywhere. The traffic was backing up. One driver, impatient, honked loudly, setting up a chain reaction of honking horns. Natalie stared at the half-eaten burrito in front of her, its insides spilling out like guts.

She didn't say it, *Too little, too late*. But she thought it.

※

You could find anything these days with Google, really, it was amazing. Hannah Morgan, Natalie's erstwhile best friend. There was more than one Morgan in Newburyport—no surprise there, very common name. But Natalie had described Hannah's house, its basic place in the town (she had indicated this the day Kathleen drove her home), its size. So, the day after Christmas, through a combination of the online white pages (thank you, People Search!), an online real estate database that was new to her (thank you, Zillow!), and a satellite service called Google Earth (you too, Google Earth, thanks very much), Kathleen was able to pinpoint the house. One click, and she had at her disposal a set of directions, which she painstakingly copied onto a piece of scrap paper—no printer. Luddite was right.

It was not lost on her that her last trip to Newburyport, with a similar goal, had ended badly, but she was fired up. All around them girls were in trouble, and here was one she could help. Not could: had to help, because nobody else was going to do it. She was a solitary crusader, shield and surcoat at the ready, trekking toward the Holy Land.

She practiced:

"Your daughter is hurting someone."

"Your daughter is hurting someone I care about."

To get to Hannah Morgan's house, you took a left off the highway exit, not a right, away from the downtown, and you wound through newer neighborhoods — nothing historical here, no secrets locked in basements or attics. Nothing, really, to see at all, save the houses themselves, and the ghostly outlines of massive play sets in the weak light coming from the quarter-moon above. No cars visible, no mess. People in houses like these kept their cars in garages, their mowers in sheds or faux barns, not like in Southie, everything out on the street for the world to see, all fair game.

No hesitating this time, no standing at the door recalling the sensation of dunking under the water. Just the doorbell, which chimed musically somewhere deep inside the house, not just one chime but several, part of some classical piece, must be.

Somehow Kathleen had expected Hannah herself to answer but, no, this must be the mother; she was dressed in some sort of black yoga outfit, hair pulled back from her face with a matching headband, and holding a sweating glass of white wine (the word "Muscat" came into Kathleen's head, a remnant from the wine-tasting class, but she couldn't remember what that was; Carol would remember, she remembered everything).

The woman looked at Kathleen, warily expectant, or expectantly wary, Kathleen wasn't sure which.

Kathleen cleared her throat. "Mrs. Morgan?"

"Yes…"

"My name is Kathleen Lynch. I've come on behalf of one of your daughter's friends, or one of her ex-friends, I should say."

Mrs. Morgan said, "Huh?"

Kathleen wavered for a minute. She looked down. She recognized the intricately tiled foyer from the photo of Natalie on the website, and she found in this recognition a modicum of strength. She said, "Your daughter, and her friend Taylor, they're hurting someone named Natalie."

"Natalie Gallagher?"

"Yes."

The woman sipped from her wineglass. "What do you mean, hurting?"

"I mean bullying. They're bullying her."

"I think you must be mistaken." She slurred a little bit on *mistaken;* it was Kathleen's guess that this was not her first glass of wine, perhaps not her second either. "Nobody's doing any bullying. Natalie was just here the other day."

Kathleen remembered, suddenly, a feeling from her youth, of being called on in class and being either ill-prepared to answer or downright wrong when she did—this made worse, of course, by the visage of the nun who had asked the question, Sister Mary This-or-That, a wrinkled white face under the wimple, a dash of peach fuzz above the lip. She cleared her throat. "Where is she? I'll talk to her myself."

"She's not here. She's on a ski trip."

This was a blow.

Mrs. Morgan added needlessly, "In Vail."

Mrs. Morgan had not asked Kathleen inside the house, so Kathleen continued to stand awkwardly between the storm door and the porch.

Surely the Crusaders faltered sometimes, right? Surely it did not all go smoothly for them all the way. There were stumbles, and they forged ahead.

"If I were you, I'd look it up, there's a website. 'We hate Natalie Gallagher,' it's called."

"Who are you again? Where's Carmen?"

"I'm Kathleen Lynch," she said. "And I'm worried about your daughter's behavior."

Around the edges of the headband, Kathleen could see gray roots that were at odds with the blond hair. Mrs. Morgan narrowed her eyes, took another sip of wine. "I think you must be confused. Maybe you have my daughter mixed up with someone else."

She had said almost those exact words to Deidre Jordan's

mother. "Look it up," said Kathleen as the door closed in front of her. She stood at the door for several seconds. The doorknob was some sort of antique copper affair, very posh. She spoke to the doorknob, hoping her voice carried through. "Look it up," she called. "Look up the website, and do something about it."

She remembered standing in her kitchen talking to Deidre Jordan's mother on the phone.

Do you know what our daughters are doing?

And Kathleen had told her she must be mistaken. Not her daughter: not her Susannah, never.

※

Taylor sent a text, with a photo attached from Vail, the view from the chairlift, little dots of skiers below. WOULD SAY WE WISHED U WERE HERE BUT WE R GLAD U R NOT

Delete.

※

What did a Crusader do when a Crusade failed? *Did* the Crusaders fail? Kathleen's knowledge of that period of history was fuzzy at best. But if they did, probably the Crusaders did what all people did when faced with failure: they regrouped, pushed forward, called upon some inner reserve of toughness. Human nature being what it was, and probably mostly unchanged from then to now.

Back at home, she opened her computer. Shouldn't she know more about medieval history? All the history she knew happened in the past two hundred years.

One website called the Crusades "an unmitigated disaster." She read on. God! She hadn't known about the Children's Crusades, mini-Crusaders starving to death or being sold into slavery. What a mess. Bodies laid out on roadsides, Crusaders cooked like roast chickens inside their heavy armor.

So they didn't regroup. They were dead dead dead, as dead as doornails, dead like Ashley Jackson.

She took the notebook from the place she'd given it on the bookshelf. "You and me, Bridget, my dear," she said. "You and me. We've got each other, and that's about it."

She found the page that she'd marked, and she set the notebook beside the computer so she could continue to transcribe as she read.

Declan Callaghan was on a ladder tipped against the side of the house when I returned from my walk. I had James in his carriage, and he had fallen asleep, tired from running up and down the grass at the park. Anna was unwell and had gone back to bed while Harry and Edward were in school.

"You look like you could use the rest," I told Anna, and Anna's face opened briefly in such gratitude and relief that I felt an unexpected tenderness toward her; I nearly cried.

I nearly cried at a lot of things then.

The day was warm, and the sky was the sort of blue that was so clear it almost hurt to look at it. Summer was not far away, and with summer would come the trip to Nantucket.

I sat for a moment with James, still asleep, on the front steps. There was a staggering amount of work awaiting me inside: the week's ironing, plus the sheets hanging on the line that needed to be brought in and put back on the beds, plus some mending of Harry's pants, and then the dinner food to prepare. The thought of completing even one of those tasks wearied me beyond belief, and I rested my elbows on my thighs and my head in my hands.

When I did that, my arms pressed against my breasts, which were so sore that I gasped from the pressure.

"Bridget!" said Declan Callaghan, climbing down from the ladder. He was sweating; his face, like mine, reddened easily, and was red now. When he was nearly down, he dropped his hammer on the ground and said, "Jesus!" Only he pronounced it "Jaysus," and I felt a longing for my father, and for Ireland, and for anyone else who might say "Jaysus" in just that way.

Declan sat down next to me. "He looks peaceful enough," he said, looking at James.

I shrugged. "Sure he is."

"What do you hear from home?"

"Oh, the same," I said. I was dressed too warmly for the day; all I wanted to do was lay my head down on the bricks and fall asleep. Still, Declan was being kind, and I wanted to try. I would try. "Marriages, babies, farming, the dances, all the rest of it. You know."

He waited a beat, and I said nothing, and into the silence he said, "Ah, marriages."

I looked at him and then down. I could see the sweat coming through his shirt. His work boots had a semicircle of mud on each tip.

"I'm a citizen now," he said. "I'll never go back. This is home, now."

"Is it?"

" 'Tis."

I thrilled to that too, I missed my father.

"I'm buying a house, I've already bought it."

"You, Declan Callaghan? You've bought a house?"

"I have. A lovely house, a lovely white house with a gambrel roof. I just need a wife to complete it." He winked. "Do you know of any good little Irish lasses looking to live over on Milk Street?"

I shook my head; I couldn't help smiling. I thought of my father playing the fiddle, my sisters dancing to it, all of them in the parish dancing to it. My father was one of the best fiddlers for miles. The phrase came to me suddenly: around the house and mind the dresser.

Declan stood up. "I must get back to work. I don't want to get on the wrong side of Dr. Turner. But you know that, living with him."

I felt a strange sensation behind my temple: a rhythmic throbbing. "What do you mean?"

"The temper! The man may as well be Irish, the way he flies off."

I said, "Oh, now."

Declan nodded. "And I guess I'll check my wages too, when I get them, to see that I don't get cheated."

"Cheated?"

"He's a cheap one, he is. Some lads I know did work for him in the past. But never again is what they told me."

"Then why do you?"

"Because it allows me to see you."

It was difficult for me to reconcile this image of Dr. Turner with the Charles that I knew: the soft hands, the gentle voice. "I don't believe you," I said to Declan.

Yet working out anything in my mind proved difficult at that point anyway. My head was too heavy for my neck. Oh, I was so tired.

Declan rose.

He said, "Chin up, Bridget O'Connell. You're too pretty to look like that on a day like this."

I thought again of all the work waiting for me inside. I thought I might be sick. I wanted to call Grainne, but I was not permitted to use the telephone.

"Girl like you," Declan said. "You could have any man you wanted, you know. You just need to point and choose. Think about it, will you? A lovely little house over on Milk Street, a real roof, a far cry from the thatch you'd have at home."

I said nothing. James, waking, pointed at the sky and said, "Birdie!"

Anyway, why did I need to call Grainne? What was I calling to ask? I already knew the answer.

Declan said, "Little lads and lasses running about, enough for our very own ceili."

Not long after that, Charles told me that in July we were going to Nantucket. As a family.

"Everyone?" I'd said. Meaning, me too?

"Everyone. Elsie and Arthur will join us for a week of it too," he said. "You'll continue your duties. But you see the place is smaller—you might be in with the children. At night." I felt something coil in my stomach at that: I remember it like it was yesterday. In with James, that would have been fine, that would have been lovely, but in with Harry and Edward, their stealthy tormenting of me, the thought of that was too much to bear.

He said, "Anna must never know about this. You understand that."

I said, "I know." Then I said, "Of course I know that." Because what did he take me for?

He reached for me after that, but I pulled away. He thought it was because of the conversation about Nantucket, but really it was something else—my body felt different, not like mine, and I didn't want anyone near me.

It was too early for the quickening. But looking back I believe that is when I felt something. I knew.

From the gravy boat smashed on the floor to this moment— the blink of an eye, a world turned upside down, a doctor's hand reaching out to touch a swollen ankle, and all my fault after that because I was greedy.

Natalie's mother was working every day now, and Natalie, who thought she'd been at loose ends before, was now really at loose ends, with school out until after the new year. (Thing number twenty-one: loose ends.)

On Monday she wandered around downtown, hoping to run into Christian Chapman, but she didn't: he had probably gone up to Vermont or New Hampshire with his snowboard, with his divorced and guilty father.

Once she walked by Talbots downtown and stood peering inside, watching her mother folding shirts; her mother was looking down, the little tip of her tongue sticking out of the corner the way it did when she was concentrating hard.

On Tuesday she went for a walk in Maudslay Park. Everyone she passed, it seemed, had a dog or a friend to walk with, and the openness of the sky above her, the tangle of the tree roots on the ground, the crunch of the frostbitten grass and leaves under her feet, all of these seemed to underscore her solitariness. (Thing number twenty-two: solitariness.)

On Wednesday she called Kathleen Lynch, but nobody answered. She didn't leave a message.

On Thursday her father called her. "We're taking you out tonight, me and Julia. Remember? New Year's Eve. We talked about this, right?"

"I don't know," said Natalie, lying. "Yeah, I guess so, maybe."

"We'll wine and dine you," he said. "Wear something nice."

In spite of herself, she smiled. "Dad," she said. "I'm thirteen. I don't drink wine."

"We'll stick with the dining, then," her father said, and his voice took on a jovial quality that she found hard to resist.

"Okay," she said. She nodded, as though her father could see her. "Okay, you got it."

She pulled a dress out of her closet. It was from the summertime; it would be too short, because she had grown since then, and it was inappropriate for the weather, but she had nothing else: she'd wear her coat.

After she closed her phone, she opened her computer. She had bookmarked the page with her photograph on it, and even though she told herself she would never look at it again she looked at it all the time. She looked to see who had said what about her, to see what they'd said, to see how bad it was getting. She had bookmarked it! *What a loser,* she said to herself sometimes, pulling it up, her stomach churning, her guts tied into knots. She was an active participant in her own grim fate.

This day, though, New Year's Eve day, she hit the link and got a perplexing *page not found* message. Refresh. Nothing. Again, refresh. The page was gone.

⁂

Kathleen didn't know if children even learned cursive these days. She remembered Susannah bent over the kitchen table, the tangle of her ponytail, one leg bent beneath her in a triangle, working at the penmanship sheets that came home with her every Tuesday. What grade was that? Second? Third? Did it matter? No, it did not.

She remembered her own cursive instruction at the hands of the nuns. Even now her penmanship was perfect, it had been drilled into her, rulers firmly applied to the backs of her prepubescent knuckles.

All that week, the week between Christmas and New Year's Eve, Kathleen read the notebook. When she wasn't working, she read; when she was supposed to be working—she read then too. It was slow going because she was transcribing as she read, continuing the notes Natalie had made.

Carol called a couple of times: post-Christmas blues, she said, the grandkids had left, and my *God* they were annoying when they were here but when they were gone there was sort of a hole.

"Carol," said Kathleen. "I can't."

"You can't what? You can't do anything? Drink? After-Christmas sales at the Atrium?"

"The *Atrium?*" said Kathleen. "I don't think they put anything on sale at the Atrium. No. Thank you, but no. I'm buried with work."

Neil stopped by her desk at odd times of the day, just as he usually did. He hadn't heard from Adam, then he *had* heard from Adam, but something seemed off. Then everything seemed great with Adam, but Neil was panicking that he'd never get Henri's room done in time. He hadn't hung the curtains. Would Kathleen like to come over and hang curtains with him? He would make fondue—

"Neil," she said firmly. "I can't."

He peered over her shoulder. "Wait," he said. "Isn't that..."

She felt like a child taking a spelling test, covering her paper with the crook of her elbow. "Maybe," she said. "Now shoo."

"Didn't you—"

"Neil!" she said. "I'm busy. I love you to death, you know that, but I'm *busy.*"

※

She brought the notebook to and from work with her. The light in the living room wasn't terrific, so more often she sat at the kitchen table, Lucy sleeping beside her.

I began having more strange dreams — dreams about my family back in Ireland, dreams about little James, much bigger than he was, ten or eleven years old, talking to me in another language, a language I didn't speak.

Elsie and Arthur came around more, it seems they were always around. Lots of whispered conversations between Charles and Arthur, doors closed while they were talking.

"You know how it is," said Elsie, laughing. "Men and their business dealings." She said this in the same way she once said, "Men and their cars!"

I don't know where Anna was during all this time. She was lying down, she was writing letters, she was sitting in the straight-backed chair in the living room looking out the window for long periods of time while the boys ran in and out. But anyway she was absent enough for Elsie to be able to observe me, and for her to be able to come up behind me in the kitchen when I was working at the sink.

She said, "You don't have to tell him, you know."

Carefully, looking at the water, at the silverware from breakfast I was washing, I said, "I don't know what you're talking about." I turned. Then she laughed, right in my face, her mouth open so wide I could see the strings of spittle at the back of her throat, so close to me that I could smell her breath, her perfume, see the way her makeup caked in the fine lines around her eyes, I could see the outline she put around her lips to change their shape.

"Oh, don't you?" she said. "I think you do."

"You don't know me at all," I said. "You don't know anything."

"Bridget," she said. "Don't get your fiery Irish temper up with me, I'm on your side. Probably the only one who is."

I paused at that. She was right.

"Arthur is buying a new car," she said. "A Rolls-Royce Silver Ghost. He's just ordered it from the plant in Springfield. We'll have it by the summer."

Was I supposed to react to this? I knew nothing of cars, didn't know one from another. Back at home we used horses to draw the hay home for winter feed. We used horses for everything.

But she pressed on: "Do you know how much that costs?"

I didn't, of course. I shook my head.

"Fifteen thousand dollars."

Still I had nothing to say. I couldn't even begin to understand that kind of money.

She leaned even closer, if this was possible, and said, "Do you know what I'm saying to you, Bridget? I'm saying that I have" — here she cleared her throat, which she did often, because she had one of those smoky cigarette voices, she smoked all the time (drank, too, she showed me once that she kept a flask in her garter) — "that I have money. Lots of it. I'm not afraid to spend it. And if you need help, well, then I'll use my money to help you. Charles has no money to help you."

This was an added blow, and she saw it on my face because she said with some pity, "You didn't know that, did you?" She sighed. "You don't know much, my darling girl."

I said, "I know that he loves me."

She laughed long and hard at that, so long and hard that Anna called from the other room to see what was the matter, so Elsie lowered her voice when she said, "Oh, Bridget, silly Bridget, if you believe that, then you are not as clever as I assumed you to be, not by half."

Kathleen closed the notebook, marking her place carefully with a scrap of paper. Reading the cramped writing was making her head hurt, and her eyes felt like they were straining in their sockets. She remembered her mother, in the months before her death, her litany of ailments always at the ready: can't see like I used to, can't hear like I used to, can't taste like I used to. "Lucy," she said. "Come on, let's go for a walk."

The walk was short, and though it was nighttime she thought she saw from the glow of the streetlamps that Lucy was limping. "Can't walk like you used to, eh, old girl?" she said. Add it to the list. Neither of them was getting any younger.

Elsie arranged the whole thing. For a Thursday, my day off. But of course she couldn't pick me up at the house; she said she would meet me down at the corner of Titcomb Street, which was far enough away to make it unlikely for anyone I knew to see us. And we planned to meet early enough that most people weren't out anyway. There was something about the light that reminded me of home, of the morning grass on my bare feet, the sounds the horses made when my father hitched them to the plow.

Elsie was late; I stood there for a good long time, watching the light grow brighter and brighter, the long, thin strands of pink and orange in the direction of the river. I started to think that I'd made the whole thing up, that she wasn't coming, that she had no need to come.

But she came, and I sat in the car, and we drove for miles and miles and miles, all along Route 1, and then into the city, to Commonwealth Avenue, a grand street lined with grand homes. She pulled up in front of one of these and pointed to a little door just visible through an alleyway.

I thought she would bring me in, but she didn't. I was shaking and shivering; my heart was clattering away. Elsie waited while I got out. She pressed bills into my hand and said, "Don't bother counting it, it's right, I've already checked." She said, "They're expecting you." She said, "I'll come for you in a while."

When I got back in the car later she said, "Is it done?"

"It's done."

She looked at me appraisingly. "You're looking well enough," she said. "Better than I did, coming out of it, anyway."

I was too tired to answer her, too tired to register what she'd said, too tired for anything except resting my head back on the seat and feeling them both inside me, the lie and the baby, the baby and the lie, the lie and the baby...

I hid the money inside my shoe. It was more than I had been expecting. I thought of it as a start for myself, a little bit of salvation.

⁂

On New Year's Eve, Kathleen went to the grocery store after work. She wanted to make a Bolognese sauce. She looked in vain for Melissa Henderson and took her failure to appear as a sign of betrayal: Where are you when I need you, Melissa? Where is Natalie? Where is anyone?

With the sauce bubbling on the stove she realized the futility of another meal for four or six laid out before a party of one. She was definitely going crazy. That was the problem. "And herein lies the problem," she said aloud, to nobody. Talking to herself: was that an official sign of insanity, or was that just what sane people thought about going insane? *Just because you're paranoid doesn't mean there isn't someone looking over your shoulder,* somebody had told her once. That sort of thinking twisted her mind in knots.

"I'm heading for the loony bin, Lucy," she said. "Want to go to the loony bin with me?" Then she said, "Sorry," because she realized that she had confused Lucy, who thought they really were going somewhere together. "Sorry, sweetheart," she said, and she bent to rub the wide white stripe on the bridge of Lucy's pointy nose. "I didn't mean to tease."

She sat there for a moment on the floor with Lucy and took stock of all the different ways she might be losing her mind.

a. Professor Paterson had never answered her email. She was out of her league; she didn't know what to do about the bullying, and yet she couldn't pull herself away. Professor Paterson didn't like her; Natalie didn't like her; nobody liked her.

b. She had wasted fifty-three dollars and twenty-four cents on her last culinary effort, and now she was in the process of making another meal nobody would eat. Waste! She was a waster. If the planet went to hell it would be mostly her fault.

c. She had become careless at work. She had a stack of letters on her desk, letters from real people seeking real answers to their questions, and she had not answered them. She had fallen behind because all she wanted to do was concentrate on Bridget's notebook. The Archives was the only place in the world where she shone, where she had ever shone, and even there she wasn't shining. She might never shine again.

d. She had driven all the way to Newburyport to deliver Bridget's notebook to Natalie and she had neglected to leave it behind. While there, while trying to help, she had gotten the girl in more trouble. She hadn't helped. She had done the opposite; she had un-helped.

e. Susannah. Was she ready to think about it? No, she wasn't. She needed more wine.

f. Was she becoming an alcoholic?

g. She had also failed dismally with Hannah Morgan's mother. She had failed *as* a mother, and she had failed *with* the mothers. Failures, failures, all around her.

h. Her only true friends were Lucy, Neil, and Carol. Neil was about to become a father, and he would no longer be able to be her friend; little Henri would gobble up all of his time, and Adam's too — and there, in a blink, would go the architects of the only social life she had. Lucy was a dog. Carol was wonderful, really lovely, but she was so far above the world's disappointments that you felt obnoxious dragging her down into the sewage of your own blunders.

i. More wine (f!).

j. She had never imagined, when it all happened, that she would lose her daughter forever.

k. Was it forever yet?

l. No. But it was close.

The gourmet pasta she'd bought ($9 a pound, astonishing, and she had bought it anyway) took a full fourteen minutes to cook — the more you paid, the longer you waited, apparently, so Kathleen turned back to the notebook. She was almost at the end.

This night is the hardest thing for me to write about. I've hardly let myself think about this night — through most of my life I've kept it tamped down, tied up, stored in a little box in my mind that I never let myself open.

I am opening the little box now, and after I write this I will close it again; perhaps I will keep it closed forever and ever.

I was in my room when it happened. I was sleeping, the sleep of a poor girl, lonely and exhausted, the sleep of the dead, the sleep of the guilty.

The first noise was the one that woke me. The crash, the fall that came after. It seemed like the falling went on forever. It takes a long time for a little body to make its way down a flight of stairs.

Then the screams. Not James's—he was silenced. It was Anna's screams I heard, and that's what sent me running, and sent the boys running too, from their room, and also Charles, and so we all arrived at the same time to see Anna on the floor bending over James, whose head was turned at a strange angle, an angle that couldn't be right.

Anna looked first at me, pure venom. "You left the gate unlatched."

To Charles, who was pushing past me to get to James, "Do something." Then, louder, hysterical, "Do something!"

But of course there was nothing to be done.

I started to say, "But I didn't...I wasn't...I know—"

"You stupid child," Anna spat at me. "You don't know anything." Then she began to wail. "Take her away!" she said. "Get her out of my sight. Take her away from me forever. Do you hear me? Get her out of my house."

Charles didn't look at me; he too was bent over James. He said, "Bridget. Go."

It was the middle of the night, but what could I do? I gathered the few things from my room, and I obeyed. All the way to Milk Street in the dark, stumbling every now and then, crying.

"Declan," I said, banging on his door. "Let me in. Let me in, Declan. I've got nowhere else to go."

I hadn't left the gate unlatched. Charles must have done so, returning to his room.

⁂

New Year's Eve, seven o'clock, Natalie in the back of her father's pristine Lexus, feeling very much like the child who had been driven up and down Route 95 making sales calls to doctors' offices.

They went to Mistral, which was the fanciest restaurant Natalie

253

had ever been to, and Natalie watched as her father paid thirty dollars for the valet parking alone. While they waited for their table—it was an eight o'clock reservation—her father drank a martini at the bar, and Julia had a seltzer water with a lime in it. Natalie and Julia sat on the barstools while Natalie's father stood behind, hovering, like a mother hen (a father hen).

Natalie drank a Shirley Temple, which she thought was horrifically juvenile, but her father ordered it without asking her and in fact she did enjoy it. When she and Hannah were younger they had practiced tying the cherry stems in knots with their tongues. Over and over again they practiced until an entire jar of cherries was gone. Hannah learned to tie the knot and Natalie never did.

Julia asked Natalie questions: about school, about what she had done over the vacation (nothing, was the honest and mortifying reply), about what she wanted to be when she grew up (Natalie hadn't thought about this in such a long time that she went with her default answer from fifth grade even though she no longer really believed it: a vet). Natalie felt her dislike of Julia begin to dissolve: she was lively, she was interested, she was, in the yellow glow of the restaurant's lights, pretty. Sort of.

When Julia rose to go to the bathroom Natalie's father said, "So, Nat, how's your mother doing?"

She said, "I don't know. Okay, I guess." She chewed her lip and looked around the restaurant. When she turned back to her father, the expression on his face was one of such despair and consternation that, in an effort to erase it, she found herself saying, "I think she's better. Getting better. She's taking some medicine—"

"Really?" Her father brightened.

"Yeah. And her job, that'll be good."

Her father said, *"Job?"*

"At Talbots, downtown. Didn't she tell you?"

Her father took a long sip of his drink. "No," he said. "She didn't tell me."

"Oh," said Natalie. "I thought *you* told her to do that. I thought you made her."

"Made her? Natalie, believe me, it's beyond my power to make your mother do anything." Natalie wasn't sure what that meant. It was bewildering, the grown-up world, everybody hinting around but not really coming out and saying anything.

Natalie sucked at the remains of her Shirley Temple. She had saved the cherry for last, as she always did, and she ate it now, savoring it, chewing on the stem to get all the juice. She didn't try to tie the knot.

She said, "Dad—"

Suddenly she wanted to tell him everything she'd told her mother, but with the hope of a different reaction: about the texts, the bewildering transformation of Hannah Morgan, the website that had appeared and then disappeared, Bridget's notebook. She wanted to ask him what he knew about their house and who had lived there; she wanted to talk to him about the family tree, scratched out on the yellow legal pad.

She thought, there in the restaurant, with its buttery walls, its bright-white tablecloths, its bustling waiters, that she could open up to him. She wanted to tell him about Hannah Morgan and Taylor Grant in Vail. He would throw back his head and laugh: they'd laugh together. "God, how pretentious," he'd say. "Vail? Are you kidding me?"

She said, "Dad—"

But he was talking at the same time, talking quickly, and he was saying, "Listen, Natalie, I wanted to tell you this on my own, before Julia gets back, Julia and I..."

She felt an ominous black ball forming in her belly.

"We're going to have a baby!"

The room was spinning.

"In the summer we're going to have a baby, at the end of July."

Now he was watching Julia, who was weaving her way back from the bathroom. When she reached them he caught her hand briefly before letting it drop. Natalie had the sense of watching two people on a stage from the back of the audience.

Her father said to Julia, "I told her our news."

Our news. Natalie could have vomited. She shook her glass so that the ice cubes clinked together.

Julia flushed and turned to Natalie. "Isn't it exciting? A baby! I never thought I'd have a baby." Natalie thought of the black bra in the bedroom. "And you'll have a little brother or sister."

Her father said, "Natalie?" but she didn't look up from her plate.

She could hardly eat her dinner—prime sirloin with corn whipped potato and golden chanterelles, and for dessert, a warm chocolate torte with vanilla ice cream and crème anglaise. Anytime she looked up, she saw Julia's head tipped toward her father. When the check came her father reached for it, and Julia said blithely, "It's my turn to pay," sliding a card into the thin black check holder. All around them there was the low and steady buzz of a restaurant filling up, the mysterious rhythm of adult laughter. It seemed that in all of this there was no room for Natalie.

When she got home she left a message for Kathleen at the Archives. She could have called the home number, IN CASE OF EMERGENCY, but she didn't. She said, "Can I come down to get the notebook back?"

⁂

"Oh, my God," Kathleen said. "Oh, my *God.*"

She read the line again: *Let me in, Declan, I've got nowhere else to go.*

The timer for the pasta sounded. Kathleen strained it too quickly, nearly splashing some of the scalding water on her arm.

She checked the Bolognese. It looked delectable. And it seemed to be pleading with her for a better fate than that of the pot roast she'd made the previous month: shoved into an inadequately sized refrigerator, later thrown away. Food couldn't plead, though. (She was hallucinating. Add it to the list.)

She wanted to call Natalie to tell her what she'd just read. But Natalie didn't want to talk to her, and even if she did she didn't have her phone; her mother had taken it away. Because of what she, Kathleen, had done.

She turned on the television. In Times Square, thousands and thousands of people stood shoulder to shoulder. How could they stand it? What if you had to go to the bathroom, needed a sip of water? She wouldn't have been able to stand it. She was positive that, had she been in Times Square on New Year's Eve, she would have given up long before midnight and would have run screaming through the crowds.

The camera focused in on a child wearing a pair of glittery glasses with the number 2010 cut out around the eyeholes. The glasses were too big for the child—a girl—and she had to hold her chin at an impossible angle to keep them on. How old was she? Six, maybe seven: front teeth missing. Was this child expected to stay up until midnight? What kind of parents were these?

You should talk, Kathleen Lynch, she told herself morosely. You should talk.

She had a little more wine, and then she called Neil. Surely he was out, but she called anyway.

Neil was not out. Neil was at home, staining Henri's outrageously expensive crib with Australian timber oil. "I blew everything else off, to finish this," he said. "It's supposed to be sheer. But I'm not sure it's supposed to be completely *invisible*. That seems sort of like it defeats the purpose. Why, what's up?"

"Nothing," she said. "I've just...well, I made a bunch of food, and it's sitting here on the kitchen counter, and I'm not that hungry."

"Oh, sweetie," said Neil. "I just stuffed myself with Upper Crust. Slice of the day. It's the Fenway: sausage, pepper, onion. I'm completely bursting. I went on a total binge."

Kathleen took a deep breath. "Oh," she said.

Neil said, "*Damn* it." Then, "Sorry, Kath, I think I just messed up. Good thing the goddamn stain is invisible."

Nobody called her Kath. That was even less common than Katie. She liked it. She took a deep breath, exhaled. "Also," she said. "I'm...well, I guess I'm a bit low." Another breath. "I guess I could use a friend." This was hard to say, and after she said it she waited.

"Kathleen? Don't say another word. I'm on my way."

Kathleen pictured a cartoon character leaving tracks behind him.

She was agitated, waiting for Neil. She was shaken by what she'd read, but she didn't want to talk about that with Neil. She wanted to put the notebook away, and talk about it another time with Natalie. She went into her bedroom and took out Susannah's First Communion picture. She brought it back to the kitchen and placed it on the counter. It looked incongruous next to the pot of Bolognese sauce, with a bunch of aging bananas bordering it on the other side, but she didn't care. She spent some time admiring Susannah's wide eyes, the hopeful quality to her smile. Heartbreaking. She felt the memory of Susannah at that age — second grade, it would have been, spring of second grade — tumble into the great, yawning hole inside of her.

She picked up the notebook and read the end again, just to be sure she had it right. (She did.) She put it away, underneath the pillow in her bedroom.

Neil arrived without ceremony, without even knocking, and for that she was grateful, because she wanted to get right to it. She had a glass of wine waiting for him. She served them both giant bowls of the pasta and the sauce. "Stop grimacing," she told him. "You don't have to finish it. I just want to serve it."

"Give it to Lucy," he said. "She's looking sort of svelte, don't you think?"

She ran her hands along Lucy's sides. "She is, actually. We've been walking a lot. Haven't we, Luce?"

"She looks like she's actually going to answer you," said Neil. "God, I swear that dog is part human."

"Not part," said Kathleen. "All." Lucy retreated to the living room and Kathleen motioned for Neil to sit at one end of the table while she sat at the other end. She brought the First Communion picture over as well and placed it in the center of the table.

"Do you know what the detective told me when Susannah disappeared?"

Neil shook his head.

"He told me that there's nothing scarier than a teenage girl, nothing more dangerous."

Kathleen fixed her eyes on Susannah, looking at the gap between her too-big teeth, the glimpse of the lace along the neck of the dress borrowed, Kathleen remembered, from a neighbor with a daughter two years older. It had been hard to find a dress to fit Susannah because she was tall for her age, as Kathleen had told Natalie.

And even though the neighbor's girl had been tall too (what was her name? Kathleen couldn't remember), Susannah was taller; the dress was supposed to fall to midcalf but instead hit just at the knee. Kathleen remembered the shoes, too: white patent leather with a buckle at the ankle. Brand-new, and worn only that one time.

It bothered her that she couldn't remember the name of the neighbor's girl.

Her hands were shaking. She pressed them to the table to steady them, but the shaking seemed to be traveling through her whole body.

Her bowl of pasta sat untouched, as did Neil's. She took a tiny bite. It was delicious (another culinary triumph), but she had no appetite.

Erin! That was the girl who had lent them the First Communion dress. Of course. Erin. In those days, in their neighborhood, you couldn't throw a stone without hitting at least one person named Erin. This Erin had become a nurse, married a cop, moved to Quincy. She probably had a gaggle of children by now, spots on her chest from too much sun on the Cape in the summer.

Kathleen leaned toward Neil. She thought that, had they been closer in age, to somebody passing by outside they might look like two parents discussing a troublesome toddler, or two lovers having a conversation about something intimate and complicated.

"I think he was right. Let me tell you how scary girls can be, Neil, girls that age. You have no idea. The hold they have over each other: God, it's terrifying. Really, truly, there's nothing scarier than a teenage girl."

Neil, sitting there, made Kathleen think of a schoolboy taking in a lesson.

"Kathleen, you don't have to tell me all of this —"

She held up a hand. "I was seeing this therapist, you know, to help me through it. I had nobody else. Every week I climbed the stairs to her office — she was on the third floor, an old three-family on Broad Street, it was turned into a medical building, peeling brown wallpaper on the stairs, some sort of flowery design. Every week I sat there, as dutiful as a puppy, on this blue couch with cushions that were too big to sit back against. You know the kind I mean?" She paused and waited; it seemed important that Neil understand about the cushions.

He nodded. "Too puffy," he said. "I hate that."

"Me too." She nodded vigorously. "This therapist, I've forgotten her name now, I guess I blocked it out, told me that it was her job to make sure I was taking care of *myself*. She told me I had to get

Susannah out of my mind, that I had to release myself from responsibility for her. She told me my survival was at stake."

"And?"

"Of course I couldn't follow her advice." Kathleen looked around the house. "How could I? Susannah was all I had, she was my one and only. I mean, this therapist's job wasn't to take care of Susannah, but mine was. I changed Susannah's *diapers,* Neil. I remember a happy, skipping three-year-old with this laugh that strangers would turn around to smile at. I remember the way her hair smelled — the way her hand felt holding mine when we crossed the street, her hot little hand. I remember her at *this* age" (she pointed at the photograph) "and as a preteen, and then as a teenager. Learning to drive, learning to cook, braiding her hair, all of it. I remember all of it. I was the one who got up with her in the middle of the night when she was sick or scared, the *only* one who got up with her, the only one here, all the time." This seemed to bear repeating. "The. Only. One. And I'm the one who let her go."

"*You* didn't let her go. She just went. It wasn't your fault." Lucy returned from the living room, padding into the kitchen and standing in the center of the room. "She looks like she has an announcement to make," said Neil, watching her. "I wouldn't be surprised if she cleared her throat."

Kathleen could see that he was trying to lighten the mood, but she didn't want it lightened. "She never said good-bye. She just… left. She just left."

"I know," he said.

"You don't know," Kathleen answered. "I mean that with all due respect. But you don't know. You can't know."

Neil shifted, took a sip of wine. "How did you get over it?"

"I didn't. I'm not over it. I'll never be over it. I went to support groups, I went to more therapy, different therapists."

"Better cushions," said Neil sagely.

"Exactly. You name it and I went to it."

"Did it help?"

"Sometimes. Yes. No. I don't go anymore. I probably should. I was in this support group for a while, and this woman who was the leader of it, she had this thing she used to say. *Another moment, just like this.*"

"I don't get it."

"That's how you get through the days. One moment, then another moment, then another one after that—"

"I see," said Neil.

"Technically, I shouldn't be talking to you about this. They told us, in one of the groups I belonged to, not to talk about this kind of stuff with people who haven't been through it themselves. You know, not to talk to *normal* people about it."

"Civilians," said Neil.

"Right. That's why I don't talk about Susannah at the Archives. People who have been there for a long time, they know I used to have a daughter and now I don't, but they don't know any more than that."

"But you still *have* a daughter."

"No," she said. "No, I don't. I can't think of it that way. But every so often I wake up in the middle of the night, and this phrase goes through my mind: *I lost my daughter.*"

"Kathleen."

"Can you imagine what that feels like? I lost her."

Neil shook his head slowly. "No. But it sounds to me like it's the other way around, like she lost herself."

"Well." Kathleen poked at the bowl of pasta. Lucy lay down in the middle of the floor and let out a low whine. "I know, yes, that's true. But there had to have been something I could have done, something I didn't do, something I could have protected her from."

"But there wasn't."

"I don't know. Maybe, maybe not."

✳

Later, with both of them looking straight ahead at the television, it was easy enough for Neil to say, "Kathleen? What made you tell me all this now? Tonight? I mean I'm glad you did, but I'm just curious about the impetus."

"Impetus," she said. "I like that word." She didn't say it, but she knew the answer had something to do with Natalie, with Ashley Jackson, and with Bridget's story too: girls alone, girls struggling. "I don't know," she said. "Something about the new year, I guess."

Neil said, "Good enough."

Just then the ball began its descent down the pole.

"Oh God," Neil said softly. "Did Dick Clark just *count* wrong? Oh, that's awful. I can hardly watch."

Kathleen, lost in her reverie, hadn't heard. When the ball reached the bottom, Neil leaned over and kissed her on the cheek.

And it was the kiss, ultimately, after all they had talked about that night, that brought the tears, though she tried to hide them from Neil when she said, "You, sir, are a true friend."

He smiled. "Don't go all maudlin on me, boss."

"No, I mean it." She put her hand on his arm, his smooth, gym-toned arm. Baby skin was what it reminded her of. "Really, Neil. Little Henri is so lucky to have you and Adam."

"You think so?" He looked so eager and childlike that her heart, which she already thought was well wrung out, twisted once again.

"I do," she said softly. "Happy New Year, Neil."

"Happy New Year, babe."

⁂

Kathleen saw the light blinking on her phone at work: a message. She listened to it. *"Kathleen? Can I... can I come get the notebook back?"* This time she left a number. "That's my cell," she said. "I got it back from my mom. I think I want to do the project. Let me know."

Kathleen lifted the notebook from her bag. She thought she had finished on New Year's Eve, but she flipped through it again and saw that after a few blank pages were two more pages of writing.

⁂

My story didn't end there, when I knocked on Declan Callaghan's door in the middle of the night. No story ends like that. Mine was a life, like any other—it kept going and going, the way lives do.

I named the baby James.

Declan didn't want to, but I insisted.

He was nothing like the first James. He was more serious and knowing—wise about the world. It seemed he came out of my womb that way.

"Imagine when I tell them at home!" I said to Declan, just after he was born. "That I had him in a hospital, with nurses and a doctor and food brought to me after on a tray."

The Turners moved away. I heard they moved to Boston, I do not know the details of that. I never saw them again. Probably Charles is dead and gone now; Anna, most likely, too—and the boys, who knows, I bet they are around somewhere, unaware of all the rest of it, that part of their family lives on through me.

So then what?

You keep on going, day after day. You learn things. You learn how to quiet your baby in the middle of the night. You have two children, and then three, the last one a beautiful little girl who looks so much like your favorite sister that you name her after that sister: Fiona. Your little Fiona's face is a map of Ireland, that's what people tell you, and sometimes you are surprised by how true that seems; looking at her, you can see your mother bent over the hearth, you can feel the heat of the fire, you can hear your sisters' laughter when they do the bonfire dance, around the house and mind the dresser.

Every now and then you go back and you reread the letter you were writing to Fiona all that winter and spring and summer, the letter where you told her everything that happened, the letter where you told her not to come to America. You never send the letter, but she never comes anyway. And when you learn of her death you cry harder than you've ever cried for anything in your life, harder than you cried for little baby James, so hard you feel as if your body has turned itself inside out. You die a little bit yourself that day.

There are happy times too. Even a life with its share of tragedy is made up of small happy moments as well: the pleasure of diving under a wave in the ocean, a thunderstorm in the middle of the night, a perfectly folded fitted sheet, teaching your daughter the treble jig, eating ice cream from a cone in August, the first smile of your last child.

One day, when you are forty-five years old, you go to Nantucket. It is as beautiful as everyone told you it would be. You stand with your bare feet in the sand looking out at the ocean and you remember who you were nearly a quarter of a century ago, and what you did, and what you didn't do.

And then your husband will take your hand, and press it to his cheek, and you will stand like that for several minutes, and you will think that this is happiness, that maybe you didn't miss out on it after all. Five years later, when he dies from a cancerous growth on his liver that nobody knew about, you will remember this moment. You will remember thinking it: This is happiness.

You drop a gravy boat; a doctor touches your swollen ankle; your world changes forever, the blink of an eye, a lost girl, found.

You learn things. You learn that solace can come from unlikely sources.

It's a life, like any other. You're not finished living it.

Bridget O'Connell Callaghan, Newburyport, Massachusetts, 1975

Kathleen called the number Natalie had left. Voice mail. "Absolutely you can have your notebook back," she said. "Of course you can. And I have a question for you — the notebook mentions a letter, a letter from Bridget to her sister Fiona. Is there any chance you have that letter? Was that letter with the notebook when you found it? I know that's a long shot. But call me back, and we'll figure out how to get this to you. I don't want to mail it, too much risk of its getting lost. So call me back."

Next she looked up the number for Dr. Quinn, Lucy's vet. Nobody answered the phone there either. Voice mail! Was the entire planet going to voice mail? Was nobody answering phones anymore? She left a message there too. "I'm calling about my dog," she said. "Lucy Lynch." It always felt strange to give a dog a last name, but there you were, the world was basically a proper place where certain formalities were expected. "She's been coughing," she said. "I'm not sure if I should be worrying. But. I am. Lucy Lynch, a border collie. Please call me back."

※

January, and with it the chill and low gray skies: a New England winter. Natalie, trudging to school on the first day back after

Christmas vacation (they were supposed to call it winter break, but nobody did), longed for the sunshine. She thought, Global warming, where are you now? But the best the earth could do was to spit rain instead of snow, and it did so vengefully, so that inside the school as well as outside all felt damp and sodden, with wet footprints marking the hallway and coats stuffed inside lockers never quite drying before it was time to put them on again.

Hannah Morgan and Taylor Grant came back with suntanned faces and lift tickets hanging from the zippers of their coats.

Natalie thought about what Kathleen had said about waiting for the longest day of the year and then missing it. That made her think about something else Kathleen had said on that same car ride: *into the gloaming.* Here we go, she'd said. Into the gloaming.

The countdown to the independent-study projects: eleven days. "I'm expecting really great things out of you," Ms. Ramirez said. She was looking at Natalie. Natalie looked away.

Then, suddenly: this. The principal announced, over the loudspeaker, an assembly for the entire school. The nature of the assembly was not disclosed, and Natalie, who had just come from a futile game of volleyball ("Use your *height!*" the gym teacher cried. "Natalie, your arms are a mile long. *Reach* for that one!"), sat flushed, still breathing heavily, in a chair in the darkened auditorium as first one school administrator, then another, stood at the podium and talked about the following:

It had come to their attention *that*—

There had been some stories in the national news recently *saying*—

Some students in this school appeared to be engaged *in*—

The recent suicide of a girl in Des Moines, a girl named Ashley Jackson, was significant *because*—

The administration was issuing new rules *having to do with*—

Natalie felt everything inside of her body constrict.

Ms. McPherson, the guidance counselor, got up and said a few words. She was available; her door was always open; anyone who wanted to discuss the issues could come and talk to her. It was time, according to Ms. McPherson, to take the bull by the horns when it came to bullying (here she held her hands up as though she were indeed wrestling with a recalcitrant bull).

Bull, bullying, Natalie figured that it was supposed to be a pun.

Blown up large on a screen on the stage was a photograph of this girl, this Ashley Jackson, who had killed herself, asphyxiated herself in her parents' garage. Natalie had never heard of her. Des Moines was so far away, another world, and yet Natalie couldn't stop staring at the girl, trying to read her history.

But what? Who? *How?* Not Natalie; she had never breathed a word to anyone at school. Not her mother. Kathleen Lynch? It could have been, must have been. *Was* it?

The texts came during the assembly. This was strictly not allowed, using cell phones during an assembly, so they must have been subtle about sending them, as Natalie was subtle about reading them.

U WOULDNT DARE, said the text.

Another one: BUT U DID

U R A RAT

U WILL PAY 4 THIS

Delete, went Natalie's fingers on her phone's keypad. Delete, delete, delete.

She noticed that there was a voice mail, and inadvertently she deleted that at the same time. Delete delete.

※

At home that night Natalie put her cell phone in her nightstand drawer. Then she took it out again, removed the battery, put the phone in a shoebox under her bed and the battery in a seldom-used drawer of her dresser, which held tights, long outgrown, and a gold necklace with a tiny cross that had belonged to her father's mother, long dead. Everything was outgrown, everybody was dead.

There was a word she had learned recently from a vocabulary list in Ms. Ramirez's class, and it had stuck with her because it sounded foreign, exotic, and at the same time completely apt. The word: *nadir*. Surely this was the nadir.

She took the phone back out of the drawer, replaced the battery, put it in her backpack.

·⁖·

Natalie, walking home from school, tried to remember the old rhyme they used to say, something about a crack. *Step on a crack, break your mother's back.* What a terrible thing to say. And yet she stepped right on the next crack she came to—easily, almost gleefully.

Then, from behind, a voice, her name: Christian Chapman, hair flopping, unzipped jacket flapping, sneakers slapping the sidewalk. "Hey! Hey, Nat." Nat. Nobody called her Nat. Well, sometimes her mother, occasionally her father, but aside from them, nobody. She turned.

"Oh," she said, trying to garner every drop of self-confidence at her disposal, watching his bungling progress (to be so beautifully and unself-consciously *clumsy*—she envied him that; he must save the grace and athleticism for the snowboard).

"Hey, Christian."

He caught up to her finally and stood facing her, chest heaving, cheeks slightly pinked from the cold and the exertion. She said, "What's up?"

"Where you headed?"

She told him: home.

"Where's home, again? I forget."

She told him: Milk Street. "Oh," he said. "That's kinda far. You walk?"

"Yeah," she said. "I used to take the bus, but I hate the bus."

"Me too," he said. "I hate the bus. I'll walk with you."

"You will?"

"Sure," he said. "Part of the way, anyway. Why not?"

She trained her eyes on the sidewalk; she thought that if she looked up he would see her furious blushing. They were walking together down High Street—she, Natalie Gallagher, was walking with Christian Chapman down High Street.

Christian was close enough to Natalie that she could see the rise and fall of his chest as he breathed. The day, having started off cold and gray, had warmed up considerably; underneath Christian's jacket he wore a thin gray T-shirt that looked regular but that Natalie guessed was made out of some fantastically expensive technical material.

"So...did you study for the Science test yet?"

She had forgotten about the Science test: shit.

She said, "No, not really, I'll probably do it today."

"Yeah? I have to start a few days early or I'll never get it all. But not you—you're one of the smart kids!"

Insult or compliment? She couldn't tell. A thirteen-year-old freshman was what she was, flat-chested, awkward, too young, *too damn tall*. She said, "Uh—"

Christian said, "Hey, Natalie. Follow me." He backed up against the stone wall that ran parallel to the street and pushed himself up until he was sitting on it. "I like to sit up here," he said, shrugging. He looked adorable when he shrugged, like a little kid who didn't know what he wanted at the ice cream store.

"Come over here," he said. He patted the stone beside him, and she clambered up too, though the wall was not all that accommodating, because the stones were set more for aesthetics than for comfort, and she could feel an oddly angled one attacking her through her jeans. "See?" Christian said. "That was no problem for you. That's because you're tall."

Was Christian Chapman leaning toward her? Was he going to *kiss* her? It didn't seem possible. But the way he was looking at her—God, she would have no idea what to do if Christian Chapman kissed her, no clue about how to respond. But *was* he?

A name flicked through her mind: Kathleen Lynch. Then another: Bridget O'Connell Callaghan. Then: Ms. Ramirez. She remembered, strangely, the sensation of being tucked in at night by her father, her insistence on having the sheets pulled so tightly around her body that she could scarcely breathe. All of these thoughts were hitting her so quickly and with such intensity that she would have been unable, if asked, to articulate them, and yet each seemed to stand individually, in alignment, like soldiers in her head.

The mind was a strange instrument, somehow she had time to reflect upon that, but only just enough time, because a car swerved over from the center of the street toward them, not hitting them, but bumping briefly up on the curb and onto the sidewalk. Certainly it came close enough to cause them to react, and then it was gone, but not before its driver pressed the horn so loudly that the sound seemed to reverberate visibly.

"What the hell was *that?*" said Christian.

Natalie, mystified, bewildered, a little frightened, her heart battering her rib cage, said, "I don't know." But of course later, after the rest of it happened, she realized that she should have known, she should have known all along. And maybe she did. They weren't old enough to drive; they'd brought others into it.

Christian Chapman, who had disembarked from the wall and had walked a few steps away, turned and said, "Natalie? What are you doing up there still? Come on down. Follow me."

Follow me! Follow him. She would follow Christian Chapman anywhere. She was shaking, she was weak, but she would follow him to the moon, if only he'd ask.

⁂

Dr. Quinn, the vet, was away, it turned out. Skiing. "Vail," said the receptionist. "Lucky duck. But we have someone else in, Dr. Ryan."

"Okay," said Kathleen. She led Lucy into the exam room. When Dr. Ryan entered and extended his hand in greeting, she said, "Geez. You're just a puppy yourself."

He flushed at that. "Not really," he said.

"How old *are* you?"

"Old enough," he said. "Twenty-eight."

The age Susannah would have been. Was, was. Not would have been.

He crouched next to Lucy. "What's been going on?"

Dr. Ryan felt all along Lucy's back, along her sides; he placed his palms against her chest. He lifted her onto the examination table and looked into her eyes, her ears. "This cough," he said. "Harsh and dry, or moist and productive?"

"Harsh and dry," said Kathleen. She felt a little dizzy. She sat down in the chair.

"I do feel something," he said. "Close to the chest wall, some sort of a mass." He paused. "I think we need to aspirate this."

"You need to what?"

"Aspirate," he said. "We pass a needle through the chest wall, remove microscopic cells for evaluation." Lucy was looking seriously at him.

"Evaluate them for what?"

"Cell abnormality."

"You mean cancer?"

He took a deep breath, nodded. She had the urge to hug him—

to comfort *him*. Wasn't that strange? He was so young; he looked a little bit lost.

"Today?"

"No, we'll need to sedate her for that. We'll need another appointment."

"Do you think that's what it is?"

He tented his fingers. "A dog of her age, urban environment, it's not out of the question." He paused. "I mean"—he looked down at the chart—"Mrs. Lynch, we can't confirm for certain without aspirating, but if I had to hazard a guess now I'd say, yes, it is likely to be cancerous."

Mrs. Lynch. Dr. Quinn always called her Kathleen.

"And if it is...what do we do about that?"

Dr. Ryan inhaled again. "That depends. If. There are options, but none is extremely promising, and for an older dog—"

Kathleen couldn't breathe; she felt like *she* was the one with the mass close to the chest wall. She said, "Is that all, for now?"

Dr. Ryan didn't answer; he was writing on Lucy's chart. He had lifted Lucy down from the table, and Kathleen picked up her leash from the floor.

"Ma'am," said Dr. Ryan. "Don't forget to stop at the desk, make an appointment..."

Kathleen didn't stop.

Dr. Ryan said, "I'm sorry...," and he made a movement toward Kathleen as if to stop her. But Kathleen was out the door, and Lucy was too.

※

"Do you have children?" Kathleen had asked Detective Bradford the last time he came.

"Yup," he said. "But they don't live with me. They live with my wife." He rubbed his chin. "Nasty stuff, divorces."

"But you have children."

He nodded.

"How many?"

"Two. Boy and a girl."

"Then you understand," she said, "that I'm not giving up. I'll keep looking for her until the day I die."

"I understand," Detective Bradford said. "But—"

"That's all," answered Kathleen. "I know you're done. I just wanted to make sure that you understand that I'm not."

※

This time there was a single text, only five words long.

It came minutes after Christian Chapman left her; she heard the *ding,* and with shaking fingers she dug her phone from her coat pocket.

WE WILL TAKE U DOWN

Delete.

Natalie kept walking, but she didn't put the phone back in her pocket; she kept her eyes trained on it, waiting for what was coming next.

Nothing came. It was recycling day; the blue bins were scattered across the sidewalk like so many dead animals. Natalie had to cross over or pass around them with nearly every step.

The neighborhood was sheathed in a heavy, gray, midafternoon silence. The high school got out first, so the kindergarten and elementary school parents had not yet begun their vigilant school-bus watching. Natalie felt like she was alone on the street, in the town, maybe even in the universe.

She checked the phone again, in case the rattling of the recycling bins she had to step over had caused her to miss an incoming text. But there was nothing.

Now she was scared. Before, she had been troubled, bothered, saddened. Lonely! But now she was scared. The car on the sidewalk, the horn honking so loudly. Just a few more inches and it *could* have taken her down. *We will take u down.* Christian Chapman had departed quickly after that. It must be that he sensed some bad luck around her, some invisible but radioactive element on her skin.

She thought of the school assembly, of Ms. McPherson, the guidance counselor, with her poodle puff of hair, her unfashionably waist-high khakis, the earnest way she spoke. She thought of the photographs of Ashley Jackson, her smile wide and welcoming: innocent.

Natalie knew what people said about kids like Ashley Jackson. They said: Why would she do something like that? What could be that awful? Someone that young, that normal. People didn't understand, didn't know. But Natalie understood. She knew.

What had Ms. McPherson said? *My door is always open.*

⁂

Kathleen felt something at her back—what was that? The wings of time? Was that in a poem? She paused to Google it and found that she had it wrong. *Sadness flies away on the wings of time* was the correct quote. (*That's not true,* she said softly to her computer screen. *Sadness doesn't go anywhere.*)

She read the last entry in Bridget's notebook again:

Solace can come from unlikely sources.

⁂

Natalie's mother had the Saturday shift at Talbots, nine to three, and also Sunday, noon to five.

Natalie said, "Why are you working so *much?*"

Her mother, dressed now in a smart black jacket, and underneath that a cream-colored blouse with ruffles down the front, shrugged and said, "The money is decent, Nat, and it keeps my mind off things."

Natalie flicked her eyes away, not saying, *What things?*

Her mother said, "Are you going to be okay alone here?"

"Sure," said Natalie. "Of course. I've got homework."

But she didn't have homework, not really.

She stood in her silent kitchen. She made a peanut butter and jelly sandwich and consumed it standing up, looking at the mound of mail on the counter.

Which was better, the mother who stayed in her room, or the mother who emerged to fold shirts and rearrange the sales rack at Talbots? Truly, she didn't know.

※

On Sunday she dialed her father's number three times. The first two times he didn't pick up. The third time he answered. He said, "Hang on, Nat," and then she heard him say, "What's that, honey?" to someone else (*Julia,* of course) before returning to her. When he did he said, "I've been meaning to call you all day, sweetie."

She said, "You have?"

"I wanted to let you know that we're going away for the week."

She said, in a hollow voice, "Away?"

He said, "To Punta Cana. We got a last-minute deal, we couldn't turn it down..."

She saw now that she had it all wrong. The Julia in the restaurant, with the kind questions, the carefully tilted head, that woman was an imposter. She didn't care a whit about Natalie.

Her father said, "With the baby coming..."

Julia, like everyone in the world, wanted to secure her own spot.

Natalie didn't say, What about your job?

She didn't say, Where the hell is Punta Cana?

She didn't say, What about *me?*

She said, "Okay, then. Have a great time." And then she hung up.

She thought, I've got to do something.

Twilight came, and then dusk. She opened the front door and stepped out, *into the gloaming,* then stepped back in. She thought about Lucy, and the way her ears pointed straight up when you asked her a question, then lay back down when you stroked her head. She thought that if she had a dog like Lucy—any dog at all, really—she might not feel this yawning emptiness.

⁂

Kathleen left another voice mail for Natalie about the letter. Could she just look for it? Could she please? This was in her archivist's nature—if there was another piece of the puzzle, she wanted to have it. And could she call Kathleen back, let her know that she was okay? Kathleen was worried about her...

Her message was cut off there, the female voice friendly but firm: if Kathleen wanted to rerecord the message, she could press the number two.

⁂

Natalie took a deep breath and pressed the code to hear her voice mail. She had deleted the last one, but this one she wanted to hear—maybe it was her father, calling from Punta Cana. Maybe Julia had drowned in the aquamarine water. (How could you drown in that, though, Natalie didn't know. She had visited the website for the resort whose name her father had mentioned, you could see clear down to the ocean floor, you could see to the ocean floor even from the open-air hotel rooms. Only an idiot could drown in that situation.)

But of course her father hadn't gone to Punta Cana yet. He'd only just told her about the trip. It was Kathleen Lynch. Natalie

277

chewed on her hangnail and listened to the message. A letter, she was supposed to look for a letter that Bridget might have left with the notebook. She was supposed to look for the letter, and then she was supposed to call Kathleen Lynch so they could talk about it. Natalie had mentioned something about that to Kathleen in the beginning; there had been another piece of paper, two or three of them actually, and they were tucked inside the box that was under her bed, alongside her mother's birth certificates, the fake one and the real one. She slid the box out from under her bed and took out the pieces of paper. This handwriting was much harder to decipher than the writing in the notebook (and that was hard enough); the paper was old, and as thin as tissue paper. It seemed like it might dissolve in her hands. She held it up to the light. She couldn't make out any of it, not a single word. She wondered if Neil could, if he was such a whiz at that stuff.

But Neil had deserted her too. Thing number twenty-three that made her sick: deserters.

A text came in while she was thinking about this. She didn't want to look.

But she looked.

Technical difficulties with your Web page, it said. *But don't worry, we will get it back up.*

Delete.

※

Finally, Monday night, a reply from Professor Paterson. He apologized for the delay. He had been out of town and hadn't had access to his email. He hoped he could still offer assistance. (That was heartily ironic, thought Kathleen, an online expert who did not check his email.)

Kathleen read on. As she read she felt her hands grow warm, then clammy; she felt the heat rise to her face. Her heart beat faster.

These situations are always *to be taken with the utmost seriousness,* wrote Professor Paterson.

Do not advise your daughter to ignore the bullying, wrote Professor Paterson. *That is a common mistake parents make.*

It is not the correct response, wrote Professor Paterson.

These things can escalate very quickly, wrote Professor Paterson.

Your daughter needs to know that she has an ally in you, wrote Professor Paterson.

Schools do not *always know how to respond to these situations,* wrote Professor Paterson. *Often there are missteps, errors in communication.*

Kathleen switched from email to Safari to pull up the Web page with the pictures and comments about Natalie.

It wasn't there.

"Gone?" she said out loud.

It was gone.

"Jesus Christ," she said (a lapsed Catholic, she was, lapsing further). "What the hell is going on around here?"

※

It took Natalie a full day to gather her nerve. The day after that, Tuesday, early, before the first bell rang, she stood outside Ms. McPherson's office. There was a light on—from a lamp, not from the overhead—and she could see Ms. McPherson's curly poodle head at the desk, bent forward, writing something. Finally she knocked tentatively, and Ms. McPherson rose and walked to the door. Natalie could see her searching her face for some sort of clue to her name.

"Natalie Gallagher," she said. "I'm a freshman."

"Of course!" said Ms. McPherson. "Natalie, of course. You're here early. You're lucky you caught me. Usually I have first period free and I'm not even here now, but I came in to catch up on some things." She motioned toward the piles of papers on her desk.

"Mount Miscellaneous, that's what I call all of this here." She smiled. "I'm forever trying to whittle it down, and making no progress whatsoever. Now, what can I do for you?"

"Well," said Natalie. She sat carefully on the corner of the slender orange chair toward which Ms. McPherson motioned her. Her hands were shaking and if she didn't hold her quads steady she thought her knees might knock audibly together. She stared hard at the wall, where there was a series of inspirational posters with words in fancy white script written across different nature photos: a waterfall, a field of wildflowers, an ocean at sunset. *If you can dream it, you can become it. What lies behind us and what lies before us are tiny matters compared to what lies within us. Yesterday is history. Tomorrow is a mystery. And today? Today is a gift—that's why they call it the present.*

Load of crap, thought Natalie so spontaneously that she almost said it out loud. But the photograph of the ocean sunset was, after all, very beautiful, and perhaps it was that that calmed her, or perhaps it was Ms. McPherson, and the way she seemed to be leaning forward. The expression *hanging on every word* came to Natalie. Whatever the cause, she felt a loosening from somewhere deep inside her. She felt it all beginning to come out. She began talking, and she told. She told all of it. She told everything, and while she was talking Ms. McPherson sat very still, her elbows resting on the desk, scarcely blinking.

And then, when she was finished, Natalie answered a series of questions put forth by Ms. McPherson, whose face, it seemed to Natalie, had undergone a transformation from sympathetic to earnest to carefully guarded.

No, she didn't have records of any of it.

She had deleted the texts.

"And there was a Web page," she said. "It was awful."

Ms. McPherson tilted her body toward the computer. "Ah," she said. "Well, why don't we have a look at that, together, and see what we come up with."

Natalie cleared her throat. "Actually," she said, "the Web page is gone."

"Gone?"

"Gone. But—"

More questions.

No, there had been no physical harm.

No, she hadn't seen the occupants of the car. But she was sure—

"I'm sure you're sure," said Ms. McPherson. "But did you *see?*"

No. She hadn't seen, not for sure. She had been with another student, with Christian Chapman...

No, he hadn't seen either.

Finally Ms. McPherson sat back and lifted her fingers to her mouth. When she lowered them, she said, "It's a delicate situation, you see, Natalie. Because without proof—without real and solid proof, and even sometimes with it—well, these things happen off of the school property, they're very hard to punish. Hard for us to punish, I should say. They're out of our jurisdiction."

"But you said..." For a moment, Natalie could not go on. "At the assembly, I thought you said—"

"Yes, well." Ms. McPherson straightened in her chair and made a great show of looking through the papers on her desk; for what, Natalie had no idea. "Of course we take it seriously. Anything that concerns our students concerns us."

Natalie thought, Bullshit.

"I mean, to a point. And when things like the Ashley Jackson case occur, when *tragedies* like the Ashley Jackson case occur, I should say, there is certainly a flurry of attention all over the country, mandates come down from on high, from the superintendent, that sort of thing. Mandates to address the problem, I mean. But the lines are blurry when it comes to how much responsibility *we* have in situations like these." When she said the word *we* she pointed to her chest, and Natalie noticed for the first time a stain in the shape of a cloud on her beige shirt. Coffee, maybe, or dried milk. She kept her eyes fixed on the stain because she thought if she looked up she might start to cry.

"Sometimes," said Ms. McPherson, "sometimes we don't understand why kids can be so hurtful to one another."

Fuck you, Natalie wanted to say. It's your job to figure that out.

Ms. McPherson said, "Have you talked to your parents?"

Natalie shook her head gently, so that the tears wouldn't spill out of her eyes. She took a deep breath, and Ms. McPherson continued. "That might be the wisest first step, to talk to your parents. And then together you can figure out what to do about this, uh, this *situation*."

"Problem," corrected Natalie.

"Problem, situation, whatever you want to call it."

Problem, thought Natalie.

"And if things get really out of hand—"

"Then what?"

"Well, then in some cases it's the authorities who need to be contacted."

"The authorities?"

Ms. McPherson cleared her throat. "The police."

"The *police?*" Really and truly Natalie was dumbfounded: Was she supposed to call the *police?* On Hannah Morgan and Taylor Grant? The police! And they would—what? Arrest them? Take them away from the school in handcuffs? That was sure to make her a lot of friends, something like that. The drumming in her ears began anew.

Ms. McPherson must have seen something in Natalie's face because she softened and relented. "Listen, Natalie. I know this is difficult."

In a hard, mean voice, harder and meaner than she meant it to be, Natalie said, "What?"

"All of this." Ms. McPherson made a balletic gesture — absurd, really, with her plump arms — to indicate the inspirational posters, the main office outside her tiny corner, and beyond that the hallway of the school. "Growing up. I've been there, believe me. I know."

Natalie thought, You don't know. You don't remember.

"Typically," Ms. McPherson continued, absorbing the tips of her forefingers between her lips, "typically, you know, bullies choose someone they feel threatened by in some way. It's a defense mechanism, really: strike or be struck."

Natalie nodded mutely; what she was thinking was, *That doesn't help.*

"And I am here for you, I really am. Talk to your parents. If you'd like, have them come in. We'll set up a meeting. We'll talk about it. We'll see where we can go from here. But without any record, without anything official, there's nothing we can *punish.* There's nothing specific we can do."

Natalie said, "But I thought—"

Ms. McPherson leaned toward her. "Yes? You thought?"

Natalie couldn't say it, that she thought the assembly had been called because of her. She thought that someone had come to her rescue. Really it was just a sorry coincidence, having everything to do with Ashley Jackson and nothing to do with her.

Natalie whispered, "Nothing." She gathered her backpack and her coat, both of which she had shed when she first entered, and kept her head steadily down while she looped her arms through the straps.

Needlessly (she thought later) she said, "Thanks." And Ms. McPherson's cheery reply: "You're welcome! Anytime, really."

At this point Natalie could hold her tears back no longer. She glanced around furtively and headed toward the girls' room just outside the office. A safe haven, she thought—the first bell hadn't yet rung—but after all it turned out not to be a safe choice but a treacherous one. She was approaching the entrance when her path was suddenly blocked by the figure of Taylor Grant, who seemed, through the blur of Natalie's tears, to have grown taller but who was actually the same perfect height as ever. She was smirking, and poised like a rattlesnake, coming in for the kill.

Natalie fled: out the door, down the hill, past the wall where she'd sat with Christian Chapman—this was a stinging reminder of the worst of it—then down High Street, toward home. The wind was ferocious and she was running against it. At home she undressed and stood in the shower, making the water as hot as she could stand it, almost scalding her skin. But she wouldn't let herself turn the temperature down. It seemed like this was a test, what she was doing to herself, and she wanted to know what she was made of.

⁖

All around them were girls in trouble. The flip side of that was girls in charge, and really it was hard to know sometimes which was which. Susannah had been one, and Deidre Jordan had been the other. Girls in trouble, girls in charge, and the delicate balance between the two.

Kathleen said to Neil, "I have to go out for a while."

He said, "Want company?"

"Thank you. But no."

She had been storing the notebook and the transcript she'd

made from the notebook in her desk drawer, plus an extra copy of the transcript she'd printed out. There was a lock on the door of the drawer, and a little key to go with it, which she used now to unlock the drawer, slipping the key afterward in the change pocket of her wallet. In her purse she put Natalie's father's family tree. She put the notebook with a printout of the transcribed pages folded inside in a plastic Stop and Shop bag. She wrote a note to Natalie on a piece of paper and stuck it inside the bag: "Glad to return Bridget's notebook to you. Your project must be due soon! I think we can take another look at your father's family tree now." She tucked one of her business cards in with the note. She wrote on the back of it, as she had that first time, her home phone number. After some thought she added the same words: IN CASE OF EMERGENCY. She'd meant it flippantly the first time, sort of, but now she meant it for real. She was thinking of Professor Paterson's email: *These things can escalate very quickly.*

All around them, girls were in trouble.

She drove to Newburyport, took the exit, bore right on the now familiar road, all the way down High Street. (Which house had Bridget lived in with the Turners? A question for another day, that, but one she knew she could find the answer to, when she had time to dig.) Left on Lime Street, right on Milk Street. She rang the doorbell at Natalie's house, but nobody answered. Natalie, of course, would be in school, but where was the not-dead mother? She rang again: nothing. When she listened closely she thought she heard the sound of water running. The not-dead mother must be in the shower.

She waited for a few minutes, but the sound did not abate.

She imagined Bridget O'Connell making her way toward this house in the nighttime, limping toward her future. Maybe not limping. The ankle certainly had healed by then, but the picture was that much more vivid if you included the limping. (Surely she wouldn't have been barefoot either, but Kathleen added that detail for a touch of color as well.)

She propped the bag against the door.

※

Around lunchtime Natalie headed back to school. She did not want to miss English.

Also, once her skin had calmed down from the shower, she was eager to get out of the house which, empty, with the light falling across the kitchen linoleum in a certain way, gave her the strange sensation that she was fading from the world.

Only half of the day left: she could do this. "I can do this," she said, out loud.

When she was coming out of the house she saw, propped next to the doorway, a Stop and Shop bag, and inside it the notebook, with some pages folded inside. With it was a note that said, "Glad to return Bridget's notebook to you. Your project must be due soon! I think we can take another look at your father's family tree now." Also in the bag was a card. Kathleen Lynch's card, identical to the one Natalie had in her room, with the same writing on the back: IN CASE OF EMERGENCY. (Did she write this on all of her cards, hand them out to every visitor to the Archives?) Natalie tucked the card in the front pocket of her backpack, and she put the older papers, the ones she'd found in the black box, in the main part, with the notebook, her gloves, and a peanut butter and jelly sandwich she had made to eat on the way.

Too late she realized that she had miscalculated the time it would take her to get to school. She had arrived too early. English was twenty minutes later, and lunch was still in progress. That wouldn't do, to arrive at this time, making her way in the crowded cafeteria, pulling her sandwich from her backpack, finding somewhere to sit.

So she didn't walk up to the school. She leaned against the stone wall to eat her sandwich. It seemed weeks and weeks ago that she had stood here with Christian Chapman, though really it had been only a few days. While she ate she studied the sky and considered her next steps.

She had three more days to finish the project. Should she go back to Kathleen Lynch? Was there enough time to do something with her father's family tree? Maybe, if she got these older papers, the ones from the box under the bed, to Kathleen they'd be able to pull something together. Or should she start completely from scratch? She had no dog, so she could write no animal autobiography à la Emily Middleton. Perhaps a poetry collection after all—something about nature. She wondered if she could be sufficiently moved by nature to impress Ms. Ramirez. She thought, looking at the clouds skidding across the sky, the slant of the midday light against the bare trees in the yards across from the school, that she could. Emily Dickinson had been. "Nature is what we see—The Hill—the Afternoon." She could do something.

Natalie was thinking about all of this, and trying to remember the next lines of the poem, which she had read for extra credit back in October, when she felt herself shoved roughly from behind, and then, when a familiar voice said, "Sorry!" she turned, feeling the sickening sensation in her gut, in her bowels: the return of the awful. Hannah and Taylor, having somehow scaled the wall (*like superheroes!* she thought, *like evil superheroes!*) were instantly on either side of her.

"Oh," she said. "Hey." She looked quickly from side to side. The lift tickets hanging from their jackets were tattered and their Colorado suntans were fading; they were, like everyone else, adopting the pastiness of a New England winter. But where this might have made them appear less threatening, in fact it did the opposite, and there was something eerie in their solemn, sullen pallor, and in the way the wind lifted their hair behind them.

Taylor said, "I saw you coming out of Ms. McPherson's office this morning."

Natalie offered a tiny "So?"

After that they began speaking in alternating lines, as though they were actors on a stage, with Natalie the hostage audience.

"What did you say to her?" (Taylor.)

"Nothing." She considered saying, *None of your business* but thought better of it.

"You must have said *something,* because she called our parents." (Hannah.)

"We got called into the office."

"We got our cell phones taken away."

"That's your fault, Natalie."

"Thanks a lot, *Natalie.*"

As they spoke they moved closer and closer to Natalie.

"Hey," said Taylor. "Maybe we should take *her* phone. Then we'll be even."

Roughly she pried Natalie's backpack from her and unzipped it. She dug through it, and Natalie remembered the notebook and the papers. Uselessly she said, "Don't—" but it was too late. Taylor pulled the notebook from the backpack and waved it theatrically at Hannah. When she did that, the thin papers, the older ones Natalie was saving for Kathleen Lynch, spilled out onto the sidewalk and were taken immediately by the wind. Natalie made a move to grab at them, but it was futile. "Oooooooh," said Taylor, holding the notebook. "What do we have here?"

"That's mine," said Natalie. "Give it back."

"Nope," said Taylor. "No, I don't think so." She tucked it under her arm and continued looking through the backpack. There was a look on Hannah's face that said she thought they might be going too far, but Taylor Grant didn't notice that. She was well into it now. She found Natalie's phone and opened it, expertly tapping away. She said, "Oh, and by the way. Christian Chapman?"

Natalie felt herself go cold.

"Wait until you see the message you sent him."

"But I didn't—"

"That's what you think."

The world seemed to fall away around Natalie.

"Let's just say he's going to be surprised. I bet he thought you were more *innocent* than this, Natalie Gallagher."

Hannah said, "*Taylor.* Come on. That's too much. Let's go back in."

"And *not* in a good way," said Taylor. Gleefully. "Wait until he *sees!*"

Hannah said, more sharply, "*Taylor.*"

Taylor dropped the backpack and the phone over the wall — the final humiliation was that Natalie had to scramble around to retrieve them — and they were gone.

Natalie still had, in a pocket of her backpack unexplored by Taylor, some of the pills, her mother's salmon-colored pills. She could hardly open the baggie, her hands were shaking so badly.

How many would make her forget?

One, two? More?

How many?

⁓

There was a monkey in the tree that she could see from where she was lying, and he was wearing a red knit sweater, like a stuffed monkey she used to have when she was younger, but this was a real monkey, until he smiled, showing horse teeth, long and yellow.

Then the monkey leaned forward toward Natalie as though he were about to speak, and he became another creature, with a human body and a dog's head; the dog was not any recognizable breed, he was some sort of mangy mutt, like the kind you saw on news programs where they visited poor areas of third-world countries, dogs roaming the streets, kids eating out of gutters.

Where was her phone? Where was the card with Kathleen's number?

And then the tree itself seemed to be leaning forward, all the way forward, like it was going to topple right on top of Natalie.

And then...

※

After she dropped the notebook off at Natalie's house, after she made her slower progress back up Route 1 in the midst of the midday shoppers, Kathleen suddenly felt as though she could go no farther. She pulled over into the parking lot of the Christmas Tree Shops and sat for a minute.

In the far corner of the parking lot were towers of snow and ice made gray and ugly by car exhaust, like something from an evil fairy tale. Kathleen watched an overweight woman heave herself out of her car and make arduous progress toward the store. The woman turned to her companion, also female—but younger, leaner—and said something that made them both laugh. What did this woman have to smile about, sloshing as she was through dirty puddles on her way to poke through bins of bargains made by tots in faraway factories? Yet she was smiling. What should have cheered Kathleen—the resiliency of the human spirit!—instead depressed her.

All of it depressed her: the cars whizzing past, wearing their winter coats of grime and filth, the NPR voices on the radio, droning about civil war in some African country, even the birds overhead, coming perilously close to the telephone wires. All of it. It was all too much.

Kathleen was tired, but there was so much she wanted to do. She wanted to go back to the Archives and look up the death record for little baby James Turner, just to confirm that he'd actually existed, that he'd actually died. She remembered a line from the notebook, about James, how his head was *turned at a strange angle, an angle that couldn't be right.* She shuddered.

There was more to be done, lots to be done.

She wanted to drive to Waltham to look up the records from the 1930 census; she wanted to see the listing for the Callaghan family. If Declan Callaghan was a citizen, they would all be listed, the whole family, Bridget and whatever children had been born by then. She wanted to double-check the rest of Natalie's father's work; she wanted to complete the family tree for Natalie. She wanted to put it all down, diagram it: the fact that James Callaghan was really half Turner, which led to a whole *different* branch of the family tree. She wanted to explore that too.

Later, another time, she wanted to go deeper into Bridget's family: she wanted to find the married sister in Lynn, her children, who would be Bridget's children's cousins.

And then to the village in County Kerry—there was potential there too, all of those siblings left behind.

But she was tired. She was so, so tired. She thought she could lay her head down on the steering wheel and sleep, right there in the parking lot, if she let herself.

※

She didn't. She kept driving. This time the sign outside Prince Pizzeria said, MARY ME MARY and whether it was a spelling mistake or the missing *R* had floated from the sign and out into the traffic was anybody's guess.

Even the prospect of Neil, with his bright chatter about little Henri, did not appeal to Kathleen. So, pulling over again, this time in the parking lot of Kelly's Roast Beef, with its bright green sign (*Our sandwich platters are awesome!* was written in neon orange), she dug in her bag for her cell phone. It was an ancient thing, kept only for emergencies, incapable, as far as she knew, of texts or any of the rest of it. It was a phone that Natalie, if she were to see it, would laugh at. Kathleen left a message for her supervisor. Sick, she said in the message. Came on suddenly. Felt feverish: could be contagious. "That time of the year, you know." Out the rest of the day. Do her best to be in tomorrow.

⁂

So it was home she went, home to Lucy, who didn't rise to meet Kathleen. This was unusual, Lucy was like an English butler, always at the door but never in your face about it. Kathleen's heart was heavy with trepidation as she walked to her bedroom. But Lucy's chest was rising and falling, and her tongue was partly revealed between her lips in her familiar position of deep sleep. Kathleen felt around Lucy's chest, under the thick hair. *She* didn't feel any mass. Maybe the vet was mistaken. She'd take her in again next week, when Dr. Quinn was back from his ski vacation.

Kathleen was so tired from the events and the effort of the past several days that she lay right by the dog bed with Lucy and fell asleep. She dreamed about Bridget, and also about Susannah, and about Natalie too. In the dream, everything she touched was marred by the specter of girls in trouble, girls in danger. Ashley Jackson's mother setting out hats and noisemakers for a birthday party; Bridget O'Connell's parents saying good-bye to her when she left her little village for America, the adventure of a lifetime. She herself, tying Susannah's first pair of sneakers, pulling the tongue tight, the little rhyme she used to say:

> *Bunny ear, bunny ear, side by side*
> *Round the tree and jump inside*

Through the hole and pull it tight
If you made bunny ears, you did it right.

Then Susannah, younger, much younger, the age of Melissa Henderson's baby, her tiny satin lips pressed together in sleep, the soft down on her head, her floppy little body nestled into Kathleen's for nursing, and then for sleep. Oh, to hold that baby again, to have another chance at all of it. She was sleeping still, but she felt the memory like an ache deep in her body, in her bones.

※

The three girls were bound together so closely in her dream, intertwined, really, one becoming the next becoming the next, that when the ringing of the phone roused her she scarcely knew the decade, or who she was.

The voice on the other end was brisk, brooking no questions. Calling from Anna Jaques Hospital in Newburyport, the woman said. Kathleen's name was on a card brought in with a patient earlier that day, a patient whose parents they were unable to reach. Did she know how to reach the parents?

Kathleen felt a little dizzy. She thought briefly of Gregory, of his poor broken heart, broken in the real sense. Had he felt this way, at the end?

Of course Kathleen knew the answer, but she whispered: "Who?"

A Natalie Gallagher. Her name was written on a label inside her backpack.

Kathleen had to sit down in the chair by the phone. ("Sit down!" people said when they had bad news for you. She used to think that was out of politeness, before Gregory died, but she knew after that it was out of necessity because really your legs could give way.

She had fallen in a heap when she learned about Gregory, a little puddle of shock and bewilderment.)

She said, "What happened?"

"I'm sorry, ma'am," came the voice. "But we can't tell you anything, because you're not related to the patient. We're calling only because this card was in the backpack, and because it's after school hours now and we can't get any information from the school. We've called the only number we could find, the home number that we found in her cell phone, but nobody answered. The cell had a couple other numbers too, but nobody answered those. Nothing else in the backpack, just part of a sandwich and a card with this number."

The woman had a North Shore accent: *numbah*.

Kathleen stood and began gathering her things, putting her shoes back on, rooting for her car keys in the pocket of the jacket she'd thrown on the bed. Lucy lifted her head only inches from the bed and then settled it back down, immune to the urgency. "You have to tell me," said Kathleen. "You have to tell me what happened, and if she's okay."

The voice relented slightly. "I can't give you details. But she's okay. I really shouldn't have told you that, I could lose my job."

Kathleen didn't care a nickel about this woman's job.

The woman continued: "What I'm asking is, do you have any way to get in touch with her parents? Guardian? Whoever?"

"No," said Kathleen. "But I'm coming up there."

"We can't release her to you, it's really got to be her parents or a legal guardian."

"I'm coming up," said Kathleen. "Just tell me how to get there. I know how to get to Newburyport. Just tell me how to get to the hospital."

The woman sighed. "Okay. One-thirteen to Rawson, right at Rawson, top of the hill. But really, we can't—"

"I'm on my way," said Kathleen.

"I don't know where you're coming from, but since you're not related—"

"I'm leaving now."

She was gathering a leash and a water bottle for Lucy when she noticed the light blinking on her answering machine. She pressed the button. The call had come earlier that day, but she hadn't noticed the light when she'd come home. She'd been too worried about Lucy. Natalie's voice: "Kathleen...Kathleen, I did something. I took a pill, two pills. I feel really weird. Kathleen, can you come get me? I need you."

She rewound, played it again. *I need you...I need you.*

"Right on Rawson, top of the hill," the woman on the phone had told Kathleen.

She hadn't stopped to write that down—no time to stop, no time to do anything but get in the car and go, go, *go*—so she repeated it the whole way up: right on Rawson, top of the hill, right on Rawson, top of the hill.

In front of one of the High Street homes a boy, young and somber, four or maybe five, ski jacket zipped over snow pants, worked a shiny scooter up and down the sidewalk; his pace was glacial and uncertain but, even so, he had a bike helmet affixed firmly to his head. Kathleen thought, Parents! Careful, always, but so often about the wrong things. She should know.

Right on Rawson, top of the hill.

Ashley Jackson turning the key in the ignition in her parents' garage, Susannah lying on her bed, her face to the wall: in danger, all over, girls in danger. Right on Rawson, top of the hill.

It was a small hospital, a community hospital, sitting right in the middle of a residential neighborhood, but the emergency department, a concrete building annexed onto the red brick of the rest of the hospital, looked sturdy and dependable. Two ambulances sat idly in front; had Natalie come here in one of *these?*

⁂

Looking back on it later Kathleen felt like a character in a movie, the way she burst through the doors and into the ER's waiting room; she had run from the parking lot, she knew her hair was crazy, she knew her eyes were crazy, and crazy, too, was the way she said, "Where is she? Natalie Gallagher. Where is she?"

"Did I talk to you? You Kathleen Lynch?" This must be the woman from the phone: North Shore accent, bottle blond, all business. Her nametag said THERESA.

Kathleen nodded.

"I told you, on the phone, we can't tell you anything. If you're not related."

"I'm related," said Kathleen.

The woman's eyes flicked over Kathleen, then to a television suspended in the corner across from a constellation of fluorescent orange chairs. "You're not related. You already told me that. We're trying to reach her mother or her father." *Muthah, fathah.* "We left messages at home, we just had the one number." She peered closely at Kathleen. "You don't have another number for her parents, do you?"

No. No other number.

A twenty-something man in scrubs behind the admissions desk pointed a remote control at the television. He paused on one channel, and Kathleen saw the red CNN letters, a scene of rubble in some faraway city, people running.

"Where's that?" said Theresa, looking past Kathleen.

"I don't know." The young man had already changed the channel, some sitcom, two married people arguing in a kitchen, why did every sitcom feature two people arguing in a kitchen?

"Please," said Kathleen. "Please, can you let me see her? Can you tell me what's going on?" She was reminded of a long-forgotten feeling from childhood, powerlessness at the hands of an adult, a teacher, her mother, her father, someone who stood, like this woman, in front of the very thing Kathleen wanted most.

"I really can't," she said. "Hospital policy. If I don't follow it, I could lose my job." She tapped her nails on the counter and looked down at a clipboard that was resting there.

Then the door opened again. "*That's* the mother," said Kathleen. "That's Natalie's mother."

Theresa stepped forward. "You the mother? Natalie Gallagher's mother?"

Carmen nodded; she didn't see Kathleen at all, or, if she saw her, she didn't acknowledge her. "What the hell is going on?" she said. "I got home from work, had all of these messages—"

"Your daughter...," said Theresa.

"Where is she? Where's Natalie?"

"I'll take you to her," said Theresa. "She's okay, she's sleeping, she woke up for a little bit, and now she's sleeping again. It looks like she might have taken some pills—"

"Some *what?*"

That's when Carmen saw Kathleen. "What are you doing here?" Then, to Theresa, "What's she doing here?"

"I called her," said Theresa. "We couldn't reach anyone else, and your daughter had this woman's number on her."

Carmen said, "I don't understand. How'd this happen? What pills?"

"There were pills in her backpack," said Theresa. "In a baggie. We've identified them as Ambien. We don't know how many she took." From somewhere she produced the baggie and held it out to Carmen.

"Two," whispered Kathleen, but nobody was listening to her.

Carmen's face went pale. "Those are mine. Those are my

sleeping pills." She made no move to take them out of Theresa's hands, and so Kathleen did—she'd take them into the bathroom and flush them down the toilet, put an end to all of this.

"She was awake for a while," said Theresa, "which means it's likely she took only one or two. She couldn't remember."

"Two," said Kathleen, louder this time, and both Carmen and Theresa stopped and stared at her.

"What do you mean?" asked Carmen. "How do *you* know?"

"She called me. She left me a message."

"She called *you?*" said Carmen. "What do you mean? She called *you,* and not me?"

"Whoever she called," said Theresa. "Doesn't matter." (*Mattah.*) "She couldn't remember. But don't panic when you see her, she's got an NG tube in."

Carmen said, "A what?"

"A nasogastric tube. Standard procedure in a case like this."

Again Carmen said, "A *what?*"

"A tube in her nose," said Theresa. "It looks worse than it is, don't worry."

"Wait," Carmen said to Kathleen. "Wait out here."

The channel-surfing man settled on CNN again. (Did this man not have a speck of work to do?) "Earthquake," he said.

The screen was showing a lot of children: children everywhere, children covered in fine white dust, children wearing Catholic school uniforms with socks pulled up to their knees. "Where?" said Kathleen. She was mostly just making conversation; the tragedy at hand seemed, at the moment, bigger and more important than whatever was happening on the television screen. Closer to home, as it were.

Just then Carmen came back out, nodded at Kathleen. "She's awake now," she said. "She's asking for you." She looked to the ceiling and back down again, right at Kathleen, and Kathleen could see that her eyes were wet. "Not me," she said. "She wants you."

So it was that Kathleen didn't hear the young man's answer, didn't hear the sound track to it all—the constant wail of sirens, and the British-inflected voice of the CNN reporter, didn't hear any of it.

❋

Kathleen followed Carmen back down a fluorescent-lit hallway and into a curtained cubicle.

Natalie, lying in the hospital bed, looked even frailer and paler and thinner than she usually looked; also, her height was obscured by her position on the bed, so she looked younger too.

"Hey," said Kathleen softly. She reached out and stroked Natalie's hair.

"I dreamed you were coming, you were like this big angel..." Natalie's eyes closed and she drifted off.

Theresa peeked her head around the curtain. "Everything okay?" she said. Kathleen was beginning to soften toward her. Despite the Massachusetts accent, despite the hospital setting, there was something of the old-fashioned diner waitress in her, gruff but sincere: she'd get your egg order right, no matter what. Theresa crooked her finger at Carmen. "This way, please, I've got forms for you—"

Kathleen said, "Go ahead. I'll sit with her."

Carmen said, "Well—"

And Kathleen, firmly: "Go ahead. She's in good hands, I promise." For the first time since Natalie had walked into the Archives, she actually believed that.

When Carmen had gone, Kathleen pulled up a chair and sat beside the bed. Natalie's eyes fluttered again and she said, "I just wanted to forget for a few minutes. I just wanted to go to sleep. I just...I thought it would be easier to sleep."

"I know," said Kathleen.

"I didn't expect—"

"I know," said Kathleen. "I understand. Shhh, you don't have to explain."

"My project is due Friday. And I haven't done any of it. I haven't done anything!"

"Don't worry about that," said Kathleen. "Natalie, don't worry about that."

"I never did any of it," Natalie repeated. "I thought I was going to do this really great thing, and I never even finished the notebook. I don't even know the whole story. And the letter! I found the letter you called about."

"You did?"

"But they took it, Hannah and Taylor. It's gone, ruined."

This was a blow, but Kathleen tried not to let it show.

"They took the notebook too, it's all gone. They took everything. They did something with my phone...oh, God, I think they sent something to Christian..." Natalie tried to push herself up on one elbow and gently Kathleen guided her back to a prone position.

"It's okay," said Kathleen. "It's all going to be okay."

"No," said Natalie. "No, it's not. How am I ever going to go back to school...after all this...I can never—" Her shoulders began to shake, and she started to cry in the silent way that Kathleen learned to cry after Gregory died, because she did it so often it became second nature. Sometimes she did it in public: she had to learn to be quiet about it because she never knew when the crying would come, or if she'd be able to control it.

There was movement and sound outside in the hallway, someone ran by, someone called out, and Kathleen was reminded that there were other emergencies in the world, even in this town, that were not hers or Natalie's.

"Natalie," said Kathleen. "Listen to me. It's going to be okay."

Natalie said, "How? *How* is it going to be okay?"

And all at once it fit together. The metaphor Kathleen reached for first was the pieces of a jigsaw puzzle, but, no, that was too easy, this was something more grinding and laborious, like the plates of the earth sliding together.

And if that seemed too grandiose a comparison, who could blame Kathleen Lynch for that, because she understood, sitting in this hospital room, by this bed, beside this fragile girl, that it had all led to this. All the false starts, the bad advice, the times she'd tried to help Natalie and couldn't. That was never her role. Natalie was not a replacement for Susannah, not a do-over. Kathleen's role was to bridge the past and the present; that's who she'd been for twenty-six years, that's what she did every day of her working life, and she was being called upon to do it now. So she would.

She took a deep breath and she said, "Natalie, it's not lost, even if the notebook itself is lost. I've been reading it, all this time. I typed the whole thing out for you. I have a copy for you, back in my desk."

"You did?" Natalie didn't try to sit up again; she was looking directly at the ceiling. "You do?"

"I do. I know it wasn't mine to do that with, I know it wasn't my business—"

"No, no," said Natalie. "I'm glad you did."

Kathleen said, "How about I tell you? I'll tell you everything I know."

"Now?" asked Natalie.

"Well, I meant a little later, when you're more yourself," said Kathleen. "Another day, maybe. There's no hurry."

"No. Now." Here was something Kathleen had forgotten: in some situations, and this was one of them, there was simply no arguing with a teenage girl.

So Kathleen began to talk. She started at the beginning, and she told the whole story, everything she could possibly recount from reading the notebook, all of Bridget's story. She tried to recall it in as much detail as possible: Elsie's shoes, the way little baby James smelled, the trip to Boston for the abortion that never happened. She pulled Natalie's father's paper from her purse. She kept looking toward the doorway, waiting for Carmen to come and take it from her, or to come and take Natalie herself from her, but nobody came, so she kept talking.

"Here's the connection," she said, pointing at the paper. Natalie pushed herself up again, and Kathleen reached behind her to arrange the pillow to allow her to sit. She continued. "Your father got a good start, but he stopped with James. And even if he'd kept going, he never would have known James's story, *never* would have known that Dr. Turner was your great-great-grandfather, never would have known about the other baby James. We never would have known that without the notebook that you found." She knew Natalie was tired, but she kept going. "You see, here? Your father went just two generations back, and then he stopped. He didn't get as far as Bridget, didn't know that Bridget was your" — she paused, ticking off the generations on the paper, just to be sure — "great-great-grandmother."

"Yeah? She was?"

"She was. You have all kinds of roots now — two different families, two different directions to go in."

"Yeah," said Natalie softly. "But the project...school —" She looked stricken.

Kathleen thought of Bridget, walking in the darkness from the Turners' house to Declan's house, away from one life and toward another. "Listen, Natalie," she said. "Look at Bridget's story. *She* thought everything was over that one awful night, she thought there was no hope left, nothing to live for, and then look what happened. There was a whole other life for her, a new beginning, children, life, love, all of it, waiting for her. She only had to reach out and take it."

She watched Natalie absorbing this.

Then she said, "I want to tell you something, Natalie. I want to tell you about the night Susannah left."

It reminded her a little of confession, except in place of the priest and the rosary was a girl with an NG tube. No forgiveness, not here, but not really there either. It didn't really exist, forgiveness, did it?

Kathleen told Natalie the whole story and then she paused. Natalie was listening, rapt. Kathleen said, "My daughter fell, Natalie, and I didn't catch her. If I hadn't left that night, if I hadn't gone to the store..." Then she said, "Everyone has a moment they would go back to if they could, to make things different. That's mine. Maybe you had yours today, but that doesn't mean things are over."

Kathleen had been standing at the kitchen phone when she learned about Gregory. This was in the days when phones were tethered securely to the wall. Kathleen thought if she went back to that apartment in Marblehead she'd find the same phone on the same wall—or, if it had been removed, at least its ghostly outline, the telltale rectangle. They wouldn't say anything specific over the phone, only that she had to come to the hospital immediately. But she knew it from the way the person on the other end spoke, a woman, maybe a woman just like Theresa. "As quickly as you can," said the woman. So Kathleen had gathered Susannah, and she'd gone. This was before car-seat laws were the way they are now. Susannah and a jumble of blankets in the backseat, Kathleen driving as fast as she could. She dared the cops to stop her, and none did.

She didn't see Gregory die, didn't see Susannah leaving: she'd missed everything.

She looked again at Natalie, studied the freckles on her cheeks. She said, "You think this is where you are forever, all of this high school stuff, all this stuff with your friends or not friends, but really you're just at the beginning of the rest of your life, all the good things that are coming. All of this will be just a blip for you one day. I know it. Do you believe that, Natalie Gallagher?"

Natalie didn't meet Kathleen's eyes, and her voice was so low that if Kathleen hadn't been listening very carefully she might not have heard Natalie's whispered affirmation. But Kathleen was listening, maybe as carefully as she'd ever listened to anything, and so she did hear it.

Natalie's eyes were closing, closing...closed. Kathleen watched her. Her face, in repose, looking so young and innocent that Kathleen could imagine what she looked like as a child, maybe even an infant, rocked to sleep in the same house where Bridget O'Connell Callaghan had rocked her own babies to sleep, little James, and the rest of them, the ones that came after. Kathleen stopped talking and she sat very still and watched Natalie breathing, watched her chest move up and down, watched her eyes twitching underneath her eyelids. She watched her the way you watch an infant, when every breath is precious and new.

All around her, girls were in trouble, but here was a girl who was safe, and Kathleen would watch over her, while she slept, and then some.

※

Kathleen returned to the waiting room in time to hear Theresa say to Carmen, "We're going to have to admit her overnight, you know, for observation, a room with a cardiac monitor."

Carmen said, "*Over*night? Really?"

"A precaution," said Theresa.

There were a lot of things Kathleen wanted to say to Carmen, none of them particularly nice.

But she looked at Carmen, and she saw herself. Struggling. Doing her best on her own. The two were more alike than not.

Theresa said, "I mean. I got two kids myself. It's not my business, *technically*, once she leaves here. But. If this was my kid, I would look into what's going on, at school and whatever." Theresa squinted. "You got that? If it was more pills, if it was a bunch, we'd have to admit her to a psych ward, inpatient, any psych ward that had a bed available. You know that, right?"

Carmen nodded, and Kathleen nodded. They hadn't known, neither of them had known that.

A phone on the desk rang. "For you, Terry," said the guy in the scrubs, and Theresa turned to take it, her attention shifting away.

Kathleen thought again of the women in the Christmas Tree Shops parking lot—battered, maybe, but not beaten down. Resilient. She looked again at the television.

"What a mess," said Carmen, sighing, looking past Kathleen. At first Kathleen thought she was talking about them, about Natalie, but then she realized that her attention was fixed on the television screen. "Did you see that? Haiti?"

Kathleen said, "What? *Where?*"

"Haiti," said Carmen again.

"Oh God," she said. "Oh *God!* Neil."

※

This time she *did* get a speeding ticket, $198, just before the turnoff to Route 1, the cop immune to her explanations, not that she tried that hard. She took her punishment like a lady, holding out her knuckles to be rapped, like the good Catholic girl she once was. And then she drove even faster. She was tempting fate, but she had to get home, because she thought Neil would be there waiting for her, on her porch, head in his hands: he had nowhere else to go.

※

For how long could they sit there in Kathleen's living room and watch the wrenching images? Forever, apparently. As evening turned to night (the gloaming came and went without ceremony), they kept watching. Over and over they saw the shots of the buildings tilted crazily, like a child's diorama carelessly knocked over. (Kathleen kept thinking of a fifth-grade project of Susannah's, a model town with buildings made out of egg cartons and toilet paper rolls.) The same reporter who had been speaking when Kathleen was in the hospital was speaking now.

"What is she so *fucking* calm about?" said Neil through white lips. "Isn't she *there?*" He didn't turn to apologize for the curse, and if Kathleen needed proof that he was in pain there it was. Not that she needed proof.

They kept showing the bleeding children.

Neil had his cell phone and every now and then he picked it up and pressed buttons frantically. "Nothing," he said over and over again. "There's nothing going through."

"Of course there isn't," said Kathleen. "There's probably no point in *calling* now. I mean the entire infrastructure—"

"I know," said Neil. "But I have to do something. What else can I do?" He looked at Kathleen as though he expected an actual answer, and that's when she remembered the pills, which she hadn't given back to Carmen, and hadn't flushed down the toilet.

"Take one," she said. "To help you sleep. You need to sleep."

"Here?" croaked Neil.

"Yes, here. That way I can keep an eye on you." This gave her something to do: she gathered extra sheets from the linen closet, and a pillow from her under-bed storage box. The sofa in the living room was a hide-a-bed, and she worked at the creaky springs until she had the whole thing pulled out and ready to be made up. She would have put him in Susannah's old room, but she was storing things in there; it needed a good clean-out before receiving a guest.

"All this trouble," said Neil. "I can just go home."

"Absolutely *not*," she said. "I'm not leaving you alone."

The buildings were continuing to crumble, the reporter said. There was dark commentary about the building codes—they didn't exist. The presidential palace had gone down.

"Oh, *God*," whimpered Neil. "Look at that."

Kathleen reached for the remote.

Neil said, "Don't. What if they show Adam. Or Henri. *Don't.*"

Kathleen said, "Oh, Neil. What are the odds?"

"But they might," he said. "It's possible. They might."

※

Kathleen had thought that the letter to Fiona would explain something, some missing piece from Bridget's life, but really that was probably just the terrier-like nature of the archivist, unwilling to let any little detail go. Fiona herself was of course long dead and gone. When, and how? Maybe Kathleen would find out someday, maybe she'd send herself over to Ireland to do some real research, the hands-and-knees, wiping-mud-off-a-gravestone sort, down and dirty. You weren't a real archivist if you'd never done that, were you?

She sat on her bed and made a mental accounting. Bridget's notebook: gone. The letter to Fiona: gone. Maybe they'd be found someday, waterlogged, washed up on the banks of the Merrimac, indecipherable. But for now: gone.

She had thought, this whole time, reading the notebook, trying to find the connections to Natalie, that she was doing something for Natalie, for her project. But that's not what the notebook was for, in the end; it wasn't a story all by itself, no beginning and end to it, really. (It made you wonder how many other genealogies had a missing piece to their stories.) Bridget's notebook was an instrument, a device planted by someone to bring Natalie into Kathleen's path. (Not God, Kathleen didn't believe in God, at least not the God of her youth and young adulthood, the incense, the crucifix, the stained glass Stations of the Cross, all that kneeling and asking for forgiveness. But she believed in something.)

She tiptoed out to the living room to check on Neil. He was sleeping deeply, his mouth open, his limbs sprawled across the sofa. He was the second person that day to have fallen asleep under Kathleen's watch. You didn't do that, you didn't fall asleep in someone else's care, unless you felt safe. That was something.

She took Lucy out in the little scrap of yard, not wanting to leave Neil for too long. There was a spectacular moon, nearly full, and she stood for a moment looking at it—same sky watching over Natalie and her mother, same sky over Haiti, over Ashley Jackson's grieving parents, same sky that not so long ago had watched over Bridget O'Connell, then Bridget Callaghan, it was all the same, the sky above them.

Yes, that's what she'd do, she'd take some time off from work, Lord knows she had enough vacation time saved up; she'd give herself a trip to Ireland as a present. Not right away, not until she knew what was going to happen with Lucy. She wasn't going to fail anyone else who needed her, wasn't going to abandon anyone.

"A present," she said aloud.

She hadn't saved Susannah, but she had saved Natalie, sort of; she'd saved Neil, in a way.

A present for what?

A present for surviving.

Lucy lifted her head and regarded Kathleen and it seemed that they exchanged an important thought.

Was it wrong to see something in any of this?

Was it wrong to believe?

⁂

Natalie's mother thought she should wait until the following Tuesday to go back to school, that Monday being a school holiday; her father, returned from Punta Cana with the peeling remnants of a sunburn on his face and along the upper reaches of his neck, thought so too. But Natalie didn't want to wait any longer, she was too anxious, the waiting gave her a feeling of permanent unease in her gut, so off she went on Friday, but not until after lunch. She couldn't quite imagine walking in in the morning, part of the rest of the school, the waves of bodies, all those stares and whispers.

Her father showed up to escort her in the Lexus "just to make sure you're okay," but she made him drop her across the street, on the corner of Kent, where she waited until he drove away before heading into the building. Though she would have bet real money that he was circling the block and zipping down Merrimac to come up a different street and observe her from another angle.

Her legs were trembling. She almost turned back; she wanted, very briefly, to run to the safety of her father's car. But she thought of the notebook, and the story Kathleen had told her, and she thought of Bridget O'Connell walking through the dark streets of Newburyport, the same streets she had just traveled, and she forced herself to go on.

She got to English as early as she could, earlier even than Ms. Ramirez, and she stood by her desk, waiting for her, listening to all the sound and movement in the hallway. She'd forgotten, already, how loud all of that was. But it was Hannah Morgan, not Ms. Ramirez, who came in first.

"Hey," said Hannah, and softly Natalie answered back: "Hey."

They studied each other for a fraction of a moment: they could have been two animals waiting to pounce, or two long-lost relatives ready to embrace. It was anybody's guess, really.

Hannah said, "Natalie—"

Natalie surprised herself by how hard her voice sounded when she said, *"What?"* It sounded like a stranger's voice.

"I just…"

"You just what?" Natalie considered her, and it was like they were nine years old again, facing off over a game of Monopoly: Boardwalk for Park Place. "You just what, Hannah?"

Hannah said, "I just didn't think you'd be back already."

"Well. I wanted to tell her why I didn't finish my project."

Hannah looked down, then back up, and her voice caught. "Natalie, she knows why."

"She does?" Natalie fixed her eyes on the back of the classroom, on the view Ms. Ramirez had from where she stood.

"Everybody knows."

Of course Natalie had expected this. You didn't get driven away from high school in an ambulance in the middle of the day without people knowing about it, it wasn't exactly a slow news day when that happened, but hearing the words opened the wound anew; Natalie felt a little nauseous.

Something was missing from Hannah—but what was it? Oh, of *course,* it was the space around her, the space around her was empty; Hannah was alone.

Natalie said, "Where's Taylor?"

"Didn't you hear?" said Hannah.

"Hear what?" (And from whom was she supposed to hear it? She'd been holed up like a hermit all week—so bored, in fact, that she'd finally hooked up the Wii.)

"She might not be coming back. She might be transferring, to this private school down in Manchester."

Natalie took a moment to absorb this, then said, carefully, not really sure she wanted to hear the answer, "Because of me?"

"I don't know." Hannah made herself busy with her notebook, then looked up at Natalie, squinting. "Yeah, I guess so. I mean, yeah, of course because of you. A lot of shit went down because of what happened. A *lot* of shit. Taylor's parents found everything on her phone, and they got the school involved—the principal, everyone. The parents are doing something, there's all these committees..."

"What about your phone?"

"What do you mean?"

"Didn't you have your phone taken away too? Didn't someone look at your phone? Your mom or something?" Natalie thought of Mrs. Morgan, all that Christmas baking, the clean, dry socks, the slippers fresh from the package.

Hannah studied her. "Yeah, she took it away," she said. "But she never looked. And then she gave it back. Anyway, most of it was on Taylor's."

So, thought Natalie, it would end like this, Hannah getting away with everything, slipping away like a criminal in the dead of the night.

The bell rang then, and there was a great chaotic push from the hallway into the classroom, a mélange of colors and shapes and sounds. Ms. Ramirez entered with the students. Speaking over it all, Hannah said, "Natalie?"

"What?"

Natalie saw that Hannah's eyes were wet. Her mascara smudged in the corner of one of her eyes when she reached up to wipe at it. By then the classroom was nearly full, although Christian Chapman hadn't come in yet. He was always late. Natalie didn't take her seat. Neither did Hannah. And Natalie waited, they all waited, to see what would happen next.

EPILOGUE

For two solid weeks Neil stayed with Kathleen, all but abandoning his condo. He didn't want to go back there, didn't want to see the crib stained with Australian timber oil, the coffee table corners carefully housed in pieces of foam, the pale green curtains decorated with pictures of small smiling elephants. Why elephants? Why smiling? Kathleen, who went by there daily to pick up the mail, to gather clothes and books that Neil needed, didn't know. She made up Susannah's room for Neil, and she liked, late at night, to stand outside the door, hearing Neil's steady breathing.

He had his own stash of Ambien, prescribed to him by his primary, and dutifully he took one before bed each night. He slept so heavily that when it was time to get up for work, Kathleen sometimes had to shake him by the shoulders.

The vet called to schedule Lucy's procedure. Kathleen didn't call back. She was nothing if not a researcher, and she had done her research. She knew there was nothing to be done; she knew that sedating a dog Lucy's age was a risk in itself. She knew that if the news was what she expected it to be—what Dr. Ryan had all but told her it would be—there wasn't much to be done then either. She left the Archives at lunch every day and drove home to see to Lucy. At night, while she and Neil watched terrible television and drank red wine together, she brushed Lucy, paying special attention to the thick coat over her chest. She walked with Lucy around Castle Island, and when Lucy rasped and stopped to rest, Kathleen stopped to rest too.

She knew that when Lucy showed discomfort she would march right in to that puppy-faced doctor and ask him for whatever drugs would make the dog feel better.

"And then," she told Neil, "I'm going to march right in to my own doctor and ask for the same thing."

"I'll go with you," he said. "Both places."

Three times a day, because she'd told Neil she would, she called in to his home voice mail to check the messages. She did it when he wasn't there because the expectant look on his face, and then the crush of disappointment when there was nothing, was too much for her to handle. He carried his cell phone everywhere he went; he slept with it under his pillow, and when he went to the bathroom (he told Kathleen) he rested it on the edge of the sink.

Kathleen kept saying, "Neil, honey, anything is possible. You may hear from him yet—"

"Yeah," said Neil. "I know."

Every day Kathleen made breakfast for them both, practically spooning oatmeal into Neil's mouth the way she would for a child—the way she had when Susannah was eighteen months old and on a self-imposed hunger strike. Even so, he lost weight. His pants hung off him. He tightened his belt to its smallest hole. He wore the same gray T-shirt and boxer shorts to bed each night; Kathleen snuck them away every few days to wash them. She suggested he take some time, a week, more if he needed it, without going to the Archives.

"No," he said. "What am I going to do alone all day here? I'll go crazy."

So they drove in together, listening to NPR—there was other

news going on, there was the swine flu and the Australian Open and the Taliban. When stories about relief efforts in Haiti came up, Kathleen reached for the dial to turn it off and Neil always stopped her.

When the news came through about the American Baptist missionaries from Idaho, they both sat up straighter.

One day Kathleen searched through death indexes (a gloomy name, that!) for 1926 until she found James Turner. Town: Newburyport, Mass. Age: eighteen months. Cause of death: fall down stairs. Here it was. It was real, then. A real person. At the Department of Public Health in Dorchester, there would be a real death certificate. And only three of them alive today — Kathleen, Natalie, Neil — who knew the story behind it. She would call Natalie, they would go together to the Department of Public Health. She'd made Natalie promise that they'd keep working on this together. Any weekend day she could make it down, and when she couldn't, Kathleen would go to her. No more fake early releases, though, Kathleen had made her swear to that.

She couldn't find a listing for Bridget Callaghan in the death indexes. The only explanation she could think of for that, of course, was that Bridget hadn't died in this country, that she had, somehow, made it back to Ireland, that she'd died there.

She went to find Neil to tell him that. He was sitting at his desk, white-lipped, gripping his phone. He leapt up when he saw her.

"Oh, Neil," she said, misreading his expression for grief. "Oh, Neil, sweetie." She moved toward him. "Come here," she said, although by then she had reached him, and when he started to cry, she said, "Oh, honey, it's okay."

"That was Adam," he said. "That was *Adam*. He just called."

"What?"

"He just called. He called from the embassy..." His words tripped over themselves. "There are kids everywhere, kids lined up in hallways...the staff is overwhelmed, it could take weeks more to get out, Adam lost his passport in the quake, it took forever to get his identity verified at the embassy, he was separated from Henri, but then he found him—"

Neil was talking so quickly it was difficult for Kathleen to make out each word.

"All the paperwork is gone, everything is gone, I have to make copies from what we have at home, thank *God* he's so anal..."

Kathleen said, "Oh, *Neil.*" She tried to maintain composure, but a tear leaked out.

Finally he took a breath and they regarded each other. "You saved me, Kathleen Lynch. These last two weeks, you saved me. You kept me alive, I mean it."

She said, "Oh, come on. Stop it." But she felt some latent emotion, something she had thought long dead, rebloom inside her.

"I've got to go home!" Neil said. Home to the pale green room, the cushioned corners, the clothes folded inside the dresser. Now he could prepare for homecoming.

⁕

And Kathleen could prepare for...what? First to help Lucy through what was to come, and then she'd book the trip to Ireland. She would take a month to do it. No, she would take six weeks. A compromise: five weeks. She had that much vacation; she had acres of vacation. She had plenty of money saved. She hardly spent anything on herself.

The more she thought about it, the more it seemed odd to go all the way there and research someone else's family, so she would pull out her own research and prepare that too. She'd visit both places. She'd go to Galway, where her family was from, after County Kerry and do some of her own digging.

"Won't you be lonely?" said Neil when she told him on the

phone. It was going to be at least a week—maybe longer—before Adam and Henri came home. Neil was refolding the clothes and putting them back in the dresser drawers. He told Kathleen he was walking around the house in circles, making sure everything was perfect. Lucy was sleeping in the middle of Kathleen's kitchen.

"No," she said. But would she be? She didn't know.

In fact she didn't want to go to Ireland alone. She wanted to go with Natalie.

That was crazy, right? That idea was insane. You couldn't take someone else's child to Ireland.

But. What if she waited until summer. That would give her plenty of time to get Carmen used to the idea, to explain the plan. Carmen wouldn't have to pay a penny for it—it would be on Kathleen's dime, all of it. They could go to the village where Bridget had come from; they could find Fiona's gravestone, maybe Bridget's too. They could stand inside the church where the O'Connell family would have gone for Midnight Mass. And the next time Natalie had some sort of independent-study project to do—well, she'd really blow them all away with this.

Was it really so insane? There was only one way to find out.

She picked up the phone; she dialed.

Author's Note

I set *So Far Away* in Newburyport, Massachusetts, the town in which I live, because it has an abundant history and it felt like the right place for my fictional Irish immigrant to have landed. Bridget's story, though based in part on the experiences of actual Irish immigrants in the early 1920s, is my own creation. So, too, are the cyberbullying incidents depicted in this book, as well as the responses by school officials and other adults in the community. Cyberbullying, and bullying in general, are problems that I take very seriously, as do school officials in Newburyport and towns across the state, especially since the passage of antibullying legislation in May 2010 by the Commonwealth of Massachusetts. My intention in this book was to illustrate the experience of one fictional teenager, not to predict or depict any specific community's response to such a situation.

Acknowledgments

Somehow I thought the second book would be easier to write than the first. I was wrong, and I thank the following people for helping me see this through from messy first draft to final manuscript. At Weed Literary: Elisabeth Weed and Stephanie Sun, two of the sharpest agents in the business. At Reagan Arthur Books: Reagan Arthur, for her wise editorial eye and her copious amounts of patience; Andrea Walker, for her willingness to read multiple drafts and offer sound advice each time; Sarah Murphy, for being ever reachable, smart, thorough, and upbeat; Marlena Bittner, for having the energy and optimism of a hundred publicists; and the eagle-eyed Jayne Yaffe Kemp. Also thank you to Crystal Patriarche for taking on my books with such enthusiasm.

Outside the publishing world, I thank the incomparable Janis Duffy, formerly of the Massachusetts State Archives, who welcomed me into her workplace more than once, tirelessly answered my questions about genealogical research, and helped me bring my Irish immigrant to life. Justin Patchin of the Cyberbullying Research Center and the University of Wisconsin–Eau Claire answered my many, many questions about cyberbullying and proved himself to be infinitely more responsive than any fictional expert in the field. Thomas Bracken, who was certainly not alive in the early 1900s, nonetheless talked to me about the history of Irish step dancing in his native country. Drs. Michele Burns and Michael Pilz answered my medical questions. Dr. Douglas Gross, founding executive director of the University of California Haiti Initiative, talked with me about Haiti. Jay Williamson of the Historical Society of Old Newbury answered my questions about life in Newburyport in the 1920s.

I also found the following books helpful: *Life in Newburyport, 1900–1950,* by Jean Foley Doyle; *When Youth Was Mine, A Memoir of Kerry 1902–1925,* by Jeremiah Murphy; *The Irish Bridget: Irish Immigrant Women in Domestic Service in America, 1840–1930,* by Margaret Lynch-Brennan; and *The Irish: A Photohistory,* by Sean Sexton and Christine Kinealy; along with John Lagoulis's articles in the *Daily News* of Newburyport.

On the home front: The community of writers I've found online and locally who make a solitary pursuit a little less solitary. The lovely ladies of Lucey Drive, Jana Schulson and Karen Mascott, with whom I share carpools, bus stop waits, and running schedules. Iara Santos, for coming back for a summer. Katie Schickel, my localest writer friend. Elaine Cummings, who throws a heck of a book party. The two independent bookstores in my town, the Book Rack and Jabberwocky, whose staffs have welcomed me with open arms. My sister, Shannon Mitchell, who has cheerfully attended more book events than any one person should have to, and who always brings friends. My parents, John and Sara Mitchell, who have taken their appointment as the Vermont publicity arm seriously. My in-laws, the Moores and the Destrampes, for south-of-Boston support. Margaret Dunn and Jennifer Truelove, who are willing partners in research and road trips. My daughters, Adeline, Violet, and Josephine, who keep the clothes hampers full, the house alive, and my ego soundly in check. And my husband, Brian, who has handled my writing of this book the way he does everything: with patience, grace, and an impressive willingness to celebrate the small steps along the way.

About the Author

Meg Mitchell Moore is the author of *The Arrivals*. She worked for several years as a journalist, and her articles have been published in a wide variety of business and consumer magazines. She received a master's degree in English literature from New York University. She lives in Massachusetts with her husband and their three children.